I THINK I LOVE YOU

Allison Pearson

**WINDSOR
PARAGON**

First published 2010
by Chatto & Windus
This Large Print edition published 2011
by AudioGO Ltd
by arrangement with
The Random House Group Ltd

Hardcover ISBN: 978 1 445 85487 8
Softcover   ISBN: 978 1 445 85488 5

British Library Cataloguing in Publication Data available

Printed and bound in Great Britain by the MPG Books Group

I THINK I LOVE YOU

For my son, Thomas Daniel

And in memory of my beloved grandfather,
Daniel Elfed Williams

It panics him. He always keeps the curtains drawn. 'They are out there, Mother, they're out there.'

Evelyn Cassidy, on her son David's reaction to his fans

PROLOGUE
1998

The wardrobe was double-fronted, with a full-length mirror. Inside was her mother's tweed suit with the mink collar. There were tailored skirts, and blouses on hangers. There were sweaters in soft colours, carefully folded, with layers of tissue paper in between. At the bottom were the racks of shoes.

It was there that she found it, behind the racks. She wasn't looking for it. She wasn't looking for anything. She was reaching for a pair of black patent heels, the shine still on them after thirty years, when her fingers brushed against something colder than leather. She took it out. A tin with a lake and mountains on the lid. A Christmas gift from Austria. Inside, she found cards and photographs, and a sheaf of letters, tied together with a red ribbon.

The pink envelope was out of place. It had smiley faces and a rainbow on the front. It was addressed to her, but there was something strange about the handwriting. It took her a moment to recognise it as her own. Not her own now, but the way she used to write, a long time ago, with flowery loops. The envelope had been opened and it was easy to slide out the letter inside. She read it for the first time in her life. Then she read it again to make sure.

She got up and walked across the landing and pushed the door into her old bedroom. The brown coverlet was still on the bed, soft and slightly damp to the touch. She knelt down, reached under the bed and pulled out a grey transistor radio. She flicked the switch.

PART ONE

1974

How To Kiss—Part Two

You have kissed him, the one important boy, for the first time. Was it a successful kiss? Was it a kiss he'll always remember? Was it a kiss that made him kiss you again? Or was it a kiss that he'll remember for all the wrong reasons? That is the last thing in the world you would want to happen. So, when the time comes to kiss again, it's important to bear a few things in mind.

Don't make these mistakes:

1. Don't be nervous.
2. Don't spend too much time practising, so that's all you can think about when the time comes.
3. Don't look flustered or nervous, don't look as though you're afraid.
4. Don't close your eyes all the way until you're sure your lips are going to meet his and his lips are going to meet yours. He may be just as nervous as you and might close his eyes and wind up kissing your nose or the side of your mouth, unless you see what's happening and move your head so your lips will meet.
5. Don't put your tongue into his mouth. Not this time.

You are going to think this—these exact words—then think it again and again.

'He wouldn't want to kiss me unless I looked pretty to him. I look pretty to him. I look pretty to him. That is why he wants to kiss me. That is why he is kissing me now.'

'Loving Fashions', *16* magazine

1

His favourite colour was brown. Brown was such a sophisticated colour, a quiet and modest sort of colour. Not like purple, which was Donny's favourite. I wouldn't be seen dead in purple. Or in a Donny cap. How much would you have to like a boy before you went out wearing a stupid purple peaked cap?

Honest, it's amazing the things you can know about someone you don't know. I knew the date of his birth—12 April 1950. He was a typical Aries, but without the Arian's stubbornness. I knew his height and his weight and his favourite drink, 7-Up. I knew the names of his parents and his stepmother, the Broadway musical star. I knew all about his love of horses, which made perfect sense to me because when you're that famous it must be comforting to be around someone who doesn't know or care what famous is. I knew the instrument he learned to play when he was lonely. Drums. I knew the name of the dog he left behind when he had to move away from New Jersey. I knew that when he was a boy he was small for his age and he had a squint and had to wear an eyepatch and corrective glasses, which must have been hard. Harder than for a girl even. I didn't wear my glasses if I could help it. Only in class for the blackboard, though I couldn't see well without them and it got me into trouble a few times when I smiled in the street at total strangers who I mistook for members of my family. A few years later, when I got contact lenses, I was stunned by the trees. They had leaves, millions of leaves, with edges so sharp and defined they looked like God had made each one

3

with a pastry cutter. Basically, before I was sixteen, the world was one big Impressionist painting, unless I screwed up my eyes really tight to bring it into focus. Some things, as I would discover, were best left a blur.

Back then, I wasn't interested in the real world. Not really. I answered my parents' questions, I gave the appearance of doing homework, I lugged my cello into school on my back, I went down the town on Saturday afternoons with girls who sometimes felt like friends and sometimes didn't, but I was living for Him. Each night, I spread my long dark hair out on the pillow and made sure to sleep on my back so my face was ready to receive a kiss in case he came in the night. It wasn't that likely, obviously, because I lived in South Wales and he lived in California, which was five thousand miles away, and he didn't even have my address, although I had once sent a poem for him to a magazine. Choosing the right colour paper took longer than writing the actual poem. I settled on yellow because it seemed more mature than pink. I thought all the other girls would choose pink and part of loving him was finding better ways to please him so he would know how much more I cared. They didn't sell brown writing paper or I would have used brown because that was his favourite colour. Some time later—three weeks and four days if you're counting, and I definitely was—a reply came in the post. It was seventeen words long including my name. It didn't matter that the letter said they were sorry they couldn't publish my poem. In some crucial way, I felt as though I had made contact with him at long last. Someone important in London, someone who had been in the same room as him, had touched the yellow paper I had touched

4

and then typed my name on an envelope and licked the stamp. No rejection slip has ever been more treasured. It took pride of place in my scrapbook.

I knew exactly where he lived in California. In a canyon. A canyon was like one of our valleys, only much bigger. We said much bigger. David said way. Way bigger. Way was American for much. America was so big that Americans would drive one hundred miles just to have dinner with someone and they didn't think that was a long way to go. In America, way to go means you've done something well. Way to go, baby! And they have gas instead of petrol.

Other words I had learned were cool, mad and bathroom. You have to be careful because a bathroom is not a bathroom in America, it's a toilet.

'The Americans are a most polite people who are not standing for vulgarity,' said my mother, who was German and beautiful and disapproved of many things. You might say that my mother's whole life was a battle to keep the vulgar and the ugly at bay. In our town, she had found the perfect enemy. I just liked knowing American words because they brought me closer to Him. When we met, it would be important to retain my individuality, which was one of the top things David looked for in a girl.

In every interview I had read, David said that he preferred a girl to just be herself. But to be honest I was unsure of who myself was, or even if I had one, although I still maintained a touching faith that this unknown and as yet undiscovered me would be deeply appealing to David when we eventually met. How could I be sure? The understanding in his eyes told me so. (Oh, those eyes. They were deep green pools you could pour all your longing into.) Still, I reckoned that meeting David would be awkward

5

enough without any unnecessary confusion, so I did my best to pick up American. It would be tricky to go to a bathroom in his house in Los Angeles, for example, and find there was no bath, wouldn't it? Or imagine saying someone was mad. David would think that I meant they were angry. Crazy means mad in America. Back then, I couldn't imagine David ever being angry, he was so gentle and sensitive. Sorry, do I sound mad?

'Donny Osmond's a moron,' Sharon said firmly. She was kneeling on the floor, picking at the staples in a centrefold with her thumbnail trying to free a male torso. The slender, headless body was naked to the waist and practically hairless, except for a fine golden down just above the belt, which boasted a heavy bronze buckle. It looked like the door knocker to an Aztec temple. Sharon eased the poster off the frail metal pins until it rested on her hands, trembling a little in the hot air blowing from the small heater beside her. Sharon's bedroom was small, painted in a sickly shade of ointment pink and reeked of burnt hair, a bad candyfloss smell that got in your nostrils and stayed there. Sharon had dried her hair in front of the heater and a few strands got sucked into the back, but we didn't really notice the smell, so absorbed were we in our work.

'I don't think Donny's a moron, to be honest with you,' I said carefully.

'All the Osmonds are morons. I read it in a mag,' she insisted without looking up from the poster. Sharon was an expert restorer. The best artist in our class. When she grew up she could probably get a job in a museum or an art gallery. I loved to watch her work. The way she rolled her tongue into a little tunnel when she was concentrating and applied her

6

attention to the tiny puncture holes in David's stomach, soothing the torn paper with her fingertips until the flesh appeared to seal up.

'There you go, lovely boy,' she said, and placed a noisy smacking kiss on his belly button before adding the poster to the pile.

There was a prickle in my throat like a piece of trapped wool. I badly wanted to correct Sharon about the Osmonds being morons, but our friendship was still too new to risk disagreement. We liked each other because we agreed. We agreed because we both thought David Cassidy was the most wonderful boy currently alive and maybe in all of human history. At thirteen years of age, I couldn't imagine the luxury of having a friend you could disagree with. If you disagreed with her you could fall out. Then, before you knew it, you'd be back out there in the playground by yourself, sighing and checking your watch every couple of seconds to indicate that you did have an arrangement to meet someone and were not, in fact, the kind of sad, friendless person who had to pretend they were waiting for friends who did not exist.

Even worse, you could find yourself entering into anxious negotiations with some other borderline outcast to be your partner in PE so you didn't have to be in a pair with Susan Davies. Susan Smell, who had a disease of the skin no one could spell. Her face, her arms and her legs were all cratered like the surface of the moon, only some days the holes were filled in with the chalky dust of calamine lotion. We knew exactly what it was because our mothers dabbed the lotion on us when we got chickenpox. The angry, itchy spots were like tiny volcanoes around which the soothing pink liquid hardened into

7

a tempting lava crust. Mustn't pick it, mind, or it would leave a scar. The worst thing about Susan Davies, apart from the way you felt really sorry for her but still didn't do anything to help her, was the pong. Honest to God, Susan smelt so bad it made you retch in the corridor when she went past, even though she always walked on the side with the windows.

'Donny's a *Mormon*. I think it's a religion they founded in Utah,' I said cautiously, trying the sounds in my mouth.

Ooh. Ta.

I knew exactly what Mormons were. Donny Studies were part of my deep background research on David. I knew everything about the other Osmonds too, just in case, even Wayne. At a pinch, I could have given you the star sign of every member of the Jackson Five, and details of their difficult upbringing, which was in such contrast to their carefree, joyful music. Twiddly diddly dee, twiddly diddly dee. Twiddly diddly dee. Dee dee!

You know, I can never hear the opening chorus of 'Rockin' Robin' without a spasm of regret for what became of that remarkable little boy and all his sweetness.

Even as a child, I had this overdeveloped taste for tragic biographical information, a sort of twitching inner radar for distress. I may have been the only one not to be in the least bit surprised when Michael Jackson began to take leave of his adorable black face in painful cosmetic stages. You see, I understood all about hating the way you looked and wanting to magic away the child who made a parent feel angry or disappointed. When you grow up, they call this empathy. When you're thirteen it just makes

8

you feel like you're not so horribly alone.

'D'you reckon Mormons all have to wear purple because it's Donny's favourite colour?' I asked.

Sharon giggled. 'Get away with you, Petra, you're a case, you are!'

We thought we were hysterically funny. We laughed at anything, but lately boys had become a particular target for our witticisms. We laughed at them before they could laugh at us, or ignore us, which curiously felt even more wounding than being teased or insulted. You know, I always liked Sharon's laugh better than mine. My laugh sounded like a nervous cough that only starts to let itself go too late, when the joke has passed. Sharon made that happy, hiccupy sound you hear when you pull a cord in a doll's back. She looked a bit like a doll, did my new maybe friend. She was round and dimpled and her eyes were an astonishing bluebell blue beneath the palest barely there lashes. Her hair was that bone-dry flaxen kind that bursts out of a person's head like a dandelion clock. When we sat next to each other in Chemistry, her hair would float sideways on an invisible current of hot air from the Bunsen burner and stick to my jumper. If I tried to sweep it off the static gave me a shock that made my arm swarm.

Sharon was pretty in a way everyone in our group could agree was pretty without feeling bad about it. It was a mystery. Her weight seemed to act as a sort of protective jacket against jealousy. When she lost her puppy fat I think we all sensed it might be a different story. In the meantime, Sharon posed no threat to Gillian, who had got the two of us together in the first place and who was the star of our group. No, that's not right. Gillian was our Sun. We all revolved around her and you would do anything,

9

anything at all really, really humiliating and shameful things, just in the hope she might shine on you for a few minutes because the warmth of Gillian's attention made you instantly prettier and more fascinating.

As for me, the jury was still out on my looks. I was so skinny that next to Sharon I looked like a Victorian matchgirl. And don't go thinking, 'Oh, get her, she's proud of her figure.' Skinny is not the same as slim, no way. Skinny is the last-girl-but-one-to-get-a-training-bra because you've got nothing up top. God, I hate that expression. Up top. 'Hasn't got much up top, has she?'

Where we lived, girls had Up Top and Down There. You don't want to let a boy go Down There, but sometimes he was allowed Up Top, if you'd got anything there, like.

Skinny is always being late for hockey and being made to run five times round the games field because you keep your blouse on until the others have left the changing room so they don't see your sad little girl's vest. A vest with a single shaming rosebud on the front.

The magazines told us to identify our good points. Mine was eyes. Large and grey-blue, but sometimes green-blue flecked with amber, like a rock pool when the sun is shining on it. But my eyes also had these liver-coloured smudges under them which no cucumber slices or beauty sleep could ever cure. I never stopped trying though.

'Petra's dark circles are so bad she could go to a masked ball and she wouldn't need a mask,' Gillian said and everyone laughed, even me. Especially me. Be careful not to show her what really hurts or she'll know exactly where to put the knife in next time.

10

My worst feature was everything else really. I hated my knees, my nose and my ears, basically anything that stuck out. And I had pale skin that seemed even paler because of my dark hair. On a good day, I looked like Snow White in her glass coffin.

Expertly, my mother took my face in one hand, chin pinched between thumb and forefinger and tilted it sharply towards the bathroom light. She squeezed so tight my jaw ached. 'You are not unattractive, Petra,' my mother said coolly. 'Bones really quite good. If you pluck the brows when you are older, here and here, like szo, revealing the eyes more. You know, you are really not szo bad.'

'It's *too* bad, Mum, not so bad. I don't look *too* bad.'

'That is exactly what I am saying to you, Petra. Relax, please. You are not szo bad for a girl at her age.'

*　　　*　　　*

My mother believed she spoke perfect English and my dad always said now was not the time to tell her. Did I mention my mother was beautiful? She had a perfect heart-shaped face and eyes that were wide open yet sleepy at the same time. I'd never seen anyone who looked like my mother until one Saturday night I was round Sharon's house and there was a show on TV. This woman was sitting on a high stool in a dress made of something that shone like foil with a white fur cape draped around the shoulders. She looked glamorous and hard, but her voice was like a soft purr.

'That's all woman, that is,' Sharon's dad said,

11

which made me wonder what the rest of women were. Were they halves or quarters? Marlene Dietrich didn't look like she had kids, but then neither did my mum. Put my blonde mother in a gathering of my father's dark, stocky Welsh relatives and she looked like a palomino among a herd of pit ponies. Guess which side of the family I took after.

*   *   *

'Got it! Knew it was here somewhere.' Sharon was grinning in triumph. She had found the legs to match the torso. *Jackie* was giving away a free life-size David poster, but it came in parts over three weeks. Last week was jeans and cowboy boots, this time it was the body. They always saved the head till last.

'So you got to keep buying the mag, isn't it? Do they think we're blimmin' stupid or something?'

I couldn't see Sharon's face, but I knew she was frowning and funnelling her tongue as she lined up David's belly with his jeans. This was the hard part. Once she'd got them in position she flipped the shiny pages over and I handed her the strip of Sellotape, ever the dutiful nurse to her surgeon. We both stood up to get a better view of our handiwork. It wasn't a typical David pose. Among the thirty or so posters on Sha's walls there wasn't another quite like it. His thumbs were tucked into his waistband, the top button of his flies was undone and the jeans wrenched apart so you glimpsed that inverted V of hair that the zip normally hid. I tried to think of something funny to say, but my mouth felt dry and oatmealy. The absence of his head was definitely a problem. We urgently needed David's smiling face

12

to reassure us about what was going on down below. I felt a flicker as a tiny pilot light ignited in my insides and a warmth like liquid spread across my stomach and trickled down into my thighs.

Sharon had seen a penis, but it was her brother's so it didn't count. Carol was the only girl in our group who had touched a real one. Chris Morgan's in the tree house down the Rec where the boys went to look at dirty mags. Carol said the penis felt like eyelid skin. Could that be right? For weeks after she told us, I would brush a finger over the skin above my eye and I would marvel that something which was made of boy could be so silky and fine like tissue paper.

When we went through the mags, Sharon and I always flicked past the bad boys. Mick Jagger and that David Bowie, he was a strange one. We sensed instinctively that those stars were not for us. They might want to come down off the posters on the wall and do something. Exactly what they would do we didn't know, but our mothers would not have it.

'It's really weird,' Sharon said contemplating the headless, semi-naked David.

'Weird,' I agreed.

It was our new favourite word, and we used it as often as we could, but it really bothered me that we weren't saying it right. When David said it on *The Partridge Family* it had one syllable. Whirred. Our accent put the stress in the wrong place somehow. However hard I tried it still came out as 'whee yad'. On the cello, I could play any note I liked. I knew if it was wrong the same way I knew if I was cold or hungry, but controlling the sound that came from my own mouth was different. Funny thing is I didn't even realise I had a Welsh accent. Not until our year

13

went on a school trip to Bristol Zoo and some English girls in the motorway services mimicked the way I asked for food.

'Veg-e-tab-ils.'

I pronounced the 'e' in the middle, but English people didn't.

They said 'vedge-tibuls'.

Why did they bother putting an 'e' in there, then, if you weren't supposed to say it? So people like me could sound *twp* and they could have a laugh.

Sharon and me were doing our top rainy Sunday-afternoon thing to do, listening to David's *Cherish* album and flicking through magazines for any mention of him. After Sunday school, which lasted for two long hours, there wasn't much else to do in our town on the Sabbath, to be honest with you. Everyone abided by some unwritten law that people should stay indoors and keep quiet. Even if you didn't go to chapel, which we always did because my father was the organist, it felt as though chapel had come to you. My Auntie Mair never used scissors on a Sunday, because God could see everything, even the wax in your ears and the dirt under your nails. You could grow potatoes under there. *Achafi!* Disgusting. And you didn't hang your washing out on the line because of what the neighbours would think. The judgement of the neighbours might not be as bad as that of the Lord Thy God, Dad said, but you knew about it sooner.

Sundays lowered the temperature in the rows of grey-stone terraced houses clinging to the mountain which rose steeply above our bay, and even the sea became a bit subdued. It always made me think it was a good day for Jesus to walk on the water. People shivered on the Sabbath and went upstairs to put a

14

cardigan on and came down to watch the wrestling on TV, but always with the sound down, out of respect. It was really 'whee yad' looking in through the windows as you ran down the hill towards the seafront, using your back shoe as a brake till you smelt the rubber, and seeing the big men in their leotards throwing each other about, silently bellowing and stamping their boots on the floor of the ring.

Going round Sharon's house was like a holiday for me. She had an older brother called Michael who teased us, but in a funny way, you know, and a younger sister, called Bethan, who had a crush on little Jimmy Osmond, if you can believe it. (We called him Jimmy Spacehopper because he had these little bunny features stuck in the middle of a round face like a balloon.) Sha also had a baby brother called Jonathan who sucked Farley's Rusks in his highchair till he got a crusty orange moustache which you could peel off in one piece when it got hard and there were visitors who dropped in for a chat and stayed because they were too busy talking to notice the time. As for Sharon's mum, well, she was lovely, you couldn't ask for a nicer person. She knocked on the bedroom door, really respectful, and came in and offered us squash and Club biscuits. Always remembered that I preferred the currant ones in the purple wrapper, not the orange. Mrs Lewis said she liked our David posters and she told us she still had a book of matches and a cocktail stick from the night Paul McCartney dropped into a club in Cardiff. 1964 it was. Sharon's mum was absolutely crazy about Paul. Said she had hated Linda for marrying him.

'He was mine, you see.'

Yes, we saw.

My favourite thing was the David shrine on the back of Sharon's door. She got it in a *Tiger Beat* her Auntie Doreen brought back all the way from Cincinnati, America. Four pictures fixed at mouth height so Sha could snog him on the way out to school in the morning. Like she was saying goodbye to a real lover boy. In the first picture, David had that shaggy haircut and a naughty smile. The second was this look—you know. In the third, his lips were puckered up, and in the fourth, well, he just looked really happy and pleased with himself, didn't he?

Over time, the four Davids became smeared and blurry with the Vaseline that Sharon used to soften her lips, a trick we copied from Gillian. Sometimes, Sharon let me have a go at kissing David Number 3. I wasn't allowed posters on my wall at home because my mother believed that popular music could make you deaf and was really common and therefore appealing only to people like my dad, who worked down the steelworks and was a big Dean Martin man on the quiet, though that's another story and I'm meant to be telling you this one.

Well, at the start of that year, several things happened. Gillian—she was never just Gill—lent Sharon to me as my special friend. I was really happy, you know, but I sensed the loan could be called in any minute if Gillian's infatuation with Angela, the new girl from England, ever cooled. The uncertainty gave me this feeling in my stomach like I was on a ferry or something and couldn't get my balance. Most nights, I woke with a fright because my legs were kicking out under the sheets as if I had to save myself from falling, falling. Another thing was the headmaster told me after assembly one morning that I was going to play the cello for Princess Margaret when she came to open our new school hall. She was the Queen's sister and the Lord Mayor and some people called dignitrees were coming. But the really big news was that David Cassidy had postponed his tour of Britain after having his gall bladder removed. Two girls in Manchester were so upset they set themselves on fire, according to the mag.

On fire! My God, the thought of the passion and the sacrifice of those girls, it burned in our heads for weeks. We hadn't done anything that big for him. Not yet anyway.

Another couple of fans wrote to David asking if they could have a gallstone each as a souvenir. Sharon and I pretended to be shocked and disgusted by the gallstones story. *Achafi!* Secretly, we could not have been more delighted. The blimmin' cheek of it! Honest to God, where were their manners? It was in bad taste and unladylike. David, as any true fan knew, liked girls to act really feminine. We shook our heads and crossed our arms indignantly, as we had seen our mothers do, resting them on the invisible shelf where soon our breasts would be. Asking for David's gallstones!

Feeling superior to your rivals was one of the sweetest pleasures of being a fan, and maybe of being female in general.

We found out all about the tour cancellation and the gallstones from *The Essential David Cassidy Magazine*. It was brilliant, our Bible really. God's own truth. At 18p, it was way more expensive than any other mag.

17

'Dead classy, mind,' Sharon said, and so it was with its thick, glossy paper, gorgeous recent pix and a monthly personal letter written by David himself actually from the set of *The Partridge Family* in Hollywood, America. You couldn't put a price on something like that, could you?

From David's letters, we collected facts like eager squirrels, putting them by for some vital future use. If you'd asked us what that use was we couldn't have told you. All we knew was that one day it would become magically clear and we would be ready.

'David writes lovely, mun,' Sharon sighed.

'David writes *well*.' I heard my mother's voice correcting Sharon's speech inside my head. She looked down on people with bad grammar, which was everybody except the lady who did the tickets at the library and the announcers on the BBC.

'Don't talk tidy, please talking the Queen's English, Petra,' rebuked my mother whenever she caught me speaking the way everyone else in town spoke.

But there in Sharon's room, with the little heater filling the place with sleepy warmth and David on the turntable singing 'Daydreamer' I could tune out the voice of my mother and start learning how to be a woman all by myself.

'Nothing in the world could bother me
Cos I was living in a world of make believe . . .'

The cancellation of the Cassidy tour at the start of 1974 was a bitter blow, but it also came as a relief. It gave me more time to perfect my plan for meeting David when he came later in the year. Maybe

18

autumn. He would call it 'the fall', which seemed perfect to me. I knew that somehow I would have to travel to London or Manchester because Wales was so small it had no concert venue big enough to hold all the fans. I wasn't sure how I would get there—no money, no transport, a mother who thought any singer who wasn't Dietrich Fisher Dishcloth shouldn't be allowed—but once I got there and was safely outside the concert hall I knew that everything would be fine.

I would be hit by a car. Not a serious injury, obviously, just bad enough to be taken to hospital by ambulance. David would be told about my accident and he would rush to my bedside. Things would be awkward at first, but we would soon get talking and he would be amazed by my in-depth knowledge of his records, particularly the B-sides. I would ask him how he was enjoying the fall and if he needed to use the bathroom. It would not be at all weird, it would be cool. David would be impressed by my command of American. Jeez. He would smile and invite me to his house in Hawaii where I would meet his seven horses and there would be garlands round our necks and we would kiss and get married on the beach. I was already worried about my flip-flops.

*   *   *

Yes, it was a kind of madness. It didn't last all that long, not in the great scheme of a life, but while I loved Him he was the world entire.

*   *   *

The next day was school. I hated Sunday nights,

19

hated the melancholy hour after getting home from Sharon's warm funny house, hated having to revise for the Monday morning French test.

I love, I will love, I was loving, I have loved, I will have loved. *J'aurai aimé*. Future perfect.

The only thing that made it bearable was reading the David mags I kept under a floorboard by my bed and listening to the Top 40 in a cave beneath the sheets.

My mother's voice drifted up the stairs: 'Petra, finishing your homework, at once, and then cello practice.'

'I'm *doing* my homework.'

And so I was. Lying on the brown candlewick bedspread, reading by the light of the bedside lamp, I studied that week's words and committed them to heart.

Dear Luvs,

I guess I'm like everyone else. I just dig getting letters! I like to know who you guys are. That's why I'm totally thrilled when I get a letter and YOU tell me something about yourself—your favourite colour or where you live. Pretty soon, I feel like we're old friends. That's so nice.

I reckon I should return the favour. Well, you probably all know what I look like by now . . . But the thing is I'm sitting in my trailer in between takes of *The Partridge Family*. It's a real home from home, with family photographs and all my favourite sodas.

Hey! I've just caught sight of the amount I've written—and this was supposed to be just a short letter! I guess I must have had so much to say to YOU that I got carried away.

See the effect this has had on me? I never used to like writing letters and I used to have to stretch my literary efforts to get them to seven or eight lines. Now I can't wait to make contact again next month. Till then.

Luv,
David

2

Hey! I've just caught sight of the amount I've written—and this was supposed to be just a short letter! I guess I must have had so much to say to YOU that I got carried away.

See the effect this has had on me? I never used to like writing letters and I used to have to stretch my literary efforts to get them to seven or eight lines. Now I can't wait to make contact again next month. Till then.

Love you loads,
Loads of love,
Loadsaluv,
Lvu—

'God's *bollocks*.' Bill pulled the paper out of the typewriter as hard as he could. It made that sound he always thought of as Writer's Hiss, halfway between a rip and a zip. He balled the paper up and hurled it at the waste-paper basket, or, rather, at the cardboard box that was all the office could afford. 'Wagon Wheels 184 pkts' it said on the side. Bill's aim was untrue, like many things about him, and the missile struck Zelda amidships. She turned very slowly, and her paisley kaftan billowed like a sail.

'Now now, William. Don't despair. Man has to suffer for his art,' Zelda said. Bill had never understood the word *chortle* until he heard the noise that his editor made when she was amused, preferably by the misery of others.

'What's art got to do with it? I am making up absolute rubbish to put into the mouth of some cretinous pretty boy who can't sing, probably doesn't shave yet and certainly couldn't write a letter to save his own grandma.'

'It's a perfectly respectable branch of fiction,' Zelda replied, unperturbed.

Bill sometimes wondered what she would do if— as seemed increasingly likely—he climbed up onto his desk, took off his tie and hanged himself from the ceiling in the middle of work. First she would wash the teacups, then empty the pencil sharpener clamped to the edge of her desk, and finally, with everything in order, she might consent to call the police and ask them to take away the remains.

'Look at Cyrano de Bergerac,' she went on. 'He wrote love letters on behalf of a numbskull so that he could win the heart of a fair lady. The numbskull, that is.'

'I know who Cyrano is, thank you, Zelda. And the whole point is that he loved the lady himself, but didn't think he could make her love him back because of his enormous conk. His target audience was one. Roxanne was a pearl beyond price. Whereas I am writing to a million girls who wet themselves at the slightest opportunity. And I know you won't believe this, but I do not love them from afar. Not one of them. And why don't I love them? Because they are roughly as intelligent as that cardboard box. And how do I know that? Because they seriously believe that the rubbish I produce on my Smith Corona here represents the actual, sacred sayings of Saint bloody David bloody Cassidy. That's what they're like. They're like peasants in 1321. You give them a bit of dead badger skull and tell them it's

23

the funny bone of the Blessed Virgin Mary and they fall down in a dead faint and give you everything they own including the cow. I am writing for peasants.'

There was a pause. Zelda smiled, as she would at a child who was nearing the end of a tantrum.

'It means a lot to the girls,' she said quietly. 'We provide a service. We are making them happy.'

'But I don't want them to be happy. I want them to fall down a mineshaft.'

Zelda looked at the young man with the scruffy beard. He was tipped back as far as his chair could go with a pair of what appeared to be coalminer's lace-up boots parked on his overflowing desk. What was he—twenty-two, twenty-three? She couldn't remember what he'd put on his application, but she did recall that his CV had suggested he could make things up from unpromising raw material, which was a perfect fit for the job. Roy said he was a stuck-up little ponce and didn't want to hire him. A journalist of the old school, Roy was the proprietor of Worldwind Publishing and he recommended the applicant make a visit to the barber to take several inches off his hair. It hung in a lank, dirty-blond curtain obscuring his face. Zelda thought it a rather wonderful face, but she would never have said so. In fact, when he forgot to be cynical, Bill had a rascally charm and a grin that reminded Zelda very much of that lovely young man who she had seen only last week in some film at the Odeon. *Thunderbolt and Lightfoot*. Anyway, Zelda had insisted they should give Bill a chance and she was right. In the three months he had worked as the chief, indeed the only, feature writer for *The Essential David Cassidy Magazine*, William Finn had shown a real flair for his work. The readers seemed to love him. Sales of the

24

David Cassidy Love Kit had gone through the roof since Bill had tweaked the advertisement with some well-chosen, poignant observations about the many ways a fan could demonstrate her devotion.

His exclusive story about how two fans in Manchester set fire to themselves after learning David's tour had been cancelled was touched with genius, although Zelda conceded that a certain poetic licence had been applied to an incident which had involved a single poster and a box of matches. But consider the postbag. It was so heavy poor Chas could no longer get it up the stairs in one go. There was some quality in Bill that made the girls actually believe they had a direct connection to David. No, she very much didn't want to lose the goose that laid the golden prose, so Zelda tried again in her best, soothing kindergarten-teacher voice.

'Now now, William. You don't really want to throw our lovely young lady readers down a mineshaft, do you?'

He rewarded her with a smile of truce. 'OK, I want them to grow up strong and sane and to realise that they have wasted the best part of their youth having pointless dreams about a wanker in a cheesecloth shirt.'

'All girls do something like this, William. They wouldn't be girls if they didn't. Fantasy is an important part of growing up. We can't all sit around and read Shakespeare, you know.'

'At least Shakespeare wrote Shakespeare.'

'If you say so.' Zelda narrowed her eyes, like someone thinking over a dark rumour.

'Oh, for God's sake.' Bill stared at Zelda. 'You're not serious. You don't really—'

'*Bacon!*'

'Oh, come off it, Zelda, just because—'

'On toasted white, please! With a dollop of brown sauce. And if they have any Twiglets. Thanks, Chas!'

Zelda sang out her instructions to the office dogsbody, who did what he was told but did it with such unrepentant surliness that you ended up half wishing he would say no.

'Bill?' He groaned the name from the narrow doorway to the stairs.

'Um, turkey mayonnaise if they've got it. You know, the one that looks like sick. Thanks, Chas. Use the change from yesterday. And a drink.'

'Cherryade? Passed your Corona Fizzical yet?'

'Bog off.'

Chas turned and lumbered down the stairs. It sounded like a piano being moved.

Zelda turned back brightly to Bill.

'Where were we?'

'You were about to make a complete ar—'

'Thank you, William. All I was trying to say was that these girls you are so rude about have certain dreams and longings that we are able to fulfil. That is our business. The wish fulfilment business. There are plenty of creative people who would leap at the chance.'

'*Creative*.' Bill lowered his head in shame and stared at his boots.

'Certainly. And I know you won't accept a compliment, being too grand for the rest of us, Mr La-di-da Bachelor of Arts from the University of Suffolk—'

'Sussex, actually.'

'But I happen to think, William, that you have a certain knack for writing these letters of Mr Cassidy's. I would go further than knack. I would

26

say a gift.'

'*Gift.*' His head sank lower. His nose was level with his navel. There was a stain on his trousers the shape of Venezuela.

'Absolutely a gift. I would kill for such a talent. As it is, I am left to lay out the magazine and paste it together and arrange picture credits and all the other things that you would consider beneath you.'

'I never—'

'Oh, I'm not complaining. I enjoy my work, which is more than you ever seem to do. All I'm saying is that you have proved yourself surprisingly good at pretending to be somebody else. You could have been an actor. Or a spy.'

'Or a contender.'

'I beg your pardon?'

'Nothing.' Bill heaved himself up in his chair, looked up at Zelda and smiled. 'Sorry. I know I should be grateful. But really, Zelda . . . like I say, it's not just the writing, it's who I'm writing *for*.' He stuck a hand into the heap of loose papers on his desk and pulled out a sheet of A4, light pink in colour and stained with what he hoped were meant to be tears. A stale yet aggressively sweet metallic smell rose to Zelda's nostrils.

'Charlie,' she said.

'Who's Charlie?'

'Charlie the perfume. The ones who really love him tip their favourite scents on the letters. There's one girl from Truro who writes eight letters to every issue—'

'Jesus.'

'Yes, I suppose she's trying to wear us down by sheer force of numbers.'

'Like carpet-bombing.'

27

'Sort of, except it doesn't work.'

'Like carpet-bombing.'

'What?' Zelda wrinkled her nose. The wider world was offensive to her, like a blocked drain.

'Forget it. So does this Cornish girl get her stuff in?'

'Once, and that was enough. My mistake. It only encouraged her. She sent sixteen more by the following Tuesday. And they really stink. Gallons of Old Spice. We think she gets it from her dad.'

'Could be worse. Could be Hai Karate.'

'Or Tabac.'

'No,' said Bill solemnly. 'That would burn through the paper.' He seemed to lose his thoughts for a moment, as if following the memory of old aromas. Then he shook his head, to clear it, and held up the pink correspondence. He gave a cough, and read out loud:

> 'I want to let you know I care.
> So much I find it hard to bear.
> I see your photos on the wall,
> But I know you're not there at all.
> I think about you night and day,
> And all the time I hope and pray
> The day will come when I shall see
> Your own eyes, David, look at me.
> They say you have no actual zits
> And no desire to feel my tits.'

Zelda gasped in shock and put a protective hand to her own ample bosom. She had gone the same colour as the letter.

'I made up that last bit,' said Bill, with modest pride.

28

'Mmm, sometimes,' she said at last, gulping the word out, 'I wonder if—'

'I mean, don't they *realise*, these daft kids, I don't even *own* a cheesecloth shirt, let alone a necklace made from puka shells. What kind of sea creature is a puka anyway? Look at me. I'm wearing the bottom half of a brown suit from John Collier that cost eleven quid. I don't want to wear a suit, but you keep telling me this is a proper job. I want to wear jeans, except that my jeans aren't like David Cassidy's. I don't unbutton the flies at the top so you can see my pu—'

'William!'

'Well, I don't. I do them up properly. And I'm not sure I even have any eyelashes, let along long ones. He looks like a Jersey calf. And I don't have mirrored shades because I would look a total spaz and because it's always dark here anyway, unlike sunny bloody California, and because people would take the mickey and look into the mirrored bits and try to brush their hair. The only thing I can do like David Cassidy is sing. I was in the school choir and I did a solo on "Morning Has Broken". My aunt made me sing it into a tape deck afterwards. Christ almighty.'

'All of which proves what a good mimic you are. My point in the first place.' Zelda had recovered her composure. 'Anyone who can make a girl sit down and write a poem as heartfelt as that must be doing something right.'

'Heartfelt? Zelda, they don't *have* hearts. They have a bucket of raging hormones and a need to follow whatever their friends are doing and not fall behind, whether they want to or not. They think they're in love, but it's just a projection. They're like . . . like illusionists, deceiving themselves.'

Zelda was out of her depth here. She felt the conversation slip its moorings and drift from her grasp, into areas where she had no experience and even less wish to go. Almost three decades in the magazine business had taught her what worked, and that was that. The year she started as a typist on *Picture Post*, thousands of bobby-soxers had gone crazy for a new kid called Frank Sinatra at the New York Paramount. The girls refused to leave their places between shows, even to go to the lavatory. 'Not a dry seat in the house,' one reporter joked. That phrase had stuck in Zelda's mind, witty yet strangely animal and unpleasant. What did it tell you about the young female that she was prepared to wet herself in order to deny another girl the chance to get near her hero? Poor William was a bit of an intellectual. He hadn't woken up to the power of what he was dealing with. She would have to send him to a Cassidy concert where he could observe the little lionesses when their prey came into view. The February concerts had been cancelled because David had to have an operation. Roy was furious, of course, what with having a whole vanful of memorabilia to unload. Now he'd have to store it in a lock-up on York Way till spring, when there were two concerts pencilled in. One for Manchester, one for Wembley.

Zelda smiled. Imagine William standing like Gulliver with all those teenies surging around him. She loved the idea of the pretend David coming face to face with the real one. Wouldn't mind being there herself actually.

'Chas will be back with the sarnies,' she declared, and moved away from the features area, in stately fashion, heading for the safe haven of her desk,

30

which indicated its superiority to the rest with a partition made of pot plants. In its bottom drawer was a pack of John Player Specials and half a bar of Old Jamaica, for after the bacon sandwich. Nice cup of Nes. All would be well.

*   *   *

Bill had not wanted the job with Worldwind Publishing, but when Roy Palmer made him the offer even he could see that he didn't really have a choice. Eleven months after leaving college with a degree which was lower than his abilities but still far better than he deserved—given that he had spent his final year honing his pinball skills in the arcade on Brighton pier—he had pretty much reached the end of the road. That long, glittering road marked Graduate Opportunities. After that, he stumbled onto the potholed, dusty path where the unchosen have to accept that, instead of a career, they will be lucky to end up with a pay cheque.

The closest Bill had got to an occupation worthy of his potential was being shortlisted for a traineeship with one of London's top advertising agencies. He had endured a two-day assessment at a hotel in the Cotswolds with fifteen ruthless individualists all competing to show how well they worked in teams. Bill had shone in the copywriting exercise, but during the product pitch he had become insanely irritated by a girl called Susie. You could actually see the agency's directors watching Susie and writing down adjectives like 'bubbly' and 'warm'.

After a brand-recognition exercise for a disgusting new fruit cordial, one of the directors said, with

31

unfeigned eagerness: 'Susie strikes me as being a real people person.'

It was the first time that Bill had come across the expression, and he hated it on sight. What other kind of person was there for crying out loud? A scorpion person?

It was bad, obviously, that Bill had spoken these thoughts aloud and even worse that the meeting room had fallen into a silence colder than church on Christmas Eve. So it was probably inevitable that he would be sent home early, deposited unceremoniously on Banbury station with his overnight bag and a complimentary bottle of Jungle Qwash, because he was not enough of a people person. On balance, Bill thought that he was ready to sell his soul, but it turned out he wasn't prepared to suppress everything that made him who he was just to flog an orange drink which burned the roof of your mouth and made you thirstier than a beaker full of bleach.

Not long after the advertising fiasco, there was a promising interview for a local radio station. He pictured himself at the microphone, preferably in the late slot, playing a roster of obscure but addictive songs to sobbingly grateful listeners. He would wear headphones the size of boxing gloves. He would become a cult. Instead of which it was made clear, by a claret-nosed station manager named Dodge, that Bill's gifts would be dedicated entirely to filing—to the plucking of discs, not of his own choosing, from the station's record library, and their careful replacement after airplay. He was offered the job on the spot, with an extra five pounds slapped onto the weekly pay packet 'if you don't mind a bit of cleaning', which he did, actually. 'Pride comes before a fall', his mother used to warn. It was not a saying that Bill had ever understood, but at that moment, as he refused the offer with alacrity, he felt both proud and fallen. He remembered looking back at the figure of Dodge, who stood in reception, unsurprised, blowing his nose and staring long and hard at the contents of his handkerchief.

There were some rewards. Over the barren weeks of applications and rejections, Bill had time, at least, to improve his fingering on the guitar. He also grew a small experimental beard, which he hoped would be construed by those in the know as an affectionate tribute to Eric Clapton, but which was described by his sister Angie, whom he ran into just off Denmark Street, as 'seaweed clinging to a rock'.

It was around this time that his girlfriend, Ruth, started to lose patience with him. When they first met, in his final year at Sussex, Ruth thought she had a catch. She thought she had bagged herself a boyfriend who was going places in the world, and those places clearly did not include the Camden dole office.

As the weeks dragged on, Bill had time to develop a theory of jobs. He reckoned you could get an accurate measurement of how far your prospects had dived by the number of stairs you had to climb to the interview. Great jobs came with lifts. Banks of lifts standing to silver-buttoned attention like the guardians of an ancient citadel. Lifts which arrived with a geisha's sigh and opened with the delightful ching of money. And beside them there were receptionists, who asked you to please take a seat and Mr Porter would be right with you. He still dreamt about one receptionist, an Ali MacGraw brunette in a tight red merino wool sweater, who had

33

offered huskily: 'Tea and two sugars all right, William?'

One by one the jobs with lifts slipped from his grasp. He had just reached the basement level of despair, when, sitting with a pot of tea and a round of toast in a Chalk Farm cafe, he spotted a small ad in a corner of the *London Evening Standard*. 'Publishing Opportunity for self-starting graduate. Knowledge of pop music an advantage. Lively writing style essential. Desirable central London location. Perks.'

The desirable central location turned out to be the groin of Tottenham Court Road, a junction where the whores competed for trade with the unlicensed minicab drivers. Both professions looked equally taken aback if a punter took them up on the offer of a ride.

It took him a while to locate the tall, narrow building because there was no number and the nameplate for Worldwind Publishing was a business card, taped between Bunnyhop Personal Services and Kolossos: Importers of the Finest Greek Cooking Oil. Where once must have stood an impressive Georgian door, there was now a flimsy hardboard replacement with a handle improvised from parcel string. Bill pushed the door gently and fell into a dark hallway. It took a few seconds for his eyes to adjust to the gloom. There was one light fitting on the ceiling, a crystal dome the size of a washing-up bowl, but such light as it shed was filtered through a gauze of dead insects. He spotted some stairs in the distance and set off in their direction, the carpet squelching underfoot. It was like walking on mushrooms. By the time Bill got to the sixth floor, his ears had popped and his lungs were banging noisily on his chest demanding to be let out, but, unbelievably, there was another set of steps to go. Ascending to the seventh floor, the staircase became so narrow that you had to spiral your torso in a sort of corkscrew motion to get round; there was a real danger you might end up holding your right hand over your left shoulder.

Once at the top, before entering the office itself, it was necessary to squeeze past a battlement of cardboard boxes. Some were open, and inside, spilling out, was a selection of magazines. They bore different headlines, but they all had the same girl on the front. Definitely not his type. A shy smile, shoulder-length mousy hair, hazel eyes, lashes you could wipe a windscreen with. Bill heard a rasp of breath; some sort of office boy, who was either a wizened teenager or a perky pensioner but couldn't possibly be anything in between, had come to hover at his side. It could do no harm, Bill thought, to be friendly.

'Not my type.'

'Who?'

'That bird there, on the cover.'

The rasp did something strange, writhing and wheezing into a cackle.

'I should friggin' well hope not.'

'I beg your pardon?' Two minutes in, and Bill was already floundering.

'Cos that's a fella.' The goblin was richly enjoying the moment, storing it up to recite at the pub round the corner: 'So this nancy comes in for a ninterview and he thinks David Cassidy's a bird . . .'

Bill leaned down to the open boxes. 'Blimey.' A fellow it was, but only just. Certainly nothing that he would recognise as a man. The guy, whoever he was,

35

had a waist smaller than Ruth's. Bill's own musical heroes were Clapton, Jimi Hendrix and the Stones. Before the interview he had riffled through his record collection and done a bit of homework. Nothing too ostentatious. Just enough to show them that he knew his stuff. If he were called upon in his first week to conduct an interview with, say, Keith Richard, he would be ready. Mind you, there was a rumour of this *NME* journalist who had gone to talk to Keith in March and not come back till August.

The goblin, who turned out to be called Chas, ushered him through to what he called the 'inner sanction'. There was nobody there. Bill sat for ten minutes staring at the signed photograph of Tony Jacklin and two bottles of Johnnie Walker on top of the filing cabinet. Did he really want to work for a golf-loving dipsomaniac?

'Don't think we've forgotten you, dear,' said a large, flustered woman who had clearly forgotten him. Her long grey hair was loosely pinned up in a bun and she wore a garment that could have been modelled on a teepee. She introduced herself as Zelda. After her came a man wearing the largest pair of glasses Bill had ever seen: they were like two TV screens soldered together and they magnified the man's eyes which were as blank and beady as a blackbird's. He stuck out his hand. 'Roy Palmer,' he said, as if issuing a threat.

The Worldwind proprietor had slicked-back hair that was too black to be his original colour and one of those rubbery comedian's faces which immediately made you think he must be a friendly, likeable guy. In this case, that was a mistake. Roy thought he was funny, but nobody else did.

Bill should have walked out the minute he

36

discovered that the magazine he'd be working on was targeted at girls aged eleven to fifteen. He'd done puberty already and done it badly. He knew absolutely nothing about the female version of it, and that suited him fine. Once, searching the bathroom cabinet at home for shaving foam, he had come across sanitary equipment belonging to his sisters. Some sort of belt affair with hooks and a box of Tampax. There was a puzzling diagram of a girl standing like a stork on one leg. Bill read the word 'insertion', shut the door and never opened it again.

'Think of the teen-idol phase as a sort of corridor between girlhood and womanhood,' Zelda had said. 'Our magazine's role is to guide a girl on that journey.'

'Our profit,' Roy interjected, 'comes from targeting the girl and her pocket money between the cute furry animal stage and heavy petting, if you get my drift.' When he laughed, Roy's mouth revealed a Stonehenge of ancient teeth.

While Zelda examined his CV, Bill studied the highly polished shoes he had borrowed for the occasion from his mate Simon, a trainee accountant in a firm with three lifts. Bill had taken a few liberties with his details and was almost certainly about to be found out.

'You seem to have done very well in your final college dissertation, William. May I ask what the subject was?'

He coughed and covered his mouth. 'Er, "The Romantic Sublime—Voice and Desire in English Love Poetry 1790 to 1825".'

'Keep it clean, keep it clean,' snapped Roy.

Swiftly, Bill changed the subject. 'So what exactly would I be doing here?'

'Well, dear, think of a thirteen-year-old girl in Manchester or Cardiff,' Zelda said brightly. 'What are the things she wants to know as she lies in bed and stares longingly up at the posters of David on her wall? That's where you come in with your romantic poetry and creative writing.'

He did not hide his astonishment. 'I'm supposed to make it up?'

'Oh, not all of it. The record company PRs will provide certain materials of course. If D.C. comes over in person there'll be a big press thingummy, you can go along and ask some questions, bring back as many facts as you can. Stock up the larder so to speak, then pad it out for the next few months. I think you'll find it starts to write itself after a while, once you get the hang of the voice. And the desire.' Zelda smiled encouragingly.

'Will I have the opportunity to speak to Mr— David?'

'Heavens, no, dear, but we can get all kinds of nuggets from his people in Los Angeles. They're awfully helpful, though you have to call them at funny times of day. Then it's up to you. All the kinds of things girls like to know about boys, you know.'

Bill nodded. He hadn't got a clue. The job was an insult. He wanted to be a rock journalist, not a girly-boy impersonator. Anyway, there was something sick about mucking around with little girls' dreams. You would have to be some sort of desperate pervert to even consider it. The salary was £2,750 per annum plus luncheon vouchers.

He started the following Monday.

Within a fortnight, Bill had begun to familiarise himself with David Cassidy's family history. There was a charismatic stage-actor father who, despite the

Steinway grin, seemed to be not entirely enraptured by his son's overnight superstardom. David, Bill guessed, had wanted to impress the old man who had walked out on him as a kid, but such shattering success probably only made matters worse. Bill thought of the distant relationship with his own father. At twenty-two, the age Bill was now, Roger Finn had not been struggling to thread a new typewriter ribbon through the miniature horns of a Smith Corona. He had spent his days in the sky over the South Downs fighting the Battle of Britain against the Luftwaffe. There may be more daunting men to have as a dad than a Spitfire pilot, but when you were trying and failing to re-arm a typewriter it was hard to think of one. Once, and only once, his dad had mentioned the war, taking Bill and his sisters on the train to an air museum. In one hangar, suspended from wires, was an actual Spitfire. So heroic and indomitable had the plane become in the boy's imagination that he was unprepared for this frail craft. It made him want to cry. It was like a sparrow made from tin.

In a desperate bid to look professional, Bill popped out one lunchtime and purchased three books in Foyles, one on California, the other on Hawaii, where the star had a house, and the third on horses, which were his hobby. It turned out David had weak eyes as a kid and needed an operation on a squint. Bill himself suffered from colour blindness, invariably confusing green and brown. It must have been tough having to wear corrective glasses and an eyepatch, especially for a boy who looked like a girl.

Honestly, it's amazing the things you can know about someone you don't know.

Are You Destined For David?

David loves every single one of his fans, and he'd love to meet and date each one of you. But as that would take round about 50 years, it wouldn't be a very practical idea!

The kind of girl David would fall for would need to have some rather special qualities—because, after all, David's a rather special kind of guy! Here are the top qualities David always looks for in his favourite girlfriends. How many of them do you possess?

David is never turned on to a girl just because she's specially attractive, or has lovely hair or a super figure. He always looks for something much more than that—the kind of thing you can only find out when you know what someone's like on the INSIDE.

David loves girls to be bright and happy, smiling and laughing easily, and always looking on the bright side of things. Of course, if you were going out with David you'd have plenty to be smiling about!

David likes girls with sparkling, free and easy personalities, with just a touch of zaniness and a great sense of humour. He likes girls who are individuals, and who never try to be like anyone else. Most of all he likes girls who are FUN!

David loves healthy girls with loads of energy—girls who enjoy going off in the country and taking long walks in the fresh air, who like to go horse-riding or bicycling.

David loves all sports, watching or playing, and likes to be with girls who share his enthusiasm—though he doesn't expect them to be great experts on the games or brilliant players!

David never likes to see girls wearing lots of make-up—he always goes for the fresh, natural look. He doesn't like to spend time with girls who are constantly looking in the mirror and adding a spot more eyeshadow, or rushing off to comb their hair after they've been in a slight breeze.

David loves girls who can cook!

David likes girls to have a mind of their own and he'd never expect a girl to agree with everything he said. And that brings us on to the subject of arguments—the kind of friendly little quarrels that everyone has from time to time. David doesn't mind good-humoured arguments like these, but his ideal girl would always be ready to 'kiss and make up' as soon as the discussion was over. Sulking and brooding for hours on end is guaranteed to turn David off any girl!

David's favourite girlfriends always share his love of music.

Well, those are some of the qualities David is looking for in his ideal girlfriend. Does she sound like you at all? Could YOU be the future Mrs Cassidy?

3

Of course, I dreamt about him all the time, but I didn't tell the others that. You have to keep some things back for yourself. Just like I never told them the truth about my favourite song. When Gillian said 'Could It Be Forever' was David's best record, I said she was absolutely right. So fabulous. So romantic. The way that David kept you dangling and waited a whole stomach-flipping beat before slipping in that final 'But'. And his voice just *melted* that word. I swear you can hear him smiling as he sings it. He must have known he had us exactly where he wanted us and he kept us waiting until we screamed and pleaded for him to say it . . . 'But?'

We tended to chew these things over at lunchtime, which was spent huddled round the big old throbbing radiator in the science-lab corridor. When it was wet, anyway, which was most of the year where we lived. In spring, Gillian's group moved its centre of operations outside under the horse chestnuts at the far end of the playing fields. I was still new to the group, a recent substitute for Karen Jones, who had offended Gillian after Stuart Morris did the slow dance with her at the Christmas disco. I mean, danced with Karen, not Gillian. Fair play to Karen, Gillian never let on she fancied Stuart before she saw them dancing together so Karen couldn't have known, could she? Cried her eyes out when Gillian called her a slag in the car park.

Compared to David, boys of our own age seemed like pathetic cretins.

'Look at him, he's just a kid, he is,' Sharon would

jeer if one of them dared to approach.

Experts in romance, we had never been kissed. We just knew David was a gentleman who would never try any of that stuff the boys did at the Starlight disco on Saturday nights. Grabbing a feel before they even got you a Pepsi. But Stuart Morris was three years older than we were and in the lower sixth. He was acting captain of the school first XV while Gareth Pugh's knee was on the mend. Rugby was the local religion so that made Stuart a god. Without needing to be told, almost as if we were born knowing it, we had grasped a key mathematical proof of the female universe: the more desirable a boy is the less chance you have of getting him. The less chance you have of getting him the more desirable he becomes. Therefore, boys who like and want you are not desirable. QED.

Anyway, Gillian was going with Stuart now and Karen was out and I was in, or almost. I was so desperate to keep in with them I needed to make the right impression without having a clue how.

' "But" isn't a very sexy word,' I announced that lunchtime, trying to sound as though sexy was a word I used every day, although this was the first time I'd tried it out loud. 'But in "Could It Be Forever", David makes "but" sound sexy.'

'David's got a sexy butt!,' shrieked Carol, overjoyed. 'Sexy butt, sexy butt!'

Carol was the most advanced of all of us. She had meaty swimmer's shoulders and a bum that stuck out so far you could balance a paper cup on it. Not only had she started her periods when she was ten, her breasts had developed overnight as though she'd got fed up of waiting and used a bike pump. You wouldn't put it past her, to be honest with you. Carol

43

was on really friendly terms with her breasts. She handled them like they were hamsters, even getting them out occasionally and petting them. Me, I would hardly dare glance at my own shy swellings in the bathroom mirror at home, not unless it was steamed up. My nipples were flat and soft and dusky pink like rose petals. Carol's were closer to walnuts; brown and nubbly, you could see them clearly through her blouse.

'Secondary sexual characteristics,' that's what the Biology teacher called breasts. And with the blimmin' boys right there in the same room with us. Thanks a lot, Sir. They never let us forget it. SSCs. Secondary sexual characteristics.

Carol's breasts were hard to ignore because she knotted her white blouse tight under them, even though she was always getting told off by the teachers for showing her stomach, which was the colour of Bisto all year round. Carol's eyebrows were apricot; so fine they were practically invisible. When the sun shone, the skin underneath looked like bacon, so she drew the arches in with a brown Rimmel pencil. It made her look hard. Harder than she was really. And she had this way of wearing our school tie with a long dangly end so it seemed less like a boring tie and more like a lizard tongue for licking up boys.

Carol was sexy, before we even knew what sexy was, is what I'm trying to say.

'Sexy butt! David's got a sexy butt!' Sharon took up Carol's chant, delighted by my mistake.

'That's not what I meant,' I said quickly. 'It's just the way he pauses in the song and leaves you hanging on for the but . . .'

Too late. Even to my own ears I sounded stupidly

earnest and pedantic. No fun Petra. Learn to take a joke, why can't you?

The others were all falling about. Even Angela and Olga, who had gone to fetch the drinks and the KitKats from the machine, and had missed the sexy but conversation. Carol's honking piggy laugh moved into its final snorting stage and hot chocolate shot out of her nose and spattered all down her blouse so she looked like she'd been machine-gunned. My mum would've killed me, but Carol couldn't care less. There was something animal about Carol that scared me sometimes.

'Petra wants a feel of David's sexy butt,' she leered, puckering up her sink-plunger lips and grabbing at my skirt.

I pushed her away. 'No, I don't.'

God, don't you hate blushing? Once a blush starts you can't stop it; like a spilt glass of Ribena it goes everywhere. Obviously, I had noticed David's backside. You couldn't very well not notice it, could you? It stuck out of all the photos of his concerts when he wore those slinky catsuits. But I didn't want to hear David's bum being joked about. Joking about ordinary boys was one thing, like having a laugh about Mark Tugwell, the double-bass player who sat behind me in county youth orchestra. Tuggy Tugwell. Carol said he kept a spare oboe down his pants, and I couldn't stop myself looking whenever he uncrossed his legs. But this was different. I was in love. I loathed crude or disrespectful talk about David. I pictured myself riding to his defence in a long cream cheesecloth dress with a high collar, pin-tucks on the bodice and frothy lace trim, like the one Karen Carpenter had. I'd be sitting on that palomino pony David was riding in my favourite poster on

Sharon's wall. But I'd be riding side-saddle like the Queen, so I didn't spoil the dress.

Smutty jokes about David really upset me. I suppose they were an unwelcome reminder that he was common property. Stupid, really. I don't know how you can get the idea that someone who has the biggest fan club in history, bigger than Elvis or the Beatles, is yours and yours alone, but you can, you really can.

The hard thing was I loved talking about David, and everything connected to him, even in a silly way. Wednesday nights, I would take the long way round to orchestra practice just so I could walk past David's the ironmongers, behind the bus station. Seeing his name written in big letters over the shop felt like a sign. I mean, it *was* a sign, you know, but a different kind of sign. Like the world knew that I loved him and put his name up there special. Just saying his name out loud was a thrill after hearing it a million times inside my own head. Talking about him to friends made him more real, but at the same time it meant I was sharing him, which hurt. I preferred it when we were alone together in my bedroom.

'David is sexy but what?' demanded Gillian twitching her delicate, Beatrix Potter-bunny nose.

She was in her usual perch on top of the radiator, slender legs dangling down, navy sheer socks pulled up to her thighs, leaving only a few inches of pale flesh exposed. I tried not to look at the flash of white panties, which made me think of her new boyfriend and of what he might be doing to her. How I longed for those long socks of Gillian's. My socks came to just below the knee and my mother insisted I wore garters to hold them up. The elastic burrowed into the skin leaving an angry red bracelet round my calves. It took ages to fade. Sometimes, when I lay in the bath and looked at the marks on my legs, I liked to pretend I was a tortured saint. One who had courageously kept the faith and endured the red-hot irons of sadistic torturers with pointy beards, giving absolutely nothing away. Stigmata rhymed with garter.

'What's so funny then about David singing but? I don't get it,' Gillian demanded.

God had made Gillian perfect, but in His infinite wisdom He had left out a sense of humour. Maybe if you're that pretty He reckons you don't need one. God probably thinks it's only worth giving a sense of humour to those of us who have to laugh at all the rubbish bits that are wrong with us.

'It's not funny,' I said, trying to silence Sharon with a pleading look.

She was supposed to be on my side, not Carol's. When we were at her house doing our David scrapbooks, I felt we were getting really close, but at school I never quite knew whose friend she was. Sharon's shifting loyalty stung more than Carol's crude taunts.

'I was only saying "Could It Be Forever" is David's best song, like you said, Gillian,' I went on, hoping that saying Gillian's name would make them stop. They were all scared of upsetting her, even Carol.

Gillian took a pot of Vaseline out of her bag and dabbed a blob on her bottom lip. She had this way of moving the jelly, flexing and rolling both lips to push it along and get an even coverage without needing to use her finger. Like all of Gillian's actions, it was seductive and mesmerising. We all tried to copy her, but ended up with jelly on our teeth.

Gillian was looking at me as though I was something in a shop window she might seriously consider buying. For one brilliant moment I thought she was going to smile. Maybe even invite me round to her house to listen to records. Then she slid off the radiator, yanked down her skirt and said: 'That's the aggravating thing about you, Petra. You're always agreeing, aren't you?'

*   *   *

Our form room was out in one of the Terrapins next to the netball court. Better known as the Cowsheds. Freezing in winter, baking hot in summer. Walls so thin you could hear a chair being scraped back in the class next door. They called it the temporary block, but it had been there since the war.

On the way back to afternoon registration, Angela told us she had some news. I could tell from the little secret twitching smile on her face that she'd been saving it up like the last sweet in a packet. Her cousin, a girl called Joanna Crampton who lived in London, had phoned the night before. David was coming over to the UK to do two concerts at the end of May. It was for definite. Her cousin had read it in the Cassidy mag, which she got a week earlier than us because she lived in Hounslow. Everything took so long to reach South Wales. The whole world could have ended, London could be destroyed by a nuclear bomb and we'd still be stuck in Double Geography for all we knew about it.

The concert was on 26 May at a place called White City.

White. City. It sounded like a beautiful marble

palace to me. Like the Taj Mahal maybe. I pictured the glittering paved road leading up to the turreted entrance and the sound of softly trickling fountains. The date was instantly imprinted on my brain like it was my wedding day. 26 May.

'They're saying it's his last public performance ever,' announced Angela with a quiver of pride.

'He's not coming again? *Never*! We gotta go then, Petra,' shrieked Sharon, slipping her arm through mine. 'David's gonna be looking for us, mun. We stopped biting our nails and everything. We got four hundred and thirty-nine photos of him and now he's saying it's his last concert. There's gratitude for you!'

It felt so nice to hear our laughs twining round each other, her hiccupy soprano, my scratchy alto. I knew Sharon was sorry about Carol and the sexy 'but'.

'If we want tickets,' Angela said, 'we got to get a move on and send a postal order. One pound each, it is.'

'I got one of them from my auntie for half a crown,' Sharon said.

'What's a pound in the old money then?' someone asked.

Olga did the calculation while the rest of us were still counting on our fingers. She had a fantastic head for figures, did Olga.

Before we went decimal, it used to be twelve pennies to the shilling. Three years later and I was still scared of the decimal point. Put it in the wrong place and you could be out by hundreds. My thirteen-year-old brain clung on stubbornly to pounds, shillings and pence. I particularly mourned the passing of the threepenny bit, which felt heavy

49

and hot in your hand, and had a really satisfying bumpy edge. It was definitely the best coin to play with in your pocket if you were nervous.

'Ach, only the British are such idiots they would really be counting in twelves in the first place,' my mother said. Evidence of the backwardness of her adopted homeland was one of her favourite things.

Gillian announced that she had twenty-five pounds in Post Office savings. A small fortune, it made us gasp. Carol said she could nick a load off her dad who ran the amusement arcade down by the pier and always had a big bag of change.

'So we've got a tidy bit already. Problem is we have to think about the train fare now and the Underground the other end,' Olga said, appointing herself treasurer of the trip, though she didn't have many rivals for the post.

As the girls added up the money they had, plus the money they thought they could get, I felt the panic rising within me. A salty tide that reached the back of my mouth and made me feel my lunch was about to come up. This couldn't be happening. I'd always felt there'd be plenty of time to see him. Every cell in my body was getting ready for that meeting. He'd wait for as long as it took, I knew. Until the spots across my oily T-section were gone. Until my breasts were worthy of a proper bra. (Playtex trusted intimate apparel for the Woman You Want to Be. Pink, underwired. Page 78 of the *Freeman's Catalogue*.) Until I had got the Bach cello suites exactly how they were supposed to sound. Pain and joy braided tightly together, like my mother plaiting my hair until my scalp squealed for mercy. Pain and joy, pain and joy. One day, I planned to play my favourite pieces to David. Even if words failed me, music never would.

50

But now there were no more untils. David's final concert in Britain was less than a month away. After that, he was never coming back. I'd be like that girl in the play we were doing in English. She never told her love but let concealment like a worm in the bud feed on her cheek. That's exactly what it felt like. Something gnawing away at your insides. I knew more about David than anybody. All of my preparations could not go to waste.

Somehow, I would get a ticket and go to him at the White City.

*   *   *

There were things my mother didn't know. My mother didn't know that she had chosen a really bad name for me because Petra was also the name of a famous dog on children's TV. She didn't know that whenever our teacher called the register and got to me, the whole class started barking, or at least most of the boys did.

My name came next but one to last, so I always had a couple of minutes in which I pretended I was too busy to care about what was coming up. Fitting a new cartridge in my pen, carefully wrapping the old one in blotting paper, searching my satchel under the desk for a sharpener I knew perfectly well was in my brown furry pencil case.

First Mr Griffiths had to get through the Davieses, including poor Susan Smell, all the Joneses, one Lewis (my Sharon), one Morgan, mad Gareth Roberts, then all the Thomases—

'Karen Thomas?

' 'Ere, Sir.'

'Karl Thomas?'

'By'ere, Sir.'

'Siân Thomas? Susan Thomas?'

There were six Thomases altogether, including two cousins who looked like speckled brown eggs. Their dads were identical twins who took it in turns to work the ham machine down the Co-op wearing nets over their sandy hair so the dandruff didn't fall in the meat. After the last Thomas, there was a pause that always felt like an eternity in hell to me before . . .

'Petra Willi—?'

'Woof! Woof! Awooooo.'

'Petra Williams. Quiet! I said, QUIET!'

The class became a kennel. Yapping, snarling, barking. In the back row, Jimmy Lo threw his head back and howled like a wolf under a full moon.

My new friends in Gillian's group shot me quick, encouraging smiles. The smiles said they were really sorry and embarrassed for me. Mostly, though, I think they were just glad it wasn't them who had the name of the TV dog.

'All right, that's enough, class,' Mr Griffiths snapped.

If the barking carried on when he tried to read out Steven Williams's name, which came straight after mine, Mr Griffiths began to change colour. You could watch the blood travel upwards from his shirt collar and suffuse his face as though red ink were being injected into his neck.

'I said, that's enough of that. Let's be having you. I said silence NOW, class.'

Mr Griffiths was a nice man, but he was young for a teacher, and good-looking with sideburns, pleading spaniel eyes and a floppy moustache and I just knew it would be better if he was older and ugly so that his anger was scary instead of funny.

The barking wasn't really my mum's fault. My mother didn't know that Petra was the name of the dog on *Blue Peter* because we didn't have a TV set. My mother didn't agree with television.

'It is a box for idiots,' she said.

In fact, my mother claimed that scientists had proved that if you stared at a television set for long enough, rays from the inside could destroy your vital organs, even the kidneys which are located at the back of your body beneath your waist. When I first told Sharon about the danger television rays posed to internal organs we were in her lounge, sitting on the Lewises' new mustard Dralon three-piece suite and waiting for *The Partridge Family* to start. We had our favourite clothes on. Well, we had to dress up for David, didn't we? Barred by Mrs Lewis from watching the show because of their disrespectful comments, Sharon's big brother, Michael, and his friend, Rob, were outside the door, keeping up a sniggering commentary and threatening terrible violence against David.

'Hello, poofter, hear the song that we're singing, / C'mon, he's crappy,' the boys sang tunelessly to the *Partridge* theme tune.

'Shut yer face, yer only jealous,' Sharon bellowed back.

She laughed about the rays from the TV, but a few seconds later she went into the kitchen and came back holding two baking trays high in the air like they were cymbals. We both lay back on the settee with the trays covering our chests and stomachs.

'The trays will deflect the poisonous rays,' Sharon said in a metallic Captain Scarlet voice. 'Don't panic now, will you? Your kidneys are safe with me, Petra

53

fach.'

The baking trays made us look like Roman soldiers who had died in battle.

In the lunch queue outside the hall, Jimmy Lo, whose parents ran the Chinese takeaway on Gwynber Street, shouted: 'Petra is a German shepherd.' He pronounced German as Jermin. 'Geddit? *Jermin* shepherd. Petra. Woof-woof!'

And then the boys with him—Mark 'Tuggy' Tugwell and Andrew 'Amor' Morris—started to sing:

> 'Hitler has only got one ball,
> Göring has two but very small,
> Himmler has something sim'lar . . .'

(Years later, after I had gone to college in London, Lo's Chinese restaurant was closed down by health inspectors for serving Alsatian meat in the chop suey. This is known as poetic justice.)

The Germans bombed our town during the war and people don't forget something like that in a hurry. They had a display on the bombing in the central library, in the main corridor with old photographs the colour of tea. Night after night, the planes came back to hit the steelworks and the docks. The explosions lit up the sea like a giant flash photograph, and you could see as far away as Ireland, people said. If the pilots couldn't find their target, they just unloaded the bombs anyway so the planes would have enough fuel to make the journey home to Germany. I knew all about it because Mamgu and Tad-cu, my grandparents, had a farm up in the hills behind the town and they were shutting up the cows one night when they heard an incredible piercing sound.

'Well, ye Dew, Dew, you'd have thought the Almighty Himself was wolf whistling,' Mam always said when she told her grandchildren the bomb story. We knew it was true because the crater was still in the top field. It was so big you could fit a whole house in there.

I found it hard to believe that my mother was on the other side during the war because our side was right and we won. In our house, it was my mother who was right and she always won.

When my grandparents, my dad and his two sisters, Auntie Edna and Auntie Mair, were running towards the byre in their nightclothes with buckets of water, the plane that caused the fire was already on its way back to the country where my six-year-old mother was sleeping. A pregnant cow lost her calf and, for five days after the bomb, the entire herd's milk came out as cheese.

See, even before my parents met, they were already fighting.

*   *   *

In my favourite David dream, the register was being called when David opened the door and strolled into our classroom. It was always after the six Thomases and just as Mr Griffiths said my name. David was wearing that white open-necked knitted shirt with the outsize collar and pearly buttons he wore on the album cover of *Cherish*.

My God, has he ever looked more beautiful? David Cassidy was the only human, male or female, who could make a feather cut seem insanely desirable. Looking out of that album cover, his gaze is so intense his hazel eyes are practically black; like

55

the *Mona Lisa*, his eyes make you want to look and look and never stop looking.

Once he was in our classroom, David would introduce himself to Mr Griffiths, smile his gorgeous, easy Keith Partridge smile and say, 'Hey, Petra. What a cool name! I really dig it.'

That would shut them up. They would be so impressed that a world superstar had turned up at our school. And David, being American, wouldn't know Petra was a TV dog. He'd think Petra was just a name like any other, maybe even a pretty name. When I was older I would live in America in a canyon and no one would bark at me ever again.

My friends never spoke about the barking. It was probably hard to think of what to say. Only two people mentioned it. One was Susan Davies.

I was coming out of a cubicle in the toilets this break-time, right, and Susan was over by the paper towels; she'd folded one of the towels in this really clever way to look like a dove and she stood there working the wings so they opened and closed. We were alone.

'Mustn't let them get you down with that barking, must you?' Susan said, almost to herself.

'No,' I said, turning on the tap and pumping the button on the soap dispenser. You always tried to get a drop even though the hard pink bubblegum gunk over the spout stopped any coming out. Susan's unmistakable odour—the smell-shock of her that forced you to breathe through your mouth when she was near—merged into the sweet stink of the toilets.

'There's lovely your hair's looking with you, Petra,' she said.

I glanced up and saw her face in the mirror. If you forced yourself to withhold judgement for a few seconds, it was possible to see that a girl with thickly lashed brown eyes and sweetheart-bow lips was under that disastrous pock-marked mask. Susan's own hair was fair and shiny like in an advert and so long she could sit on it. The hair was her only claim to beauty and I knew in that moment, when she praised mine, how well she took care of it, how it was lovingly conditioned and brushed every night so it would be perfect for school in the morning. If you saw Susan Davies from behind and you didn't know, you'd be waiting for a real looker to turn round. I wondered what that would be like, to turn to acknowledge a wolf whistle with a Silvikrin swish of your long flaxen hair and to see the shock and disgust in a boy's eyes.

'Your hair's—' I began, but the door to the toilets slammed open like a cowboy was coming into a saloon for a gunfight. Carol. She ignored Susan, pulled her pants down, plonked herself on a toilet and didn't even bother to lock the door as the pee sluiced into the pan and she let off a squealy, pressure-relieving fart.

'They're dead mingy in that canteen,' Carol said, addressing the toilets as if it was just the two of us. When I turned round, the only evidence Susan had been there was a paper dove perched on the top of the bin. I pushed it down under the other towels. I didn't like it; Susan acting like we were both in the same boat. I didn't want her pity. What did it make me if I was being pitied by Susan Smell?

'You bin talking to Susan Davies, then?' Carol said.

'Gerraway with you,' I said, holding my nose and pretending to faint at the imaginary pong.

Carol honked her approval.

Unpopularity was like a germ you could catch. It was better not to get too close.

* * *

The only other person who mentioned the barking was Steven Williams. It was that same afternoon we decided to get tickets for David's concert, and everyone was charging in a mad bundle out of the class after registration when Steven came up and handed me a copy of *Twelfth Night*.

'Hi-ya? Think this is yours,' he said.

Steven was tall and he stooped slightly when he spoke to me. I knew he was one of the rugby boys and a mate of the evil barking Jimmy Lo. He had a scratch on his cheek beneath his right eye, which was the same blue as warm summer sea. The width of his shoulders was amazing close up. I felt like a Barbie doll next to him.

It wasn't my copy of the play, I knew that. Mine was in my bag. I'd seen it when I was hiding my red face in there during registration.

'Thanks,' I said, and took it.

'Sorry, like, about the barking,' Steven Williams said, 'Boys're a bit mental, that's all.'

I nodded.

'Rose-red city, is it?'

'What?'

'Petra. Rose-red city, half as old as time.' He spoke the words clearly as if he were an actor reciting a poem.

'Dunno,' I said.

Why? Please God, why? I'd never said dunno in my life before. Dunno was common. Dunno was the vocabulary of morons. My mother could drop down

58

dead in the street if she knew she had a daughter who said dunno. The woman who devoured *Reader's Digest*'s 'It Pays to Increase Your Word Power' could not have produced a child who said dunno.

'Remember your manners, Petra, for Gott's sake,' my mother chided.

'Thanks a lot,' I tried again and nervously cracked a smile.

Steven picked up his red-striped Adidas sportsbag and slung it over his shoulder as if ready to go, but then he stayed where he was, moving his weight from one foot to the other.

Was it a trap? I looked around to check if Jimmy and the other boys were lying in wait, but they were already a hundred yards down the path, booting their bags into the mud and falling on top of them.

'Thought you'd like to know—about the other Petra like.'

'Thanks. I didn't. Know. Rose-red city.'

Which was the colour of my cheeks by then, of course. The blush travelled faster than the feeling that was driving it; a feeling for which I did not yet have a name. One of the most powerful feelings in the whole wide world.

'So long, then,' Steven said, gesturing with his free arm to show me he needed to catch up with the other boys. He raised his eyes from the floor and smiled. The smile said the barking wasn't going to stop, but that he didn't agree with it.

'So long, then.'

I think we'd just had our first conversation.

*　　　*　　　*

'What did Steven Williams want with you, then?'

Gillian demanded when I caught up with the girls in Needlework.

She put the emphasis on the you. As though I was the last girl in the world any boy would want to talk to.

'He had a book of mine by mistake,' I said.

I hated Needlework, or rather Needlework hated me. I'd been trying to put a zip in a midi-skirt for three lessons and Miss kept telling me to unpick it and try again. Each time I gently depressed the foot pedal on the little Elna sewing machine I felt like a rodeo rider forced to ride a giant bee. Just the faintest touch on the pedal and the needle went crazy. Bbbzbzzbbzzzzz.

'Steven Williams can get between my covers any day,' Carol smirked, raising herself half out of the chair and making thrusting motions with her hips. Olga rolled her eyes at me. Unlike me, Olga actually wore her glasses in school and could see.

'Good-looking boy, fair play to him, keeps himself tidy,' Sharon said, licking the end of a piece of cotton before threading it through a needle. She began to manoeuvre a sleeve into place in the bodice of a pink satin bridesmaid dress that she would wear at her auntie's wedding in August. It already had darts on the bust, an assortment of pin-tucks and an invisibly stitched hem. The long puffed sleeves, lying like amputated limbs on the table ready to be sewn in, had perfect crimped-pastry tops. What I am telling you is that Sharon's dress looked like a *dress*. A feat more astonishing to me than writing a symphony or docking a spaceship. That dress was so professional Sharon could have sold it in a shop.

'Anyway, that Steven Williams is a terrible kisser. Bethan Clark 'ad him,' confided Gillian. 'Spits in

60

your mouth, he does.'

*   *   *

We were walking down the street, arm in arm, our group. Gillian was in the middle and that Saturday she allowed Sharon and Angela to link arms with her. The second favourites got to hold the arms of the girls holding onto Gillian. I was on the outside, but oddly exhilarated and grateful to be part of the line-up at all. Because the pavement was narrow, I had to let go of Olga's arm every time we came to a lamp-post, step into the gutter, then quickly hop back onto the pavement and grab her again. The conversation moved on, so I was always a beat or two behind. In my hurry, I failed to notice the dog mess.

'*Ach-a-fi*, Petra, is that you? Got something on your shoe? For God's sake, girl.'

Gillian said I could catch them up once I'd got the poo off my shoe.

'Come up my house after, OK?' yelled Angela without looking round. My friends moved off, not breaking formation, their backs like a wall.

I found a lolly stick in the hedge and started to flick out the claggy orange shit from the sole. It took ages because the smell kept making me gag; the last bits were stuck deep in the rubber criss-cross pattern and I tried to rub them off with a dock leaf. God, my hands really stank and I didn't have any tissues. It was OK, though, because I could wash them at Angela's house in her downstairs cloakroom. I ran my fastest up the hill to catch them up and I got a stitch; the pain ripped into my left side and I had to sit on a wall for a while till it died down: then I picked

61

the wrong turning, didn't I, and I had to go back to the main road again to get my bearings. I was so late. The pungent, gritty smell of melting chip fat started to come from the houses where the women were putting the dinner on. The girls'd be worrying and thinking I'd gone home or something. Eventually, I found the horseshoe-shaped close of detached houses where English Angela lived. It was lovely, really new with all these young trees planted in circles of soil cut in the front lawns. The trees were just sticks tied to a post really, with a single branch of pale pink blossom like the kind of feather boa I always wanted. Angela's place had a patio and a cloakroom and everything. Lucky I remembered the number. I was so relieved and happy that I knew which house was Angela's I almost started crying when her mum opened the door.

The woman was carrying a baby girl who had damp ringlets stuck to her head and looked grumpy, like she'd just woken from a nap. Angela's mum seemed surprised when I said why I was there.

'Oh, sorry, love, the girls aren't here. They're over Gillian's tonight. Bit of a party. Forget, did you?'

*　　　*　　　*

I did forget something. I forgot to tell you my favourite David song. It wasn't 'Could It Be Forever', not even with that gorgeous, sexy dangling 'but'. It was 'I Am A Clown'.

The single only made it to number three in the UK charts, but it was always my personal Number One tearjerker. I loved it because it was so sad, so soulful, so sensitive and deep all at the same time. Probably what I thought I was. David sang about being a clown in a circus sideshow. He had to keep smiling no matter what, even though it was killing him on the inside. The first time I heard 'I Am A Clown' I got the shivers. Honest to God, I felt that he was speaking to me in code. David felt lonely and trapped in his pop-star life and only I could hear him. And you'd never have guessed it, but being able to feel a bit sorry for him was even better than thinking he was perfect. It was like noticing he had bad skin and not minding. (Which he did, as it happened, and I didn't mind because David's spots came up when he suffered with his nerves and all that make-up he had to wear for filming. It wasn't acne or anything. He was just sensitive, that's all.)

If David could be pitied, it meant that he needed me. I had a role to play in his life. Despite all of his wealth and fame and all the millions of girls he could choose from, he needed *me*.

David Cassidy was lonely. The thought was strangely thrilling. With me he would not be lonely any more.

That's why I never revealed my favourite song to the other girls. If I told them then they could copy my idea. It might cost me some crucial advantage when David and I finally met. He was going to be so impressed I hadn't chosen one of his obvious hits, wasn't he?

'Gee, that's amazing, Petra. You dig "I Am A Clown"? Wow. No one else ever noticed that song and it means so much to me. It happens to be my personal favourite.'

And what would I say back to him?

Believe me. You really don't have to worry. I only want to make you happy. And if you say, Hey, go away, I will. But I think, better still, I'd better stay

63

around and love you. Do you think I have a case? Let me ask you to your face.

Do you think you love me?

I THINK I LOVE YOU.

4

Twenty to six, and Bill was staring at his second pint. They had only arrived at the pub, he and Pete, seven minutes ago, but already he had ordered and consumed a large, smeared glass of the usual. He didn't know what the usual was; his own usual was whisky when he could afford it, or Guinness when he could not, or even, on a spring evening, with sunglasses on, and no male acquaintances within ten miles, a gin and tonic. But now, in the Cat & Fiddle, not wanting to appear different, or to be mistaken for posh, he had listened to what Pete had asked for and carefully followed his lead. And the usual, it turned out, was most unusual: a pale, brackish draught of what appeared to be canal water, topped with a drift of industrial scum. He had forced it down, then more of the same to take away the taste. Each man was paying for his own; Pete had not paid for Bill's, and Bill, slipping easily into the habit of meanness, had returned the lack of favour. He had, however, bought a packet of crisps, which sat between them, and into which Pete was now freely plunging his fist. He seemed worked up about something.

'I mean, it's bollocks. Just complete and utter bollocks.'

He paused for effect. Bill, whose mind had been elsewhere, wondered if he was meant to lend support.

'Well, it's certainly—' he began.

'Right. Total. And the worst thing is, they don't even know they're doing it.' His fingers rustled among the crisps. 'D'you think it's a girl thing?'

'Well, it might—'

'Has to be. I mean, the way they take one tiny detail and go completely mental over it. Like it's life or bleedin' death. You wouldn't get a bloke doing that, would you?' Pete pulled his fingers out and licked off the salt. He had been to the Gents when they first entered the pub—too quick a visit, Bill reckoned, to have spent time washing his hands.

'Oh, no, no,' said Bill, who had resolved to agree with everything his new colleagues said. As a strategy for fitting in it was imperfect, but it would do until he came up with a better one. They paused to drink in unison. Pete offered Bill one of Bill's own crisps, which he declined. There were hardly any left.

'You're right,' Pete continued, as if he and Bill were in the midst of a constructive discussion. 'It is just girls. They get the record home and play it like a million times, and then their dad comes in to tell them to turn it down, and when he slams the bedroom door the needle jumps, so that there's this bloody great scratch across, I dunno, "Can It Be Forever" or whatever—'

' "Could it".'

'Could it what?'

' "Could It Be Forever". That's the name of the song, actually.' Bill was on safe ground. For a fraction of a second, he was appalled to discover in himself a sliver of pride: the righteous pride of a man who knows his special subject and is not afraid to correct anyone who doesn't. In great haste he drained his glass, almost to the lees.

'Sod off,' said Pete, without rancour, or not much. 'Anyways, for about a fortnight they go totally spare, like somebody died, and they hate their parents and

66

won't eat. And then, this is the mad bit, they sit around with their girlfriends, who are just like them but worse, and they egg each other on, so they get their rockers in a twist—'

'Knickers.'

'Pardon?'

'Knickers,' said Bill. 'You get your knickers in a twist, you go off your rocker. They're different things.' As he spoke, he could hear his voice growing smaller and starting to die. Pete must have heard it, too, because he leaned a bit closer and said: 'It's true, then.'

'What's true?' Bill smiled, trying to keep things light. He helped himself to a crisp.

'What they said, that you're one of them university wankers.'

'Who said?' Bill asked in genuine curiosity, but Pete just sniffed. The crisp tasted damp. There was salt on his gums. Not for the first time he felt the full horror of being English: sitting in a packed pub, drinking swill, with someone you don't care about, being quizzed about your social class. He asked himself—again, not for the first time—what it was like for David, living in California. Even if it was only a tenth as good as the songs made out, only a hundredth as sunny and relaxed as it looked in the films, it had to be better than this.

He reached for his pint, downed the dregs and used them to rinse his mouth. As he did so, he shook his head, as if trying to rid himself of a thought, like a cow with flies on its eyes. Here I am, he reflected, a graduate, an adult, more or less, and I am jealous of David Cassidy. In his first three months of employment at Worldwind Publishing, Bill had devoted most of his waking hours to studying the life

67

and style of David Bruce Cassidy—or, as Bill had described him to Pete, 'that lucky sonofabitch'. The curse sounded false coming out of Bill's mouth, he knew that. He had to take a run up at it, like a horse attempting a four-bar gate.

Sun-nuv-vuh-bitch.

You really needed the proper twang, like someone out of *Dirty Harry* or *The Dirty Dozen*—a dirty movie, anyway—to get the full effect, and Bill's version of a twang was worse than useless. He had never been able to do accents, and his American was especially pathetic; he sounded, and indeed looked, like a man trying to dislodge a shred of meat from a back tooth with his tongue. But, for all that, and despite the fear of making a fool of himself, he loved 'sonofabitch'. He loved it because, for a second, even if it didn't make him come across as American, it made him *feel* American. And that was obviously better than being a twat from Tolworth, two stops down from Wimbledon.

'Sorry, go on about the record,' he said, trying to restart. He could see Pete struggling between the urge to tell his story and the well-worn need to pick a fight. Eventually, he sighed, brushed the empty crisp packet onto the floor and carried on. The fight could wait.

'Like I said, there's this scratch, and they decide that's an omen. Like it means something. Didn't people used to look at guts to tell the future, Greeks and that?'

'Absolutely,' said Bill, who let his neck slacken so his heavy head nodded and nodded like one of those toy dogs in the back window of a car. Who on earth had the strength for a fight on a Friday evening, with your spirit sapped by a week of slog at the premier

David Cassidy fanzine? Pete could have denied the moon landings, at this moment, or the Holocaust, and Bill would have nodded along.

'So, they decide that the scratch, which was only caused by her dad, is a message from Cassidy.' Pete would have broken his beer glass and chewed the shards rather than call a pop star, any pop star, by his Christian name. They weren't friends, him and Cassidy. He didn't know the bastard. Didn't have him round for tea. And it wasn't just pop stars, nancies like that. It was any fella. Surnames, all the way. To Pete, the tragedy of James Bond had come the previous year, when Connery had given way to Moore. The Aussie bloke didn't count.

'And because the scratch is on that song, the "Forever" one,' he went on, 'it means that Cassidy is striking it out, or some crap like that, or changing his mind. Instead of Can It Be'—he glanced at Bill, daring him to a challenge—'it means, sod the question, It Will Be. You Will Be Mine. You, you girls, sitting there with your purple hot pants and your stupid gonks.' For Pete, this was rhetoric enough, and he made a swiping motion, one hand across his face, as if to brush away the blame. 'I read it,' he explained. 'In that bloody rag we put together.'

'And in Amsterdam,' Bill said, firing back, 'he wore this stupid red stuff along the edges of his suit.' He thought it was a good idea to borrow some of Pete's outrage, even though he couldn't feel it himself. What Pete took as an insult—to England, to his manhood, to his certain knowledge of women— Bill treated as mildly intriguing. But he couldn't admit as much, so he pretended to be picking up the thread. 'He had on this white *catsuit*,' (Pete reacted to the word with a vigorous air show of mock

69

masturbation, the other hand gripping his glass), 'and it was trimmed in scarlet. And I promise you, we had more letters about that—what's it called? Frogging?'

Finally, they both had something to laugh at. Bill was warming to his theme, surprising himself in the process, and he went on.

'And these letters told us what the red meant. One girl had taken the photo we had and traced it, on greaseproof paper, and she sent us the tracing to prove that he was actually trying to spell out her signature in red braid.'

'Christ.' Pete was bent low, for some reason, as if grieving at all this female folly. His nose was almost touching the beer mats.

'And another thought that the frogging, the stuff on Cassidy's suit, was a dragon.'

'What?'

'She thought the pattern looked like a dragon's head.'

'What?'

'And that was meant to signify the Welsh dragon.'

'What?'

'And she was from Pontypool, so she thought Cassidy's "catsuit" design was aimed at her.' Bill waited for Pete to reply, like someone hitting back a tennis ball, but even Pete was flattened into silence. Swiftly he finished his drink, slipped from the bar stool and made for the door. Bill shrugged and followed him. They stood outside the pub, on a slender one-way street, where the air was no more breathable than within. Traffic fumes spilled from the road and met the yeasty waft of beer. Bill could barely move.

' 'Lo, mates.'

70

A bent figure was suddenly by their side, grinning up at them. It was Chas, the ageless office boy, scampering and talking through his teeth. He looked like an old English elf from the cover of a prog-rock album.

'Bin in the pisser?'

That was the office nickname for the pub, derived from rhyming slang. Bill had been stumped for a while, and Pete had had to spell it out for him, wearily, as if explaining a sum to a child. 'Cat & Fiddle, piddle, pisser. Jesus, I thought you were s'posed to be the clever clogs.'

Chas was angling now, in the brewing dusk. 'Drowned 'em?'

'Yeah, we're done,' said Pete. He was even less keen on buying a drink for Chas than he had been for Bill. He would not have bought him a drink after a month in the desert.

'Hello, Chas,' said Bill, looking down at him.

'Heard the big news?'

'No, what?' Bill had a weakness for the catastrophic event. 'Plane crash? Queen been shot? Peter Purves gets off with Val?'

'Hnyah, no such luck,' said Chas, giving a short snort. 'Just in. Schedule for the tour. Seems like our Mr Cassidy will be performing his miracles all over the shop. White City. 26th of May.'

'So?' This was Pete, with all the sourness he could muster.

'So we have to tempt the little misses even more, that's what.'

'Whatcha mean, even more? They don't need tempting, they need a bloody fire hose to keep them off,' said Pete. 'Me and Bill here were just talking about it. You could ask them for anything, I mean

71

anything, and they would lie down and let you have it, just for one more look at their lovely . . .' He stopped, wound himself up, until his whole body was a sneer, '. . . Daaaaayvid.'

'But this isn't just a look,' said Chas. 'This is London.'

'White City?' echoed Pete. 'What's he doing in that dump?'

'How many can you get into White City?' asked Bill. 'Twenty thousand?'

'God no, thirty, easily,' said Chas.

'Thirty-five, with those little girlies,' said Pete. 'Pack 'em in nice and tight. Squeeze the little darlings till they snap. Love that, they will.'

'And we get hold of some tickets and give them away as prizes? Is that the idea?'

'That's it.'

The three men stood on the kerb, jostled by drinkers and passers-by.

'Can you imagine?' asked Bill at last.

'Not much, hnyah,' said Chas.

'I mean, imagine being one of those girls. The ones who win our tickets.'

The other two peered at him, not quite sure if they liked his drift, let alone his imagination.

'Come again?' Chas was wrinkling his nose and rubbing the tip. He was getting thirsty, almost to the point of using his own cash.

'Well, they sit all day in, in, Hartlepool, or Worthing, or, or—'

'Fife. We've had some loonies from Fife.'

'—And then one day, they get chosen to go and see the guy in person. I mean, these girls feel chosen anyway. They feel he's waiting for them.' Bill looked at his colleagues. 'Believe me, I know, I read their bloody letters. That's my job, OK? And now they will be chosen. Some girl will already be able to tell you Cassidy's favourite colour and the colour of his eyes, and whether he likes cornflakes or Rice Krispies, whether he has freckles—'

'He doesn't.' Pete sounded firmer than normal, like a defendant denying the charges in court. 'No freckles. He has spots. Scores of the buggers. Believe me, Bill, I know, I scrub them out. That's my job.' He glanced down at Chas, who snickered on cue.

'Touché,' said Bill.

'To what?'

'Doesn't matter. Point is, if I already knew the poor bloke's star sign, and I could read my future in his stars and all that palaver, I would open my envelope from the magazine, as licked and sealed by Chas'—whose tongue stuck out at this, again on cue—'and I would just, you know, faint. Or die.'

For a moment, neither of the others spoke. Then Pete enquired:

'What is it, anyway?'

'What's what?'

'His star sign?'

'Aries, but that's not the point. What I'm trying—'

But he had gone too far, and the others leapt.

'Ayr-ries? You *are* a wanker! I knew it,' said Pete.

So great was Chas's glee that he actually bunched his bony little fists and beat them together, like a wind-up monkey playing the cymbals. They had a fellow worker who knew the horoscope of a male pop star: you could sit next to someone for five years and not find anything as juicy as that. They might as well have discovered Bill sleeping with a teddy bear, or combing a doll's hair.

Bill let their pleasure rise and subside. Nothing he

73

could do about it; they would stash his confession away and use it in the future, whenever he needed embarrassing. Could be any time.

He had only himself to blame. That morning Bill had completed a feature about David's star sign under the headline: MIRROR MIRROR ON THE WALL, WHO'S THE GROOVIEST ARIAN OF THEM ALL? Bill despised astrology, although, to be fair, it was hard to hate something that didn't exist. It was like reading a travel article about the best hotels in Atlantis. But girls liked it, he had noticed, even sensible ones; even clever ones, girls with degrees in philosophy or history who could pull apart the basis of the Christian faith over a prawn curry but would still take their biro, on the bus-ride home, and draw a careful red circle around the prediction that, come Tuesday, Sagittarians would feel an upswing in their private life that could be risky but which, handled wisely, might produce a major change. Ruth, for example, was on the cusp between Cancer and Leo so she read the forecast for each sign and picked which one she liked best. Bill was astounded that the future of their relationship might hang on whether his girlfriend woke up feeling more like a lion than a crab.

No constellations wheeled above the street. No stars, however bright, could beam their messages of encouragement and caution through the soup of London air. Bill shook himself.

'All right, you two,' he said, 'I'm done. See you on—'

But he never named the day. He had paused, on the brink, to stare past Pete, and over Chas's head; his shame forgotten, his focus locked elsewhere. Down the street came something that was not meant to come down streets; certainly not small streets off

Tottenham Court Road, with a low breeze blowing used sports pages onto the roadway, and wads of Juicy Fruit stuck to the kerb. It was vast and flat, and as it prowled along it growled at the drinkers on either side, who instinctively leaned back to let it pass, raising their drinks to shoulder level. To Bill, it was as if he were six years old, on horseback, beside a castle moat, with a dragon coming over the drawbridge, breathing flame.

'Jesus,' he said. 'An Espada.'

Chas, who was unimpressed by the vision, and, more importantly, could see no good reason why anyone else should be impressed, picked up the sound.

'Ay vee-va, Espadya,' he sang, to no one in particular.

'That's not a car,' said Pete. 'That's an aircraft carrier.' His breath came out in a rush as he spoke, and Bill realised that he must have been holding it.

'It's an S2,' said Bill.

'Could even be an S3. Try and check the steering wheel as it goes by. They updated it last year.' Pete and Bill had been seeking common ground for some weeks now, something that would lead them beyond the habit of rubbishing office life, and Bill, for one, who feared friendlessness more than most things, had almost despaired of establishing any point of contact. Now they had found one.

'What's all this S bollocks?' asked Chas.

'Well, the engine's pretty much the same, but they've changed it a couple of times since '68, and you can only really tell from the interior,' Bill said.

'Who's they?'

'Lamborghini.' Bill was genuinely astonished. He thought that such a passion was obvious, infectious,

75

and shared by every man. 'Don't you recognise it?'

'Bog off.'

There was a stifled laugh from beside him. Two women, holding gin and tonics, were listening. When Bill looked at them they glanced away.

'Christ, look at it,' said Pete. 'It's so low.'

The car was almost alongside now, moving warily, between the drinkers on either side of the street. They almost stood to attention, as if making way for a hearse. The roof barely reached Bill's chest, and he had to duck down to look inside. He couldn't make out the steering wheel, but he did catch a flash of sideburns, and a roll-neck sweater that matched the cream interior. Chas, bent almost double, had seen it too, and for him that decided it. He straightened up, with a curling lip, and said out loud, 'Tosser.' Bill knew he was right, but he couldn't keep his eyes off the car. As it cleared the mob, it quickened, the growl becoming a low roar, then turned and was lost from sight.

'Never seen one before.' Pete stood staring down the empty street.

'Me neither,' Bill said.

'So how d'you know about the inside and all that bollocks?' Chas asked. He seemed perplexed.

'Read it in *Autocar*. They had a Lambo special couple of months ago,' said Pete.

'God, yeah, did you see that bit where they took a Miura P400SV and put it against the Daytona?'

'Fantastic. Just brilliant. But I hate the way they took the eyelashes off the SV. I mean, I know it's got better carbs and everything, but the lashes were the best bit. Give me the S any day.'

'I know.' Bill had more to say on the subject, but even as he spoke he was conscious of having crossed

76

a line. Pete couldn't care less—as far as he was concerned, he had witnessed a miracle, and would feel free to tell everyone about it for the rest of his days—but Bill had just noticed the two women screwing up their faces in bewilderment and scorn.

'What bloody eyelashes?' Chas was still there, shifting from foot to foot as if he needed to pee, though all he really needed was a drink. Bill felt uneasy. He spoke dismissively, trying to win back lost favour.

'Oh, some crap about the headlight surround on the Miura. Earlier ones had these kind of black strokes at the top and bottom, and they were supposed to look like, you know, when a girl does her eyes, and . . .' He tailed off. Chas didn't reply, at least not with anything resembling a word. He puckered his mouth and blew a spitting sound, like someone ejecting an apple pip. Then he lowered his head, turned and melted into the throng around the entrance to the pub.

Pete, too, shook himself, as though coming out of a trance, and said brightly, 'Well, mustn't hang about. Dinner on the table. See you Monday.' He walked up the street towards the Tube. After a minute or so, Bill, who had not said goodbye, went the other way, digging in his pockets for a cigarette that he knew he didn't have. He was suddenly unhappy, though why he couldn't say. It was like being a small boy, unable, for a second, to find his parents in a crowd. The two women watched him go. One of them, her hair piled high, reached into the bottom of her glass, retrieved a slice of lemon and began to nibble.

'Like I said,' she told her friend. 'Men.'

*　　　*　　　*

77

He was supposed to take Ruth out on Friday nights. Friday nights were girlfriend and curry nights, but he hadn't been able to face it. Not tonight. Ruth was thrilled with his new job as a rock journalist. Not only was Bill off the dole and no longer an embarrassment, scrounging food out of the fridge in the Bloomsbury mansion-block flat she shared with Lesley and Judith, a couple of trainee solicitors; he was also doing something that lent Ruth herself a certain cool. For a museum assistant, who spent her days photocopying layouts of Anglo-Saxon burial mounds while dreaming of something less dead, it was thrilling to be able to say the word 'boyfriend' in the same sentence as the name 'Mick Jagger'. Bill had never known her so proud or so happy. It was hideous.

Obviously, he would never set out to deceive the girl he was supposed to love. It was just that when Ruth asked for more details of Bill's brilliant new writing job, he had been physically unable to speak the words *Essential David Cassidy Magazine*. Until that moment, he had not realised that the one thing he truly feared about women was their disappointment. Worse than anger, worse even than tears, female disappointment seemed almost operatic in its power to make the male feel worthless.

When you asked them what was wrong on their birthday and they said, 'Oh, nothing': that was the worst. For some reason, 'Oh, nothing' was to be even more feared than a simple 'Nothing'. A long apprenticeship as little brother to two older sisters, who alternately petted him or told him to get lost, had not prepared Bill for a girlfriend who expected you to read her mind, often it seemed before that

78

mind was made up.

Ruth was kind enough to be glad for him about the job. But mainly, he suspected, she was chuffed that choosing Bill as a boyfriend had finally paid off. The loser known as 'Socks' by her flatmates, because of the cheesy trail he left around the flat, was suddenly a man to be reckoned with. Lesley and Judith were both engaged, one to a civil engineer, the other to a wine merchant in Parsons Green. He had seen Ruth struggling bravely through the flatmates' shared rapture over Lesley's engagement ring—a sapphire with flanking slabs of diamonds. 'White gold,' she reported. 'They had it made to order at Hatton Garden. Chose the diamonds and everything.' So when it came to telling Ruth about his work, Bill had settled for 'journalist' and 'music business'. Not untrue, though not exactly true either.

He thought there would be loads of time to put her right later. But the night he accepted the offer from Roy Palmer, Ruth had given him a hero's reception when he got back to the Bloomsbury flat. There was a whole chicken cooked in some kind of brick with baked potatoes followed by roasted peaches. He had only ever tried tinned with condensed milk. After the afters, there was sex of a kind Ruth had never offered before; if not quite the kind of sex that rock stars had, or even the kind that he thought they had, then certainly the kind that he thought she thought they had. Which was rock star enough for him, to be getting on with. He felt like a peach. Fuzzy with pleasure. So, after that, Bill was in no real hurry to set Ruth straight about how he spent his days. When would be the best time to reveal to your girlfriend that you composed flirtatious letters to lovesick thirteen-year-olds?

79

Never would be the best time.

The lies Bill had told weighed heavily on him, though even worse was the thought of all the lies he would have to tell in the foreseeable future, with larger lies brought in to bury the smaller fragments. Bill was up to his neck in layer upon layer of untruth, as though interred in one of Ruth's burial mounds. He had already had to pretend that he was writing under an alias when Ruth asked to see the reviews, which he hadn't written, in a magazine he didn't work for. Plus there was the constant threat of discovery. The museum was only ten minutes on foot from Worldwind Publishing. Ruth could easily turn up in her lunch hour. Only the monstrous portrait he had painted of Roy Palmer—a volatile compound of Reggie Kray and Lord Beaverbrook—had thus far kept her away.

Men who lead a double life must get satisfaction from it, or why would they take the risk? That was the theory, but Bill was the sorry exception: his double life had all the dangers of being found out but none of the practical pleasures. Could there be— had there ever been—anything more humiliating than having David Cassidy as your other woman?

'You don't know how many times I wished that
    I had told you.
You don't know how many times I wished that I
    could hold you.'

Bill caught himself singing under his breath. Christ. That was the trouble with Cassidy songs. Once they got into your brain they stuck there like chewing gum. Long after he had forgotten all of Tennyson and Keats, he would be able to give a confident

80

rendition of 'How Can I Be Sure'.

There had been a nasty moment, a couple of weekends before, when he had gone round to Ruth's flat, to pick her up on the way to a party, and for once—unusual for her, since she was so much more punctual than him—she wasn't ready. 'Give me five mins,' she had said, which meant fifteen. So he had idled the time away in the girls' living room, read the spines on the bookshelf, and sneered at some of the titles, then felt guilty about the sneer. I mean, why shouldn't a woman read *Jonathan Livingston Seagull* if she wanted to? It was a free country, wasn't it? Just so long as it wasn't his woman. Please, God, not Ruth. Please, Ruth, not that.

And then, from one of the other bedrooms, a voice began to carol: 'I'm. Just. A.' The notes climbed, and as they reached the top a second voice joined in from the bathroom. Absent-minded voices, as of singers happily busy with something else, clipping on an earring in front of the mirror; no more than a musical doodle, really. Lesley and Judith, too, were getting ready to go out, for an orgiastic evening with the civil engineer. And into the doodle there cut a third voice, well out of tune: 'Will whoever is singing that bloody song please stop it right now.'

Bill stood there in horror, listening to Ruth as if he'd never heard her shout before—as if he hardly knew her. 'I can take almost anything. I can manage Brotherhood of Man. I can manage Terry Jacks and his "Seasons in the Sun", I can even manage Demis Roussos, if you buy me a kebab. But I will not sit in my own flat and listen to David bloody Cassidy, thank you very much. Thank you.'

This was followed, of course, by peals of delighted laughter from the other girls, thrilled to have

81

discovered a sore spot in their fellow lodger. Bill, however, did not laugh. He saw no comedy in Ruth's outburst against David. He looked into the future, and covered his eyes.

COULD YOU BE DAVID'S WIFE?

David's the first to admit that he has unusual habits, likes and dislikes that might just take a while to get used to! Yes, the girl who falls in love with David will have to like a lot of the same things David does, or at least understand some of the things he does—things that could be a little strange!

For instance, it isn't unusual for David to be almost ready for bed when suddenly he'll get back into his clothes! Why? For a midnight stroll of course!

David's dating habits could be thought of as strange. It could be common for David to call you at six in the morning, wildly enthusiastic. Let's go fishing!

So, if you become Mrs David Bruce Cassidy you might be awakened at three in the morning to the sounds of guitar music.

David's also fussy about the way his girl would dress or look for him. He can't stand hairspray—he wants to run his hand through your hair without that sticky feeling. And when he thinks about the wife he'll have some day he pictures her getting into bed wearing a fluffy negligee and with a freshly scrubbed face and a beautiful smile—NOT in flannel pyjamas with a head full of curlers and a face full of cream!

5

'All right, have I got:

   a. high colouring that is prone to stubborn spots
   b. delicate pale skin that flushes easily
   c. sallow skin with greasy patches or
   d. none of the above?'

We were in the Kardomah, just off the market square, drinking frothy coffee which they served in Pyrex cups and saucers. We didn't like the coffee much, but we thought it was American so we swallowed it down. The coffee came scalding hot and burned the back of your throat, then it got cold and scummy without ever being nice to drink. The Kardomah was the coolest cafe in town, in our opinion. All the flashest motorbikes were parked out the front. Service was slow and the ashtrays only got emptied every other day, but there was a pinball machine next to the door and plastic flowers in a vase on the tables. Coffee was expensive, but Sharon and I could make two cups and a shared toasted teacake last most of the afternoon. You just had to avoid the waitress's eye, that's all. That Saturday, the place was packed and we could hardly hear ourselves talk with the noise of the steam machine clearing its throat every few seconds.

We were wearing our ponchos over pointy-collared shirts and cord flares. Mine was brown-and-cream honeycomb, knitted by Mamgu, and I had a crocheted cap, with a two-tone appliquéd flower in lighter chocolate, which I had reluctantly removed to come indoors. I also wore a brown velvet choker, which was a bit tight, but I believed it to be an elegant accessory, plus it added length to my neck. (My neck was one of my weak points.) Sharon was sitting opposite me in a red poncho with a long white fringe and a big smiley David badge on the front. She was reading aloud from the multiple-choice quiz on the Beauty Dos and Don'ts page.

'Well, what d'you reckon, Pet? What skin type am I then?'

'None of the above,' I said cautiously.

'You're a b, definitely,' she said circling the answer.

That week it was Gillian's birthday and we were all in town shopping for presents. We had left Olga and Angela rummaging grimly through the sale bin in Boots. Privately, I was determined that my present would be the best. I thought I had hit the jackpot with the purchase of a Mary Quant blue eyeshadow kit. The colour palette went from the pale, almost duck-egg blue of Gillian's own eyes to a gorgeous rich indigo. In its lacquered black case with the Mary Quant logo, the kit was a thing of giddy beauty and part of the giddiness came from thinking how much it cost. More than I had spent on Christmas presents for both my parents, a concept that made me slightly ill, but I was so excited by the idea of Gillian's surprise and gratitude that any expense was worth it.

Even when she wasn't with us, Gillian filled our conversation. She belonged to a type of girl who must always have existed, but that didn't make her any less fascinating. Gillian returning a smock top to Dorothy Perkins because the embroidery on the bust had unravelled was more riveting than any of the rest of us going over Niagara Falls in a barrel. An entire

85

afternoon could be whiled away speculating on whether she was getting back with Stuart. Gillian and Stuart had more break-ups than Elizabeth Taylor and Richard Burton. They were our personal film stars.

'Hey, Susan Dey. Deydreamer? Wakey-wakey. Are we doing this quiz or not?' Sharon tapped the red Formica tabletop with a teaspoon to get my attention.

'Don't mention *her* name, please,' I protested.

'Susan Dey, lucky bitch,' hissed Sharon without malice, or not much.

Every group needs a common enemy. For Cassidy fans, it was Susan Dey, the actress who played David's sister in *The Partridge Family*. I wouldn't say we hated Susan Dey exactly. I was just annoyed because I wanted to be her, and there couldn't be two of us, plus she was insultingly pretty and—this really was the final straw—clearly a sweet person. In magazine interviews, Susan always denied there was anything going on between her and David. Although she was working with David every single day, she claimed not to be affected the least little bit by the charms that had worked on half the girls on Earth.

Sharon and me, we had our suspicions, but we preferred to give Susan the benefit of the doubt. The alternative was too upsetting to think about. We spent quite a lot of time studying pictures of her and, although we never said it aloud, I think that we would have conceded that, in a straight contest, David might prefer Susan's stunning Californian beauty to two Welsh chicks who had to be in bed by eight thirty.

It wasn't just Susan Dey, mind. Any other women in David's life were a source of anguished speculation. Last August, our magazine had this photo of a really slim pretty girl with short brown hair who was wearing a bikini and sitting next to him by a swimming pool. The caption said: 'David relaxing with a friend.'

What friend? *What kind of friend?* The girl made me sick with jealousy. Her name was Beverly Wilshire. I couldn't rest easy until the September issue when the mag ran another photo of the same girl, this time wearing a man's shirt and jeans. Turns out she wasn't called Beverly Wilshire after all. That was the name of the hotel where David was staying! She was Jan Freeman, who was David's stand-in on the set of *The Partridge Family*. So that was OK, you know. Never thought he'd like a girl with such short hair anyway.

'Listen to this, then.' Sharon was pressing on with the Beauty Dos and Don'ts, swiftly circling the answers as her pen moved down the page.

One of the things I loved about Sharon was how definite things were for her, how it didn't seem to occur to her that the world was bewildering or scary in any way. We were forever doing these multiple choices that were supposed to reveal how to make yourself prettier or more attractive or to pinpoint your personality type. Boys weren't sitting there doing quizzes about what they could do to make us fancy them, were they? But we carried on doing the quizzes anyway. I suppose we were so hungry for clues about how to grow up and be desirable.

Sharon always ringed the answer she felt was right. Fearlessly told the truth about herself. Me, I stared at a, b, c and d for ages, then tried to sneak a look at the upside-down answers at the bottom of the page. Always weighing up which choices would prove that I was the best kind of girl to be, and then going back to change my answers if I didn't come out as the right personality type. When I finally made a choice, even if it was the right one, I wondered where the others would have led.

Tell you the really chronic thing, I even cheated at multiple choices when I was by myself. Pretending to be better than you really were to other people seemed normal, but trying to kid yourself was weird. I felt furtive and ashamed, just like the time I copied most of Olga's answers when she sat next to me during a physics test and, by a complete fluke, I got a better mark than her and she knew what I'd done, but she never said a word. Just took her glasses off and rubbed the bridge of her nose in a really disappointed way. I couldn't seem to stop myself. How can I put this? The fact was other girls seemed real to me in a way I didn't feel real to myself. I felt as though I was still making myself up in a hurry, improvising from minute to minute. But the funny thing was I didn't mind feeling scared and unfinished when I was with Sharon: she was strong and definite enough for the both of us.

My thoughts were disturbed by a loud squawk: 'Oh, you're not gonna believe it, Petra. Listen to this: "You scored 8 to 13. You are very casual with your looks!"' Sharon laughed and took a bite of teacake before passing the last bit to me. The currants were burnt and tasted like coal, but I was starving.

'Sha, stop reading, will you? It's bringing me out in a rash.'

'Hang on. Here's a good bit now. It says, "Even if you feel you are the plainest, most problem-plagued girl in the world, these days there's no excuse—it's easy to create a new image for yourself because it's character and tequi—" '

'Technique.'

'—technique that really matter.'

Sharon always asked me about words. I did words and she did pictures, that was our deal. She slapped the mag down. The dirty tea things from the previous customers were still on the table and an open packet of sugar scattered over a wide area. 'What's technique when it's at home?'

I dipped a finger in the froth of the cold coffee, then rolled it in the spilt sugar and slowly licked it clean.

'Mm. The way you do something. Like you drawing a picture or me playing the cello. Good technique is holding the bow right and sitting up properly. Bad technique is slouching, only using a bit of the bow, playing all tense and hunched up. Basically, if you've got good technique you get a richer sound.'

Resonance. I remembered the word Miss Fairfax had taught me. When the cello resonates it sounds as beautiful as a forest, if forests could give up their secrets.

Sharon nodded. 'You got to play for that Princess Margaret, 'aven't you?'

'After we get back from seeing David. Got to plan our outfits for the White City first. Think I'm gonna wear my cords and my cream top under my brown bomber jacket. What d'you reckon?'

I was an expert when it came to dodging enquiries about the cello. I loved my instrument as much as I hated talking about it. I wanted to talk about things that made me feel the same as the others. Let me tell you, a cello is not a good instrument if you want to be invisible. Stick to the flute, is my advice. The

89

standard response to me carrying the cello was: 'How you gonna get that violin under your chin?' Not funny after the twentieth time; not that funny the first time. Then, I was lugging my big case onto the school bus a few weeks before and a boy on the back seat stood up and shouted: 'Oi, skinny, give us a tune on yer banjo.'

Since then, I'd stopped taking the cello home and kept it behind the upright piano in the small music-practice room at school. My mother and Miss Fairfax both thought I was practising for the Princess Margaret concert every break and every lunchtime, and I wanted to, I really wanted to, but I couldn't take the risk of leaving my friends. They might wonder where I was. Worse still, the worry that couldn't be admitted, not even to myself, was they might not miss me at all—and I would come back one day to find my place was taken. Like a room where they've removed a chair and rearranged the furniture so you don't know the chair was ever there. Karen Jones had been vanished overnight like a lamp no one liked any more. The other day in PE, Karen had to be partners with Susan Smell. It was a warning and maybe an omen. Plus I didn't want Gillian to see me as Miss Hoity-Toity up-herself classical music.

Impress Princess Margaret or Gillian Edwards? It was no contest.

'You two finished by any chance?' The waitress stood by our table with a hand on her hip.

'Still going strong,' said Sharon. She had poured the cold tea from the previous customers' pot into her empty cup and she raised it with a cheery grin towards the waitress, who stalked away.

'That woman's got a face like a smacked arse.'

90

'*Shar-rrron.*'

'She has. Just cos we're too poor to have proper food. If you have gammon and chips they let you be. Spend a lot on Gillian, did you?'

'Not really. Not much to play with after buying the concert ticket.'

My foot touched the carrier bag under the table and I got a jolt of pleasure thinking about its precious cargo. I was positive that the classy Mary Quant eyeshadow kit would soon change my life for the better. In my head, I was already foreseeing various heart-warming scenes. Gillian ushering the other girls into her legendary bedroom on her birthday. 'Have you seen what *Petra* got me?'

Gillian receiving admiring comments for her make-up on Saturday night at the Starlight disco. 'Yes, it's indigo, actually, from the Mary Quant eyeshadow palette that *Petra* gave me for my birthday. It was recommended in *Jackie*.'

When the camera swivelled round, it was me who was centre stage for once. Petra being promoted to Gillian's best friend to the astonishment of the rest of our group. Petra as the wise and effortlessly funny confidante in Gillian's legendary bedroom. Petra maybe even invited to accompany the Edwardses on their summer camping holiday to France. They were the only people we knew who went abroad.

The Gillian fantasies sort of muddled in with my David dreams, filling up a lot of my waking time as her birthday drew near, and Bach had to take a back seat. I had always been conscientious about practising. Now, every time I looked at my cello, I felt guilty, as if the cello knew it didn't come first any more.

'I got her Ponds Cold Cream,' Sharon was saying.

91

'Cleanses without drying the skin, leaving it radiant, that's what the ad says.'

At thirteen, our notions of sophistication were drawn entirely from magazines. We were the perfect consumers, Sharon and me, believing absolutely everything the mags told us. I had an oily T-section which I dutifully tried to tame with Anne French Cleansing Milk. A bottle cost a lot, but the pointy blue cap with its pleasing ridges felt good and purposeful as you opened it. It made me feel like I had a skincare regime, which Beauty editors said was vital. It was never too early in life to start a skincare regime.

We bought one of those little brown barrels of Linco Beer shampoo because Sharon had read that it gave your hair incredible shine. Did we look like the brunette in the advert with a curtain of hair so glossy you could see your reflection in it? Not a chance. We smelt of hops, which, if you ask me, is in a dead heat with bad eggs for the most sick-making smell in the world. That smell is so bad it makes your *ears* hurt. During our Linco Beer period, Sharon's Uncle Jim asked if we'd started brewing our own. It was not the kind of male attention we'd had in mind.

There were so many problems girls like us could have. And those posh women up in London, well, they had all the answers:

The current trend is for delicate, highly curved brows, unlike your own which grow thick, dark and bushy! Which of the following do you do?

a. Pluck them fiercely into a thin, fashionable line
b. Leave them just as they are, unfashionable

or not

    c. Trim up the untidy bits at the inner edge, thin down the outer edge to a narrow line and lighten the general effect with some brow colouring of a lighter colour

    d. Pluck them evenly along the whole length, taking hairs mainly from underneath

A surprising amount hung on that question. We worried about eyebrows a lot. Mine were a pair of hairy caterpillars straight out of the Ugly Bug Ball, from Dad's half of the family. Not like my mother's. She had Grace Kelly arches, of course. But I didn't want to make the same mistake as Angela. Plucked hers from on top and now they wouldn't grow back. Eyebrows were like the punctuation marks of a face; you didn't realise how they made sense of the rest until they were missing.

The magazines generally had seven pages of things you had wrong with your looks, followed by an article called 'Confidence and How To Get It'. One day, when we were much older, we might have a laugh about that, but not yet. If our skins were still problematic and subject to uncontrollable eruptions, then so were our hearts; agonisingly tender and so easily hurt.

Mags could make you do really crazy things, mind. That afternoon in the Kardomah, Sharon announced she was getting a perm. She'd been reading about Problem Face Shapes.

A round face can easily look like a full moon, especially if you have the wrong kind of haircut. Fringes don't improve round faces and neither do short cuts. Hair is crucial so aim for width at the side. A light perm will give body to your hair and need only make it slightly wavy if you don't fancy a head of curls.

'Go on, you've got gorgeous hair, what are you on about?' I said.

Sha's sunny face was suddenly shadowed with doubt. Her baby-blonde mane was so fine I couldn't imagine it in any other style. Out of all of us, Sharon came closest to the ideal Disney Princess. It wasn't just the long golden hair that flicked up happily at the ends. There was such a sweetness in her, any minute you expected her to throw open the window and start singing to the birds, who would come in and help her make a dress. ' 'Sall right for you with your cheekbones.' Sharon sucked in her cheeks till they were concave. She looked like Mamgu with her dentures out. 'My face looks like the blimmin' moon.'

'Stop it. I look like a whippet that needs a square meal, I do.'

'You want your 'ead examining, you do, Petra Williams. You're like a model, you are. I'm fat,' she said flatly.

'No you're not. You've lost loads of weight, mun. Look at that top, it's baggy on you.'

And so we carried on the game, the eternal ping-pong of female friendship, the reassurance that never truly reassures, but we crave it anyway. The game that always ends in a score draw, if you want to keep your friend.

The waitress came up and banged down the metal plate with the bill. 'It's not a hotel, you know.'

We paid and walked along the street to the seafront. In a few minutes we were on the concrete steps that led down to the pebbled beach. After the warm, soupy air of the cafe, the sea breeze was like a slap. When I opened my mouth wide the salty air blew all the way down to my lungs. From across the bay came the mournful sound of the hooter that told you it was tea break at the steelworks. In the distance, I could see the flame flickering on top of the gas tower. It never went out. My dad would be eating the sandwiches my mother made for him. Ham and cheese every day. *Schinken mit Käse*, my mother would say under her breath as she wrapped them in greaseproof paper. Dad asked for less butter, too thick a layer turned his stomach. Mine too. He never asked for anything else.

Sharon was scrutinising the pebbles on the beach and I sat next to her, knees tucked under my chin, poncho pulled tight around me. She was always searching for the perfect pebble, especially the ones she said looked like thrushes' eggs. Very pale greeny-blue with a sprinkle of black spots. She liked to draw them. Filled page after page of a sketchbook with them.

I told Sha I was afraid my plan for going to see David would never work. The small white lies I'd told my mother were already getting bigger and greyer. I had written the story I'd told my mum so far in my diary and put it in the hiding place under my bed so I could keep track of all the fibs. The thought of my mother finding out that I was going to a pop concert was as painful as the thought of not going with the others to the White City.

Sharon said everything would be OK, she and her mum would cover for me. That was one advantage to my mother refusing to mix with any women in the town because they were all common and went out to

95

the fish van in slippers with curlers in their hair. At least she couldn't compare notes with the other mums.

I loved it down there by the pier. My mother claimed the sea was depressing. Ach, always coming in and out, reminding you that it had been going in and out before you were born and would be going in and out centuries after you'd died. The sea was indifferent to human suffering, my mother said. But I found comfort in the things she hated. The sucking of the sea as it drew breath to come in and then the roar as it pulled back, dragging the pebbles with it. Nature's lullaby, like a mother saying hush for ever to a crying baby. Shhuuussssh. Shhooooossh. If you laid your head right back and moulded your arms and legs into the pebbles you could feel yourself disappearing. That was a good feeling; not being there any more. I liked to do it in the summer when the warmth of the stones got into your bones.

Every time we went down to the beach the sunset was different. Sometimes the clouds were so beautiful and crazy that if you painted them like they really looked people would have said you were making it up. That evening, the sun was like a lozenge that had been sucked until it was so thin it was about to break.

'Look,' I said to Sharon, 'a Strepsil sunset.'

*   *   *

I told my mother we were going to see Handel's *Messiah*.

I knew she'd approve. She liked high culture. In fact, she approved of altitude in general. High heels, high opera, highball glasses that she got from the

Green Shield stamps catalogue and filled with lime and Cinzano Bianco and loads of crushed ice. 'The poor woman's cocktail,' she called it. Tall men in high places would have been my mother's ideal.

It wasn't a complete lie about the *Messiah*. There would be singing and worship of a kind and we would need to take a train and money for something to eat. I had found the concert in the Forthcoming Events section of the *South Wales Echo*. Same night as David's White City concert, 26 May, only it was in Cardiff, not London. So it was perfect, really.

Except this was the first big lie I'd told her in my life and I was scared from the start. If I hadn't wanted to go so badly I'd never have dared. My heart felt like a fish flubbing around in a net that was gradually being pulled tighter and tighter.

'Handel is sublime,' my mother had said when I told her. 'What is the choir, Petra?'

'The Cwmbran Orpheus,' I said.

'Not bad. Really not of the highest, but not szo bad,' she said, removing a leather glove and raking a hand through her wavy blonde hair. 'I am glad you make this effort, Petra. Your friends are nice girls, really I hope, good families and so on?'

'Yes.' I tried to think of my mother meeting Sharon's family, but my mind blanked at the prospect.

We were standing in the narrow, stepped bit of land at the back of the house that my dad had turned into a fruit and vegetable patch. It was a garden to feed us. The only concession to decoration was a row of sweet peas along the brick wall that divided us from Mr and Mrs Hughes next door. (Even after seventeen years my parents were still not on first-name terms with their neighbours, and never would be, not in Wales.) The green stalks of the sweet peas twirled upward around wigwams made of bamboo. When they appeared, the flowers—in pink and white and violet—looked like the finest paper rosettes. Sweet peas were the kind of flowers fairies slept in. Carol told us one day that she didn't believe in God. He had just been invented by old men to stop young people enjoying themselves. But, I ask you, why would Nature go to so much trouble to make something so pointlessly beautiful as the sweet pea?

The scent was delicate and strong at the same time. 'Intoxicating.' That was a word from 'It Pays to Increase Your Word Power'. '*Noun:* intoxication, an abnormal state that is essentially a poisoning. The condition of being drunk. A strong excitement or elation.'

My mother taught me to cut the flowers every single day of summer; if you did that they kept coming back. She admired the sweet pea for its abundance, I think, but also for its determination not to let beauty die.

To anyone else, I suppose it wouldn't have looked like much of a garden, but I loved being out there with my dad. It was our place. He would smoke his pipe and, when it went out, I ran back indoors to fetch his matches. He had a pouch for his tobacco, and we would sit on the top step behind the compost while Dad scraped out the sticky black stuff from the pipe with a match, then he would take ages pressing the new stuff in, tamping the brown leaf down till it was like a nest. Dad said I was clever like my mother, because I could read music and got all the grades. But he was the clever one, I'm telling you.

When Dad was my age, he taught himself the tonic sol-fa and he could play anything he liked.

Bought the piano in our front room out of the wages he'd saved until he was eighteen. I didn't think it was right that when my father was a boy he went down the pit and had to crawl on his elbows and knees to get the coal. But Dad said they were champion days.

'Best men in the world, *cariad*, you couldn't ask for better.'

He was sorry when he had to come back to the surface, a job at the steelworks, on account of his bad lungs. Six syllables. New mow cone ee owe sis. It was the longest word I knew. Pneumoconiosis. Occupational hazard.

Out in the garden, where we wouldn't disturb my mother, my father would warm up his voice. 'Doh, ray, me, fah, soh, lah, te, doh.' You had to breathe from the diaphragm, see, give each note its full weight.

At the bottom of the garden steps, there was a small brick outhouse that was a toilet before they took a corner of one of our three bedrooms and made it into a bathroom. When I was small, Dad used to carry me out there at night, hitch up my nightie and sit me on the wooden seat. I tried to hold the wee in and let it out quietly because I didn't want to wake the spiders. The spiders were huge and their webs festooned the brick walls like net curtains for ghosts.

Climb to the top of our path and you got the most incredible view. The sea was spread out like a glittering cloak all the way across to Pendine Sands where a man set the world land-speed record. You could always tell when a storm was on its way in. The sky over the sea was the colour of saucepan and the clouds turned a sinister yellow as though the sun behind them was sickening for something.

99

'Quickly, please. Hold this bush while I tie it, Petra.'

The blackcurrant bushes were threshing around in the wind the Saturday before we went to White City. My mother got me to hold each bush while she fixed it with a small piece of twine to a cane. The twine was kept in the front pocket of her suede jerkin and she cut it with a knife. Even when she was gardening my mother appeared chic. That morning, she was wearing some Land Girl-type jodhpurs, which would have made any other woman look like a water buffalo, and a man's shirt tucked in under a belt that was two shades darker than the trousers. A paisley scarf was loosely knotted at her breast. She looked as dashing as Amelia Earhart standing next to her aeroplane.

'Right as rain,' my mother shouted at the sky. 'What is so right about rain? Why are the British saying this? Fruits they need sun.'

She snatched up a hoe and appeared to point the rusty tip accusingly at my dad, who was sitting on the top step smoking his pipe and just looking at her. The weather was his fault. Everything was his fault. He smiled and threw his hands up in surrender.

'It's only a saying, Greta. Don't take it personal, love. It's May. There's plenty of time for them to ripen.'

'Ach, but they will have no flavour. Only rain flavour.'

If he could have gone up to the sky and fetched the sun down for her on his back he would, I knew that. My father worshipped my mother, though he never found the right sacrifices to appease her. As far as she was concerned, he had won her by false pretences, and she would never forgive him for it.

100

When they met, Glynn Williams was the star of the town's operatic society and my mother was a young soprano. Their duet from *Kismet* got a write-up in the local paper.

My mother made a mistake. She thought Dad was going up in the world, when it turned out he had just climbed a hill for a while to take in the view.

My father had a look of Clark Gable, or so Gwennie in the grocer's told Mrs Pricc the Post. I'd never seen Mr Gable so I didn't know. Every morning, when Dad left home for the steelworks on his motorbike, I would stand by the upstairs landing window and watch him. The deal I struck with God was that if I watched my father till he got right to the end of the road, and never took my eyes off him for one second until he disappeared round the corner, then God would bring him back safe to me. It always worked, so I never dared stop looking.

The family on my father's side were short and dark. In old wedding photographs you might take them for Sicilians. My mother mistook Dad's stocky good looks for manly purpose, while he mistook her angelic blondeness and full lips for sweetness. Her disappointment with him coloured our days.

The story went that her parents had bought a passage from Hamburg to New York, but the boat docked at Cardiff one night and they got off in a hurry thinking it was Manhattan. (Fog, tiredness, a baby crying at the wrong moment.) It was an embarrassing piece of bad timing for a celebrated family of German clockmakers. Growing up in four rooms over a watch shop in the High Street, my mother felt she had been cheated of her destiny. She craved a bigger stage, the one her face deserved. The life her beauty had been designed for was out there

101

somewhere, ebbing away as the shop's clocks ticked and tocked.

It's so hard for a child to understand their parents' unhappiness. Mine, if only I'd known it, were infected with the virus of incompatibility. Nobody died from it, but nobody lived either. My mother stayed put and, well, you'd have thought she was a normal wife and mother, but her offended spirit got its revenge. Anything could set her off. Me reading a book. Me not reading a book. Greasy hair, spots, which she regarded as self-inflicted although everyone got them, girls and boys. I used to wonder if I was an only child because I'd been such a disappointment.

There were so many times I wanted to tell my mother about the boys barking at me in class, but it would have meant mentioning Petra the TV dog, and I knew how angry that would make her. She would suspect I had been watching the idiot box. Instead, one night after a really bad day at school, I asked her if I could please be called by my middle name, Maria.

She raised the palette knife she was using to free a cheesecake from its tin and swiped it at me, narrowly missing my cheek. 'No, why are you asking this, you stupid, stupid girl? I told you Petra is a fine name, it was the name of my aunt, who was really a most elegant person in Heidelberg. If you ask me one more time you will be punished, you stupid girl, do you hear?'

When she went out, my dad liked to dance me round the front room. We weren't allowed in there with our shoes on. There was a big black radiogram with mesh on the front with a gold surround and three cream Bakelite knobs. Normally, it was tuned to live classical concerts, but on Sunday mornings we were allowed to turn the knob to *Family Favourites*. My mother approved of *Family Favourites* because the show was sometimes broadcast from Germany. Soldiers stationed out there sent record requests for their loved ones back home.

Every Friday night, my mother took my father's wage packet from him and gave him an allowance to go down the club. Your father, he can't be trusted with money, she said. He was always *my* father when she was angry. You should have heard him sing, though. Even in a land famous for song, Dad's baritone stood out. 'I've Got a *Cruuuussh* on You, Sweetie Pie.' That was one song he sang to me. One day, with Dean Martin crooning 'That's Amore' on the radiogram next door, Dad took me in his arms and whirled me round the kitchen. I imagined being in a hot place with my hair pinned up by a single red flower. I imagined being glamorous.

*   *   *

'Well, we are going to see the Messiah. Kind of.'

Sharon cracked up. She thought the alibi I had given my mum for where I'd be on 26 May was brilliant.

We were sitting with Gillian on the grassy bank just above the rugby pitch, talking about our plans for White City.

'Genius, Pet,' Sharon said. 'David is a god to us and you can wear your Sunday-school clothes to go out the house and after you can get changed into your gear round mine. Then you can stay the night when we get back so your mam'll never suspect, will she?'

Sharon's Uncle Jim worked on the railways, in the signal box at Port Talbot, so he'd given her the time of the late train coming back. It was specially for people who went up to London for the shows. We were sure we could get the 11.45 p.m. if we left the concert the minute it ended.

'What are you two wearing to London?' Gillian asked. Her blue eyes were fixed on the game below, where Stuart was acting captain of the school team.

Sharon let out a groan. 'Oh, God help us, just think what Carol will wear to meet David.' Puckering her lips into a familiar sink-plunger pout, Sha gathered her small breasts in both hands and pushed them up until they were like two blancmanges wobbling over the top of her school blouse. She stood up and started strutting around with her chin jabbing forward and her bum pushed out in imitation of Carol's stroppy cockerel strut.

'She'll wear a blimmin' bikini and get us all arrested,' I said.

We both laughed, not unkindly, at the thought of our sexy friend. Gillian ignored our fooling. She was doing that ladylike poise thing she did whenever there were boys around.

Down on the pitch, the game was turning nasty. Our team, in red and white, were playing a school from the Valleys. Great hulking brutes, they were. The ruck was peeling apart and one ox came bellowing out from the tangle of limbs and lashed out at our prop, till both had blood on their mouths.

Suddenly, the ball was free and one of our boys got a hand to it. He hugged it to his chest, sidestepped the ox and put on a burst of speed. God, he was fast, mind. The guys who hurled themselves at him looked like they were diving at thin air. For a moment, in the thick of the action, the boy somehow made time for himself. It was magic, the way he seemed to be running in slow motion inside his own private bubble while the other players flailed around him. He got over the line, lightly touched the ball to the ground and turned round, a grimy grin splitting his fair face. Steven Williams.

'Hey, he's waving at you, Petra,' Sharon said.

'He's waving at *us*,' said Gillian, who was on her feet, clapping and cheering.

All my life I would remember that try. See Steven running down the wing, making a mockery of the blundering beasts around him.

Some things never die.

6

'It's you. You are David Cassidy.'

Zelda was standing next to Bill's desk in the office, holding up a sweater. It was sleeveless, knitted in stripes of red and white wool, with a row of buttons down the front that winked silver in the light. Around the hem was a strip of wobbling blue, with small stars uncertainly picked out in white. 'And look at the back.' She flipped it round to reveal a large capital D in silver satin, stitched somewhere between the shoulder blades. 'Stand up,' said Zelda, and Bill, feeling ten years old, did so without hesitation. What power did this majestical woman wield over him, he wondered, that he should rise at her call? She pressed the sweater against his chest. Bill had the second button of his shirt unbuttoned, like someone in an aftershave commercial, and for a second he could actually feel the hairs on his chest stick to the silver D. It was not a pleasant feeling.

'And it fits, Billy!' she went on. 'Like I said, it's just you.' Billy? Nobody had called him Billy since a boy called Newsome in the third form, who had veered away with a nosebleed.

'Don't call me Billy,' he said, in a low voice. 'Please.' He could see Pete the Pimple, at the far end of the room, working up a smirk.

'Sorry, William dear,' said Zelda. Everything bounced off her, including slights and hurts of every description, whether given or taken. She shook the sweater. 'Look at it glitter, though. And have you realised how the stars and stripes are meant to look like the American fl—'

'Yes, I did notice. Though it's sort of upside down.' Together, they marvelled at the wondrous object. Here, at last, was proof that knitwear could ruin your eyes. It had arrived that morning in a brown box, plastered with 1p stamps. The box sat now at her feet. 'Who's it from?'

'Clare Possit.' Zelda put down the sweater and produced a rose-pink envelope from some concealed pocket of her floor-length tangerine dress, which looked like it came from Marrakesh and jingled as she moved. 'Clare Possit, 47 Lucknow Road, Shrewsbury. Aged fourteen, brown hair, twenty-seven posters, one rabbit called Partridge.'

'Christ.'

'Yes, well. Likes toasted sandwiches and knitting. Hence this lovely sweater. Would like to be Mrs David Cassidy when she grows up.'

'If she grows up. If *he* grows up.'

'Now now. Clare has been very busy, I'd like you to know. As well as a sweater she encloses a woolly hat, for Manchester you understand.'

'Of course. In May.'

'And also a pair of socks.' Zelda delved into the box and held them up gingerly, away from her, as you might a pair of poisonous caterpillars. Bill leaned closer, genuinely interested.

'That one says "CHE" on it,' he said. 'Like Guevara. Is Clare Possit a Maoist? Does Mrs Possit know about it? Do they even do Cuban liberation in Shrewsbury? I never knew.' He paused, and his face fell. 'Oh, I see.' Zelda was holding up the sock's sad twin. It bore the legend 'RISH'.

'Together,' said Zelda, brightly, 'they spell out—'

'Yes, I geddit.' Bill considered the socks. To his surprise, he had not yet ceased to be surprised by the

107

madness of Cassidy love. David was still basically a kid, and the likelihood of his ever being allowed to become a man seemed slimmer by the day; either he would be torn asunder by his fans, like a stag among hounds, or else he would be frozen in eternal youth, the way that rich Californians had their corpses stowed in dry ice. And he couldn't sing; not like Jagger, anyway, or Bowie, or any of the grown-up gods. Next to Cassidy, even Marc Bolan was a proper adult male, and he wore eyeshadow, for God's sake. And a feather boa. But—and the thought of this niggled Bill, and wouldn't go away—you had to hand it to the Cassidy guy: he could stir up love. He was like a witch with a cauldron. Bill had fancied, at college, that he knew a bit about love—not as a condition of the heart (God help him), but as a tactic that poets and painters used, an artist's strategy for getting women into bed, or getting yourself into their head. But this boy, this American pansy; he could manufacture an emotion out of nowhere, out of nothing, and sort of squash it into a song, like Clare Possit cramming socks into that brown box. And when the girls unwrapped it at the other end—when they heard it, alone in their bedrooms—they not only believed it, they believed he had believed it in the first place; they even believed it was directed specifically at them.

The fools, the uncountable fools. Shakespeare had his Dark Lady, maybe a bloke on the side, but how many could David win over with one verse; one yelp of that watery voice, one sideways nudge of the bum? Millions of them, tens of millions of Clares and Judiths and Christines, all utterly convinced that they were cherished, both che'd and rish'd; that they were in love, as you might be in Shrewsbury or Wigan or

108

Weston-super-Mare, but also, in return, that they were loved. Pop ruled the world. Poets were left for dust.

'Zit city.'

He came out of his reverie with a start. For an instant, his head spun. Pete was beside him, pushing a picture into his frame of vision. Where was Zelda? While Bill was dreaming, she must have sailed away.

'Look at that.' Pete poked at something with his finger, which was grey with graphite at the tip; he had flecks of white in the nail, too, which Bill's grandmother used to say was evidence of a bad diet. Well, she got that right. Two days ago, Bill had seen Pete force a KitKat into the hollowed-out crust of a Cornish pasty, and then eat the whole thing. Had he already eaten the meat and veg from the middle, or simply scooped them out with his slaty fingers and thrown them away? And here he was, bent over, rich of breath, showing Bill a photograph. No, two photographs.

'Before and after,' he said. 'Like one of them weight wanker ads.' He sniffed hard, and rubbed his nose with a knuckle. 'Normally I wouldn't take a copy, you know, just tart up the one. But this was so good I thought you ought to see the original, before I got to work. You being new and everything.'

For all Bill knew, that may have been a kindly offer, wise counsel from an old hand, but somehow it came out sounding like an insult. So did everything that dripped from the lips of Pete.

'Afters first.' It was a black-and-white head shot of David Cassidy; his back was to the camera but he had turned round, coy as a deer, glancing over his shoulder to tell the world's females to come hither. Or, if they were minded, just to come. Sex must get

109

in there somewhere. His lashes, with their graceful curve, were absurdly long—could they be forever?—and his skin was as flawless as a saucer of milk.

'OK, now what? It's a girly-boy.'

'Now look at her.' Pete gave a terrible grin, and slid another image into view. 'Before.' Bill looked.

'Oh Jesus.'

Every teenager had spots, but this guy had a problem. His erupting, pitted cheeks might have aroused the professional curiosity of a vulcanologist.

'Jesus,' Bill repeated. 'It's like looking at the moon.' Then, realising that praise would be in order, he turned to Pete. 'Great job, mate. Magic wand and all that. Cassidy doesn't know you, but he bloody well needs you.'

'Fuck off,' Pete said, to indicate that he was pleased.

'How d'you do it?'

'Ink, whitener, chronic little brush. Pencil and rubber, sometimes. You kind of . . . stipple over the bumps.'

Without ado, wary of talking about his art, or anything that might smack of art, he pulled the images from Bill's grasp and marched off. He had come over to show off his handiwork, received due credit, yet gone away angrier than he had come. Like many workers in the office, Pete conducted himself like a sour, superannuated child. Was that the fault of management, Bill asked himself, or was it just the job: the inevitable result of spending too much time up to your neck in other people's adolescent dreams?

The phone rang. It was beige, all angles instead of curves, and too light to stay in one place. Bill picked up the receiver, and the cradle, responding to his tug,

110

fell off the edge of the desk.

'Shit,' said Bill, very loudly. Zelda, who was passing, gave him a stern look. Other people could only purse their lips, but she could do it with her whole face.

'Don't swear,' said a voice on the other end of the line.

'Who is this?' Bill asked. 'Oh, Ruth, hi. No, sorry, I dropped the, hang on, wait a sec.'

He retrieved the cradle and tried to balance it on a pile of letters. 'No, it's not a bad time at all. I just— Yes. Yes, fine. Sorry?'

Zelda had stopped now, and was watching him struggle with the phone. Suddenly she stuck out her tongue.

'Christ,' said Bill. 'Sorry, no, love. It's just Zelda's doing something with her tongue. No, her tongue. Zelda. She's my. Sorry? No, my boss . . .'

Zelda had put one finger to her mouth, pretended to lick it, then used it to make little swirling motions in the air. Bill didn't know where to look. Why was his immediate superior choosing this moment, above all, to offer what looked like intimate sexual services? Did she bear a grudge against Ruth? Neither of these options seemed likely. The week before, after all, Zelda had refused a Cadbury's Flake on the grounds that it was 'a bit rude'.

'No, love, I'm, I'm, I'm busy with—tour schedules, setting up interviews. Yes. Who with? Oh, you know, big names. No, not that big. I mean not yet.'

He was conscious of starting to squirm. Zelda was looking at him oddly, still doing something unfathomable with her hand.

'No, but God I'd love to. Or Jimmy Page. Yeah, I know. You know they banned the last album in

111

Spain? Cos of the kids on the front? Yeah, I know . . .'

Bill watched as Zelda reached out and took the cradle of the Trimphone from the paper pile. The letter on top had the legend 'I HATE LITTLE JIMMY OSMOND' pasted down the side in blue Dymo tape. Zelda licked her finger again, turned the phone over, then used her fingertip to moisten the round rubber feet on its base. Finally, she cleared a patch of space on Bill's desk and plunked the cradle down, firmly pressing until it stuck. 'There,' she said, with pride, and walked off, singing, in her deep, vibrating alto, 'Stair-air-way to heh-uh-ven.' Bill put his head in his hands, the phone against his skull. Dimly he was aware that Ruth was still talking. Her voice hummed in his head.

'Mm, yup. Well, I'm meeting the boys after work. What? You know, the other guys.'

He lowered his head, sneaked a glance around the immediate area, sank his voice to a whisper. 'The band. What? I *am* speaking up. I said the band.' Someone two desks away looked up. Nobody he knew, a newcomer holding a giant stapler; but still, couldn't be too careful.

'No, I'll be done around nine thirty, ten,' Bill continued, voice back to normal now. 'Yeah, the Grapes. See you then. Better go. Oh, you know. Rock never sleeps and all that. Yep. OK, bye.'

Bill tipped his head back and thought about Ruth for a while. Outside, the sunlight had paled, and showers tapped on the window. The office was growing darker, but the lights hadn't been turned on; not because of the note that had circulated last week, warning of electricity costs, but because no one could be bothered to reach for a switch. Some of them, like Chas, openly preferred the gloom.

112

Bill bent to his keyboard again and became another person. He wrote of his sun worship, and how he couldn't live without his musical instruments ('if anyone wanted to torture me, they'd only have to take away my drums and guitar'), and apologised for his raggedy scrawl. Then he stopped, and counted the words he had produced so far. Eleven hundred and thirty. Perfect. Should he be proud, as a journalist, or ashamed, as a man, to bring the stuff in like this—on time, to length, right on the button? Just room for a sign-off: *'Don't gorget . . . Keep a place warm for me in your hearts till I can get there to fill it. Till then, Love—'*

He was aware of a shadow moving in front of him, around him to his back, but so rapt was he in the act of impersonation that he couldn't be bothered to look up. So it came as a shock when four words were breathed beside his neck, in a low growl.

'Let me fill it.'

Bill jumped, half up, half backwards, trying to halt the spinning in his head. 'Whawha,' he said.

'Sorry, cock,' said Roy, mightily pleased by the effect of his interruption. The publisher had come to call.

'No, sorry, my fault,' said Bill, struggling to his feet, like an old man in a pub being introduced to a girl. Why had today, which hadn't started too badly, ended in a litter of apologies? 'Sorry, you were saying . . .'

'I was say-ying,' Roy went on, in the leery tone that he preserved for slower, younger employees, 'that you ain't seen nothing, son. Your pretty boy there, Mr Cassidy, butter wouldn't melt, but they say he melts all over the shop, them little ladies sticking their faces through his gate.'

113

'Surely not. He's not like that,' Bill replied, unexpectedly turning into his own grandmother.

'Anyway, now you'll have a chance to find out, won't you? Cos Mr Squeaky Clean is coming to dirty old England—'

'Yes, I know. We have tickets.'

'Ah, but you have tickets to the concert, sonny Jim. I'm talking about the press conference before. And not just that. I'm talking about you and Mr Maytime, head to head, top to toe, just the pair of you, fifteen lovely minutes. You and Cassidy, alone together in a hotel room. There are girls in this country, let me tell you—there are girls at the North bloody Pole who would give their furry knickers for one minute with that nancy in a hotel suite. And you get a quarter of an hour, my son. Don't waste it. Not queer, are you?'

'I—'

'Good. Cos I'm not sending a poofter to see the bloke when all our readers want to snog him, am I? Don't want you putting your grubby mitts down his brown clothes, do we now?'

'Come off it, Mr—'

'All right, all right. You're doing a grand job, anyway. Born to it. Just don't ask him what he really thinks or any of that arty bollocks. Nothing about his soul. Doubt if the poor bugger's got time for it, anyway.'

'Time for what?'

'A soul. He's just a voice in a shirt, isn't he? And he can't be arsed to do the buttons up. Like some people I could mention.' And, with that, Roy idled away, making a chewing sound. Bill surreptitiously reached a hand to his chest and did up one of the buttons. He knew what the boss thought of him. Roy, he knew full well, looked at him and saw a fancy-

114

pants: a smart-arse with a poncey shirt and a college degree (as if that was any use), a hireling too scared of life to get his nose into it, too innocent to admit what happens when, as in Roy's favourite and much-repeated phrase, 'pop shit hits the fans'.

He was probably right. All the same, Bill didn't know what to believe about someone like David Cassidy; he didn't know what to want to believe. In idle moments, maybe with Ruth asleep at his side, he had wondered what went on when a male of twenty-four years found himself on the receiving end of mass adoration; what literally went on, not in the young guy's head, but in his bed and at his feet, in hotels and swimming pools and the green rooms of stadiums and television shows. When the worshippers met the boy-god, what was the likely result? Did they swoon or shy away, like the heroines of romantic fiction, unable to bear the fantasy made flesh; or did unromantic fact get the better of them, and force them to their knees?

Bill had heard the rumours about David, couldn't exactly avoid them, yet something in him chose not to listen: something not just prim and prudish, but protective of the rights of dreamers everywhere.

He must have spent years of his life, after all, thinking about Paul McCartney—not about being McCartney, or becoming McCartney, but holding fast, nonetheless, to an image of Paul somewhere there beside him, larky and quick, showing him the fingering on 'I Wanna Hold Your Hand' and egging him onward: 'Aright, mate, take your time, no hurry. That sounds great, Bill, I can see you've been practising.'

And if Bill had stood there, dreaming of that nonsense, and knowing in his guts that the nonsense made sense, more sense than anything else; well, then what right did he have to mock the silly girls, knitting their DC sweaters and sending their poems and their locks of hair?

'Tread softly, William, for you tread on their dreams.' Zelda's words which, at the time they were uttered, had made him choke on a Polo mint, came back to him with the full chiding gentleness of their speaker.

He looked at his watch. Almost three o'clock. Two more hours and he'd be done. In three hours' time, if Zelda didn't try to keep him late, and if the Tube wasn't clogged, and if he could manage to grab a quick Scotch beforehand to steady his nerves, and his fingers—all being well, come six o'clock, the music journalist would make music of his own.

*   *   *

Bill played bass in Spirit Level. They were not a well-known band, even to their extended families. Nor would they ever be well known, not unless they were accidentally caught up in a hostage drama, or played a heroic role in evacuating a pub during a bomb scare, or were, indeed, bombed themselves. That would be bloody typical, wouldn't it? To achieve immortality instead of fame, selling truckloads of records on the back of having died. All those groupies, wandering round in a daze of admiration, and no one to sleep with . . .

They had formed at school. 'You're still a bunch of schoolboys, aren't you?' Ruth had said, on the single, deeply ill-advised occasion when he had invited her to a gig. They had played for twenty minutes above the Duke of York's in Acton, and Ruth had stood there, shandy in hand, immobile; never had a human being, Bill thought, been less stirred into deep, liberating rhythms by the pulse of popular music. She hadn't even blinked. Afterwards, once they had trudged off to make way for Space Hopper or Spikenard or whoever else was up next, he had sipped his pint and, summoning his courage, asked what she had thought.

'What can I say?' she asked in return, with rather too wide a smile, and the phrase had hung over his head, ever since, like a double-edged sword. But she was right about one thing: they were kids, still. Not just adults reliving their youth, which would have been sad enough, considering what youth was like, but adults using the weaponry of youth—shouting, singing, arguing, mucking around—to pretend that they could fend off the unwanted responsibilities of adult life.

The lead singer was called David Crockett. People would come up to him after a gig and say, 'What's your name again?' and he would answer, 'David Crockett.'

'No, your real name.'

'Crockett, really. David Crockett.' Then, without exception, they would say, 'Oh, piss off,' and turn away, with a shake of the head.

At school it had been different; everyone knew his name, and the band had decided not to conceal the fact but, more cunningly, to make it their selling point. 'You could be David Crockett and the Wild Frontiers,' said Mrs Crockett, his unflappable mother, as they sat at her kitchen table one afternoon. She always insisted on David, not Davy, which—or so Bill believed—made it slightly harder to maintain the pose of American pioneers.

117

Tolworth was a long way from Oklahoma. It lacked a Gold Rush, for one thing. The suburb was on the south-westerly fringes of London, clinging to the capital's hem.

They had all been upstairs at the Crocketts', discussing the swiftness of their path to glory, now that Derek, a psycho in waiting, but also the best guitarist in the school, had joined the band. Their first number one would enter the charts in 'early April '71', according to the drummer, Colin Hobbs, who was the best at maths. Mrs Crockett had knocked on the bedroom door, put her head round and said brightly, 'Tea and Battenberg when you're ready, boys!' They had interrupted the conversation about private jets and dutifully trooped downstairs, like Scouts.

Bill didn't know where the original band members were these days. After school, where everyone was afraid of him, Derek had started to run up against kids—young men—who bore just as much resentment as he did, for reasons that none of them could grasp, let alone sort out. In the winter of 1970, just as Bill was starting to think about the use of kissing in Keats, Derek had got into a fight on Wimbledon Station. The other boy had ended up on the tracks, with half his chin scraped off, and only just scrambled free. Derek had got eighteen months in a place for young offenders and none of them heard from him again. Bill worried about him sometimes, late at night.

Derek's guitar case might have had two Stanley knives Sellotaped to the inside, but, of all the pupils who tried, and failed, to play the weepy Harrison riff from 'Something', Derek failed least. But he had vanished from their lives, and—more importantly—

118

from their line-up, and his place had gone to Colin Dougall, who smoked more weed than anyone Bill had ever met, often appearing from a kind of cloud, but who was also the only person he knew who still went to church. The combination seemed unlikely, or plain wrong, although drummer Colin had some elaborate theory about the warm front of cannabis meeting the moist air of incense, and it starting to rain in the nave. Colin Hobbs's problem, apart from being clever, was that he was called Colin, and, as David pointed out, you couldn't have a band with two Colins in it. Everyone accepted the logic of this argument, even Colin Hobbs, who went off to Southampton and became, so his mother said, 'very into computers'. His place, behind the drum kit, had gone to John Priscumbe, who was too young, then to Michael 'Stinky' Sturrock, who smelt, then to a creature called, simply, Brillo, who had lasted a week, and finally, to everyone's relief, to a solid Lancastrian, Geoff Hymes, who had come to London to make his fortune and wound up mending fridges in Maida Vale. No one could call him a great drummer, and nobody did, but he was genial, and punctual, and, best of all, every other weekend, he had the use of a Ford Transit.

In the meantime, the band had changed its identity, even more often than its players. No one had liked the Wild Frontiers, and even Mrs Crockett went off it after a while. So, for no reason, they became Black Coffee ('the whitest group I know,' said the DJ at the school disco). Then Jetlag. Then Eagle, in tribute to the lunar module, just after the moon landings. ('If we had stuck with it,' David would say, pretty much every month ever since, in the pub, 'we could have waited till the Eagles were

119

famous, then sued them for stealing our name.' 'But they're plural,' Bill would reply. 'That's different. And there's that "the".' It was, he often thought, the most pointless conversation of his career.) Then Mandrake Root, once the second Colin was in place. Then, very briefly, the Stitches (the idea being that, at the close of a triumphant career, they could release a Greatest Hits album entitled *The Stitches: In Time*). And now they were Spirit Level, and, as Bill announced with something more than modesty to anyone who would listen, they were still as bad and unfocused as they had been when Mrs Crockett gave them all a slice of Battenberg, with a cake fork each. Names could come and go, talent could rise and fall, but Spirit Level were, and always would be, underperformers. Their cover version of 'All Right Now', repeated, yet unrefined, over many drunken weddings, still sounded, as Bill had confided to a friend at university, 'like a double-decker bus running over a herd of cows'. The band was the one dependable constant in his life, but it was more than that. It was—though he would never admit as much to himself, let alone to Ruth—his one true love.

*   *   *

'Gorget.'

'I'm sorry?'

'Gorget.' Zelda held out the sheet of paper. She had swanned by, seen Bill sipping a cup of coffee, and plucked the letter from his typewriter, with a zipping sound. 'Typo near the end. You've got "gorget" instead of "forget". And you haven't signed it.'

'I think they'll know who it's from.'

120

'Don't you be too sure,' said Zelda, who looked as if she might at any moment wag a finger at him. 'The boy we had before you, no, two before you, not counting the pervert, he once finished a letter from David and signed it "Brian".'

'Why?'

'Because that was his name, silly. He was so . . . into it, as you might say, that he forgot who was who.'

'Like Method.'

'I beg your pardon?' To Zelda, the word sounded suspicious, as if it might be connected with sex.

'Nothing,' said Bill. 'So was he the pervert?'

'No, the perv— Look, I don't have time for this sort of, of, tittle-tattle.' Zelda was flushed. 'Please just make the corrections.'

'What did he perv about?'

'William, really, I have far better things to do . . . If you could just go through this one more time.'

'So it's all right then?'

'A lovely piece of work, just lovely.' Zelda was on safer ground now. 'I particularly like the part about him being a medieval minstrel. Very . . . imaginative.'

'Well, he said something about that once himself. I'm just following his lead. I'm not really, you know, making it up. Am I?' he went on, more in blank pleading than in curiosity.

'You're doing an excellent job. Much better than Brian, who, if he had a fault, did rather let the whole thing go to his head.'

'In what way? Did he start wearing the kit?'

'Sorry?'

'You know, the catsuit? The shell necklace? Did he wear it here, at this desk? On a Tuesday?'

Zelda chose not to reply. She merely picked up a

121

bottle of Tipp-Ex and handed it to Bill. 'Correct.' And with that she moved on.

The top of the Tipp-Ex had stuck tight. Bill twisted it, swore, and twisted again. It flew off, and a blurt of white liquid flew over Bill's right hand and up his wrist. Chas, as if on cue, picked this instant to stroll past.

'Filthy little bugger. Right where everyone can see.'

'Sorry?'

Chas wheezed and cackled, like the sidekick of a stage villain, and slunk towards the Gents. Bill sat there, wiping his wet hands. The phone rang, and he reached for it. As he took hold of the receiver, the cradle popped unstuck, with a faint squelching sound, and fell off the edge of the desk.

'Sod. This,' said Bill, very loudly. 'Soddit.' The phone was covered in correcting fluid, so he just said, 'Sorry,' and dropped the receiver on the floor, where it went on squawking for a while. Using his left hand, he fed the sheet of paper back into the typewriter, rolled it down and, with a single finger, stabbed the word 'David'. 'And sod you,' he said, again out loud. 'Little prick.'

'Who you talking to?' said the man he didn't know, a couple of desks away.

'No one.'

The man gave a quick, jeering grin. 'Rock never sleeps, eh?'

Bill had run out of the strength to be angry. He just looked over and sighed.

'More like pop never wakes up,' said the man. He laughed at his own joke, and lowered his head to his work. The rain outside was thicker now: angry but bereft of rhythm, like the drumming of Colin Hobbs.

Suddenly, Bill had no desire to make music among friends. He wanted to go to sleep.

The squawking wouldn't stop. Bill retrieved the phone from under his feet. 'Yes?'

'William, it's Zelda.' This was not good. Zelda's office was only twenty seconds away, and, as a rule, she liked to launch herself through the gap in the potted-plant partition and cruise around the desks of her colleagues. The other day, Bill had introduced her to the phrase 'shooting the breeze', which had never come her way before—Zelda's language, and indeed her world, stopped short at the frontier of the Home Counties—and she had mulled it over, tasting the words, and pronounced at last, 'I like that.' From now on, if there was a breeze to be shot, she would shoot it; and the only thing to keep her from shooting was unwelcome news. When forced to bear bad tidings, she would deliver them over the phone.

'William, I'm so sorry. There has been an editorial meeting'—that meant she and Roy had shared the scrapings from the end of a jar of Coffeemate—'and it has been decided to bring the quiz forward to the next issue. As you may know, we were planning to run it for our readers in midsummer, but now that David has announced his dates, we feel the time has come—'

'What quiz?'

'Oh, it's nothing, really.' This was even worse than Bill had thought.

'What quiz?' he asked again.

'Well, seeing how many fans of David's read our magazine, which as you know is the premier publication on the subject—'

'What quiz?'

'The Ultimate David Cassidy Quiz. Two pages,

123

highly specialised, not just for the passing girl in the street. The kinds of things only real fans would know. So Roy and I thought, in fact we pretty much decided, that you have shown such dedication to your work, and already know so much about David, that you would be the obvious—'

'When by?'

'Monday.'

'No.'

'I beg your pardon?'

'Can't be done. All that research . . .'

'Yes, well, it will mean putting in a little extra work, and we fully realise—'

'I can't do the weekend.'

'And that,' said Zelda, triumphant in her logic, 'is why I am calling you now. So that you can make a really super start on it right away. I shall be working late, too, and so will Peter of the Photographic Department.'

'Late?'

'And I thought, if we're all done by nine or ten, we could all three pop round the corner to the Odyssey Grill. Company treat, courtesy of Roy. Super squid. Very generous, I think you'll agree.'

'But this evening was . . .'

'Was what, dear?' There was a pause. Bill was dumb.

'Well, whatever it was, I'm sure you can do it another time.' Zelda was speaking brightly now, through the worst of it and hurrying to a close. 'Thank you so much. Knew we could rely on you. Layout will stop by in just a mo and have a word.'

The phone went dead. Bill put it down. He didn't know what he dreaded more: calling David Crockett to say he couldn't make band practice, or eating late-night, badly kebabbed goat with Pete the Pimple. Both had to be done, in any case; to turn down Zelda's demands, this early in his career at Worldwind, could mean no career at all. A tempting thought, in many ways; but he was saving for a car, and a trip to Greece with Ruth, and though he couldn't name his future, or give it any form or shape, he knew that he wanted one. Anything but time hanging heavy as iron in his hands.

Bill dug for a handkerchief and blew his nose. He reached for the phone again, but it rang as he touched it. He jumped, and snatched it, half in anger.

'Yes, what?'

'Forgive me, William, this is Zelda again. I forgot to add the really important bit. Something to put at the top. If you could, you know, make it a bit splashy. You can do poetic, of all people.'

'Yes?' He found himself crouching forward, as if for a fight.

'Top prize for this quiz of yours.' It was his quiz, already?

'Go on.'

'Well, normally we give away records or posters or tickets and so forth, but on this occasion, what with it being so special, the lucky winner and a friend will get to meet David himself on the set of *The Partridge Family*.'

'That's lucky?'

'Come now. Picture yourself as a girl of thirteen. Imagine how thrilled you'd be.'

'I can just imagine.'

Just.

7

The Ultimate David Cassidy Quiz dominated our lives in the days leading up to White City. Sharon and I gave every spare minute we had to it. We dragged all our scrapbooks and shoeboxes out from under her bed; the layer of dust on them felt like suede. Spring was going absolutely nuts that year, bustin' out all over like the song says, and the weather was so warm the little heater that smelt of burnt hair had been put away. Both windows in Sharon's pink room were thrown wide open and we stripped to our cap-sleeved T-shirts, kneeling on the carpet as we combed through thousands of cuttings, some of them as familiar as our own family photographs. I liked to think of us going about our task like an army which knows it is in a state of battle readiness. So this was it, the moment we had been training for. Our devotion to David was being put to the test. We would vanquish our enemies, like Annette Smith who told *Jackie* magazine she had 9,345 pix of David. Huh. Those of us who were in possession of every single issue of *The Essential David Cassidy Magazine*, including the rare limited edition special commemorative birthday supplement of April 1973, had nothing to fear from show-offs from Sevenoaks, wherever that was. Defeat was unthinkable. Mrs Lewis brought us Lucozade and Jacob's crackers and cheese to keep up our strength.

Summer took us by surprise. The candles on the horse chestnuts flared overnight. Gillian's group had already left the science corridor and moved to its meeting place beneath them, at the far end of the playing fields. It was the best spot to pretend to be ignoring the boys from. With superb disdain, we watched—or deliberately looked away—as the lads booted the ball over the posts, ducked and dived and generally pretended to be Barry John or Gareth Edwards, who had gone to school in Pontardawe, just a few miles up the road. Only the year before, our local hero had scored the greatest try in all rugby history at Cardiff Arms Park. Many centuries later, creatures in far galaxies would still be hearing the shout of joy our town gave that afternoon in 1973. Ours was a small country, and a poor one, but when I was a child we always felt rich because men like Gareth Edwards were on our side. Until the day he died, my father loved to quote the match commentator, imitating the exact quiver of pride in his voice: 'If the greatest writer of the written word had written that story no one would have believed it.'

So, secretly, we watched the rugby boys from under the cover of the trees. I was still madly in love with David and counting the days till I met him in London: what I couldn't know was that things would soon change.

At break time, Sharon and I lay in the dappled shade, propped up on our elbows, scouring the magazines she brought into school in a carrier bag. We were getting very close. Only four answers out of the forty still eluded us.

'I know I've seen David's signet ring mentioned somewhere,' said Sharon, ticking another mag off our master checklist.

'What do you get if you win?' asked Olga, who had just got back with Angela from the snack machine and handed out the cold drinks and the chocolate.

'Pet and me are going to Los Angeles to hang out with David on the set of *The Partridge Family*,' announced Sharon with total conviction in her voice.

'Geroff. You two're never going to Los Angeles,' Carol objected with a loud, prolonged raspberry. She was sunbathing flat on her back a few feet away, her blouse tucked into her bra, her skirt tucked into her knickers and her legs akimbo. The boys were looking over at her like jackals watching an antelope.

'We *are* going to Los Angeles,' said Sharon. 'We've only got four more answers to go.'

Olga handed me a Curly Wurly. I tried to break it neatly in half to share with Sharon, but the centre was rock hard. I kept twisting until the coating shattered, exposing the caramel skeleton within, and sending splinters of chocolate all over my clothes. I licked my finger and used the damp tip to collect the chocolate pieces, one by one, before handing Sharon the bigger piece with a flourish.

'Even if you get all the answers right, statistically it's very unlikely you'll win,' said Olga, who, even then, was not one of life's dreamers.

'Yeah, millions of girls will enter,' taunted Carol.

Angela said that her cousin, Joanna, who we would meet in London, was entering.

'This isn't just *any* old quiz.' Sharon was exasperated at their sheer ignorance. 'It's like an A level in David Cassidy,' she said. 'Even if you think you know David backwards it's really, really hard. Anyway, Pet's come up with something fabulous for the tiebreaker. The mag said that the fan who writes the winning tiebreaker must display a certain Johnny. What's it again, Petra?'

'What?'

'What's that saying. I don't know what?'

'What don't you know?'

'French. You know. Johnny says something.'

'Je ne sais quoi.'

'That's the one.'

'What is Petra's tiebreaker, anyway?' Gillian rolled over on the grass, turning her back on Stuart and the rugby. Through lowered eyelashes, she had been surveying her prey, but now, once again, we girls were briefly of interest to her.

'Not telling,' laughed Sharon with a flash of defiance. 'It's our secret. Petra's and mine. We'll send you lot a postcard from Beverly Wilshire if yer lucky.'

'Who's Beverly Wilshire when she's at home?' demanded Carol.

Sharon caught my eye and we burst out laughing. I suddenly realised what the unfamiliar feeling was I'd been struggling to put a name to. I was happy. It wasn't just the horse chestnuts that were full of surging hope. We were going to win the quiz, but, better than that, I had begun to be accepted for who I was, maybe even liked, one of the best feelings you can have. Had Gillian sensed it? Did she decide there and then to take it away from me?

Just because she could.

*   *   *

When you first start learning the cello the sound you make is raspy and tuneless. This instrument is a challenge. It hurts your fingers and leaves bright red points on the tips. I cried. My mother told me I must persevere. Her Aunt Petra had been a cellist in Berlin. Aunt Petra made a sound so beautiful, she said, it made the whole family cry. I wondered what it would be like to make my mother cry. The skin on my fingers grew hard. I persevered.

Miss Fairfax was my cello teacher. My best teacher, but also the weirdest. She had short grey hair, and a whiskery, wrinkled face, and she was one of those people who are so old it's hard to tell whether they're a man or a lady. She taught Latin as well as music, but no one listened. In class, Jimmy Lo said that Miss Fairfax looked like a tortoise in a wig. Even as I was laughing along with everyone else, I knew it was a terrible betrayal. She deserved better from me. In fact, she deserved everything I had to give. People said Miss Fairfax lost her fiancé in the Great War, which was so long ago that she couldn't possibly still be alive. She played the cello in London for a long time, in a quartet that appeared at the Wigmore Hall. I'd seen a poster in a frame at her house. *Jane Fairfax: cello*.

After I passed Grade 8 when I was twelve, she said: 'Now, Petra, we are entering another country.' She didn't mention the country's name. But once she'd introduced me to the Bach cello suites, I think I knew it was the country I wanted to live in.

Before I got in with Gillian's group, I used to practise at least two or three hours a day. I had not been practising hard enough for the Princess Margaret concert and Miss Fairfax knew it.

'Your cello is not a donkey, Petra. It's a racehorse. I want to hear that cello resonating. At the moment, that poor cello is very glum and sad.' Miss Fairfax pulled a tragic-clown face.

Her downturned mouth, with all the wrinkles around it, was like a drawstring purse. I thought: that is what she will look like when she is dead.

We were in the small music-practice room, ten

days before White City and just under three weeks before Princess Margaret. Behind her glasses, Miss Fairfax's blue eyes had a milky glaze that made them look like marbles. I wondered if she was pretty once.

'I can't do it, Miss,' I said miserably. I wanted her to say I didn't have to.

She made a soft tock-tock sound, adjusted my hand on the bow, pulled my shoulders down and back and let her hand rest there awhile. It was no weight, her hand; the bones as light as a mouse, but the sinews were still powerful from all the years of practice. Blue veins stood out from the crêpey, mottled skin like electrical wires.

'Petra, I want your back to be as strong as a tree trunk, and your legs and feet like roots going into the floor. Good, much better. That way the head stays free and your ears can listen to the room. During the concert, there are going to be lots of distractions and you will have to find a still point of calm in the hall. And your right arm—like this—the right arm to be as free as flowing water. Can you feel the difference?'

'Yes, Miss.'

'Good. So that way your body will be moving naturally, but your ears and mind are totally focused. You know, Bach never wastes a single note. You *must* play every single note consciously.'

She must have felt my doubt because she placed a finger in the middle of my forehead. 'All the notes are in here,' she said. 'Now we must use our imagination. In music, you never say the same thing the same way twice. Do you understand, Petra?'

I shook my head. She asked me to think of a song title. 'The first one that comes into your head.'

'Do you mean, um, normal music or classical?'

131

When she smiled, I thought I saw the girl. The one who said goodbye to her soldier boyfriend more than fifty years ago and never married. She sat like Patience on a monument smiling at grief, like in the play. How sad that was. To sit on a war monument with your boy's name written on it.

'Normal will be fine,' laughed Miss Fairfax. 'What's the song title?'

' "I Think I Love You", Miss.'

'It's a popular song?'

'Yes.'

'Perfect. So the first time we play 'I Think I Love You', just plain, exactly like that. I think I love you. The second time it's *I* think I love you. Because certainly nobody else loves you in the same way. The third time it's I *think* I love you. The cello is saying, Hmm, maybe I love you, maybe I don't, let's wait and see. And the time we play the phrase, what do we say, Petra?'

'I think *I* love you?'

'Good. Certainly nobody else is going to be allowed to love him, are they? He belongs to you. Or it could be, I think I *love* you, not I quite like you. I feel passionately. Or, last one, I think I love *YOU*.'

'Yes, and there's nobody else,' I said.

'Precisely,' said Miss Fairfax with a brisk clap of her hands. 'Good girl. One little phrase and all those different ways of saying and feeling it. Now, when you play the piece I want you to think of trying to make each note like a pearl, then make each phrase like a string of pearls.'

She asked what I imagined when I played the Bach. I said I thought of a sad story, maybe someone dying. (I didn't say what I really thought of, which was a girl trying to bring back a boy who had gone

132

away, urging the music on to bring him back to her so she could hold him one more time and he comes back and he kisses her and they fall into each other's arms and they sort of *explode* with joy and sadness and then they die of ecstasy because their love is too perfect for this world. I couldn't tell her that, could I?)

'Yes, loss. Mourning.' Miss Fairfax took off her glasses and rubbed her ancient eyes. 'But we can mourn people who are alive, Petra. Princess Margaret. We look at her and we think, she's beautiful, she's the Queen's sister wearing fine clothes, she arrives at our school in a Rolls-Royce and all the people cheer and applaud. What does she know about sadness?'

Miss Fairfax told me that Princess Margaret once loved a man, Captain Peter someone and she had to give him up because he was divorced. She *renounced* him because it was her duty. The Church said so.

A real live princess with a broken heart. Here was thrilling news from another planet.

'Is she happy now, Miss?'

Miss Fairfax took some rosin and drew my bow across it, giving an extra little shudder at the beginning and the end. 'No, my dear, I don't think she is.'

Love was so hard to learn about. It was lucky you didn't have to do a quiz on it.

'Now, from the beginning if you don't mind. Bach doesn't want you to be afraid of him, Petra. Let's show respect to him by playing each note as you imagine he wanted it to be. One pearl at a time.'

I began to play, trying to do exactly as she'd told me, feeling her hand guiding mine. She stopped me after twenty bars and said that was better. Much better.

'Now keep practising exactly like that. For the next twenty-five years.'

*   *   *

When I saw Gillian's bedroom for the first time, I wanted to raise a white flag.

'OK, you win,' I said under my breath.

Just thinking about Gillian with her perfect bedroom and her invincible prettiness made me want to surrender. To her new stereo with its smoky glass cover and separate speakers, to the white fitted shaggy carpet, to the other girl's obvious superiority. Above all, there was her dressing table with the three mirrors in which Gillian could see herself front, side and back. It was the size of our Hillman Imp.

The Mary Quant eyeshadow present seemed to have worked its costly magic, just as I'd hoped it would. In the lunch queue, the day after her birthday, Gillian invited me round to hers for tea to listen to records. My mother was so impressed I had a friend who lived in Parklands Avenue that she made my dad wear a tie to drop me off, even though he wasn't invited in.

You know, I had been fantasising about that invitation for so long. I had scripted whole conversations in which Gillian and I suddenly discovered how much we had in common. I saw us sitting on her bed giggling together; we would try on her clothes and leave them scattered in careless heaps on the floor and she would curl my new pageboy haircut under with her heated tongs and knot a scarf around my neck while giving advice on what suited me. 'That green top is fabulous on you,

134

Petra.' I saw us like two girls in a cartoon strip in *Jackie*, with the speech bubbles waiting to be filled in.

When it really happened, suddenly I wasn't sure I wanted to go. It wasn't that Gillian's legendary bedroom would be a disappointment—how could it be? It would be me that was the disappointment. I would fail to sparkle in girly chit-chat, I would remain myself, instead of being transformed into the fashionable, fun, fantasy Petra who other girls liked to be with—girls like Angela Norton, who was still supposed to be Gillian's best friend, but who looked like she was about to cry when she heard I was going round there for tea.

As it turned out, I needn't have worried about my side of the conversation. All Gillian wanted to talk about was Stuart.

Did I think he really fancied her?

I did.

But why would Stuart fancy her when he could have any girl in the school he wanted?

Because she was so incredibly pretty and fabulous.

OK, but was I really really one hundred per cent sure that Stuart fancied her?

There could be no doubt about it. He'd be a complete idiot not to, wouldn't he?

But Gillian said she'd chucked Stuart on Friday and thrown his locket in the road because he had wanted to go too far, and she didn't feel ready. Letting them undo your bra, that was OK, but what did I think about boys getting in your knickers? Would that make her a slag?

I didn't really know.

Oh, so I thought she was a slag, did I?

No, of course I didn't. No.

135

Did I think Stuart would call her and say sorry or would he start going with a girl in his own year like Debbie Guest, who would let him do whatever he wanted?

I thought that he would definitely call her and say sorry.

So, did I think she should ring Stuart up right this minute and say she forgave him and give him another chance?

I wasn't sure.

'Yeah, I think you're right,' Gillian concluded happily. 'I'll call him right now.' Unbelievably, she had a phone of her own by the bed.

'Yeah, I've really missed you too, handsome,' she whispered breathily into the receiver. While Gillian snuggled back onto her lacy pillows for what was clearly going to be a long heart-to-heart, I perched at the end of her bed, one foot tucked under me, the other on the floor, wondering when would be a good moment to get up and make my excuses.

'No, I'm not, *you* are. Yes, course I want to. Naughty boy.'

With difficulty, I managed to catch Gillian's eye and pointed first to myself and then to the door, semaphoring my wish to slip out, but she shook her head twice in a businesslike manner and carried on cooing into the phone. Whatever drama was unfolding between her and Stuart, it clearly required an audience. Wordlessly, willingly, I accepted my part in it. Gillian had three mirrors to look at herself in and now she had four.

I lowered myself awkwardly off the bed and bum-shuffled over to the rack of records next to the stereo, trying to be invisible. The first single I picked up had a bright orange centre. Harry Nilsson's

'Without You'. I could remember when it was number one. For five whole weeks. Five Sunday nights, chart night, when the forlorn opening piano chords came out of the windows of all the teenage bedrooms in all of the houses in all of the streets in all of the world. By the fifth week, we got pretty sick of it and started to think the song was whiny and even a bit boring. I played the chords over in my head and remembered how great it was.

That 'No' at the beginning was perfect, mind. Like Harry was in the middle of a conversation with himself and had just started singing it out loud. I thought of Miss Fairfax. Never play the same phrase the same way.

Gillian's tinkling laugh cut into my memory of the music and I looked across at her. She was reclining against the purple padded headboard, twirling the phone's curly cream flex around her index finger, which had shell-pink polish on its tip. Everything about her was exquisite. She looked like the most expensive kind of girl ever made. Like a porcelain figurine. Compared to Gillian, other girls seemed crude and misshapen, like we'd all been turned out by some amateur potter at evening class.

Whichever way you looked at her, Gillian scored higher in every way—marks for looks, marks for figure, marks for just being. When Gillian blushed it seemed an act of the utmost delicacy, like some swoony heroine out of a romantic novel. When I blushed, it was hot and red and humiliating. Even the fact that her breasts were nothing special—they were still stranded in that no-woman's-land between bee-sting and apple—somehow made her seem mysterious and desirable. The graceful swelling beneath Gillian's white school blouse made me think

137

of the plumage of a swan.

No one would dare call Gillian Edwards a flat-chested cow, which is what Ian Roberts shouted after me last winter as I ran out late onto the hockey field. A remark which stung, stung worse even than that spiteful hockey wind which flays your cheeks and your knees. No matter how I tried, I couldn't forget it, because every time I forced the remark to the back of my mind, it would spring up again like a leery jack-in-the-box. Flat-chested cow. A remark which made me realise how lonely I was, back in the days before Sharon, because there wasn't a single girl I dared share it with. Not one friend who would help laugh away the unkindness and join me in speculating on the tragic proportions of Ian Roberts's itsy-bitsy teeny-weeny peeny.

It's easier being beautiful. Not deeper, not better, just easier. I figured that out over those months in 1974, when I got to study Gillian Edwards up close. Beauty made her lazy, though, like a pampered pug on a sofa that's only been fed the choicest morsels. People came to lay tributes to her loveliness and she took them as her due. Boys made complete prats of themselves in front of her. Tranquilly, she would watch them out of her fine blue eyes.

When a girl isn't beautiful, people say, Oh, you've got beautiful hair, you've got lovely eyes, you've got great legs. Every female wants a little piece of beauty to call her own; a slender ankle she can admire while trying on new shoes, or peachy skin that friends remark on; but Gillian's beauty was whole, it had an absolute rightness and completeness to it: it all fitted together. She didn't have beautiful eyes, beautiful legs, beautiful hair; she was beautiful.

When it came to Personality, I could see Gillian

138

would not get top marks, not even close. But, as a keen student of multiple-choice quizzes, I knew full well that the Personality category was a consolation prize, something left over for the girls no one wanted to snog. Sitting in that bedroom, listening to Gillian flirting on the phone with Stuart, and feeling like such a lemon, such a *baby* without a boy of my own, I knew that I badly wanted to be kissed. I didn't want to be in the audience. I wanted to see that look on Captain Von Trapp's face when he takes Julie Andrews out on the terrace during the ball and he knows, he just *knows*, and she's gabbling away nervous as anything, because she knows it too, and she thinks, If I just keep moving my mouth he won't be able to kiss it.

And he starts to sing to her, saying that he must have done something good in his life, because Julie Andrews, who can clothe all of his seven children from a single pair of bedroom curtains, adores him.

Proud, arrogant men humbled by love, who buckle under its intoxicating influence; oh yes, I would always be a sucker for those. I hoped there might still be a chance with David; I would be seeing him for the first time in person in just four days at White City. I was sure I would always love him, but I didn't want to kiss Sharon's Cassidy shrine any more. The paper was gluey and cold. I wanted a real boy to pull me towards him and say, 'Come here, *you*.'

'What d'you think of these?' Gillian had finally put down the phone to her reinstated boyfriend and was rummaging in the white fitted wardrobe that ran the entire length of the wall opposite the window. She came out smiling. Gillian's smile only made rare appearances and I was struck by how tiny and white her teeth were, like a baby's teeth.

139

'Here we are,' she said. 'Try these on, Petra—you're size 4, same as me, aren't you?'

These turned out to be a pair of platform shoes, in a shade of gorgeous burgundy-brown, the very same shoes that I had worshipped for at least two months in the window of Freeman Hardy Willis. Frankly, there was more chance of becoming Mrs David Cassidy than of my mother buying me such trendy, towering footwear. (Although she always wore heels herself, my mum preferred to keep me in the kind of sensible, round-toed flatties that looked like Cornish pasties and were worn only by old women with walking frames.)

'You can keep them,' Gillian said, just like that, as though a pair of shoes that cost £9.99 were just loose change. She flung open another door and started pulling out tops and skirts. I was startled to spot a poster of an alien tartan life form hanging on the inside of the wardrobe.

'Didn't know you liked the Bay City Rollers,' I said, unable to conceal my astonishment.

Gillian gave a yelp of laughter. 'Best to be prepared. Keep your options open where lover boys are concerned,' she said. 'David's on the way out, isn't he? He'll be chip paper by Christmas. The rest of the Rollers are scrotty, but Les McKeown, the lead singer, he's a bit of all right, isn't he? Anyway,' she said, 'I like "Shang-A-Lang".'

'Shang-A-Lang'? The song was a shocker. A rinky-dink excuse for rock 'n' roll. Was this the same Gillian who once refused to stay over at Karen Jones's house on principle because Karen had a poster of Donny Osmond on her bedroom ceiling and she thought it was disloyal to fall asleep looking at another pop star's face?

Other people's heroes are always mysterious. But to swap David for a group of pasty-skinned boys with tartan trousers worn so short they revealed a few inches of hairy white leg? Impossible. While I was still trying to absorb her treachery, Gillian threw a bundle of clothes at me. There were sky blue hot pants with a red anchor design on the bib, two psychedelic dresses with swirly patterns, one in orange, the other in hot pink; there was a chain belt made up of gold links and fake precious stones, a silky pink bomber jacket and a purple choker with a cameo brooch. It was the kind of gear girls wore on the cover of *Jackie*. It was the kind of clothes you could call gear.

'Put something on, quick,' she instructed, 'Stuart's coming by with some of the boys. Taking us down the beach. Car'll be here in five minutes.'

It was a school night and we hadn't eaten anything, not since lunchtime, when I'd just had a Twix because I was saving my dinner money for White City. I felt faint with hunger. The sensible thing to do would be to say I had to get home, but apparently under some kind of spell, I pulled on the pink swirly mini-dress and the pink bomber jacket and added the choker as an afterthought, to add length to my short neck. In the largest of Gillian's three mirrors, I caught sight of an unfamiliar figure. A groovy chick with long, pipe cleaner legs which ended in a pair of gorgeous burgundy-brown platforms. I barely knew her.

Gillian had got her jacket on and switched off her bedside lamp so the room was dark, apart from a beam of light from the landing, when she said: 'Pet, I was thinking we could go in for the David Cassidy quiz.'

141

'How d'you mean?'

'Well, we're cleverer than the others by miles and I think we'd be a great team. It'd be such a laugh if we won. Get our picture in the paper an' everything. What d'you reckon?'

The sensation of being wanted by Gillian was so new and delightful that I hadn't examined it too closely. Now, the nature of the bargain came home with such speed that I felt physically winded, like that day I got thumped in the chest by a monster wave down at Three Cliffs Bay. My mind was whirring. It was trying to work out how many moves back she'd planned this. I felt the sudden desolation of coming up against a superior opponent.

But there was still time. There in front of me, within easy reach, was a branch with various good and decent replies dangling from it. The replies said things like 'No', 'I can't', 'I'm afraid that's impossible' and 'Sorry, but Sharon and I are entering the quiz, we're a team'.

Later, I told myself that I had tried to reach the branch. The truth was the ambush had been so swift and skilful that resistance felt almost rude. Even that's not the whole truth. When it came to it, I was more scared of saying no than I was of saying yes. I had wanted to be in Gillian's shoes for so long. Now I *was* in her shoes, stuck in a pair of burgundy-brown platforms and condemned to dance to her tune.

'I'm not sure,' I said, my tone of voice already admitting defeat. That was all I could manage in defence of the hundreds of hours that Sharon and I had spent building our precious archive and trying to solve the Ultimate David Cassidy Quiz.

How much did you betray your sweet, kind friend for, Petra?

Nine pounds and ninety-nine pence. To a girl who reckoned that, come Christmas, David Cassidy would be finished.

8

'Remind me,' said Bill. He stared into his coffee cup. Something was hiding in the dregs.

'Of what, dear?' asked Zelda.

'Oh, sorry. Remind me never to go near the Skyway Hotel again, in my entire life. I mean, I'll be going there anyway, after I'm dead, like everyone does, and spending ten million years there, being purged.' He sipped at the coffee, hoping not to swallow whatever lurked. 'All the more reason not to go while I'm still alive.'

'Well, you didn't have to stay there, did you? It was only a press conference. How long did it last?'

'Under an hour.'

'Well, there you are, then.' Zelda clapped her hands lightly, as she tended to do when a point had been settled—not scored, for that was not her game, but laid politely to rest.

Bill stood in her office behind the spider plants, from where she had spied him as he crept in, and to which she had summoned him, as she would an errant child. Word had it that Zelda had been a primary-school teacher in her younger days, but word was wrong. She had wanted to be a nurse.

'No,' said Bill.

'I beg your pardon?'

'No way.' He fished into his coffee. 'Zelda, I'm very grateful for this job, and I do understand that it's good experience and all that, but, really, I cannot be expected to drink drawing pins.' He held up the dripping pin.

'Crumbs.'

'Well, that's what I thought it was. A bit of ginger nut. Even a pencil shaving wouldn't have been too bad. I mean, it's all carbon. But that thing could have killed me. Lucky I'm not a Yank, or I'd have sued you.'

'Crikey, yes.' What would it take to make this woman swear—swear properly, that is, like every other journalist on earth? Was it worth dropping a filing cabinet on her big toe, just to see? Bill toyed with the idea of leaving the drawing pin on her chair, as he left, then listening out for what followed. But she would probably just jump up and squeal 'Lawks-a-mercy', like someone out of Dickens, and save the offending pin for future use.

'Have a biscuit, William. I have Playbox or custard cream. Over there, in front of the felt tips. No? So, then. Mr Cassidy. Was he forthcoming? Anything you can use?'

Bill sat down, without being asked.

'I think he's had enough.'

'Come again?'

'Well, you know he's said this is his last tour. You know he's giving up touring.'

'So he says.'

'He does say. And I believe him.'

'Well, let's not get carried away. It's only one side of his appeal, the live performance.' Zelda shifted in her chair. This kind of talk made her uneasy. If David Cassidy's appeal waned, so would *The Essential David Cassidy Magazine*, and with it all their jobs—Bill's and Chas's and Pete's and everyone's, all the service industry that clustered round the glowing star. And where would she go then? *Mott the Hoople Monthly*? *The Wizzard Fanzine*? Imagine working to promote a band which wasn't even spelt correctly.

145

'I'm glad it's over.'

'Excuse me, it is most certainly not over. And for you to say so, William, is frank—'

'No, *I'm* not saying it's over. He said that, Cassidy said it.' Bill dug into the pocket of his jacket and took out a pad. Ruth had bought him a bulk order of six from WHSmith. They had the words 'Reporter's Notebook' on the front, in slightly larger letters than Bill would have liked, and he had been in two minds about taking the pad out at the press conference, in front of real reporters. Then he had seen the real reporters.

' "I'm glad it's over, I'm glad I've almost finished doing that." Then someone asked him for the reason he's not doing stage shows any more, and he said, hang on, got it somewhere here . . .' Bill flipped pages. Zelda smiled, and glanced at the custard creams.

'Here we are. "The only way that I can really grow"—this is still him—"The only way that I can really grow, and devote enough time to making a good album, is not to be touring six months a year, being . . ." Sorry, just trying to read my own writing here. Looks like "blow something".' Zelda's smile held steady.

'Oh yes, "being blown out, tired and wasted". Unquote. See what I mean about him having had enough? I mean, I can't just bung that in next month's letter to the fans, can I? "Hello, lovely girls, let me tell you, I am just so blown out and wasted right now, it's a killer. Wanna come and help me blow those cares away?" ' Bill had adopted his best American accent, which was widely held to be the worst in the office.

'No, I see your point.' Zelda tapped her nails on

146

her desk blotter. 'But that bit about growing, you could do something with that, surely? I'm sure our girls would love that.' She sounded like a headmistress, talking about a new drinking fountain in the corridor. 'It's so . . .' Zelda tipped her head on one side, searching for the most extravagant adjective. '. . . so Californian.'

'Oh, of course,' Bill replied, only half conscious of the complete absurdity of two British adults calmly discussing a state—a nation, in fact—which neither of them had ever visited. They might as well talk about the moon.

'Anyway, what was he like? Do tell.' Zelda was brighter now, back on safe ground.

'Hard to say. Nice enough bloke. Couldn't always tell what he made of the whole thing, cos whenever the photographers started flashing away, which was basically every time he looked up, he would blink a bit and then put on a pair of these mirrored shades.'

'Mr Cool!' said Zelda, who liked to think she was tuned into her readers' minds.

'Mmm. Yup. Anyway. So what he said was, he talked about all these, what was it, yes, "these little things, things about our personalities, that we hide and keep inside ourselves".'

'Perfect!' Zelda held her hands together, as if preparing to pray. 'And what were they? The little things?'

'That's just it. He said, and I quote, "I'm certainly not going to reveal them to 850,000 people".'

'Ooh, the meanie. And where did he get that number from, I'd like to know? Why aren't they all reading this magazine?' Bill couldn't tell whether Zelda was being serious. Everything was upbeat to her, even bad news. Especially bad news. When the end of the world came, she would announce it like a jingle for Rise & Shine.

'Anything about England?' she went on.

'Yes, he said he was enchanting. Sorry, that it was enchanting and he was enchanted.'

'Excellent. There's half your piece written for you, practically. The home-grown interest.'

'Except he said exactly the same thing about Australia. And Germany. And he thanked the fans for their support.'

'Lovely. I do like it when stars are polite.'

'And someone asked him about the hysteria, you know, the trail of destruction he leaves wherever he goes. Not actual destruction, nobody dies, but the stuff we deal in, broken hearts and what have you.'

'And what did David say?'

'He said he hates being blasé about it, the hysterics, but it's just there, it's part of his life. And, what was it, hang on a sec . . .' Bill flipped pages again. 'Yes, this is it: "I think eventually it's going to pass on, as all things do".' Bill closed the pad. 'Quite the philosopher, our boy Dave.'

'Quite.' Zelda was unsettled, he could see. She gazed down at the blotter. Talk of passing on made her feel as if they were discussing the deathbed of a loved one. Then she remembered something more cheering, and looked up at Bill.

'And what about going to his hotel suite afterwards, for a heart-to-heart? Just for our girls. Did that work out all right?'

Now it was Bill's turn to hesitate. He swayed a touch, steadied his nerve and replied: 'No dice, I'm afraid. They cocked up the timings. Couple of people had a quick shot and then they sent the rest of us away. I was livid, I can tell you. Kicked up a fuss, but

148

by then he'd left the building, apparently. Last seen heading down Queensway in a Bentley, with a couple of convent girls hanging onto his exhaust.'

'Thank you for that, William. What a pity. Anyway'—Zelda rose from her desk—'we must use what we can. You've got enough to go on, haven't you? You don't have to make an awful lot up. The feeling of David is what we aim to convey, after all, the essence, and that should be easier now you've seen him close up. Am I right?'

'Completely.'

'It's a funny thing to say, William, with your job being what it is, but . . .' Here she stretched out her arms, as though about to burst into song herself, and said, 'Do try and tell the truth.'

*   *   *

'David *Cassidy*?' Ruth sat up in bed. 'David Cassidy?'

'Well, as I say—'

'David *Cassidy*?' It was like someone paging his name at an airport. 'You went to see David Cassidy? What are you, a twelve-year-old girl?'

She got up and walked to the basin, ran cold water into the tooth mug, and drank it down. Then she turned to face Bill. 'David Cassidy?'

'That is his name, I admit.'

'Don't get smart-arse with me, Bill. I mean, I know your job has a wide brief or whatever it's called, you have to cover a load of stuff, but . . . David Cassidy?' Ruth made motions with her hands, which he could hardly see in the half-light.

They had woken up, with spring rain on the tin roof of next door's garden shed, and, since they

149

happened to be awake, made love. English to a fault, Bill thought as he lay there: sex not as mad urge, as a pulse of something irrepressible and strong, but as something brought on by weather—bad weather, at that—to fill the time. On the other hand, to do it at three o'clock in the morning (that most mysterious of hours, when you normally woke, if you woke at all, to fret about having no money, or dying young) gave it a strange and suspended air, and Bill wondered if, come the morning, he would find it hard to remember, like a dream. On the other hand, that meant drifting back to sleep, and thus far there had been no drift; they had lain there, twined in one another, and talked of nothings, sweet or otherwise, and Bill had somehow convinced himself that now would be as good a moment as any to broach a delicate matter. That, he now saw, had been his first big mistake of the day, and it wasn't yet dawn. Too early for an error, surely, even by his blundering standards.

'David Cassidy?'

'Look, love, as I said, it was a one-off. Normally, someone else handles all that stuff. You know me. I really only function when I'm working on things that I know about, you know, bands I really like.' He coughed, as if his breath couldn't bear the sheer flow of lies that were tumbling out of him, in the wake of one small truth. 'I mean, I was slated to do this Led Zeppelin thing, fantastic chance to talk to them, nothing to do with a show, so no hurry involved, just me and them sitting around.' Ruth was sitting on the end of the bed now, looking at him. She wore one of his T-shirts, the one with a burn on the hem. Some unlucky encounter with a joss stick, just before his final exams.

150

'And, and, and then this guy Scott, in the office? He comes up and says, do us a favour, Bill. I've got a doctor's appointment that my girlfriend can't know about, and it's got to be today. Some medical bollocks. Probably about bollocks, actually.' Ruth sighed, and Bill hurried on:

'Anyway, he says, will you go and sit in at a press conference for me, maybe a one-on-one? David Cassidy, the one all the girls like. Just take a few notes, bring them back here and I'll work 'em up into something for the mag. Please please, and all that. So, being a sucker, I say yes, and he says he'll switch with me one of these days. You know, take my place on the Stones tour bus for three days in Sweden. Which of course I'll be more than happy to give up.' Bill paused for a laugh, which didn't come. Ruth was quieter than the rain.

'So I go and, you know what? It's actually quite interesting, in that way that, you know, it's like a wildlife documentary. See the pop star in his natural habitat. You go into the press conference, and all those total weirdos are sitting there with their lists of questions. I mean, Ruth, you should see them. These people from, I don't know, magazines called *Tune Up!* and *The Rock Files* and *Sha-La-La-Weekly*. Not just *NME* and *Melody Maker*, those blokes are relatively normal, but mags you've never heard of. And none of them smile, and none of them wash, and you just know they all go back home in the evenings and get stoned and listen to Kraftwerk. Honestly, I was like the most normal guy there. You'd have been proud of me.'

Ruth pulled up the sleeve of her T-shirt and scratched her shoulder. And she yawned.

'And everyone asks Cassidy the same old

151

questions, what do you want to do next, what kind of sound were you trying to achieve in the new album, rhubarb rhubarb, and the poor guy, I mean the guy, just sits there and bats back these answers, and you can see how totally not into it he is. And then this woman with Carole King hair gets up and asks what he really hates about his life, which I thought was kind of daring, none of us men would ever ask a question like that. I mean, for one thing, we think it's a bit rude to get that personal. And second, all of us just think, great life anyway, trillions of records, get your own jet, shag-o-rama, what's to complain about? And David gives her the eye, and he says—'

'David? He's David now? Where is this going, Bill?' He couldn't tell whether Ruth was thoroughly angry, all the way through, or whether she was enjoying herself, relishing his humiliation for a laugh. Would she tell her girlfriends about it, over coffee? Would she ever go to bed with him again?

'OK, you win,' he said. 'Look, Ruth, I'm sorry, OK? I know you want me to spend every minute of every day writing about Pink Floyd or Fleetwood bloody Mac or answering the phone from Lennon, asking me to join him in a bed-in, but, come on, love . . .'

Bill was no good at anger. He lacked the skills for it, and the stamina, especially when his cause was weak. Deceit he could manage; envy, too, in his greener days, when other boys got off with other girls; sloth he needed to work on, put in some effort there, being still too industrious by half; but wrath would never be his weapon. He wondered whether Cassidy got mad, raged at his entourage, slammed doors and smashed guitars. Not a chance. And what did he matter, anyway?

'Cup of tea?' said Bill. Thus had Englishmen, for the past two hundred years, gently sought to douse the flames of argument. When in doubt, when in a stew, when in disgrace with fortune and men's eyes: put the kettle on.

'Bit early,' said Ruth, annoyed with herself for accepting the offer of peace, but dying for a cuppa.

'Well,' said Bill, chancing it, as he got up, 'thirsty work and all that. Your fault for waking me up and demanding physical exercise.'

'Excuse me,' said Ruth, and threw a pillow at him, missing by half a room. Women could do everything, and soon enough they would, and good luck to them, about time they ran the place; but still, you had to say, with the best will—they couldn't throw. Never could, never would. That was something for his sex to cling on to, Bill thought.

He filled the kettle, which shared the same plug as Ruth's stereo and hairdryer, and made tea. The milk in the small waxy carton had seen better days; he could feel the congealed lumps as he poured, but he fished them out with a spoon and stirred. Back in bed, Ruth clutched her mug with both hands and blew on the steam: another unfakeable mark of womankind. No man would ever use both hands to hold a cup of tea, unless he was one day's march from the South Pole, with one chum dead in the snow, dogs all eaten and six fingers about to drop off. And even then he would look around the empty tent to check, in case anyone thought it was girly.

'Bill, can I just say?'

'Yes?'

'I love you and everything, but—no, listen. You're funny and clever, cleverer than me in some weird way, although you know bugger all about Anglo-

153

Saxon coinage. And I think that, whatever you say, deep down you have the makings of a romantic, though someone's going to have to dig around for ages to get there. And Lord knows what they'll find.'

'Coins.'

'Shut up, I'm talking.' Ruth put down her tea and looked at her boyfriend. The dawn sifting through the blind made the light in the room golden and granular. It settled on the naked Bill, delineating his shoulder, his arm and the curve of his buttocks. Exposed to the air, his cock, which had been slack and sleepy, began to stir, curious to see if there was more. Bill was lovely-looking, but he would never make a ladies' man, Ruth thought with satisfaction. To be one of those you needed a wholly unironic sense of being male. Bill was armoured in irony. And he had this radar that detected any incoming seriousness and shot it down before it came too close. If he ever stopped joking, if he ever took the armour off, she wasn't quite sure what would be left. Some small part of Ruth, private even to herself, suspected that he didn't really love her; but she was safe because he was far too polite to walk out. Bill's everyday uniform was a leather jacket and flares, but she knew that underneath he was such a gentleman he might as well be wearing a cravat and a coat with tails. It was hereditary. His father, who worked for an insurance company after taking early retirement from the Royal Air Force, may not have read any of the poets that Bill loved, but he had the same nobility. The knowledge that Bill would never leave her, not unless he was asked politely but firmly, made Ruth feel powerful and sad at the same time.

'Go on,' he said, yawning and pulling the sheet over them. 'You told me to shut up, then you

154

stopped.'

'I was just thinking that the music thing actually means a lot to you. It may, and I'm guessing here, I think it may actually be the coins. You know, Jimi Hendrix may turn out to be your buried treasure. Your one true love. Which is fine by me, because he's dead. And he burned all his guitars. Or if not him, then someone else. But. God, Bill, I hate to say it, but, David Cassidy.' She gave a heavy sigh, and her shoulders slumped.

'I know, I know. But it was only a one-off, for God's sake.' Bill listened to himself, in some confusion. Christ, he sounded as if Ruth had caught him sleeping with a pop star, not writing down his words on a pad from WHSmith. 'And besides . . .' This was his trump card, though it could go horribly wrong. He played it anyway. 'He likes Jimi Hendrix.'

'Who does?'

'David. I mean Cassidy.'

'Really?' Ruth lifted her head and stared at him, curious despite herself. The ploy had worked. 'How d'you know?'

'He told me. Actually, better than that, he showed me.'

'You mean you asked a question at the press thing?'

'No, later on, in his room.'

'You went to his room? His hotel room? What, did he book it for the afternoon, just the two of you?' Ruth had the grace to laugh at this. 'Did he let you use the minibar afterwards? I hope he bloody well paid.'

'Well, obviously I was bitterly disappointed that that didn't happen,' said Bill. He took a sip of sweet tea, and felt himself waking up. 'So what happened

155

was, before your filthy little mind goes any further, is that they take basically a whole floor of this horrible place, and you all sit there in the anteroom of his suite—'

'Like groupies.'

'Exactly like groupies. And wearing no bras, either, like most of them. And you wait your turn, and every fifteen mins or so this guy comes out, sort of smoothie but a heavy too, tie-and-jacket type, and he ushers you in. And you get your allotted time, and ask Cassidy which direction his music is going in, and how he likes England, and does he have any message for his fans. And then you get up and shake hands and leave.'

'But that's not what happened with you.'

'That's not what happened with me. There's a bit of a break in the routine, for some reason. And then I hear music, of all things—'

'Music? From a pop star?'

'I know. The last thing you'd expect. So out comes the jacket guy and takes me in, then gives Cassidy the nod and slips to another room. And, Ruth, I swear to you, the kid is sat there, on a sofa, got his guitar across his knees and he's going . . .'

Bill began to air-strum, in the dawn light, humming a rising note. Ruth frowned, not quite getting there, and so he sang to her, in a morning croak, about jacks in boxes and happiness staggering down the street.

'You're kidding me.'

'Nope. God's honest.'

'Let's get this straight.' Ruth had her hands in the chopping position, inches apart, as she liked to when confirming a point of order. Not for the first time, Bill thought she should be running a company rather

156

than digging up a hill. 'You go to see this, this stupid little teenage munchkin, and he—'

'Well, he's twenty-four now, but—'

'And he's playing "The Wind Cries Mary".'

'Yep.'

'Which just happens to be one of your favourite Hendrix songs.'

'One of my favourite songs, period.'

'What?'

'I mean full stop. Period. It's American for full stop.'

Ruth narrowed her eyes at him.

'Does he do that for all the hacks?' she asked. 'You know, find out their top record ever and arrange by sheer chance to be doodling around with it when they come in, to soften them up so they write something nice about him? Awful lot of work. Imagine if the chap after you liked Wagner or something.'

Bill thought about this. He took a sip of tea, which was growing cold.

'No, I think—all things considered—' He looked down his nose at Ruth, over imaginary spectacles. It was a mock-legal game that they had idly, half-consciously worked up between them, over the months, in order to defuse the threat of seeming pompous. '—I think, m'lud, that the defendant has conceived a genuine and, it must be said, well-informed admiration for the collected works of the late Mr James Hendrix.'

'The gentleman of the empurpled haze?' Ruth spoke in as low a voice as she could muster, and the growl of it made her cough. It usually did.

'The very same, m'lud.'

'And what was your reaction, pray, when the

157

defendant first, ah, gave expression—nay, gave vent—to this most heated of, ah, devotions.'

'Well, m'lud. Not wanting to beat around the bush, you understand, and with all provisos and caveats taken into full consideration, I, um . . . I sang.'

'You what?' Ruth dropped the act. 'You fucking what?' She rarely swore, and Bill was mildly shocked, on her behalf, to hear the word emerge, and secretly ashamed, on his behalf, that it should turn him on. 'You sang with David Cassidy?'

'Just like I did with you now. Jacks out of the boxes, clowns, the works.'

'And he did what? Called security? Set off the fire alarm? Tell me he laughed. Tell me at least he did that.'

'Not a bit of it. He said, "Hey." Not "Hey!" like a Monkee, but just "Hey". Kind of a recognition scene.'

'Like in late Shakespeare.'

'Just like that.'

'And then what?' Ruth was hooked now, no question. He was already starting to worry if she would tell her flatmates about it, and whom they in turn would tell, over drinks at the end of work. By Monday, embellished up to the hilt, the entirely fictional tale of his duet with David Cassidy would be all over the capital. By Tuesday it would reach his parents. By Wednesday, obviously, he would have to kill himself, though God knows that would be a small price to pay. Could you go on being embarrassed after death?

'Well, we talked about Hendrix. And, shit, he really knows his stuff, David does. All the albums, obviously, plus endless rumours about bootlegs and lost recordings. I mean, close your eyes and I could have been talking to a thirty-five-year-old with thick specs and filing cards, you know, a specialist. Like my friend Carl from college, the one who has bits of Cream lyrics stencilled to the inside of his car. You're driving along, and you flip down the sunshade thingy, or open the glove compartment, and it says "Restless Diesels" or something like that, in Gothic. Total madman. And that's another thing. He didn't really know about Cream.'

'Who, Carl?'

'No, David. I mean he knew all the stuff that Hendrix knew, he knew about Muddy Waters and B.B. King—major B.B. King fan, as far as I could tell. But the scene Hendrix got involved in over here, where it led, that's all new to him. Cos of course he doesn't know the place. The kid. He comes here and stays in hotels and limos, can't even get out and buy a pair of socks in case he gets gang-banged by half a dozen Melanies on the corner of Carnaby Street. I mean, he knows the Beatles pretty well, and he told me he'll be doing a version of "Please Please Me" on Sunday night, but . . . yeah, I know.'

Ruth had made a face. 'Do we want to hear him ruining Beatles songs? Even if he is your new best friend?'

'We-e-e-ll . . .'

'Bill,' said Ruth, as sharp as his mother telling him to brush his hair. 'Also,' she went on, 'what's with Sunday night? Got a date with him? Is he going to take you to the pictures?'

'Sod off. No, it's a concert. White City. His last eh-ver.' Bill broke down into a fake sob. Ruth wasn't fooled.

'You're going to go, aren't you? You actually want to go.'

159

'Not unless I absolutely bloody have to,' said Bill, fired for once by the fervour of telling the truth. 'Besides, I wouldn't survive. I'd be gang-raped by the Melanies, just for being the only other boy.'

'You wish.'

'I mean, I would go if I thought he might go out on a high, or some sort of total freakout. "Cassidy smashes guitar." "Teen idol sets fan on fire." I'd be the only proper journalist there. His last concert, my first scoop.'

'But he won't, will he?'

'Nah. He's a pro and the record company would skin him alive. I think he'd like to, mind you: bring it all crashing down. Say to them: you made me sing these ludicrous songs about daydreaming and cherishing, nothing about drugs or screwing, and for years I've gone along with it, but now I'm gonna sing the songs I like. It's a live appearance, my last one, so you can't jump in and stop me, so here goes: "Wind Cries Mary", "Cocaine", "Killing Floor" by Howlin' Wolf, couple of filthy Stones tracks with my tongue hanging out like Mick. Jesus, love, can you imagine the teeny-boppers? Their poor little heads would come off.'

Bill got up and drew the curtains. London daylight, tired and unwashed, flooded one corner of the room. He lay down next to Ruth and kissed her hair.

'Like I said, he won't do it, but I bet he dreams about it. I dream about it.'

Ruth held her arms up, locked her fingers together, and stretched. 'So, how does it end?'

'How does what end?'

'Your beautiful friendship. You and Davey. Handshake? Swapping phone numbers?'

160

'Well, you're not going to believe this, but—'

'Oh God, here we go again.'

'He asks me a question. I mean, my quarter of an hour is up and I've yet to ask a proper question. Ace bloody reporter I am. Anyway, we've overshot, the heavy comes in and nods to say we're done, and Cassidy says no, make the next guy wait. And he turns to me and asks how I know so much Jimi Hendrix and so forth. And I tell him I'm in a band. "What's it called?", he says. "Spirit Level", I say.'

'And then of course he asks,' Ruth said, 'what you play, and you say bass, so he goes next door, fetches a bass and you plug it in, and then, for the next hour, while frustrated journalists beat at the door, you and David Cassidy jam away and smoke dope and hit on the lay-deeze. Isn't that what happened?'

'In your dreams.'

'In *your* dreams.' Ruth smiled at Bill. 'And what about the thing he didn't like about his life?'

'What?'

'That bit in the press conference, earlier on, when the woman asked him what he hated. What did he say?'

'Why d'you want to know?'

'I just do.'

'Well, first off he said he hated press conferences like this one. As a joke. Sort of a joke. Then he looks at the woman, I mean really looks at her, and she's going all googly, and there's this really long embarrassing pause, and he says, in his best come-to-bed voice, "Dishonesty." '

'Honestly?'

'Yup. "I hate dishonesty." Apparently we have to live in truth or something.' Bill scratched his armpit. 'Like he cares. Let's face it, he's a nice bloke, and pretty good on the history of the guitar, but at the end of the day, m'lud, he's a pop star. If he wanted truth he chose the wrong business.'

'Dishonesty,' Ruth repeated, lying back and looking at the ceiling. The tap dripped. Ruth thought of taking off her T-shirt, then decided not to. The room felt cold, after a long night. Then she turned her head and considered her lover once again. 'Bill,' she said.

'Mm?'

'Oh, nothing. It's just that . . .' She rubbed her face, like someone emerging from a dream.

'Just what?'

'I was just going to call you . . . David.' Then, while he lay there laughing, she swung her legs off the bed. 'More tea?'

WHAT SORT OF GIRL TURNS DAVID ON?

'Well, I like girls with blonde hair because I find fair, golden hair appealing, especially if it's long. And I like girls with dark hair because that can be so romantic. And I like girls with mid-brown hair, like mine is, because it can be kind of cute, specially if it's kept glossy and in good condition—oh, and I almost forgot to say I like girls with red hair too.

'Seems I just like girls, period!'

9

Period is not what you're thinking it is. In American, period means full stop. You have to be careful about things like that if you ever go to Los Angeles.

'LA,' I said, trying the sounds in my mouth. El. Ay.

I once explained to Sharon that in America they call a full stop a period.

'You're joking me, Pet. That's stupid, that is. Don't they know what it means?'

I got my first period—that's a British period—the day before we went to White City. It was cruel, really, the last thing I needed, what with everything else that was going on. Maybe it was the excitement brought it on, or the fear. I can tell you, I was dead scared. Loving David had given me so much energy and belief that, one day, we would meet in the real world, instead of our increasingly unsatisfying trysts on my brown candlewick bedspread. Now, as that time drew near, I felt like one of those cartoon characters who's been running so fast they don't see the cliff edge and, suddenly, they look down and realise they're pedalling in mid-air over a chasm. I kept on pedalling, but I wasn't sure how long I could delay the fall.

Up till then, the furthest I'd ever been was Cardiff, which was thirty-eight miles away. My mother took me along to help her buy a new outfit for my cousin Nonny's wedding. The suit was in French Navy Viyella, with knife pleats: chosen, I think, to show how cool she felt towards a shotgun summer marriage that would take place in a registry office. My mother had announced that God would not be present in a registry office. I said I thought God was supposed to be everywhere. (God be in my head and in my understanding, God be in my eyes and in my looking, or so it said in the anthem our chapel choir sang.)

But my mother muttered darkly that the ceiling at the registry office was too low.

'Since when does God operate a height restriction, Greta?' my dad laughed. 'He's not a bloody multi-storey car park, is He?'

After shopping in Cardiff, we had time for a cream tea in Howells and still got the five o'clock train back. That was as far from home as I'd ever been. So a journey to London, which was five hours on the train and hundreds of miles away, followed by a trip across the big city, felt about as straightforward as a day trip to Venus.

Also, there was the period problem to deal with. Sad thing is, I should have been excited about starting: I'd wanted this proof that I was a woman for so long. I'd even lied to Carol when she was mucking about in the changing room using a box of Tampax as finger puppets. Told her I had started, when I hadn't. Really stupid, I know, but I just couldn't face being the last to get a bra *and* the last to get their period.

My mother had laid in the necessary supplies in the cupboard under the sink in the bathroom and, for once, I was grateful for how little fuss she made of me. When I tried a sanitary towel for the first time in my knickers under my cords it was so thick and bulging at the crotch I thought everyone would be able to tell. The pad made you walk a bit awkward like one of those gunslingers in the cowboy films; legs parted and hips rolling. I put two extra in my bag for London in case of accidents, which I had heard

165

the others talk about.

Also, I was finding it increasingly hard to keep track of all the lies I had told my mother. When she said things like, 'Sharon's mother, does she mind she has to collect you from the train when it's szo late?' or 'What time does the concert begin?' I had to think carefully and run through the parallel timetables I held in my head for David and the *Messiah*. Over breakfast one morning, I said London instead of Cardiff by mistake and immediately started belting out 'Every valley shall be exalted' to put her off the scent.

Dad, who knew that Handel was not his daughter's composer of choice, raised an eyebrow, but I laid low behind the cornflakes packet. I think my father knew something was going on. When my mother wasn't looking, he pressed a tenner into my hand, which was all the spending money he got for a week, and he said I was to use it for emergencies. It was too much, I said, I couldn't take it; but he made me fold it inside my purse in the zipped part. I wanted to tell him that I was finally going to see David. I wanted to share all the love I had felt and the longing, such longing.

But telling Dad would make him an accomplice to the crime, and if things went wrong she would kill him. She would kill the both of us.

Also, also, there was Sharon. She was so proud and excited about the Ultimate David Cassidy Quiz. I have never seen her happier. It was terrible.

Amazingly, between us we seemed to have found answers to the two impossible final questions. From the farthest corner of the vast David library that I carried in my brain, I retrieved the name of the dog sadly left behind in New Jersey when David and his

166

mother moved to California after the divorce.

'Tips? Are you sure?' Sharon said dubiously.

'Not one hundred per cent,' I said, 'but ninety-nine per cent. I'm definite that Bullseye and Sheesh are both dogs David has had recently and Tips is the only other dog name I can remember.'

So we took a gamble and went with Tips. Then, three nerve-racking days before the entries for the quiz were due in, Sharon finally discovered a cutting down the back of the bed which answered the signet ring question. David's father had given him the ring when he was fifteen, and David would pass it on to his son when he was the same age.

It was a great answer, the answer to all our prayers in fact, yet I wrote it down on the entry form in silence, while Sharon used her best 3-D lettering to make an eye-catching border around the edge. The thought of David having a *son* was hard for us. It meant he'd also have a wife, and the future Mrs Cassidy, well, she might not be us. But David's role as a dad seemed far enough in the future not to be worth worrying about for now.

What I did urgently need to worry about was Sharon. Her joyful conviction that we were going to win the quiz and would soon be hanging out with David on the set of *The Partridge Family* was a daily torment. I kept hoping an opportunity would crop up where I could drop into the conversation what had happened the other night at Gillian's. The way she had tricked me into saying that she could be the named friend on my quiz entry. Sometimes, for whole minutes at a time, I managed not to think about what I had done. I kept busy. I worried my mother by tidying my room. I practised the Bach suites until my shoulders ached and my fingertips

167

were as red and swollen as raspberries. I ran down the hill to the front: the sea air could always be guaranteed to blow away bad thoughts, which it did for a while. Then, the next time I saw Sharon in her pink crossover ballet cardy, hugging herself with anticipation, I felt my stomach go down a mineshaft.

'Hey, Pet, you can have my other David scarf for the concert, if you want. We can wave them at him. He's gonna see us and say, "Hey, man, who are those two fabulous-looking Welsh girls? Bring 'em backstage to meet me".'

Sharon's trusting good nature caused me far more misery than Gillian's casual cruelty. Self-inflicted wounds are the most painful kind, as I was learning, because, along with the pain, you have to bear the blame.

When would be the best time to reveal to your best friend that you have told another girl that she can take half the credit for the special project you've been working on together?

Never. That would be the best time.

'Can't bear to think how this will turn out,' I wrote in my diary. 'The only person in the world I trust enough to tell what I've done is Sharon, and I can't tell Sharon because it's her that I've hurt, only she doesn't know it yet.'

Some memories can still make you twitch with embarrassment years later, but I didn't need the passage of time to make me tingle with shame over betraying Sharon. I felt it already that night before we set off for White City, sitting on the bed in the ointment-pink room, as my best friend went through her things to help fill the gaps in my meagre possessions. Gillian had always been a main topic of conversation for us. Her every movement was

168

endlessly fascinating. But gossiping about Gillian with Sharon wasn't a pleasure any more because, when it came to knowledge about Gillian, Sharon and I were no longer equals.

That same night, Sha's brother Michael, who was in Stuart Morris's year at school, burst in through the bedroom door and told us that Stuart had been two-timing Gillian with Debbie Guest. Gillian had found out, but Stuart had dumped her before she could dump him.

Any satisfaction I might have taken in Gillian's humiliation was cancelled out by the feeling that I, like Stuart, was guilty of infidelity. I had two-timed Sharon with Gillian.

Often, when I went round to Sha's house, Mrs Lewis would let us take crackers and cheese upstairs and we would sing crumby versions of David's songs, scattering bits over the carpet. That night, side by side on the bed, we worked through all our favourites, in preparation for the next day. Sharon took the tune on 'Cherish' while I harmonised around her.

'*And I do-oooo. I cherish youu-ooo.*' I broke down at that part. I was still only thirteen years old, yet I felt as though I carried inside me the heartache belonging to someone who had lived much longer.

'Hey, Pet, what you crying for? Don't cry, *bach*,' Sharon said, stroking my hair. 'We're gonna see him tomorrow, mun. We're gonna see David.'

*   *   *

Things happened so fast that day. Too fast. Maybe if we'd had more time they wouldn't have turned out as they did.

169

We had agreed that Michael would drive Sharon, me, Gillian and Olga to the station, which was at the far end of the high street. When I turned up at the Lewises', I changed quickly out of the Laura Ashley sprigged pinafore dress and white blouse, the clothes my mother believed I was wearing to the choral concert in Cardiff. Leaving them in a neat pile on the bed, I got into my outfit to meet David, which I had hidden in Sharon's drawer the night before. Brown tabard worn over cream pointy-collared shirt and cinched in at the waist with my leather belt from Brownies—it looked pretty good, I thought—brown long socks and the whole outfit set off by my new platform shoes. Judas platforms. The ones Gillian had given me for free. Then, over the top of everything, I wore a brown bomber jacket, with a David badge and the white silky scarf Sharon had donated with DAVID in huge block letters. When I was ready, I went down to the lounge to say hello to Sharon's mum and a familiar figure was sprawled on the mustard Dralon settee. He leapt to his feet. Steven Williams.

It was too much to take in. This was my Day with David. The collision of the two boys I liked felt like back-to-back Christmases. Steven said that he and Michael were going to play in a match in Bridgend, so he was hoping to cadge a lift.

'Room for a small one?' he said with the sheepish grin I recognised from the afternoon he scored the magic try.

Michael Lewis's Mini Cooper was near the ground, even before the four of us got in. Sharon, Steven and I squeezed in the back. I was going to let Sha go in the middle, but she deliberately jumped in first so I was next to Steven, which was OK, but there was no need for her to wink really slowly at me so Steven and Michael saw it and laughed.

On the way to the station, we called for Olga. Carol was getting a lift on her dad's motorbike and Angela said she would meet us at the ticket barrier. Olga got in the back so there would be room for Gillian up front. Sharon was flattened against one window, Olga was curled up in the middle. When Olga got in, Steven had lifted me across, without any fuss or strain, onto his lap and I stayed perched there in a state of delicious terror, trying to keep my padded crotch an inch or two above his jeans, where I thought I detected a commotion. At least I was facing forward so Steven couldn't see me blushing.

By the time we pulled through the stone pillars into Gillian's gravel drive, everyone was laughing in a slightly unhinged way. The laughter only got worse when Gillian came out of her house, wearing a ruffled chiffon blouse over immaculate white trousers, and peered inside the little car.

'How many David Cassidy fans can you get in one Mini?' shrieked Sharon by way of welcome.

Gillian didn't answer. I thought of offering to get out, but it would have taken ages and I was starting to relax into my position on Steven's lap. The limited space had forced his left arm around my shoulder and I didn't want to lose the novel sensation of being protected, not yet. So Gillian had to sit in the front by herself, well, apart from Michael, who was driving. At the sight of Gillian, Michael had gone slack-jawed; he sat there beaming like Goofy, only a lot less intelligent. Gillian, by contrast, took one look at Michael, with his matted ginger hair and his clashing red spots, and sank into a deafening silence. Struggling to make myself heard above the car's

171

straining engine, I addressed friendly remarks to the back of Gillian's bouffy, blow-dried head—I knew she would still be smarting from Stuart's rejection—but I got no response.

Gillian's moods were like the weather; they could instantly make everyone around her cold or hot. Not that morning. Our shared happiness at going to see David was stronger than her disapproval.

Arriving at the station, we got out and uncurled our limbs. 'See you, lovely,' Steven said, and Gillian turned to accept the customary tribute. But it was my cheek he put his hand to and touched. 'See you then, yeah.' It was a statement of intent, not a question. Gillian clattered off down the steps and I scurried to catch her up.

'No rush, Petra, hold your horses,' Sharon called after me.

Inside the station, Olga handed out everyone's tickets. We were in that mood where you feel like you've got a balloon inflating in your heart. Everything seemed hysterically funny. A fat pigeon got a big laugh, so did a porter with luggage piled on a barrow.

'Where are you young ladies off to, then?' he shouted as all six of us belted across the iron bridge, even though there was plenty of time till the train got in. On the platform, we bought crisps and chocolate and pop from the kiosk. Olga said she had a flask of tea with milk, which set us off howling with laughter again. That was Olga for you. When the tannoy crackled into life and announced the next train was for London Paddington, honest to God, we cheered like it was the end of the war.

Gillian was over by the waiting room talking to Carol. They glanced across at me and, for a second,

172

I had that feeling my mamgu called someone walking across your grave. What did the saying mean? For me on that platform, it meant the ghost of a feeling that I was about to die painfully in some as yet unspecified way. The balloon in my heart popped, leaving me winded. As the train pulled in, a bellowing dark blue liveried monster of a train, Gillian shouted across and asked if I could bring the Etam carrier bag she'd left in the waiting room. With that, she disappeared into the carriage.

Why couldn't she fetch it herself? I didn't dare argue. Perhaps if I did what she wanted now the day could still go well.

All right, take a deep breath, move purposefully towards the waiting room, don't give away how panicky you are. Notice that the waiting room is almost full, look under the tables and chairs, ask a mother to please move the pushchair her toddler is sleeping in. Trying to control the tears in your voice ask adults if they've seen an Etam carrier bag. Be aware that, outside, the guard on the platform has started to slam the train doors. Just when you're thinking that Gillian lied to you, find the Etam carrier bag over by the window, snatch it up and run out of the Waiting Room towards the train, which has just one door left open and—thank you, God— that door is directly in front of you. Jump in just as the guard's whistle blows and the door shuts with a *kerchunk* behind you. Clutch the precious Etam bag to your pounding heart and realise that it is strangely light. Glancing in you see the contents—an empty Bounty wrapper, a hairgrip and three photo envelopes for sending away films to be developed free of charge. You see also, quite clearly now, what lies ahead of you when you go to take your seat.

It took me several minutes to find them. The train seemed as long as a walk to the gallows.

They were in the furthest second-class carriage. My friends' heads were all bowed, as though they were at prayer. Only Gillian looked up. 'Oh, Petra, I was just telling Sharon that you entered me and you for the David Cassidy quiz.'

'That's not true,' I said.

Sharon, who was sitting in the window seat next to Gillian, wouldn't look at me, but I could tell that she'd been crying. She'd put mascara on for the very first time before we left the house—spitting onto the little black tray first and rubbing the brush along it, like we'd seen the older girls do in the school toilets. Sha's mascara had run and the smudges on her cheeks made her look like a baby who's been playing with coal.

'Well, you *said* you would enter me,' insisted Gillian, as though no blame in that shabby deal could possibly attach to her.

'Well, I didn't.'

'Then you're a liar as well as a bitch, aren't you?' she concluded triumphantly.

Gillian was sitting around a table for four with Sharon and Angela and Olga. Carol was by herself at the table across the aisle. I felt like running away; none of them wanted me here, but they were all I had, my only friends. I put my bag down on Carol's table and sat in the seat opposite her. Her eyebrows were thickly drawn in with brown pencil; her nostrils flared slightly. She looked ugly and frightening.

'Petra's going to play a concert for Princess Margaret on her *cello*,' announced Gillian brightly as if she was the deputy head reading out a notice in assembly.

174

'What's it like spreading your legs wide and having something so big between them?' snorted Carol. 'Not that you'd know about that, Petra.'

Everyone laughed except Sharon, who seemed to have shrunk to half her size and was busily tugging the fringe on her new sweater coat.

'Sharon, I entered us for the quiz, I did,' I said. It was too late now, I knew, but I wanted her to hear me say it.

She shook her head and turned and looked out of the window where our valleys and our hills were fast disappearing in a heartbreaking smear of green. Soon we would be in England.

*   *   *

You chose the kind of friends you wanted because you hoped you could be like them and not like you. To improve your image, you made yourself more stupid and less kind. As the months passed, the trade-off for belonging started to feel too great. The shutting down of some vital part of yourself, just so you could be included on a shopping trip into town, not have to sit on your own at lunch or have someone to walk home with. Now among friends, you were often lonelier than you had been before. The hierarchy of girls was so much more brutal than that of boys. The boys battled for supremacy out on the pitch and, after, they showered away the harm. The girls played dirtier. For girls, it was never just a game.

10

7.50 p.m. He felt like Gulliver. Around him swarmed the little people. Most came up to his chest. Others came up to his waist. Some he couldn't see at all, could make them out only by the pressure of their jostling as they flowed past, by their cries and smothered squeals. What had the Lilliputians done to Gulliver? Tied the big man down by his hair, that was it, pegged it to the ground, and thrown tiny ropes over his giant limbs. The likelihood of that happening today, Bill thought, was growing by the minute. He had come here for work, and a laugh; now, he saw, it was more a question of getting out alive.

And, needless to say, he was the only male. This Lilliput was a female community, in which men, with one exception, were neither welcome nor required. Far away, Bill had seen, or believed he had seen, the bald, bespectacled head of a St John Ambulance man, who seemed to have lost his cap, his cool and his bearings all at once; but even he had vanished into the throng, perhaps for good. Poor bloke. Most days he gathered up riders with cracked collarbones at point-to-points, or poured fresh water down the throats of cross-country runners; nothing in his experience, or his gentle faith, could have prepared him for thirty-five thousand teenaged girls, raging like bees in the hive of White City on a Sunday night. Christ, the din.

Bill had made a mistake, and he was paying for it already. 'Get down there among the little girlies,' Roy had said, rubbing his hands unpleasantly. 'You know, get there early, pack a meal, take a tent, lots of fresh water, pith helmet. Dig yourself in and ask them what they're doing there.'

'They're coming to see their favourite pop star,' Bill had replied, nonplussed.

'I *know* that, wanker. But go and ask them to their little faces, see what nonsense they come out with. Take one of them machines to measure sound, what's it called? Dumb-bell level?'

'Decibels.'

'That's the one. See if you can get a reading on their screams. We could run a little bar chart, give a prize to the loudest, that sort of malarkey. Howlin' Hannah from Harpenden. Sharon the Shouty.'

'But I thought there was a press enclosure.'

'There is, if you're a poof.' Roy had given him the same look as he gave anyone who wore a seat belt in a car.

'But it's nearer the stage,' Bill had gone on, prolonging an argument that could not be won.

'So what? So you can see up his purple shorts? Look, matey, we don't often get a chance to see our readers in the flesh, so for God's sake go and press it. Have a squeeze and report back to me. Arright?'

Bill had obeyed, in part. He had got hold of a press ticket, after no more than nine phone calls to the promoter's office. It would mean being penned in, he suspected, like a monkey, behind some sort of cage, although his even stronger suspicion was that the human activity outside would be the most animal of all. The girls would go ape, and he would end up grateful for the iron bars. On the other hand, he would, for a while, do the bidding of his boss; get there well ahead of the show, mix with them as the mood grew, get some quotes, then make his way to

177

the safe haven of his fellow journalists before the main event. The trick was to time it right.

An elbow caught him under the ribs and knocked the wind out of him. He keeled forwards, catching his jaw on the head of the girl in front.

'Hey,' she said, twisting half round, 'watch it, OK?' She had short hair and glasses, and for a second Bill thought, with an odd pang of fellow feeling, that she was a boy. But what would a boy be doing here wearing a David Cassidy scarf?

'Sorry,' Bill said, or tried to say. He was still fighting to get his breath back, and the word came out as *zerr*.

The girl had a friend with her, who giggled. She was round and pink-faced, in a yellow sweater.

'What you doing here, anyway?'

'Erm, writing. I'm a writer.'

'What, like poems?'

'No, I write for magazines,' Bill said, dropping easily and untruthfully into the plural. The sound of chatter and hum, on every side, was deafening, but the three of them were squashed so tight that they could practically talk straight into each other's ears. Bill bent his head to their level.

'D'you do pop?' the round girl asked.

He coughed, still wheezing slightly. 'Umhum, I cover quite a lot of the music scene, actually. Rock, jazz. A little bit of pop.'

'D'you do interviews?'

'Sometimes. If the editor thinks I should.'

'Is that what you're doing here, then?'

'I suppose so.'

'So why are we the ones asking all the questions?'

Bill had no answer to that. He saved face, as he often did, by raising the level of his lies.

178

'Well, sometimes doing an interview, it isn't just a matter of Q and A, you know. It's like, like, a conversation. Like you'd have with a friend . . .' The girls were screwing up their faces. Only fifteen or so, but they could smell nonsense when it came their way; they could certainly rumble a boy—or, in this case, a grown-up—who was trying too hard.

The other girl suddenly spoke, the one whose head he had bumped into. One arm of her glasses was mended with masking tape.

'You haven't done David, have you?'

There was a pause. The crowd ebbed and surged around them, with Bill stuck there like a lighthouse. The sensible thing, of course, was to deny everything, to brush the whole question aside; who knew how these girls would react if he told them anything else? It wouldn't just be vain to say he had met the man; it might be dangerous.

'Three days ago,' he said.

He didn't know that human beings could explode. He knew that they could shout, howl, hurl their wrath against the heavens; he knew that some people, once they start laughing or wailing, find it impossible to stop; but this was different. This was like a landmine. The girls flung their hands to the side of their heads, as if trying to stop their skulls from bursting wide; they stared at him in what might, from a distance, have looked like horror; and they screamed. Christ, did they scream. All that breath, in those still-unfinished lungs . . .

'OhmyGodohmyGaaaahhdd!' Other girls skewed round and looked at them, then at Bill, feeling the heat of the mania as it spread. He was already regretting having spoken. That would teach him for telling the truth.

'This bloke met *Day-vid*,' cried the girl in the yellow sweater. Instantly the gabble doubled its strength, poured in his direction.

'What was it like what was he wearing did he have his guitar did he smell nice did he have snacks were they American ones did he have Twinkles they're called Twinkies you dozy cow was he wearing jewellery did he have a necklace on any rings please don't tell us he had rings . . .'

Bill was backing away, but they pawed at him— not at him, he was no more than a vessel, but it felt as though they wanted to scrape off any residue of David that might have clung to him. Half a thumbprint would do. One girl with plaits reached out and clamped a palm against his, saying: 'If I shake your hand, and you shook his . . .' Then she took her hand away and held it tenderly against her cheek. Another had an autograph book open and was holding out a biro, with a rubbery 'Love Is' figure stuck on the end. No one had ever asked him for an autograph when he played for Spirit Level, that was for sure, though some pub landlords would make him sign for drinks before the gig, so that none of the band tried to sneak any pints for free.

Bill looked around, just to check that nobody he had ever known, loved, worked for, spoken to, lived with or slept with was in sight. But all he could see were the heads and shoulders of juvenile strangers, so he turned back, took the pen and quickly signed his name on the yellow page, using what he hoped was the kind of wild flourish that you would get from a rock star, or from someone who had met a rock star, once. The plaits girl took back the book and looked at the scrawl, then up at Bill.

'What's your name?'

180

'Bill.'

'Doesn't look like Bill. Looks like number eighty-seven.' The girl next to her peered at it, too. 'Written by a spaz,' she added helpfully.

Bill gave a weak smile, the smile that drinkers give just before they begin to throw up, and withdraw from the scene. Somewhere there was a barrier, the obvious frontier point, which divided the press corps from the fans, but to find it would mean charging forward, head down; the better option was the more illogical one—to reverse through the ranks, exit through the entrance and make his way round the outside of the stadium to another gate. Bill chose the second route, and ceased to struggle. Instead, he took a long breath, let himself fall backwards into the throng, and kept on falling. Bodies kept him upright, more or less, and momentum kept him going. Somewhere music struck up, urgent and voiceless. Somebody gave him a hug and passed him on. Sometimes you can save yourself by drowning.

*   *   *

8.11 p.m. 'Excuse me, that's my head. Excuse me, please get off me, please.'

I was used to rough handling from my mother, but this was the first time I'd been used as a stepladder. A girl with long red hair had one boot wedged in my cheek, the other was blocking my ear, which I barely noticed anyway because I couldn't hear anything, the screaming was that loud. I tried to shake the girl off, but there was no room to shake in. I could barely move my body an inch either way, so I tried to rear up backwards and unseat my passenger, like I'd seen the horses do on Mam and Tad's farm. The girl dug

181

in her heels and stood upright on the shoulders which, until a short while ago, had belonged to me and me alone.

'David, I want your baby,' the stranger on my shoulders wailed, swaying from side to side.

'Geroff, you dirty bitch,' Carol said, punching the redhead in the backside, which sent her flying off me and head first over the girls in front of us. She didn't fall because there wasn't anywhere to fall to; instead we watched as she was borne away like a surfer on the wave that was surging towards the stage.

Many times on the beach at home, I had felt the full force of the tide. I knew what it was like to be swimming along in the shallows and to suddenly find yourself picked up and hurled onto the pebbles, to feel every bone in your body jolted and to try and claw and scramble your way up the stones, away from the water's jealous grip. But this was another kind of power altogether. It was like being held in a vice. It suddenly felt like Petra Williams, David Cassidy fan aged thirteen and three-quarters of South Wales, was no more. I was a single droplet in a sea of fans and the only way to survive was to go with the flow, which was currently forcing all of us forward up against a barrier. Sharon was clinging onto my arm, her eyes shining with excitement, her mouth fixed in a permanent O of amazement.

I expect you'd be surprised to hear we were talking. The terrible scene on the train was still so close and it had put a wedge between us, but now the crush in the arena had thrown us together once more. Sharon couldn't have kept a sulky distance if she'd tried. We had never been closer, or further apart. On the other side of the barrier, which was about twenty feet away, I could see a couple of photographers who were taking pictures of us and the vast crowd of girls. One man with a beard was laughing and pointing at us, like we were animals in a zoo or something.

The frightening thought was that David hadn't even appeared yet. On the stage was a support band, with some blonde girl singing the blues. She was good, the girl was, but the sound system was terrible, all buzzy, and the screams drowned her voice out anyway. I felt sorry for her.

Tonight was all about coming to see Him, to get as near to David as possible. How I had yearned for this moment. For eighteen months, David had colonised my brain until it didn't feel like my thoughts were my own any more, yet all I could think was, thank God I'd been to the toilet and changed my towel before we came through the gate. I didn't want to have an accident. There was no way of getting out now, or in the near future. Olga and Angela, and Ange's cousin, Joanna, had struck out for the dirty bathrooms at the back about an hour ago, and there was still no sign of them.

'IS THAT HIM?' Sharon was shouting and pointing at the stage.

I read her lips.

'NO. HE'LL BE HERE NOW, ANY MINUTE.'

Gillian was holding the other end of Sharon's David Cassidy scarf, and the pair of them shifted from foot to foot so the scarf rippled like a flag. I didn't want to wave my scarf. I thought it might be unladylike, which was something David disliked in a girl. He would prefer us to listen respectfully to his songs instead of bawling our silly heads off. Gillian refused to look at me and I was avoiding her anyway. The journey to London had not been forgiven, and nor would it be, by either side, but it was temporarily forgotten because, here amongst the swarming thousands, we Welsh girls were all each other had. Finding herself surrounded by a foreign foe, Carol was doing what all famous Welsh bruisers did on away matches: she was furiously tackling to the ground any rivals who dared to invade our square foot of space.

When we first arrived, we had found our way to some seats on the terrace, although they were no longer seats by the time we got to them. Everyone was on their feet. I mean everyone. If you tried to sit down you'd be in trouble. Honest to God, standing up was hard enough. Other girls raced past us, down the steps and into the big grass patch in the middle of the arena, and we belted after them, determined not to let any of the others have a better chance of touching David.

Standing there in the middle of that huge space, I looked around in astonishment. I didn't know that love had slain so many. Of course, I understood that David had millions of fans, but you could generally put them out of your mind. Not today. Before, it had always been just him and me. Now it was him and us. So many of us, as far as the eye could see.

Outside, in the queue for merchandise, I'd got talking to this tiny blonde girl in a thin grey anorak. Moira. She had hitched by herself all the way down from Dundee, and she didn't even have a place to stay. I was in awe of her courage. Slept on a bench outside the Skyway Hotel where everyone thought David was staying. Moira said the merchandise was a total rip-off, and it was, but I handed over Dad's tenner anyway for a two-quid T-shirt with a picture of David wearing that denim jacket I had always

184

loved him in. I desperately needed proof I'd been there; that this wasn't just another daydream.

'We Want David! We Want David!' We all joined in the chant that filled White City. We were impatient now. Thirty thousand pairs of stamping platform shoes sounded like hooves.

'You're just great, a lovely audience, thank you so much,' the blonde blues singer's voice crackled over the sound system.

'Get off!' we yelled.

Straight ahead, I saw this bald St John Ambulance man lift one girl above his head like she was a rag doll and post her over the barrier into the arms on the other side. Right then, two security men in black uniforms pushed past me, muscling their way to the stage.

'There's one of the little bitches over there,' I overheard the bigger guard yell. Really nasty he was. 'They're pretending to faint so they get taken to the front.'

And then He was there. Out of the billowing smoke, he came, like a genie or a god. OhmyGod, David. Oh. My. God. Smiling his David smile and wearing an incredible red suit. David. You've never seen anything like it, that long red coat and trousers and a bow tie that sparkled with diamonds. David. And a diamond belt. He looked so unbelievably gorgeous. David. He was laughing and there was some sort of clown dog. *Dayyvvvidd. Dayyy-vvvidddd.*

Sharon started crying she was so happy. I recognised the song first, from the opening bar. 'If I Didn't Care'. And his beautiful soft voice was caressing us, turning our insides liquid. Melting us like a Rolo. Swaying side to side, the girls from South Wales, we sang along, sang better than anyone else in

185

the whole bloody place.

Then the harmonica came in and was so achingly sad that I began to move towards him. It wouldn't be easy to get to the stage, but I had no choice, did I? I had to do it. David was lonely, of that I was positive. 'I'm coming,' I told him. With me he would not be lonely any more.

Possessed by that single thought, thirty thousand girls pushed forward towards the love of their life. It was then that I felt Sharon's hand slip out of mine.

*　　　*　　　*

8.36 p.m. Red tails? You could wear red, like a Chelsea pensioner or a Liverpool footballer; you could wear tails, like Fred Astaire; but both together? The only people, until now, who had got away with it were circus clowns, pedalling around on tiny bicycles, or else—and Bill couldn't quite recall how he knew this, but it felt instinctively true—the Devil incarnate.

But that was what the Cassidy guy had decided to wear, on an evening in May. Scarlet tailcoat and matching trousers, with the lapels picked out in rows of rhinestones (or diamonds, as every girl in the place would later insist). His belt glittered with the same gems, and so—God preserve us—did his bow tie. Bill's gaze kept drifting back to that tie, both dreading and hoping that, in some final farewell to good taste, it would start to spin round, in a giddy flash of gems. What was the whole outfit meant to say? What was the message conveyed by those prim white gloves and the twirling cane: magician, megastar, children's entertainer, total prick?

Bill stood and watched beside the other

186

journalists, most of them men, none of them Cassidy fans; not in public, at any rate. How surprising it was, then, to see their lips move in sync to half the songs, as if they had been versed in his collected works by the power of hypnotic suggestion. Maybe they couldn't help it; maybe they just had the radio on all day, in the kitchen at home, beside the draining board, and then on a shelf at the office, next to an open window. Cassidy songs would come and go, through an average radio day, and over the weeks they would seep into your nervous system, whether you wanted them there or not, and you would find yourself breaking out into a song, no more able to prevent it than you would a violent rash.

For a while, it had seemed—to Bill's relief, and presumably to the fans' dismay, though they may have been moaning too loudly to let the music through—that David would not be heard that night. He was onstage all right; he had burst onstage through a billow of white smoke, as if trying to impersonate the sun coming out from behind a cloud. And he had started to sing—singing through a grin, which Bill had always thought was impossible. Noddy Holder of Slade used to have a go, but he ended up looking like one of the witches in *Macbeth*, leering into the mouth of a cauldron. As for a tune, though, who could tell? The PA system at White City was so badly rigged, or the wiring was so amateur, that all you could hear was buzz: a fearsome, brain-eating hum that burned out of the speakers, with only a faint suggestion of melody veiled somewhere behind. To make matters more infernal, the second song, whatever it was, had incorporated a comedy routine. That is how it must have been described, anyway, on the playlist, although anything less comic would be hard to devise: a dancer dressed as a dog, with whom the star cavorted. 'I call him Storm,' he confided to his audience after the idiot had gone. They had roared anyway. Music they couldn't yet hear, and a piece of funny business with a bloke in a furry suit: to them, it was all revelation. It was all David.

Then, Bill imagined, somebody backstage had rewired a plug or flicked a switch, because, without warning, the voice came alive. 'If I didn't care . . .' Not a bad voice, either, though it bumped into a croak now and then, and Mrs Holderness, the choir mistress at Bill's primary school, would have had something to say about the tuning. ('Up, David, up! We are a kite. We stay aloft with our singing, do we not?') He was helped by a pair of backing vocalists, pin-sharp pros in slit skirts who never missed a note. They buoyed him up when he went for the highs, and they shimmered as he raced around the stage, and as the yelps of longing came streaming in from the crowd.

'Right little mover, isn't he?'

Bill glanced to his left, and found a compact, ageless man in a denim shirt, with a beard that looked like a nest. He had shouted to make himself heard, but not quite loud enough.

'Sorry?' Bill shouted back.

'The kid. Look at 'im. Moves well, you've got to hand it to him. Watch this bit, he's going to come to the front in a minute, here we go, and now wait, look what he does with his arse.'

Bill looked, as he was told, and saw the red-clad figure waltz towards them, almost to the brink of the stage. The girls' cries grew stronger. The figure twirled, one and a half times, then, before setting off

188

upstage, flourished his behind and gave it a slow shake. The two halves of the tailcoat flew apart to frame the gesture. The cries increased threefold, until they sounded like lamentation. Bill felt, more strongly than ever, that he was in the wrong place here: the wrong game, the wrong profession. Certainly the wrong body.

'Tart,' shouted the man beside him. Bill frowned back.

'Who?'

'Him. It's such an act. Putting it out there for the girlies. 'Slike watching a stripper.'

'A what?'

'A stripper.'

And he was right. If Bill had had Zelda there, or even Roy, he could have pointed at the stage and shown them the reason for their work, the thing that paid their wages every month. It wasn't just the songs; sometimes it was hardly the songs at all. It wasn't the dance. It was the act. Not a put-on, or a fraud. He was an actor, wasn't he? That was where this whole palaver had started, on TV with *The Partridge Family*, and now it had spun off and grown, only this time he wasn't pretending to be someone else. He was pretending to be David Cassidy. And, you had to hand it to the sonofabitch, he was bloody good at it.

The light in the sky above had started to fail. As if in reply, the lights in the stadium came on, flooding the long, deep bowl of mass humanity. Bill looked round, away from the stage. He was close to the barrier now, the one he had come round; somewhere beyond it was the disappointed girl with the autograph book. Everyone lifted their faces to the brightness, which swept across them and reached its

189

destination—the small man onstage, slender as a quill, trapped now in a blinding aura.

Only this time, the kid in the spotlight, no fool, was doing something new. He had the cunning, Bill understood, that every artist needs a drop of, however low his art; the salesmanship passed off as innovation. The kid would give them the song because they knew and adored it, but he wouldn't simply perform it; he'd play with it, spice it up just enough to gull the girls into believing that they were tasting it for the first time.

'Breakin' up is hard to do-ooo . . .' It came out at half the speed, the star strumming softly on the guitar around his neck, lending the lyrics a kick of proper sadness, and the drummer holding back the brisk snap that the girls would have heard on the record, using a brush instead. 'Nice,' said the hairy man at Bill's elbow. 'Clever little bugger.'

The girls behind Bill reacted to the unfamiliar speed as if a wire brush were running, ever so gently, along their spines. What had he himself written, in David's voice, two issues ago? 'Y'know when you hear a slow one, and it gives you the shivers? Well, allow me to let you into a little secret. It's the same when you SING it. True! I can be up there, holding the mike, and I get that kinda feeling myself. If you've ever held anyone close, on a dance floor, you'll know just what I mean!' Which, Bill had privately thought, was as good a way as any of writing about a smooch without actually saying the word. Pete the Pimple called it 'slow fuck stuff', as if he knew what he was talking about. He would have given a filthy grimace if he had been here right now, with Bill, and heard the sobbing and the crying out.

But something was wrong with the sobs.

There is the pain of emotions that you can't hope to master, whose strength and meaning you hardly grasp, gusting around inside you on a Sunday night, with a song in your heart; and then there is pain, the real thing, as plain as a needle. And Bill, listening through the din, could no longer be certain which was which. His stomach lurched. 'What's your name?' he said to the hairy man. 'Jerry. From *Rock On*.' Why did that matter? 'Come with me,' said Bill, turning round and pulling him along. They beat a path through four or five rows of journalists, all of them facing the singer, and all annoyed at being bustled or shoved aside, telling Bill to fucking watch it. And then he and Jerry were in the clear, at the back, looking straight at the barrier.

'Jesus Christ.'

The first thing he noticed, without knowing why, was the woman in white. Not a girl, a woman, definitely, early twenties perhaps, same age as him, though she had tried to dress younger, like someone playing an angel in a school play: white gym shoes with white laces, white jeans, white T-shirt with a screenprint of Cassidy across her chest. The only unwhite thing about her was the face. Even in the shadow of the floodlights he could see that. It was pressed against the bars, but not in eagerness, and it was red. Purple red, like a plum, as if the breath were being squeezed out of her.

All the way along, it was the same. The crush of the people behind, unchecked, with nowhere to go, nowhere to be siphoned off, no direction except straight ahead, towards the source of their joy: the crush was piling up, wave upon wave of pressure, and the people at the barrier were taking the brunt. One girl in green was almost horizontal; she must have

191

crawled sideways to find an easier space and got stuck. Some girls had their backs to the bars, as if they had turned round and tried hopelessly to flee. Most girls were crying, but the noise just got sucked into the general cry and lost. Nobody more than twenty yards away would have a clue what was going on. David would know nothing, not yet.

'Help me. I've lost my friend.'

Bill looked to his right and saw a slender dark girl, close to the top of the barrier, one leg over it. If she could climb into the press enclosure, she would be safe. One of her shoes had already fallen onto his side. He forced his way towards her, started to scale the bars, ready to reach out and grab her hand, sensing the press of bodies inches away on the other side of the cage. He heard pleading as he climbed, but also, even now, voices yelling, 'Out the way,' 'I can't see.' Behind him, David went on singing. *'Re-member whe-e-en you held me tight . . .'*

He got to the girl and clumsily took her in his arms. 'Help, please,' she sobbed. 'It's my friend. Please, you've got to help us.'

Before Bill could pull her to safety, he was plucked off the barrier, and landed badly. He felt something give in his back, a muscle tearing just below his ribs.

'What you doing?' It was a security guard, bored and burly. His white shirt was stained with sweat.

'What the hell are *you* doing?' Bill replied.

'Come on, sir, don't give us any trouble. You lot're supposed to be the sensible ones. We've got enough trouble with the loonies in there.' He jerked his head at the crowd.

'They're going to die.'

'Come again?'

192

'They can't breathe, the ones at the front. They're being suffocated. Look at them.'

'Bit hot.'

'What?'

'I'll get some water. Got a bucket over there.'

'Oh for Christ's sake.' Bill watched the big man amble away, then turned back to the bars. He saw a very small girl, her face contorted, and her mouth opened wide, soundless with shock, as the crowd behind her gave another heave. One of her arms was bending the wrong way. Another heave. It was like a monster, wallowing and thrashing. Why now? Then Bill realised. David had finished his song. They were cheering, and weeping, and sending him their love. Their undying love.

*   *   *

8.59 p.m. The water hit us girls in the face. Some of the crowd had been begging for water and this was what we got. A bucket chucked at us by a security guard. Then another. I was really angry, you know. I kept thinking of a zoo, only the keepers weren't taking care of the animals. Hundreds of girls were squashed against the barrier now and no one would open it to let us through. I'd already lost a shoe trying to climb over to ask for help. One of the Judas burgundy-brown platforms Gillian had given me. This lovely-looking man heard me screaming and sort of caught me in his arms, but he'd been pulled off by one of the nasty security people.

In the distance, I could hear David still singing.

Why didn't someone *tell* him, for God's sake? If David knew what was happening to us he would stop

193

the concert and come and help. Where was Sharon? That was all I cared about now. Sick with panic, I scanned the crush of girls, but Sha's fair head was nowhere to be seen. It must mean she was somewhere on the floor. I screamed this terrible thought at Carol, who simply nodded. Carol's life had been so full of disasters, big and small, that this one couldn't take her by surprise. She knew what the worst was, which made her tougher than someone that young should be, but it also gave her the belief that you could get out the other end.

Holding her hands apart, Carol mimed that, if she made a space, I could go down and take a look. I nodded. I was ready to try anything. Gillian just stood there, her lovely face frozen with shock, as Carol turned and charged into the wall of girls behind them, planting her legs like trees and pushing the girls back with the full force of her shoulders, as though she was in a massive scrum. A small gap opened up between Carol and the wall and I fell to my knees and crawled under the mob, into a dense forest of corduroy flares. It was dark down there, but much quieter as the screams were muffled. Just to my left, I saw something glimmer. Sharon's white-blonde head. It was unmistakable. I stretched out a hand. A shoe came from above and stood on it. I screamed. The shoe released me. I reached out again, as far as I could, managed to get a hand to Sharon's long hair, and pulled. A hank came away. Now it was Sharon's turn to scream.

'Sorry,' I said. 'Sorry, *bach*.'

On the next attempt, I managed to grab Sharon's hand and pull her towards the gap that Carol was still holding open for us.

'My side,' groaned Sharon.

194

Within a few seconds, I wasn't sure how, I was surfacing through Carol's legs and Sharon was following behind, until both of us were back on our feet in the crawl space. We sort of collapsed in each other's arms, but the hug made Sharon clutch her left side and scrunch up her face. We needed to get her out of here. We all needed to get out. I was suddenly aware of something, or of something missing. David had left the stage. A man I thought I'd seen in *Jackie* was telling the crowd that if we didn't move back and control ourselves the concert would not go on. The music was over, but the sound of crying was louder.

*   *   *

9.24 p.m. About suffering he was mostly wrong, and, to be honest, he had seen very little of the real thing, but this Bill knew, for sure: whenever and wherever people suffer, they will not be helped by the presence of Tony Blackburn. If Tony had crouched at the foot of the Cross, jabbering into the mike, would the lamentation of the women have been any less profound? Might the *Titanic* have slipped down more easily, with fewer cries of distress, if a perky Radio 1 disc jockey with shoulder-length hair had broadcast a final, uplifting message from the upper deck, flashing that unsinkable grin? And, if not, then what the hell was he doing here, urging the thousands of David Cassidy fans to get a grip? In a crisis like this, with the air being forced out of them, they were unlikely to obey the exhortations of a man they had last heard telling them to go out and buy the latest single from Mud. They didn't need a DJ, for Christ's sake. They needed a traffic copper.

195

Bill stood in the middle of the press enclosure, with bodies curled and sprawled all around. Someone, finally, had had the good sense, or the compassion, to open the single gate in the barrier; either that, or it had sprung wide under the force of the throng. Girls shot through it, propelled by the stampede behind, and lay on the grass in shock. There was no music now, just the music of humanity, which was neither still nor sad. One girl was shouting for her mum, who was either on the other side of the bars, having a panic of her own, or several hundred miles away, calmly watching TV.

Bill walked through stuff. Torn programmes, orange-tinted lolly sticks, a spangled hairband, a yellow sweater with a rip in it, a tiny patch of blood. One arm of a pair of spectacles. He looked up, and then down again. His shoe had kicked a shoe. He picked it up and surveyed the scene. Two ambulance men were trying to manoeuvre a girl onto a stretcher. She wasn't moving, and her eyes were shut. At a guess, there were at least thirty other girls moaning on stretchers.

'Can I help?' Bill said.

'No, son.' The ambulance man didn't look up.

'Will she be all right?'

'Just got to get her out.'

He moved on and approached a pair of girls, who were resting against the barrier, one sitting with her back to it, another lying across her. He held out the shoe. It was chunky as a brick and scuffed at the toe, with the word 'Dolcis' just visible inside.

'Is this yours? I think you lost one.'

'Oh, thanks, no. Mine was Freeman Hardy Willis.'

'Shall I look for it? Must be somewhere around.'

'No, thanks, honest.' The dark girl smiled. 'It

doesn't matter any more.'

Bill looked at her friend. It was like a pietà. The angular dark girl holding the smaller chubby fair one in her lap.

'You OK?' He had thought they were just doing it for comfort. Now he saw the other girl's face. 'What is it?'

'My side.' She was blonde, a little girl really, with a Welsh accent, stronger than her friend's.

'Which side?'

'Left.'

'That's why I'm holding her like this. Less painful. I read in a first-aid book that you shouldn't put pressure on it when you break a rib. Bad for the breathing. Just lie still.'

'D'you think that's what it is? Broken?'

'Maybe. She got trod on.'

Bill stood up. 'I'll get one of the St John's lot over here. You need it strapped.'

'No, yer OK,' said the hurt girl.

'And we need to get you out of here.'

'*Nooo*,' she said, much too forcefully, and coughed with the exertion. Her face twisted.

'For God's sake,' said Bill. 'What is *wrong* with everyone? You're all hurt, some of you nearly died, and none of you want to do anything about it.' He stopped. 'Sorry. I'm sorry. It's just, you know, if I was hurt, and my parents weren't here . . .'

The dark girl looked at him. 'You're right,' she said, in a small voice. 'And I said we should go and get help, but . . .'

'But I said we're staying here,' said the blonde. 'He hasn't even done "How Can I Be Sure" yet, has he? Can't miss that, can we? Got the rest of my life to be ill.'

Bill smiled. He didn't get it, even now, not with all the damage done round him, but what could you do? Resign yourself to the lives of others, and their strange ideas of love. He bent down, and touched the fair kid on the shoulder. 'Take care, OK? Lie still. Let her look after you.'

'I always do, don't I, Pet?'

The lovely dark girl glanced at him. *'Diolch yn fawr,'* she said.

Dee olk in what? 'See you,' said Bill, and turned away. There were girls coming over the barrier now; they had got some sort of ladder up, and somebody was bound to fall and have to be picked up.

'See you,' came a voice behind him. He couldn't be quite sure whose it was, in all the din. The noise rose. Something was happening, up above. The screaming returned. The lights were beaming once again towards the stage. David was coming back.

*　　　*　　　*

9.24 p.m. We sat together for a while, just the two of us, me leaning back against the barrier with Sharon in my lap, trying to take in what had happened. The scene around us was the nearest we would ever get to the end of a battle, only the wounded soldiers were all girls. There were loads of them on stretchers being carried away, some were sobbing and shaking; it was the ones who weren't crying that you worried for. On the churned-up grass sat hundreds of others, wrapped in blankets, shocked less by the brush with loss of life than by the loss of David.

'You've ruined my life, David,' moaned one.

Carol had taken Gillian off to find some hot

drinks. I thought that Sharon needed tea with sugar, for the shock, and I wouldn't have minded one myself. My right hand was throbbing and my heart was taking its time to return to its normal rate. Gillian had been like a peacock throughout the whole thing, a peacock, pretty and useless. Perhaps the Personality category of those multiple choices counted for something, after all. I had seen Carol's, and I would never look at her in quite the same way again. A crisis could tell you something about people; sort out the men from the boys, or girls in this case. Way to go, Carol, I thought, way to go.

We were still sitting there, Sha and me, when the man came up, the one with the lovely face who had caught me when I climbed over the barrier. He had longish fair hair, darker than Sharon's. Not sure how old he was; anyone over nineteen and I couldn't guess their age, they just became old. He wanted to give me a shoe. Funny, he remembered from before that I'd lost mine. Anyway, it wasn't the Judas burgundy-brown platform that had kicked off all the trouble. I sort of felt it was right that I lost that blimmin' shoe while I was trying to rescue Sharon.

The man told us we should leave, but Sharon was well enough to say that we had to stick around for David. I sort of smiled and went along with her, because she'd been through enough, you know, but I didn't feel the same. Not really. All of it, the crying and the broken bodies, it wasn't David's fault, but it was because of him. Him and us. Because girls loved him so much they were being carried away in ambulances . . .

The lovely man told Sharon to take care of herself and he put his hand on her shoulder. I quite wanted him to put his hand on my shoulder too, but if he had

199

I might have started crying and never stopped.

'Take care, OK? Lie still. Let her look after you.'

'I always do, don't I, Pet?'

I was so tired and so grateful that I told the man *diolch yn fawr* instead of thank you. He gave me a funny look. What must he have thought of me, like? Welsh was a foreign language to him. I forgot you shouldn't speak it to people you didn't know. He had seemed familiar somehow. Like I knew him from before.

'See you,' I shouted after him. 'See you.'

11

We didn't know a girl died. She must have been a few feet away from us and we didn't know. Something that big, that terrible, and we didn't even know. Shocking it was. I thought about it a lot. Went over and over in my mind the part where I'd gone down to find Sharon and the crowd was thrashing and screaming above us like an animal in pain. You could drown down there, I thought, but Sha and me, we came up, through the hole in the crowd that Carol held open for us. Else we'd have been gone.

Outside the stadium, it was so cold. The clothes we'd set out in that morning felt really stupid, summery things. I couldn't stop my teeth chattering; it was like they had a life of their own, like Mamgu's dentures sitting in the glass of Steradent next to her bed smiling their creepy smile. A smile without a face made you think of death. A girl died. Could have been Sharon. She was the only one of us who was warm because she had her new sweater coat and we got that back on her straight after the doctor strapped her rib.

White City was mad, I'm telling you. Girls were still crying and some were even stopping cars to see if David was hiding in the boot. Gillian stood outside the entrance with a pair of crystal drops rolling in formation down her cheek, like a Tiny Tears doll. She said her life was over now that David was gone.

'I've got nothing to look forward to,' she wailed.

I thought about the Bay City Rollers poster in her wardrobe and of what she'd said about keeping your options open where boys were concerned. She had never loved David like Sharon and I loved him. Girls like Gillian didn't need David. Girls like Gillian didn't need somewhere to hide how scared they were to be loved by a real boy: how scared they were that no real boy would ever love them.

When we got to the Underground station it was shut, with a load of police standing outside the gate moving the girls away and Gillian said she was going to stay the night in London with her new friend, Angela's cousin, Joanna. She would call her mum and dad from the Cramptons' house. We watched as Gillian and Jo walked off arm in arm, with Angela and Olga trooping a few lonely feet behind.

By the time we managed to find a taxi and got to Paddington, the last train had gone. The next one wasn't for five hours. We had a bit of money left and Sharon called her mum from a phone box to explain what had happened. I had to dial the number because her arm was bad. With the rest of the coins, Carol got hot chocolate from a machine and we sat on a bench, just the three of us, clutching the white plastic cups to our chests to keep warm. I didn't call home. The thought of the new green telephone ringing in our hall, and of the conversation I would have to have with my mother when she picked it up, well, I couldn't do it, could I? The lies I'd told felt like a gravestone on my chest.

Once we were on the train, all I could think about was Princess Margaret. My hand, the one that got trodden on, was throbbing and there was a bruise spreading through it like ink was being injected under the skin. It hurt to clench my fist. I didn't know how I'd be able to play the Bach suites. In the seat opposite, Carol snored her honking piggy snore; she made a funny whistling at the end of each breath, like a kettle. I felt exhausted, but also really alert with a dry headache. Next to me, Sharon was dozing with her head resting on my shoulder. Her fine, baby-blonde hair settled on my bomber jacket and the static gave me a fuzzy electric shock when she woke with a jump at Swindon.

The sky over the station was the colour of Lucozade. It didn't seem real, nothing seemed real.

'Is there a fire, Pet?' she asked.

'Don't be daft, it's just the dawn, isn't it? Back to sleep, now.'

'I knew you wouldn't enter the quiz with her,' she murmured. 'Gillian doesn't even like David that much.'

'I know.'

'Anyway, we won't win,' she said, yawning.

'Why not?'

For a while I thought she'd gone off again, then she said: 'Girls like us don't win things. They'll give it to some girl up London way.'

'Annette Smith of Sevenoaks.'

'Swotty cow.' Sharon laughed, then she winced because it hurt to laugh. 'Thing is,' she said, 'Annette Smith's tiebreaker won't be a patch on yours.'

I was telling the truth when I told the girls that I hadn't entered Gillian for the quiz. My hand did hesitate over the section where it asked you to name the friend you would like to come with you to meet David Cassidy. Why didn't I put Gillian's name down? I was definitely scared enough to do it. I knew what the price for displeasing her would be and I knew that I would be paying that price for as long as we were both in the same school. In the end, it was something so small really, something small and big. In the border of the form, all around the edge,

Sharon had done this gorgeous, intricate decoration, made up of David's name and his date of birth repeated again and again, like something from a medieval manuscript, so our entry would jump out at the judges. In one corner, in the most romantic lettering I'd ever seen, she had put something that caused a stab to my heart.

PETRA CASSIDY

I was the only one who knew what it cost her to write it.

*   *   *

We made the front page of the *South Wales Echo*. GOWER WEENY BOPPERS IN CASSIDY TRAGEDY. There was quite a welcome party when we finally pulled into the station. Sharon's mum ran up and sort of hugged us and shook us at the same time. Mrs Lewis was crying and laughing. A good-looking black man in jeans was standing with her. He put a blanket round Carol who fell into his arms and sobbed like a girl I'd never met. None of us had set eyes on Carol's dad before. He was the missing piece of her and the minute I saw him the puzzle of Carol solved itself in my mind.

Over Mrs Lewis's shoulder, I saw my mother shimmering at the end of the platform. She was wearing her tweed suit, the one she wore for parents' evenings and the crematorium. Dad was standing behind her, but I couldn't see him properly.

I know what I did was bad, really bad, you know, but I still don't think she should have hit me. Not on my face, not with all those people looking and

204

everything.

For the next three days, she kept me in my room; left my food outside on a tray with a paper serviette; even Dad wasn't allowed to speak to me. Downstairs, their quarrel raged like a distant battle. Sometimes I could hear loud bangs, cries, then silence till it started up again. Sharon's mum had rung to tell my parents we'd all been delayed in London after the riot at the Cassidy concert, that much I'd picked up from what was said in the car. Mrs Lewis, well, she was only trying to be helpful, wasn't she? Any fear my mother might have felt for me caused her less pain than the humiliation of another woman knowing she had lost control of her daughter.

'You really are making a fool of me, Petra,' she said twice on the drive home. I saw Dad's eyes looking at me in the rear-view mirror.

Being shut in my room was not as bad as you'd think. I had my copies of *The Essential David Cassidy Magazine* in their hidey place under the floorboards and the grey transistor radio with its little earphone. I had no one to talk to, but I had plenty of people to sing to me. The Isley Brothers did 'Summer Breeze' and I sang along, quietly as I could, even though I didn't know how jasmine could get in your mind or what it might smell like. 'Kissin' in the Back Row of the Movies'. The Drifters, it was, and I loved it, even though I'd never kissed anyone anywhere. *Because* I never had. My favourite song in the charts was 'She'. It was like a joke: 'So, there was this Welsh girl, locked in a room crying because a French man was singing in English while she was thinking of a boy . . .' He.

Lonely as a princess in her tower, without enough hair to let down, I had time to think about what had happened, and how I should have seen the way things would work out with Gillian as my new best friend.

The Friday before the concert, I'd gone into the girls' toilet and there was Angela standing by the mirror in a prickly haze of the spray she'd just used to stick the wings of her new feather-cut to her head. You knew you'd put enough on when the wings were hard as cardboard and stuck out like car indicators. Angela could not have been happier if she'd deliberately set out to ambush me, and I soon found out why.

'Wait till you see what Gillian gave me, Petra.' There was a note of triumph in her voice as she rummaged around in her denim bag, like it was a lucky dip. 'Gillian's really generous, isn't she?'

In Angela's hand was the Mary Quant eyeshadow kit. She flicked open the black lacquered top and used the tiny, unused sponge to apply a streak of indigo above her deep-set brown eye.

'Gillian said they were just my colours.'

'Lovely,' I said.

I thought about telling Angela, there and then, that her generous gift had cost most of my Christmas money. But I could see what pleasure it gave her, getting one over on me in the battle for Gillian's affections, the battle of friendship she must have thought she was losing until she got her hands on the eyeshadow kit. Gillian herself would take too much satisfaction in this envious little drama, planning for the plot to thicken. I felt the strings attached to my limbs twitch, but for the first time I refused to respond to the tug of our beautiful puppet-mistress. Poor Angela, so hopeful and happy with that purple shadow on her eye.

Did I think about David during those three days of solitary? Well, I reviewed the concert in my head, I thought a lot about Sharon and what could have happened, you know. Funny thing was, the person I thought most about was Steven Williams. Sitting on Steven's knee in the car on the way to the station, with his arm round my shoulder, and wondering whether he meant it, about seeing me around.

On the third day, the front doorbell rang. No one ever visited our house, not really, and if they did they came round the back. The front passage was blocked with boxes and my mother had to move them out the way to open the door to the headmaster. She was so surprised she actually let him in. Gave Mr Pugh tea in the front room, from the silver tea-set her parents brought over on the boat from Hamburg.

'Petra, please come downstairs to say hello.'

She called me, as though everything was normal, and she wasn't angry, and I shook Mr Pugh's hand, so papery and cool it felt like he had talc on it, not rough and warm like Dad's hands. The Head said it would be a serious disappointment for the school if Petra couldn't play for Princess Margaret at the opening of the new hall. He understood my hand was still a bit bruised, but the programme of events had gone to the printers. You couldn't mess about with royalty, could you? My mother agreed, flattered to play her part in the VIP schedule.

'The royal family are German, you know, from Hanover,' she announced at breakfast.

'Explains a lot,' said my dad, slipping me a pink envelope under my toast plate.

Dear Petra,

For six months now you've been a great friend to me. The best I ever had. And you've helped me SO MUCH honest to God.

I'm sorry things are bad with your mum and I hope she can let buygones be buygones.

I know you will be brilliant in the concert because you always give me the shivers when you talk poetry or play your chello.

Remember what you said in the quiz tiebreaker. 'Whatever happens in our lives we will always have David.'

Love,
Sharon

They told me to start playing the minute the Princess walked into the hall, but the plan went wrong because the Princess came over and started talking to me.

'How wonderful to be able to play so marvellously well at your age,' the Princess said.

Mahhr-vellously.

I'd never heard anyone talk like that before. She was tiny, the Princess, and her hair was dark brown and piled up on top of her head, lots of curls fastened into place by maids of honour probably. She had a short red dress on with a matching red coat over and black buttons and patent shoes and handbag. I thought she looked like Elizabeth Taylor with fat knees, but Sharon reckoned more like Sophia Loren. It was really good the Princess talked to me because then it got the nerves over with and I was relaxed when I began.

208

The new hall was absolutely packed with kids and their parents. The excited chatter was so thick you could have cut it like Bara Brith. I tried not to look up, but I could see a few people I knew. My dad had the afternoon off work and he was in his sports jacket, up in the raised seats, just behind Steven Williams. It made me feel funny seeing the two of them so close; two of the best boys' faces you could ever see, my dad and Steven. I mean it.

Everything went just like Miss Fairfax said it would. My right arm flowing as free as water, back as strong as a tree trunk, feet like roots going into the ground, and my ear searching for—what was it?—the still point of calm in the hall. *There* it was. I knew where Miss Fairfax was sitting, at the side towards the back, but I didn't play towards her, I didn't need to. I carried her in my head, I always would. Instead, I played towards him. Steven. He.

The girl asking the boy to come back to her, quite calmly at first, will you please come back to me? You have no idea how much I want you to come back to me. And then the ecstasy of it. He's coming back. He's *coming* back! Control. Taking control of your emotions, Petra. Each of the notes like a pearl. *I* think I love you. I *think* I love you. I think *I* love you. I think I *love* you. I think I love *YOU.*

The headmaster said I was a credit to the school. Miss Fairfax did a little bow. 'One artist to another,' she said. My dad cried. My mother thought that Princess Margaret had put on weight and that she'd let herself go.

'Your mum thinks Helen of blimmin' Troy let herself go,' said Sharon.

A few days after the concert, I was in the small practice-room at school, behind the netball court, when I looked out the window. I was so engrossed in my new piece I had lost track of who and where I was. Walking down the cinder path outside was Steven and my heart pitter-pattered, like it always did when I saw him. I lifted my hand to wave, but pulled it down just in time when I saw who was holding on to Steven's arm.

Gillian.

Just because she could.

*   *   *

It would be several years before I went up to London on the train again. Next time, I would make the journey alone, just me and my cello, for an interview at the Royal Academy of Music. I thought I was stronger, but my strength had never been tried again, not like it was on that day with Gillian's group.

There is a photo of all of us taken on the morning of the White City concert. We are standing in front of the ticket office at the station. Angela got a porter to take the picture with her Kodak Instamatic. Carol looks amazing, like a showgirl. Common, my mother would call it. She has had blonde streaks put in the front of her tufty auburn hair, which clashes with her red hot pants. On her feet, Carol is wearing white wet-look patent boots, which reveal a chunky expanse of bare, Bisto-brown leg and she has got down on one knee in front of the group, with her hands shimmying in the air, and her expression is saying, 'Ta-daaa! Just look at us. Aren't we fabulous?'

Sharon is wearing her new cream sweater-coat. The coat looked great on the model in the magazine, but because Sha was little and round, it made her look like a sheep, particularly with that fluffy feather-cut she'd had done at the hairdresser in David's honour. The layers never worked with Sharon's baby-fine hair, even with all those cans of Silvikrin she bought to hold it in place. I reckon Sharon's hairspray was responsible for starting the hole in the ozone layer; we never heard about the ozone layer before they invented the feather-cut, did we?

She looks so joyful in that photo; that was Sharon's gift and she shared it generously with those of us who weren't born with a talent for happiness.

My hair looks even worse than Sha's. I never did get the hang of blow-drying my new pageboy style, so, the night before White City, I wore curlers to bed to make sure the ends were turned under. I slept on my back like a saint on a tomb. The porcupine pins jabbed my scalp every time I moved. I thought it was worth any suffering to have pretty hair. My hair was one of my good points. You can see a very obvious ridge where the rollers have been. I do not, as I hoped, look like Susan Dey. As for my clothes, I am dressed top to toe in David's favourite colour, which was going to help him pick me out in the crowd, obviously. With my pale complexion I look terrible in brown. I look *yellow* in brown.

Olga is behind me, standing a little to one side with a thoughtful expression, which always was her stance to the group. Blessed, or cursed, with foreign names, Olga and I were destined to be friends—she was musical too, a viola player with a strict Russian father. But we shunned each other. It was as if we sensed the combined sum of our otherness would be too much. One weird, foreign-sounding musical girl was an acceptable aberration. Two was a ghetto. I

211

think I would have liked Olga and she would have liked me. Sometimes I saw her smiling into her pencil case at the same things.

At the centre of Gillian's group stands Gillian herself. Angela is lurking alongside with the stricken, resigned look of the best friend who knows that her position is shortly to be advertised in Situations Vacant. In a ruffled chiffon blouse, pristine white flares and a cloche hat with a flower brooch, Gillian has all the sultry nonchalance of Bianca Jagger. The camera looks at her and you can tell it wants to go on looking and looking. Drinking in her beauty. Gillian is the only one of us not attempting a smile. She lets her mouth hang open just a little, as models do. Perhaps it's my imagination, but Gillian's face seems to be simmering with the resentment which was about to boil over and burn us all.

There is so much the girls in that picture don't know. We don't know that the famous White City of our imagination will be a grey concrete dump reeking of urine. We don't know that a girl will die. That nearly a thousand will be injured, and that Sharon will be among them. We don't know, not yet, what love can cost. We were in love with the idea of love. We were trying it out for size. For sighs.

*   *   *

Not long after that photo was taken my love for David would go out like the tide. Soon I would be embarrassed to admit I ever liked him, just as, for a short time, I had been ashamed of my cello. For my 14th birthday, Sharon bought me 10cc's Original Soundtrack album. It gave me such a thrill, that LP, because it meant that out there were people who heard things the way I heard things. Words and music, pain and joy.

The swollen, fuzzy opening chords of 'I'm Not in Love' with its human-heartbeat drum, were what the thought of real boys had begun to do to every cell of my body.

But I was still grateful to David, always would be, though I didn't know it then. For being there when no one else was; for giving voice to feelings in me which had barely been born; for helping me to grow up, which is so very, very hard to do. For giving me a boy to love, a boy who could never hurt me; although only because he could never love me back. Could it be forever?

Maybe it could.

At David Cassidy's White City concert on 26 May 1974, the central section of the 35,000-strong crowd of fans surged forward when Cassidy appeared; many fainted, were trampled upon or were crushed. One St John Ambulance man said the scale of the injuries reminded him of the Blitz. The director of the British Safety Council called it 'a suicide concert'.

Some 750 girls were treated for hysteria or injuries on the night. A few days later, 14-year-old fan Bernadette Whelan, who had been unconscious since the hysterical crush, became the first fatality at a British pop concert.

David Cassidy sent a letter of regret to Bernadette's parents, but did not attend the funeral for fear of causing another riot.

At the inquest, the coroner recorded a verdict of accidental death as a result of asphyxiation. He said that Bernadette was 'a victim of contrived hysteria' and suggested that 'trendy, high platform shoes' were a contributing factor to the number of girls who fell over in the throng.

David Cassidy retired soon afterwards.

PART TWO

1998

Footfalls echo in the memory
Down the passage which we did not take
Towards the door we never opened
Into the rose-garden.

T. S. Eliot, *Four Quartets*

I beg your pardon,
I never promised you a rose garden.
Along with the sunshine,
There's gotta be a little rain sometimes.

Lynn Anderson,
'(I Never Promised You A) Rose Garden'

12

The day her mother died, she found out her husband was leaving her. It certainly made for an interesting funeral.

Petra is in the front pew of the chapel wearing a broad-brimmed black hat. Her husband sits next to her, weeping. One day there will be a detective of tears. That's what Petra is thinking. She has read recently in a magazine that scientists have discovered that real tears, tears of genuine and heart-wrenching sorrow, have a different chemical composition to the ones people cry when they watch a sad movie. Or the ones people cry if they have been caught out loving someone they shouldn't. A woman who isn't their wife, for example. There are oceans of fake tears out there, when you come to think about it, and now they have a way of telling.

Petra thinks the detective would suggest a way of trapping your husband's tears. On a Kleenex you handed him, perhaps, as he explained how much he hated the thought of leaving you and his thirteen-year-old daughter.

'You are my world. I may be physically absent, but emotionally I'm still here,' the husband might say, just as Marcus had said to Petra, dabbing his eyes.

Gently, she would take the tissue from him and seal it in a cellophane bag. Later, the detective would take the Kleenex to a laboratory where technicians in white coats would reconstitute the dried tears in a test tube. A letter with the results would arrive about a week later. Then you would know. One way or the other, you would know. What your husband's tears meant. The exact proportion of grief to guilt, of regret to relief, of salt to water. He loves me, he loves me not, he loves me . . .

Petra can hear the waves outside, hurling themselves against the shingle. The chapel is just across the road from the beach. It's a beautiful summer's day out there, a fact that can barely be registered inside this brown building, which seems to have been designed to keep in the dark and the damp. She can hear the cries and shouts of the tourists, which to her ears sound more like pain than pleasure.

Petra tries to stop her mind wandering. This is my mother's funeral, she tells herself. My mother is dead. Impossible. My mother is in that coffin. Greta has loomed so large in her life that it will take more than a funeral and a coroner's certificate to convince Petra that she is gone.

She is aware of Marcus in the pew beside her. Men don't cry as easily as women. Their tears seldom come out without a fight. Her husband's shoulders shudder slightly under his good grey coat with the black velvet lapels, the one she picked out for him before he did a series of recitals in Germany and Austria last year. Petra can hardly remember him crying, at least not since Molly was born, but in the past month Marcus has broken down more times than she can count. Since that Saturday afternoon when she got home, unexpectedly, from teaching at a workshop in Chiswick and the phone in the kitchen rang twice, then stopped for a few seconds and rang twice again. Petra picked it up, expecting to hear her mother's voice. Instead a girl had said: 'You don't know who I am.'

Petra feels the wifely impulse to reach across and

comfort Marcus, a powerfully instinctive thing, but she is surprised to observe that her hand flatly refuses to obey the instruction the brain is sending it. Her fingers flex inside the stretchy black gloves bought from a market stall in town less than two hours ago. She'd only thought at the last minute that her mother would be upset if she didn't wear gloves. The gloves make her hands feel webbed. She thinks of the black plastic feet of Canada geese. For the first time, it occurs to her that she is now a source of misery to the man she has spent most of her adult life with, an obstacle to his happiness. Marcus probably wishes it was her in the coffin.

Petra shuts her eyes quickly to edit out this thought, then glances around at the congregation. For an elderly woman who kept herself to herself and who, throughout Petra's childhood, discouraged visitors by ignoring the front doorbell and only admitting people who persevered and came round the back, her mother has drawn a decent crowd. There are officials and regulars from the chapel, two immaculate ladies from the department store where her mother worked briefly in hats, gloves and bags; and there is a surprisingly good turnout from her father's family, most of whom her mother cordially loathed because they worked with their hands. Probably they've come along to hear the famous cellist.

Across the aisle, Petra's Auntie Mair, frail now with a heavily bandaged leg, gives Marcus the smile people smile at those they've seen on TV: both overfamiliar and unsure. In response, Marcus bestows on Auntie Mair the smile you would expect—friendly enough not to seem grand or up himself, but sufficiently cool and distracted to suggest that any further attempt at contact would be unwise. Petra feels sorry for him, almost. A funeral must be a grim and awkward place to be when your mother-in-law is in the coffin and her only child has recently found out that you're in love with someone else.

After she hung up on the girl, the phone in the kitchen rang again almost immediately and Petra snatched at it, ready now to say all the things she had been too shocked to say before. She bungled the receiver, which clattered off the wall and dangled by its flex a few inches above the cat's bowl. When Petra finally managed to hold the phone to her ear, she found it wasn't the girl after all; it was Glenys, her mother's neighbour.

'I'm so sorry, she's gone,' Glenys said.

'What? Who's gone? Oh God.'

No news so awful but Glenys wanted to be first with it.

Petra had felt the need to call someone. The benign June light slanting into the kitchen through the apple-green blind was the same as it had been just a few seconds earlier; the blameless washing-up brushes standing to attention in their wire basket, the picture of Molly on the pinboard next to the phone, smiling and freckled in her Pippi Longstocking costume for World Book Day. Petra had spent hours plaiting orange wool around two pieces of bent coat-hanger so that Molly's plaits would stick out just like Pippi's. Her mother had been a genius at plaits, a talent that seems to be woven into the German DNA. She used to brush the hair fiercely till it shone, then pull it tight from the root until Petra's scalp squealed for mercy.

She experiments with the idea of her mother being in

the past tense, but, no, her brain won't permit it. And what about that girl? Surely you should be able to call some kind of emergency service and say, 'Look, I'm terribly sorry, but I am unable to process these two appalling blows simultaneously. Can I arrange to have one of them taken away?'

In the chapel this drowsy afternoon, with its glowering, eagle-winged pulpit and its tall, sightless windows, two kinds of grief are twined tightly together in Petra's heart: one grief for her mother, another for her marriage. And maybe, to complete the plait, a third: some nameless hurt that is slowly starting to take shape in her mind.

'Let us pray,' she hears the minister say a long way off.

When man and wife kneel, it disturbs a cold mustiness in the tapestry cushions which smell to Petra, as they always have, of God and rain. She must know every single kneeler in the place. Her mother embroidered several of them herself until she began to curse her failing eyes. Bad eyes Petra has inherited. At the age of thirty-eight, she is now both short-sighted and long-sighted. Recently, she has found herself joining the ranks of those in supermarkets who bring tins right up to their nose and then hold them at arm's length to try and read the contents. Today, even with her contact lenses in, she has to squint to make out the words of the hymns.

Because the chapel is so close to the sea, practically *in* the water when the tide is high, the prayer books have always been briny with damp. On winter Sundays during her childhood, she remembers peeling the pages apart to find the psalm. The pages were so frail they were more like skin than

221

paper. Whenever they sang 'For Those in Peril on the Sea', the choir locked in unequal struggle with the squalling seagulls on the roof, her dad used to say the same thing: 'Champion! Well, we've got the sound effects anyway.'

Champion was her father's word to acknowledge anything which added to the sum of human happiness, that exclamation always being accompanied by a brisk gleeful rubbing together of his hands, as if he were a Boy Scout trying to start a fire. 'There's champion for you, Petra *fach*.'

People complain that the old start repeating the same stories again and again, and they do, oh they do, but Petra has learned the hard way that all irritation is instantly forgiven when the old are no longer around to tell the story one more time. She would give anything to have her father back here with her, even for five minutes, and to hear him make that lame joke about the seagull backing singers. The replacement organist, presently toiling away in the balcony at the back of the chapel, isn't a patch on Dad. After six years, she still thinks of Eric as new. He has problems with his pedalling. Each verse ends a beat or two after the singing with an apologetic, bronchial wheeze. Petra winces; she can put up with anything; bad eyes, bad weather, bad husband; but bad music, that she never will be able to bear.

> 'Eternal Father, strong to save,
> Whose arm hath bound the restless wave,
> Who bidd'st the mighty ocean deep
> Its own appointed limits keep:
> O hear us, when we cry to thee
> For those in peril on the sea.'

The English words are unfamiliar. She realises she only knows the hymn in Welsh. The translation must be for Marcus's benefit. It is exactly the kind of detail her mother would fuss about, always worrying that they would look provincial and common in front of Marcus's family, who lived in a converted mill in the Cotswolds and who went to great lengths to make the Williamses feel at ease. As if Greta could ever be relaxed with a woman called Arabella who struck up a conversation about colour schemes. Her mother disliked Arabella on sight, and neither woman knew that it was because Marcus's mother was a Jaeger- clad reminder that Greta had married beneath her station.

After the first verse, Petra can't sing any more, though her mouth continues to mime the Welsh words.

You don't know who I am, the girl said.

Didn't she? Not in person, maybe, but Petra thinks that at some animal level, some molecular level of body chemistry, she knew exactly. Not who the girl was, but of her existence. There were none of the obvious clues. Marcus was far too fastidious for lipstick on collars or suspicious florist's receipts. Far from being guilty and distracted, as men having affairs are supposed to be, he had seemed energised and attentive; he had even started driving Molly to her sleepovers and piano lessons, which had delighted Petra, always the designated family chauffeur despite her lack of confidence behind the wheel. Some things were different, though. When they were having sex Marcus had difficulty finishing and he had taken to flipping her over to get the job done. When she asked him about this, after a few glasses of wine and keeping the tone deliberately

223

light, he gave that rueful little-boy grin of his and said it excited him. She was relieved to have his explanation, at the same time as being unconvinced. Really, she thought, the truth was that he couldn't come if he saw her face. Much easier to imagine another's face if your wife's was buried in the pillow. Back late from a concert in Oxford one night, he rolled over in bed and said, 'I want to fuck your mouth.' It was not a line that belonged in their life together—it came from another play entirely—and instantly he said it she must have known what it meant, but she tidied it away neatly in the marriage drawer marked Private, and forgot.

Petra's dad was never sure about Marcus. He always said Mark, then paused before the 'us', like a horse baulking at a difficult fence, a tic which infuriated her mother, who adored her son-in-law unreservedly. Marcus's combination of talent, acute sensitivity, quick temper and arrogance were delightful to Greta, because she believed them to be the ingredients of genius. Much could be forgiven such a man. It was kind, devoted underachievers like Petra's father who could not be tolerated. Would her mother have thought that screwing a twenty-five-year-old violinist was just another perk of the artistic condition?

No, not screwing. 'Philandering,' Petra corrected herself quickly, seeing her mother's cool stare of disapproval.

Greta could not abide coarseness of any kind. She had stopped taking *The Times* after the paper started calling it 'sex' instead of sexual intercourse. You never heard the word 'bastard' pass her lips, only 'illegitimate'. Long after the concept had lost its stigma, her mother would point to some sweet,

224

apple-cheeked baby parked in a buggy outside the Co-op and murmur darkly, 'Kerry's illegitimate boy.' Her mother was stuck in the past. Bastard now meant something else entirely.

Like Petra's husband, for instance. As Marcus edges out of the pew and moves purposefully to the front of the chapel, Petra is able to observe her partner of almost fifteen years as others in the congregation must see him. Age has not withered him; in fact, age is struggling to land a finger on the man. 'Hunky *and* soulful. And there's lots *of* him. You lucky thing,' a friend had said to her, in the early days, and Petra had blushed; it was as though the friend had stood beside their bed and watched them sleep and wake. Seen Petra enfolded by those lazy, unclumsy limbs. Marcus has none of the artist's traditional pallor; he is in rude health, always has been, with strong features that will never grow gaunt or—and this, Petra has observed, is a horribly common fate for middle-aged men—fatten and droop until the handsome youth becomes a doughy, red-cheeked squire. Not Marcus, damn his eyes. Look at him. Turned forty last year, but he still has a thatch of wavy dark hair through which, now and then, he runs a distracted hand, to mess it up rather than neaten it. A dash of Ted Hughes, someone said, and it's true. Under the decency, and despite the finesse, there is something wild not far below. Something you can't trust.

Marcus sits down, pulls the cello to him and sweeps the bow across the strings in a single motion. Whoever said that music was invented to confirm human loneliness obviously never heard her husband play. When he did the Elgar in Bristol last year, one reviewer said his performance was 'at once muscular

225

and sublimely sensitive'. Yes, and who got the most out of those muscles?

As his bow moves, and the music swells, her anger rocks back and forth. Even if the detective of tears could get a sample from her husband, Petra isn't sure she'd really want to know if they were genuine. When he said that he still loved her, did he mean it? We live in such strange times, Petra thinks. Science is solving all the secrets of mankind, one by one— predispositions to disease, the brain chemistry of criminals, DNA tests to establish fatherhood, the reason why women prefer to mate with alpha males and live with beta ones. But human nature just isn't keeping up with all this information. It isn't ready for so much truth. Not all at once. Sometimes not knowing is as much as you can bear.

Petra feels a sudden longing for him. Not for the weak, evasive man who has been accompanying her to marriage counselling while moving in with a violinist who looks insultingly like Petra at the same age. Marcus, the man who always despised the clichés of bourgeois escape, has set up home with his young mistress on a houseboat near Teddington.

'A houseboat,' Petra had repeated dully. Was any love nest in the annals of adultery more designed to make you want to summon a nuclear submarine?

'Mum, it's OK. It'll be OK.'

Molly is standing next to her, stroking her arm, speaking softly. It's only when her daughter pushes the tissue into her gloved hand that Petra realises that she is the one who is crying. The tears are running down her cheeks in such profusion that they feel like they're tying a ribbon of water under her chin. She can feel the wetness seep under the collar of her new black linen jacket. Twice as expensive as

226

anything else in her wardrobe, but she couldn't let her mother down on this important day.

'Petra, taking the control of your emotions, please,' says her mother, and she feels her chin lift automatically and her spine stiffen.

Posture can do a lot for a woman, her mother was always quite specific about that. If you carry yourself well, if you pull in your tummy, using your muscles as the body's own girdle, then middle-age spread was not the inevitability some liked to pretend it was. All her married life, her mother took pride in the fact that she weighed exactly the same as she had on her wedding day. Greta took the Helena Rubinstein line: there are no ugly women, just lazy ones.

From the summer's day far away come the ding-dong strains of an ice-cream van. A tune that was meant to have been composed by Henry VIII for his future queen had ended up as tinky-tonk chimes summoning day trippers at a Welsh seaside resort to buy a 99. What were the odds against that?

'Mum?'

'I'm fine,' Petra whispers back, and lays a hand on her daughter's hair. Molly is so much fairer than Petra, blessed with her grandmother's colouring and the same angelic, heart-shaped face.

'Mamgu would love it that Daddy is playing Bach for her,' says Molly, and Petra gives a watery smile of assent.

Molly is just thirteen and grieving for her grandmother. Merciful, uncomplicated grief. It was an unexpected bonus of motherhood, the way that Petra's daughter and Petra's mother had loved each other unconditionally and had been able to show that love in a way Petra found so hard to do with Greta. On the rare occasion when her mother laid a

227

hand on Petra's arm, she experienced it almost as an electric shock.

The music comes to its solemn end, like a life well lived, and Marcus lifts his bow and throws back his head as if to shake himself from a trance. You can tell the congregation wants to applaud, but some unwritten rule says you aren't supposed to clap in church. Do they really think God would be jealous of the talents of His own creation?

Marcus rejoins them in the pew and glances sideways to see his triumph reflected in his wife's eyes. She will not look at him. *Alas, my love, you do me wrong, to cast me off discourteously*. Petra studies her webbed fingers as the pall-bearers lift the coffin onto their shoulders. What would her mother's parting advice be as she goes to her grave? She would tell her to win Marcus back, no question. Greta wouldn't let a man of that calibre go without a fight. 'Top-drawer,' that's what she called Marcus. Marcus's family was out of the top drawer. It had pained Petra to hear her say it; the way her mother, one of Nature's aristocrats, was so impressed by the class into which her daughter had married.

The family follows the coffin out. At the very back of the chapel, in a row of seats to the side of the font, Petra notices a pretty plump blonde woman about her own age. She returns the woman's smile. It isn't until they're outside by the gate, and the coffin is being loaded into the hearse, that Petra shakes herself back to life and realises she has failed to register a face she knows as well as her own.

Sharon.

*   *   *

228

They did keep in touch. On birthdays and Christmases, filling each other in on all the news, inevitably child-related as the years went by. Petra's girl, Sharon's two boys, David and Gareth. Every December, cards travelled from Wales to London, and back the other way, cards in which both women expressed the fond hope that this would turn out to be the year when they finally got together. After a while, Petra wasn't sure how long, she forgot to mark Sha's birthday, and a few years after that, she was shocked one day to find she could no longer recall the exact date. 3rd of July? 5th? When she went home for the funeral of her cello teacher, Miss Fairfax, she took Sharon's new number with her. Mal's electrical business had prospered, and the family had moved a short way up the coast to an estate of detached houses with carports and a sea view. The neighbour on one side was a headmaster, on the other was a famous Welsh fly half who had shacked up with the reupholstered wife of a plastic surgeon.

'There's posh for you,' Sharon wrote in her Christmas card.

Petra didn't call her during that visit. Time was short, she told herself, but it was the distance between them that felt too great. In the covered market, buying flowers for Miss Fairfax's grave, she spotted a familiar figure with a coronet of baby-blonde hair wearing a vivid purple mac, instinctively lifted her hand to wave—It's *you*!—and then dodged behind a pillar. Petra didn't know it was herself she was hiding from. She felt ashamed that she had avoided the best friend of her girlhood, but Sharon could have taken one look at her and read her pain and disappointment. She wasn't ready to face Sharon

229

looking at her face.

Their friendship had survived Sha leaving school at sixteen to go to the local technical college to learn shorthand and typing, while Petra stayed on to do A levels and worked Saturdays in Boots the chemist. They still made each other laugh like no one else could. Tried out all the latest beauty products from Petra's counter, including a face-tanning machine which required you to wear goggles when you sat in front of it. They misread the instructions, of course, and Sharon's face was baked to a fiery shade of terracotta, except for the white circles around her eyes. For weeks, she looked like an early female aviator.

Before she left school, for her final art coursework, Sharon painted beguiling, sloe-eyed girls on cardboard boxes, wearing the most incredible jewelled colours, always in rooms with the sea visible through a window.

Petra was awestruck. 'They're incredible. Like Matisse.'

'Who's he when he's at home, then?' Sharon laughed. 'Get away with you, Petra. Everything's got to be like something else with you, hasn't it? Some things are just themselves, mun.'

Sharon should have gone to art college, somewhere really good, but, although she had huge natural ability, she lacked any sense of entitlement for her talent. Modesty and gentle humour were among the sweetest virtues of her people, but also their curse.

'I can always paint at home, can't I?' Though she didn't.

Petra and Marcus's wedding was the turning point. After that, things were never the same

230

between them. Sharon was making the bridesmaids' dresses, but the fittings were a palaver because Petra had agreed to have the whole thing in Gloucestershire, in Marcus's village, because, well, because they would put up a marquee in the garden and the church was so old and so pretty and their friends from London could get there more easily, rather than making the journey across the Severn Bridge into Wales, which took a toll in more ways than one.

The real reason was Greta. Entertaining of any kind and, in particular, a fear of social failure always made Petra's mother angry. Greta would be bound to go on the attack, she would try and launch a pre-emptive strike against any perceived criticism or humiliation. Besides, Petra couldn't imagine putting all of Marcus's family in the cold brown chapel with her father's sisters and a Baptist minister who could be guaranteed to mention sin at least twice, and maybe even fornication. The Church of England, which saw no sin that could not be forgiven and would be far too polite to mention it anyway, was a much more relaxing venue.

The night before the wedding, Sharon arrived at the Cotswold millhouse, her ancient Mini leprous with rust and exploding with dresses packed in dry-cleaning bags. Made of a heavy bronze satin she'd found in Llanelli market, the bridesmaids' frocks were beautifully cut, almost sculptural, with a plunging neckline edged in tiny glistening beads. Marcus's sister, Georgina, was the first to try hers on.

'What *fun*,' Georgie said. 'I say, you could go to a nightclub in this.'

Marcus's mother came in and took one look at Sharon and her dresses. 'Oh, what fun. I think we can

231

find a corsage to make that a bit more *respectable*, don't you?'

Petra should have left then and there. Should have jumped in the rustbucket with Sha and sped away to the green green grass of home. But her infatuation with Marcus had stolen her away; she felt high on being wanted by this emotionally unavailable Englishman from the top drawer. Did she know she was marrying the man of her mother's dreams? Not consciously, she didn't. The taste of triumph was so strong it masked all other sensations.

At the altar, she turned to hand her bouquet to her chief bridesmaid and she saw tears in Sharon's smiling eyes. For a second, no more, Petra felt she was falling, falling, as the bonds of her best and oldest friendship began to unravel.

*   *   *

The day after the funeral, Petra goes back to the house to start sorting through the stuff. Marcus has taken Molly for a walk on the beach followed by something to eat in the new cafe on the headland overlooking the bay. The cafe serves the kind of fresh salads and filled baguettes you get in London. Marcus has always complained about how appalling the food is down here; he clutches his chest and calls it the Death Plan Diet, which is another way of saying that people do a lot of comfort eating. Personally, Petra thinks that if you find yourself living in a former mining and former steel town during a period that social historians now call Post-Industrial Decline then you are entitled to a bit of comfort. (The once proud port might as well change its name to Former: its future

232

was all in the past.) It is surely no coincidence that, at the end of the twentieth century, it's the rich who are most successful at being thin; they aren't in need of comfort, being so comfortable already. Walking down the high street, she notices people have got shockingly, distressingly fat. When she was a child, if you were poor you were thin.

'Skin and bone. There's nothing left of him,' her aunties would report with grim relish of a neighbour who had lost his job in the pit.

She's glad Marcus and Molly aren't with her. When she pushes open the front door, the smell of her mother's last illness comes down the stairs to greet her. Of course, Greta had refused point-blank to be ill. In the final few weeks, when her balance was, as even she had to admit, 'not szo good', she still insisted on going upstairs to bed by herself, even though Petra had made up the couch in the front room. Greta fought the last battle with her preferred weapons: Teutonic stoicism and Elizabeth Arden's Blue Grass.

Petra pushes the glazed door into the kitchen. The units, a buttery apricot with brass rings for handles, and the chubby Belfast sink date from when the house was built over seventy years ago. She opens the fridge and registers its contents—three slices of ham wrapped in foil, half a yogurt with a clingfilm hat, three tomatoes and some peas from the garden, still in their pods. Her parents grew up during the war—her mother in Germany, her dad on a local farm. For that generation, she thinks, it wasn't just food that was rationed. Feelings were rationed too. They were more frugal with emotion, always keeping something in reserve.

Long ago, she remembers her mother going

233

berserk in this kitchen after Petra had wandered in while revising for an exam and had absent-mindedly helped herself to a hunk of Cheddar.

'When I was your age I would have made that piece of cheese last a week,' her mother snapped, snatching the Tupperware container from Petra's hand and slamming it back in the fridge.

Standing at the foot of her bed later that evening, her dad, the peacemaker, said: 'What you have to understand, *cariad fach*, is that people who have been hungry, really hungry, mind, well, they're not the same as people who haven't known hunger.'

Everything in the house is exactly as Petra remembers. The upright in the front room has a Chopin prelude open on the stand; Petra tries a few notes, but hearing her father's piano is unexpected agony, like slicing open a finger. After Dad died, her mother had started to like and value him; she polished the memory of a man who was only ever drone to her queen bee while he was alive.

Back in the hall, the phone on the wicker table is the one her parents had installed more than thirty years ago. There was a flurry of excitement when it was first put in. So rarely did they have visitors that the telephone engineer made a lasting impression. A cheerful man in blue overalls, he warmed the house several degrees just by entering it.

'Lovely place you got here, Mrs Williams. Righto, then.'

Petra loved that new phone: it brought a little futuristic glamour to a household that might as well have been in nineteenth-century Prussia. The phone was avocado with a darker green dialling circle. Petra remembers calls she made on that phone which felt so urgent the dial seemed to take forever to come

234

back. 'Three-two-five-eight,' her mother would answer, long after such formality started to sound stilted and faintly comical and the number itself had been lengthened and relengthened by ever-changing phone companies.

It's not always easy to recognise the significant moments of your life as you're living them, but Petra understands this is one of them. To stand in that hall and to realise that neither of her parents will ever answer the phone again. Nor will she ever need to dial their number. Death itself is too big to take in, she already sees that; the loss comes at you instead in an infinite number of small instalments that can never be paid off.

Upstairs, in her parents' room, she pulls back the heavy lined curtains. The small garden below, always so neat while her dad was alive, is in open rebellion as though, freed from her mother's reproving gaze, the plants had suddenly decided to throw a wild party. Swarming up the sooty brick wall, pastel garlands of sweet peas are wilting under their own abundance. The sweet peas need to be picked so the flowers come again and again. Mum taught her that. Petra will do it later.

First, her mother's wardrobe, which dominates the master bedroom. Double-fronted mahogany, it has a full-length mirror with a pretty bevelled edge which winks like diamonds when they catch the light. Such heavy stuff has fallen out of fashion. Brown furniture, they call it these days. In Petra's south London home, Molly keeps her skinny jeans and Top Shop gear in a small canvas closet which fastens with a zip. It looks like something forensic scientists might erect at the scene of a murder. The little tent gives off an attitude that says clothes are lighthearted, cheap and disposable. Not so Greta's astonishing wardrobe, which resembles a Lady chapel constructed to celebrate eternal femininity. Petra twists the brass key and hears a satisfying click.

Inside it's like a magazine feature on How a Woman Should Take Care of Her Clothes. Neat racks of shoes and boots at the bottom. The spare shoe trees look faintly sinister, like puppets without strings. There are none of those bunched-up sweaters that Petra stuffs any old how onto her shelves when she's in a hurry. She strokes a tweed suit with a nipped-in waist and what looks like a mink collar. It could have been worn by Eva Marie Saint in *North by Northwest*. Such a delectable suit demands Cary Grant at the very least to scramble up a cliff face and pay homage to it. Petra buries her face in the dense caramel twill where she can still smell traces of her mother. Echt Kölnisch Wasser No. 4711. Eau de cologne No. 4711, the pungent ghost of gin and freesias. Now, she starts to cry properly. For all the beautiful places that this lovely suit never travelled to, for the beautiful woman who would have loved those places, if only she'd had the chance. In the drawers down one side of the wardrobe, she finds scarves, both chiffon and silk, and a separate compartment for handkerchiefs, folded and ironed into perfect miniature sails.

Her mother believed in what are now called Investment Pieces: lambswool sweaters in timeless neutrals, folded with tissue paper that crackles when you touch them, two good crisp white cotton shirts on padded hangers. Petra was planning to keep a couple of things for herself and Molly, then take a carload down to the church hall, but this is not second-hand, it's vintage. Her mother deserves a costume museum, not a jumble sale.

Petra is feeling behind the coats when she finds it. She isn't looking for it. She isn't looking for anything. She is reaching for a pair of black patent heels, the shine still on them after thirty years, when her fingers brush against something colder than leather. She takes it out. A biscuit tin with a lake and mountains on the lid. A Christmas gift from an aunt in Heidelberg. Inside the tin, there are postcards, black-and-white snapshots of her parents in their youth, and a sheaf of letters, tied together with a red ribbon.

The pink envelope is out of place. It has smiley faces and a rainbow sticker on the front. Her heart jumps when she sees it's addressed to her, but there is something strange about the handwriting. It takes a moment, and half a lifetime, to recognise it as her own. Not her own now, but the way she used to write, a long time ago, with flowery loops and hearts instead of dots over the i's. The envelope has been opened, and it is easy to slide out the letter inside. She reads it for the first time in her life. Then she reads it again to make sure.

She gets up and walks across the landing and pushes the door into her old bedroom. The brown candlewick coverlet is still on the bed, and slightly damp to the touch, though twenty-five years of light streaming through the sash window has faded the deep chocolate to a mouldy olive-yellow. She kneels down, reaches under the bed, puts her finger into the opening between the floorboards, lifts the plank and pulls out a pile of magazines and a grey transistor radio. She flicks the switch.

Ridiculous. Completely insane. She half expects to hear his voice.

237

'Cherish is the word I use to describe,
All the feelings that I have hiding here for you
inside.'

But there is nothing. She opens the flap on the back of the radio with her fingernail and wrinkles her nose; acid has wept from the batteries and eaten into the plastic.

Petra kicks off her funeral shoes and lies back on the bed, clutching the letter and the magazines to her chest. How could her mother have kept it from her? She must have known what the words would mean. *'You, Petra Williams, are the winner of the Ultimate David Cassidy Quiz.'* The magazine is delighted to tell her that she has won the trip of a lifetime to travel with her nominated friend, Sharon Lewis, to meet David himself on the set of *The Partridge Family* in Los Angeles.

El Ay.

At the bottom of the letter, a name has been typed with such enthusiasm it has perforated the paper. Zelda Franklin. The date is 22 July 1974, almost twenty-four years to the day. This new loss, so stupid and insignificant compared to the other vast, overwhelming losses, flares up inside. Her lungs feel licked by a righteous flame. Petra, such a good girl for so long, blazes with the injustice of it. Happiness had come to her in a pink envelope, and it had been stolen from her. I was the winner, she thinks, amazed. I *am* the winner.

How could she do that? How *could* she? The grief she feels for Greta is not just to do with death; mother and daughter were lost to each other long before the woman with the perfect silver perm

238

slipped away with steely grace in the room across the landing. Mingled with raw grief is the sorrow of knowing that her mother actually chose to keep such a pleasure from her. Greta saw pop music as a fungus on the face of civilisation and, worse still, a blight on her daughter's future life as an artist. Petra runs her nails up and down the furry channels of the bedspread, feeling the strength in her fingers.

'Every day, really you must practise if you want to be the best,' her mother told her, and she had never disobeyed.

Greta had been right. Practice did make perfect, but where had thirty years of practice got Petra? Perfectly sad. She's not sure how long she lies there or when a plan starts to take shape in her mind.

Sitting up, she retrieves her shoes and collects the magazines she has disinterred from her old hiding place. Who knows, they might give Molly a laugh. In the mirror above the little bookshelf, with its row of Enid Blytons, Petra catches sight of herself. It's her father she sees looking back at her. Dad would never have put a dream come true in a box and kept it like a guilty secret.

Going downstairs, the letter tucked safely in her pocket, she wonders what would happen if she were to call that magazine up now and say to them, please can I have my prize? Silly. There wasn't any *them* left to call. No magazine, no Zelda Franklin, no *Partridge Family*. Petra takes the magazine from the top of the pile so she can get a proper look at the face on the cover. The eyes had it. Deep green pools you could pour all your longing into. He was so lovely; still lovely. Once, he meant the world to her. And she had won the opportunity to tell him so. That moment was lost forever, like a million other moments in a human life. Passing the wicker hall table on her way to the front door, Petra inserts a finger into one of the holes on the avocado phone; dragging it round, then letting it go, she hears the familiar mechanical whirr as the dial returns to its position. But even if there were people to call, what on earth would they think of her?

13

It is purely by chance that Marie takes the crazy woman's call. She got in early to the magazine this morning with a hangover that made her head feel like an ostrich egg. Vast yet fragile, it might crack at any moment. She successfully transferred her head from her flat to the Golf and then from the car park to the lift and then to her office, over by the window, like someone balancing a crystal goblet on a playing card. Now, she sits at her desk with a large bottle of Evian and a triple espresso, taking alternate sips from each to suppress the nausea. Marie needs to think. But her skull, and the sudden unwanted awareness of her brain, parched and throbbing within it, makes thinking impossible.

Today is the big group editorial meeting at which she is going to have to pitch the success story of her title, *Teengirl*, against the other editors with their bullshit advertising claims, all strutting their stuff in front of the editorial director. Sasha Harper, the editor of *Babe*, will be there in her armour of choice: top-to-toe Prada with her trusty dagger, the Mont Blanc pen. At the thought of Sasha, Marie moans softly and plunges a hand into her desk drawer, groping for aspirin. Inside, her fingers find something squidgy and cool to the touch, and recoil. Opening one eye with great care, Marie sees it is the condom that *Babe* recently stuck as a free gift on its front cover. Chocolate-flavoured condoms for young girls.

Jesus. Everything about that was so wrong.

Marie and Sasha are supposed to be colleagues on

the same team; between them they dominate the teenage magazine market. It is growing by the day. Marie's *Teengirl* focuses more on pop stars, young love and music, while *Babe* specialises in celebrity gossip, sex and its related problems. Far from supporting each other, the two women have become rivals, probably because the editorial director is the acknowledged guru of their market sector. They vie for the Boss's approval like sisters fighting over a crumb of praise from a remote father. Everyone calls him the Boss, except Barry, the marketing director, who is an old friend and uses his first name.

Marie had no need of an alarm this morning. She woke feeling wildly alarmed at 4 a.m., three hours after going to bed. Marie's subconscious allowed her to admit what she would never accept in daylight: she is losing the battle to Sasha. The battle of taste and sex and hard cash. Fourteen-year-old girls increasingly choose to dress like hookers while forty-year-olds dress like teenagers. There is no doubt in Marie's mind that girls are desperate to grow up quicker. Even nine-year-olds in crop tops want to crash the party. Where once they sought advice on unsightly love bites, the readers now seem to gobble up stuff about oral sex, if gobble was the word she's looking for.

She groans and pulls the water bottle towards her, pressing its coolness into her temple. Magazines have got sexier to keep up with the girls. Or maybe crude mags had made little girls think they should be into sex? Something weird has definitely happened to being female since Marie was a kid with a Duran Duran poster over her bed and a prized collection of trolls with luminous hair, but she doesn't have the energy or the curiosity to think what. Let someone

242

else worry about it.

Generally, Marie doesn't answer her phone. Katie, who sits just outside the door, always gets it instantly. So the chirruping receiver is a novelty. It's still so early—barely eight—that Marie picks it up cautiously. The woman's voice on the other end of the line, choked with some grievance or emotion she hasn't got under control, alerts Marie to the fact that she should have left the phone ringing. Too bloody late. She's stuck with her now.

'How old did you say you were?' Marie asks. 'I'm afraid this is *Teengirl*. Yes, *TEENGIRL*. No, I've never heard of that magazine, sorry.'

She listens patiently to the woman's story, murmurs polite yet non-committal things, and finally jots down Crazy Woman's name and her address and phone number, which is outer London.

'Yes, someone will get back to you,' Marie promises. 'Yes, I can see how disappointing that must have been. No, no trouble at all.'

Jesus, it's more like handling a call to the Samaritans than a reader inquiry. At least Crazy Woman sounds a bit calmer by the time Marie puts down the phone. With any luck, that will be the last they hear from her.

Marie reaches into her bag and finds her make-up. At the age of twenty-nine and eleven twelfths, Marie O'Donnell is still young, but old enough to know that youth will not last forever. And youth is what counts in her business. Junior staff who can barely write their name with a stick are now regularly promoted to editors' chairs since the powers that be have decided that it is no longer good enough to be able to attract readers; the editor needs to *be* the reader—young, single and sexy. Marie is still single

243

herself. Too busy working and having fun with her girlfriends, whenever she can get away from the office. Like other women of her generation, Marie has told herself that love can wait. Love is out there in a holding pattern, flying around in the wide blue yonder, until the day she radios up to say she has a landing slot available. (This is the cruellest delusion of her generation, the idea that you can dictate to love, can schedule its arrivals and departures. Love has its own timetable.)

With a practised hand Marie begins to smooth on the new Chanel foundation using the tips of her fingers in light, feathery strokes. Then her favourite coral lipstick. One application with a brush, blot with tissue; then a second application so it will last: the way the magazines taught her to do it when she was the age that her readers are now. So near and yet so far, Marie's own volcanic teenage years. She wouldn't go back to being thirteen again if you paid her a million pounds.

*　　　*　　　*

The boardroom of Nightingale Publishing is on the seventh floor, with a spectacular 180-degree view of the river. The Boss is over by the window, wrestling with the new blind, when he sees Marie come in. The Thames, normally a livid rat-grey, is a strange churny brown this morning, as though someone has poured hot chocolate into it overnight. The road which runs along the other side of the river, guaranteed to be an unbroken metal strip of fuming vehicles, is almost empty. Three red buses move along it like toys being pulled by a string. Beyond, through a gap in the

244

office blocks, is the cathedral. Incredible, the Boss thinks, that after all the years working in this building he has never tired of looking at the dome of St Paul's. When he hears a vicar on the radio talking about God's grace, it's always the dome that comes to mind.

He turns round to see his staff taking their seats at the long wooden table. Recently the subject of a major redesign, Nightingale's boardroom is now a symphony in teak and glass, with various chubby figurines set into the panelling in small, spotlit alcoves. Probably got a job lot from some bargain Buddha supplier, the Boss suspects. Total waste of money, but the advertisers expect you to look up to the minute—and they're paying. If the statues are meant to give an impression of divine wisdom and tranquillity, it's a failure, he thinks. What the bargain Buddhas most resemble are those Teletubbies who have just waddled onto kids' TV.

The Boss sets his pen and notebook on the table and inspects his management team. They're all here, the group's editors, sitting on chairs as heavy as thrones. Greg Chisholm, the Tiggerish head of PR who is always three years behind Elton John in his choice of statement specs, is next to Declan Walsh, the creative director. Declan, who was once in a boy band himself, comes off the production line in that factory which manufactures lovable Irish rogues. Between Declan and Sasha Harper sits Wendy, whose magazine is aimed at hassled mid-market mums. Bit of a witterer, Wendy, but superb at her job.

Opposite Wendy sits the immaculate Louisa Becks, a distant cousin of the Queen. Her *Better You* title is picking up affluent readers among working women who can afford to fund an extended youth that takes in yoga vacations and 'me time' spent in the warm embrace of a full-body mud pack. Whenever the Boss talks to Louisa, he gets the feeling that it is she who is granting him an audience, not the other way round. It's a class thing, he reckons. Despite the Armani suit and the corner office, he is still the lower-middle-class boy who would only have encountered Louisa's family home on his paper round.

Along from Louisa, sporting identical buzz cuts and Gucci leather pants, are Gavin and Matthew. The men's market is more straightforward than the women's. There are mags for guys who like sport, drink, cars, gadgets, girls and can read—a minority increasingly as specialised as orchid growers. And there are magazines for guys who like sport, drink, cars, gadgets and cannot read, but simply want to stare at girls' breasts. Gavin does the former and Matthew the latter, and, though the Boss is aware they long to swap, he reckons they stay more motivated where they are.

Marie, the Boss's favourite editor, looks tired today, her Celtic pallor even paler than usual. As Marie nods and smiles at him, he wonders vaguely if she could be pregnant. If she were, which would win out: her Catholicism or her ambition? He would hate to lose her. She's the only one who reminds him of his younger self.

With his back to the window and St Paul's just visible over his right shoulder, the Boss asks the editor of *Babe* to get the ball rolling. Using a Silk Cut as punctuation, Sasha launches into an impassioned, jabbing speech about how *Babe* has total ownership of teen sex.

'We own teen sex in the way that *PowerPlay* owns testosterone,' she says.

According to Sasha, *Babe* is saturating the teen celebrity gossip market, and with another big push it will soon be market leader.

'We've got something really hot coming up on this new girl called Britney,' she promises.

'And where does teen-sex saturation leave good old-fashioned romantic yearning?' asks the Boss with a sardonic smile, which always keeps his staff guessing whether he is joking.

This is Marie's cue and she leaps in. 'Well, personally, I think that girls will always fantasise about boys they regard as heroes and will always want to know about the minutiae of their daily life. Society may have become more explicit about sex, but the letters I get from girls tell me that their concerns are pretty unchanging.'

'What kind of concerns?' the Boss asks.

'Oh, um, desperate to be loved, my boyfriend thinks I'm ugly, I'm scared my nipples are lopsided.'

Marie is rewarded with a big laugh around the table, and even the Boss smiles.

'Do I detect you fighting a brave, if lonely rearguard action against premature sexualisation, Miss O'Donnell?'

She flushes. 'I'm just not sure that my *Teengirl* reader wants specifics on blow-jobs before she's even had her first kiss.'

She is no longer sure that's the truth, in fact she fears the opposite may well be the case, but Marie says it anyway because she wants it to be true. If it isn't true, what has happened to young girls? They'd started acting like boys, once they were told they were equal, but someone forgot to tell them they

247

weren't cut out to be male; they didn't have the heart for it. Or too much heart, perhaps.

'I agree with Marie,' says Gavin. 'Puppy love is still out there.'

'And barking mad,' says Declan.

'For me,' Gavin goes on, 'the really big trend right now is nostalgia. It's an end-of-the-fuckin'-century thing, innit?'

He drops hurriedly into a kind of cockney matespeak to see off any charges of being a pretentious wanker. It is Gavin's bad luck that, in the strenuously egalitarian times in which they live, a first in History from Oxford is considered more of a professional liability than a coke habit.

'*Fin de siècle*,' adds Louisa, almost to herself.

'We're seeing a lot of acts from the past re-forming,' Gavin says. 'There's a huge appetite for the Way We Were features in fashion, music, movies, whatever.'

Marie laughs rather too loudly and the others stare at her. 'Don't talk to me about nostalgia,' she says. 'I had this crazy woman on the phone first thing. Says she won some big David Cassidy quiz and she asked if she can collect her prize.'

'What prize?' asks Sasha, making sure Marie's isn't the only voice being heard. She glances up at the Boss, but he is looking away and frowning at something.

Marie can feel her face reddening under her all-day cover foundation. Stress eczema playing up again. 'You won't believe this, right. A trip for two, the crazy lady and her friend, to meet David Cassidy on the set of *The Partridge Family*, which ended in like 600 BC.'

The room explodes in delighted, jeering laughter.

'Whatever happened to Cassidy, anyway?' asks Matthew.

'He still does a show in Vegas, and the odd reunion concert,' says Louisa.

'He was a gorgeous kid,' says Declan. 'Remember that nude shot of him on the cover of *Rolling Stone*? Early seventies? Poor bastard was trying to shed his goody-goody image, but they wouldn't let their teen idols break out of the box 'cos they're too valuable as they are. How old is our mad lady caller, anyway?'

Marie isn't sure.

'Well,' says Louisa, 'I was a Donny Osmond girl and David girls tended to be slightly older than us. So, let's say she's thirty-seven, thirty-eight.'

'Fokkin' hell, Louisa,' says Declan appreciatively. 'You were a Donny girl?'

She smiles dreamily. 'Oh, I absolutely adored him. I bunked off school with a bunch of girls to stand outside the Churchill Hotel where the Osmonds were staying. Fabulous. Candida Hancock got one of his sheets.'

There is a polite, but bewildered silence, which is broken by Greg. 'Wasn't Donny the toothy wet one in the purple cap?'

'He's wearing awfully well,' says Louisa loyally. 'Fantastic on Terry Wogan.'

'I was sort of a David fan,' Wendy says cautiously. She's wary of revealing her exact age among younger colleagues, but she feels some ancient memory begin to stir inside her, like a hibernating animal which senses spring is come again. In fact, Wendy Petrie of Margate, as she then was, attended two Cassidy concerts at Wembley, the twin peaks of her adolescence, and, for eighteen feverish months, she went to sleep every night with the David Love Kit under her pillow.

'He had the most loyal fan base of all,' she continues, 'bigger than Elvis or even the Beatles. My mate Paula still says she married a man called David Connor because he was American and had the same initials.'

Marie is looking at the Boss. He's always so hard to read. What the hell does he think of them prattling on about shit like this? She isn't even sure how old he is. Early forties? She knows he got divorced from some City high-flyer and that he made a mint years ago when he sold the proprietor on the idea of a new music mag aimed at teenage girls. Marie guesses that her employer might not be quite what he seems. Some men wore suits as if the suit defined who they were; the Boss wore his like he was just loaning his lean frame to the suit until he got a better offer. He reminds Marie of some actor, if only her poor bruised brain could fish up the name. In that Michelle Pfeiffer film she loves, *The Fabulous Baker Boys*. It would come to her.

'The thing about the teen idol,' Louisa is saying, 'is he morphs through time. The boys' faces and names change, but the emotional need they fulfil, well, that never changes.'

'I think,' the Boss says at last, so quietly that they all have to shut up and listen to be able to hear him. It's an old schoolteacher's trick. 'I think that we may be able to do something with this. Huge potential identification among David Cassidy fans and anyone else who remembers their own tender feelings for a pop idol. I suspect this is one for your readers, Wendy. Has our crazy woman got a name, Marie?'

'It was unusual, foreign. Petra, I think.'

He nods and squiggles a note in his notebook.

250

'Right, how about we get Petra in, give her the complete makeover treatment, then fly her to Vegas for a Cassidy show, line up a meeting between the two of them. Fix that with Cassidy's people, will you, Greg?' It's a command, not a question.

'Sure. Hey, I *love* it,' says Greg, waving his specs in the air. The cherry-red frames are the size of cheese plates. 'It's like one of those Japanese soldiers comes out of the jungle and he doesn't know the war's been over for forty years. Real time-capsule stuff. The tabloids will love it. "Mum Claims Teen Idol Prize. At Long Last Love!"'

'So, Cinderella, you *shall* go to the ball,' exclaims Matthew.

'Yeah, only twenty-five years late and two stone heavier,' says Marie, whose own faith in Prince Charming is in a bad state of repair.

'Great human interest,' smirks Declan, 'so long as Crazy Lady isn't some bunny boiler who thinks Daaay-vidd is going to tear off her Country Casuals and jump in the sack with her.'

'Shut up,' says Marie, suddenly feeling protective of Crazy Lady. The woman's voice had had a serrated edge of despair to it.

'And the friend,' says the Boss, who is pursuing his own train of thought, far away from the others now. 'The long-lost friend, she might be good value. I wonder if we can dig up the Cassidy quiz.'

His bewildered underlings make respectful noises and start to pick up their files and their cigarettes.

Marie is grateful now that she answered the phone. Declan was right; they just have to hope that Crazy Lady is presentable, not too many cat hairs. Airbrushing can work wonders these days, but there are limits. And David Cassidy, she'd forgotten about

251

him. Is he sane and nice or damaged goods like so many of those poor bastards who found fame young?

The Boss holds the boardroom door open for her. They walk together down the corridor in silence until suddenly he says: 'You know, Marie, there's a lot to be said for the midlife crisis. People are often at their best during a crisis. You see who they really are.'

Marie laughs, not sure if that's the correct response. If she didn't long for the Boss's admiration, she might be less insecure.

Through the swing doors up ahead, they see the head of marketing approaching.

'Hi, Baz, can I see you in my office for a minute?' the Boss says.

Barry gives Marie an ironic little wave, using just his fingertips.

'Sure,' he says. 'No problem, Bill.'

14

'So, what's the worst that can happen? Either you find yourself in the presence of the guy you worshipped and adored or he's a sort of pickled Liberace.'

Carrie fishes the tea-bags out of the mugs and drops them in the sink. 'Do you want milk?'

'And sugar, please.'

'Milk in tea I can just about do. Sugar is kind of against my religion as a person from San Francisco,' Carrie says, reaching for the box of Tate & Lyle, which is soggy from standing too long on the draining board. 'One lump of type 2 diabetes or two?'

Petra doesn't reply. It's the start of the working week and she is fiddling with her bow. She takes some rosin and draws the bow across it, giving a little shudder at the beginning and the end. She pulls the cello to her and makes the loudest noise she can. Lately, for some reason she has taken to playing a few bars of Led Zeppelin as a warm-up. When she was in the sixth form at school, Led Zeppelin was what all the boys who couldn't play the guitar played on the guitar. It doesn't sound all that great on the cello, but she finds the burst of aggression strangely soothing.

The rain is tapping out a furious rhythm on the windows of the centre. Inside, the two women feel as snug as if they were in the cabin of a tiny boat lit by oil lamps. The harsher the elements outside, the deeper their contentment. Carrie and Petra get a lot of client referrals from local hospitals and social services; kids from homes of scarcely credible brutality who often have an angry response to the therapy, at least at first.

'Shut yer face, woman,' one boy said to her over and over.

Karl, with a body two sizes too big for him, smashed an impressive number of percussion instruments, including a drum that, strictly speaking, should have been unbreakable. Such cases have lost their power to shock her. If you've never known harmony in your brief life and your days lack any rhythm because your drug-addict parents keep such strange hours, why wouldn't you take it out on a snare drum? Many of the children Petra sees have severe learning difficulties.

'Your nutters.' That's what Marcus called them. 'For God's sake, Petra, why are you wasting your talent on those nutters?'

Let me in, let *me in*, the rain taps irritably on the windows. The staffroom overlooks a small park, really a picnic rug of grass that functions as the local dog toilet. When people in London talk about green spaces it makes Petra laugh. If you come from South Wales, the grass on the other side never looks greener; it always looks yellow, or shitty brown. As she gets older, she finds she suffers more from *hiraeth*; a word with no exact equivalent in English, it means a powerful yearning for the place you came from. She has lived in London longer than she lived in Wales, more than half her life, yet there is some stubborn part of her that prevents her calling this city home. The *hiraeth* feels like an extra muscle of the heart that contracts painfully whenever she thinks of the hills and of the rain falling in a curtain over the sea.

It is supposed to be summer, but the south of England has been hit by freak floods. In London, it has been raining so continuously that you only notice the deluge on the rare occasions that it stops. Dogshit Park has become a lake of mud.

Carrie passes Petra her mug of tea and a packet of fig rolls, which have become the women's private joke and their public addiction. Petra takes two and breaks one in half before biting into the figgy ooze.

'Hey, since you got back from Wales you've been inhaling sweet things?'

Carrie's drawl swoops up at the end of the sentence, turning every statement into a question. It's an inflection the Welshwoman and the Californian have in common.

'Stress,' Petra says lightly. 'Death, divorce and what's the third thing that's meant to be one of the most stressful life events?'

'David?' asks Carrie.

'You're just jealous.'

'Jealous? Of you going to Vegas to meet *David Cassidy*?' Carrie shakes her sleek grey head and her hoop earrings tinkle with silvery mirth. 'C'mon, I wouldn't have given David a suck of my ice pop. I was a Bobby Sherman girl.'

'Who's Bobby Sherman?'

'Oh. Just the fluffiest, cutest-smiled, swingiest-hipped, hottest teen idol who ever lived, that's all.'

'*Bobby Sherman*?' Petra speaks the name with the incredulous condescension that the true believer reserves for any teen idol besides her own. 'How many fans did *he* have then?'

'Just thirty million plus me and Marge Simpson,' says Carrie.

Petra sets down her bow and checks her watch.

255

Nearly time for her next session. She must pop to the loo first; you never leave a class in the middle, it breaks the spell.

'Marge Simpson had a crush on Bobby Sherman? I thought she was a cartoon character.'

'They're all cartoon characters, Petra, my dear, that's the point. Bobby was my psychic pocket just like David was yours.'

'Psychic what?'

Before she specialised in music therapy and followed her husband, Don, to England, first to Oxford and then London, Carrie had trained as a Jungian analyst. In general, she speaks English around the centre, but sometimes she drops one of her more obscure psychoanalytical terms into the conversation. Petra studies her friend fondly. She can see that Carrie is about to launch into one of those melodious explanations that drop from her lips like a waterfall. Rangy and athletic, Carrie looks like she was born with a golden tan and hiking boots. With her clear blue eyes and cinnamon sprinkling of freckles over nose and cheeks, she could be Robert Redford's sister. Blessed with thick silver hair that somehow looks chic instead of elderly, she seems ageless and enviably self-possessed. At weekends, she loves to climb cliffs, and she is just as nimble at finding the mental toe- and hand-holds to get you through a difficult patch. Carrie has two grown-up daughters, one a junior doctor, the other on a permanent gap year, and she has been a lighthouse for Petra as she attempts to navigate Molly's teenage storms; they start early these days. Twelve is the new sixteen. She knows she would be lost without the older woman's relaxed assurances that bitter rows and equally savage silences are completely normal.

256

Once or twice lately, Molly has even made Petra cry.

'What d'you expect? She's a teenager. Put on earth to test the theory that maternal love can withstand any amount of shit.'

Petra envies Carrie; or rather, she wants to *be* her, to know what it feels like to live in a mind and body that certain and true. Compared to Carrie, Petra feels she is still driving with emotional L-plates. Her mother's death was such a shock. Not the fact of Greta dying; it was obvious for months that not even her mother could stare down the cancer, which had moved, without mercy, from organ to organ like an advancing army. No, it was the fact that Petra hadn't expected to feel like an *orphan*. Not at the age of thirty-eight. Not when she was an adult. Nonetheless, orphaned is what she feels. Grief for her dad has surfaced again through the grave he now shares with her mother. She manages to be glad that neither parent lived to see the break-up of her marriage. Since Marcus left, Petra likes to sit near Carrie in the staffroom, the way animals lie beside each other in a stable.

'Psychic pocket,' Carrie elaborates, 'it's like the basket into which you put all your needs and longings.'

Petra frowns. 'Isn't that called love?'

'No, it's pure fantasy. Very common, but also hopeless and inappropriate.'

'Sounds like love to me,' says Petra picking up her cello and manoeuvring it into the case. 'Hopeless and inappropriate at love. I have a degree in that.'

At the door, she remembers something and turns back to Carrie, who is busily scouring a cup with a brush. 'Why did you have to say that stuff about pickled Liberace? You know that's all I'm going to

257

be able to think about when I go and see David. You're supposed to be supportive. As my friend.'

'As your friend,' says Carrie, 'I'm not here to make you feel better. I'm here to feel envious and competitive and subtly undermine you while pretending to be real sympathetic.'

'Oh thanks. You, you—' Petra stammers towards the insult—'you *therapist,*' she finally spits out. Laughter makes her body feel better. Her shoulder has been playing up lately and she winces as she lifts the cello through the doorway.

The room she works in is a couple of doors down the corridor. Bare and tranquil with pale, clackety wooden floors, it has bulbous, pod-like windows set in the ceiling. After dragging the instruments from the wall and setting them up on a table in the middle, Petra takes a seat at the keyboard and starts to play a few chords. On the flat roof above her, the rain creates a percussive hiss; it sounds more like static on the radio than water. Why is rain so comforting when you're miserable and so damned annoying when you're not?

As her fingers fall into formation over the notes, through the static a woman's voice comes to her unbidden, one of the most beautiful voices she's ever known. It is no strain to recall the song the woman is singing, no strain at all. Petra hums the intro and hears the woman come in on an impossibly low B flat, a man's note really. A woman had no business being able to sing that well that low.

'Talking to myself and feeling old.'

She and Sharon used to sing it together. When they first learned those words they were so young, babies; they couldn't know. How could they possibly have known? What do thirteen-year-olds know

258

about feeling old?

'Rainy Days and Mondays'. Luxuriating in the song's sadness, Petra surprises herself by launching with sudden gusto into the saxophone solo. That shot of brass in the middle of such a melancholy tune, it shouldn't work, but somehow it does. Respectfully, she doffs her musician's cap to Richard Carpenter. How well she remembers the chocolate-brown cover of the album and that ornate rococo lettering. Was it really gold? The Carpenters were supposed to be cheesy, a taste you kept to yourself she learned much later at college, but their melodies had outlived nearly all their cooler contemporaries. Far more complex harmonies, with words that felt like they sprang naturally from the tune.

She and Sharon used to love harmonising on 'Close to You'. Petra took the tune and Sha did all the *waaaa-aah-ar-ahhh* bits.

Karen Carpenter, lost to anorexia at—what, thirty-two? Such a stupid waste. Petra sees that beautiful face, framed by jubilant brown curls. Critics called Karen's face cherubic so the poor woman must have decided to starve it. Her cheeks were just bonny, that's all. Karen's voice had no strain in it whatsoever, no gear change; it moved from low to high as though a voice travelled through liquid, not air. Who else could do that? Ella, Barbra. Not many in pop, that's for sure.

How she had longed for a dress she saw Karen Carpenter wearing in *Jackie*. Petra can remember it now, remember it far better than most of the clothes she actually owned. Long, frothy cream cheesecloth, with a high neck and strips of broderie anglaise down the bodice. It was the dress the sisters in *Little House on the Prairie* wore in their dreams. Didn't Katharine

259

Ross wear the same dress on the bike with Paul Newman in *Butch Cassidy*?

Bowler hat. Paul Newman, not Katharine Ross. Now she is confused. Memory can do that to you. She is no longer sure if she is remembering things as they were or as she'd wanted them to be.

She must tell Carrie; she's bound to detect some hidden meaning in that long cream dress with its hint of bridal chastity. When they first met, Petra had been quietly appalled by the American's habit of treating her like a puzzle that needed solving. She was too Welsh to feel entirely at ease with the way Carrie picked over even the most minor detail of her life, hunting for clues. Petra's bad headaches were just migraines, for God's sake, not a sign of a crippling inability to assert herself in her marriage, as Carrie had suggested. One day over lunch in their local cafe, Petra mentioned a thank-you letter which had arrived from her mother that morning. Coming from Greta, it was a no-thanks thank-you letter. Only her mother could express gratitude without sounding in the smallest bit appreciative. Reading the letter a second time, Petra felt what small reserves of confidence she had deflating, as though her soul had a slow puncture.

'Well, what d'you expect? Your mom's such a bitch,' Carrie said mildly, spearing a gherkin.

It was like a shotgun going off. The volume of the world changed. A fork that a woman put down on the neighbouring table reverberated like a timpani section.

Who dared to call her mother a bitch? It had never occurred to her that she, Petra, was allowed to judge Greta. It was Greta who judged Petra and found her wanting, not the other way round.

'What d'you think, that you have to be the good girl forever?' Carrie said as she settled the bill. She was such a generous tipper that waiters regarded her with suspicion. Petra didn't answer. For a few seconds, no more than that, she allowed Carrie's suggestion to live in her brain, and then she banished it, like a wiper clearing a windscreen.

Just the once, she had seen Karen Carpenter on a TV chat show; it must have been only months before she died. The singer laughed off the question about her weight loss. Denied it, charmingly, with that nicest-girl-in-the-school grin of hers. Then she walked across the studio and sang. Even when her body was gaunt and she had twigs for arms, the voice still poured out like cream from a jug. The voice didn't know it was living inside the body of a starving child, and maybe Karen Carpenter didn't either. There were things about yourself that you couldn't know, sometimes until it was too late.

Petra picks up the glockenspiel. Its glittering, wintry sound is a particular favourite of Sam's. With a beater, she plays the tune they always use to say hello.

Sam should be here by now. The boy has a thing about not stepping in puddles or on the cracks in the pavement, his legs go stiff and he lifts them high like a Nazi storm trooper. Petra sighs. Elspeth, his mother, must be having a hell of a job getting him here in this rain.

So many fears once you have children in the world. Every night, Petra goes in to kiss Molly when she is asleep and she feels simple gratitude and relief that her baby has survived this long. Anorexia, which killed Karen Carpenter, is her biggest fear for Molly. Petra doesn't remember it being such a big thing

261

when she was at school; now, extreme thinness has become yet another way to compete with each other. Trust girls to get into a contest to make themselves disappear. She doesn't want Molly to waste her life hating her body. Too much female energy goes into getting smaller instead of bigger and bolder. Petra switches off the keyboard and rubs her sore shoulder. She has always been harshly critical of her own body, even when there was nothing to find fault with. Now that there is plenty to despair of, Petra looks back in frank astonishment at the girl who skulked about in long, droopy cardigans, even in the thermometer-busting summer of '76, because she was under the impression she had fat thighs. Why the hell didn't she walk down the street waving a placard saying 'I HAVE A 24-INCH WAIST'? That's what she should have done.

There is a sound of two hands banging on the door and Sam's excited puppy yelp. Petra turns to welcome her client.

*   *   *

She has almost no memory of ringing the magazine company. It is the one small consolation in a sea of churning embarrassment. Blaming alcohol would be her best bet, but it had only been eight in the morning when she made the call. Things have got quite dark for Petra lately, especially during that 3 a.m. dread hour when she wakes to find all her fears congregated at the foot of the bed, offering to run a trailer of forthcoming disasters. Maybe she will lose the house. Maybe Molly will love her father's new girlfriend and find the houseboat a cooler place to stay than her mother's centrally

262

heated suburban home. She knows that Marcus, who claims he is too broke to pay her maintenance, somehow manages to find the cash to lavish treats on Molly. Butterscotch milkshake and sponge cake, enjoyed by father and daughter in Fortnum & Mason's over half-term, must have cost about a third of her weekly food budget; the thought rankles like a broken tooth. So does the fact that, as Mol let slip, Marcus swore her to secrecy; making Molly his gleeful co-conspirator against wicked, thrifty Mummy. Even so, Petra has no excuse for ringing a place that doesn't exist at eight o'clock in the morning like a crazy old bat.

To say the action was out of character doesn't quite cover the personality shift it required for Petra to ring up Nightingale Publishing. On the computer, she'd managed to find out that, in the late eighties, Nightingale bought out Worldwind Publishing, which, almost a quarter of a century ago, had declared her the winner of The Ultimate David Cassidy Quiz.

'How old did you say you were?' the woman who answered the phone had asked.

The woman said she was the editor of a magazine—*Teenworld*?—and she had been nice, more than nice, actually, but Petra could tell from the strenuously patient way she spoke, as though she were addressing either someone very old or very young, that the editor thought Petra was a loony time-waster. A view with which Petra had considerable sympathy. Still, stubborn as a child denied a balloon at its own party, she stood her ground. 'I won,' she explained.

As a teenager, she had been unable to see things far away. Recently, things close up have also started

263

to become a blur. Glasses have lost the four-eyed stigma they had had when she was a child. Molly declares that specs are hot, or perhaps cool. Petra can't keep up with the temperature that is in fashion. Nevertheless, she comes from a generation that can't quite shrug off the sense that specs make her undesirable. Reading glasses, even if they now come in a sleek dark frame that Carrie swears make her look like Ali MacGraw in *Love Story*, are further unwanted evidence that her body is in the business of betraying her. If she's honest, there is also some niggling worry about a life that has not quite come into focus, and maybe it never will.

'What became of her, then?' Sharon had asked about a girl from the old days when they talked after her mother's funeral.

'What became of me?' Petra had thought, though not said. She thinks it a lot lately. Petra Williams, what on earth happened to her?

Childhood had felt as if it was going to last forever. A single Sabbath was like a month of Sundays. Once she left home, went to study music in London, started making her own decisions, got married to Marcus, things speeded up. The years passed like water through your fingers, especially once you had a child and started to live for someone else. These days, another Christmas seemed to arrive just as she'd put the decorations from the previous year back in the loft. Dad died when he was sixty-four; she was over halfway there and she had barely got started. If she and Sharon had taken that trip to Los Angeles in 1974 and met David, life might have worked out differently. There was someone else out there she had been destined to be, and she'd never met that person because her mother didn't hand over the pink envelope. So Petra swallowed her pride, rang the magazine company and asked nicely for her prize.

Now, she balls her fists into her eye sockets till the dark screen of vision is filled with stars. Petra has done plenty of shaming things before, but never has she made a fool of herself quite like this. Her dreams of escape, and there have been many, have stayed locked firmly inside her own head. She has gone to the cinema and seen men up on the screen that she fell in love with, and sometimes she has taken those men home to her bed. It was such a comfort when your troubles were piling up, to be able to lose them all in the arms of Jeff Bridges.

'Hey, don't worry, baby,' Jeff would say with a shake of that leonine head and then he'd kiss your troubles away. But the Jeffs were illusions made from wishing. You didn't actually want Jeff Bridges to take you to Tesco and help you pick out your fruit and veg, did you?

Now she was going to meet David Cassidy, the illusion of illusions, suddenly made flesh, years after giving up the ghost. Carrie said that death and grief could have a disinhibiting effect. Loss made you trigger-happy.

Trigger-*unhappy*, Petra thinks. What made her make that call? Was it the misery of Marcus finally leaving, like a low, cramping period pain? Was it sprawling like a stunned starfish in the marital bed and realising that she liked to sleep on her back, rather than in the scrunched foetal position she had adopted every night for fifteen years to give her husband the space he needed? Was it fear that no one would ever want to have sex with her again; or was it the greater, though related, anxiety that she

265

could never bear to undress in front of a man who wasn't her husband? She couldn't imagine being looked at without the protective gauze of indifferent familiarity. The day after her mother's funeral, she went to the grocer's down the hill from her parents' house and Gwennie behind the till peered at her for what felt like a full ten minutes before saying, with dawning recognition: 'Oh, *there* we are. You were Gillian Edwards's little friend, weren't you?'

Perhaps she had been little, but no one was going to call her a friend of Gillian's. The years had dimmed and soothed many hurts, but the name Gillian—even when it came attached to a perfectly nice woman—still caused her stomach to curdle with dislike. It was unfair the way that a name could never be rinsed clean of the stain of an early hatred. All her life, Petra would approach any new Gillian like a bomb-disposal expert, primed for devastation.

So successfully did she repress the memory of that foolish phone call that she was genuinely surprised when a woman called Wendy rang from *Women's Lives* to say she wanted to do a feature on Petra going to meet her teen idol. These days, David Cassidy was doing a show in Las Vegas. Nightingale Publishing would fly Petra to Vegas, all expenses paid, and she would finally get a chance to meet her hero. Oh, and her friend could go too, the one she had entered the competition with. Did they both mind coming in for a makeover to head office? New haircut, make-up. Refresh your image, said Wendy. Everyone's look got a bit tired, didn't it? Most readers found it a really fun day out and picked up lots of useful beauty tips.

Petra, who had stopped listening after the all-expenses-paid part, said thank you, it sounded wonderful. Replacing the phone in its cradle above the cat's bowl, she felt afloat with a sense of possibility.

Not everyone shared her keen sense of anticipation.

'Tragic,' was how Molly described it, momentarily removing the Sony Discman to which she was umbilically connected. Petra explained hesitantly that the magazine had rung with a date for the 'makeover'. She found herself holding the word at arm's length, as though in a pair of tweezers. She had only a dim idea of what a 'makeover' would involve. Over the years, she must have seen thousands of Before and After pictures in magazines and sometimes wondered how the women fared when they took their glossy new haircuts, prettily accented features and rediscovered cheekbones home to their husbands. What did the New You do with the old man, and vice versa?

'Sad, Mum, saaa-d,' said Molly. 'You had a crush on him when you were my age. Most girls don't like the same boy three weeks later. This is, like, twenty years.'

Standing at the kitchen counter, preparing Molly's favourite penne pasta, Petra gives the grater a sharp tap with a knife, so the trapped Parmesan falls onto the plate in a little landslide of pollen. As she transfers the grated cheese to a bowl and sets it on the table, she tries to explain that this is not about a teenage crush. It probably isn't even about David Cassidy, not really. It's about her, Petra: the mother formerly known as cellist. The urge to claim her silly prize is as powerful as the need to swallow or urinate. She desperately wants to find a way of telling Molly this, but the girl has already pulled on her

267

headphones, listening to Destiny's Child or Robbie Williams; going back to that private musical universe where she is happy and her parents are not getting divorced.

'Embarrassing and tacky', was her husband's verdict when he came round to pick up Molly. They were standing by the open front door, Petra inside the house twiddling with the latch, Marcus shuffling on the doormat, as though he had better places to be. In this new Cold War, the doorstep with its grubby sisal mat has become their Checkpoint Charlie, the place where Molly gets handed over to the other side. Each time, Petra senses the profound unnaturalness of the exchange, and wonders how long before it will feel normal to share her child, to divvy her up like a pie. The civilised arrangement, the one suggested by the glossy magazines, is hard to reconcile with the primitive tug in her guts that tells her not to hand over her daughter and the violent desire to snatch her back again.

At the mention of the name David Cassidy, Marcus actually whinnied with distress, like a thoroughbred that finds itself entered by mistake in a donkey derby. Bad taste of any kind was a source of almost physical discomfort to him. Marcus shared Greta's contempt for pop music and its brain-rotting properties. Privately, he also had his suspicions that Petra's trip down memory lane was an attempt to get back at him for moving onto the boat with Susie, an act simultaneously so hurtful and destructive that someone else had to be blamed for it.

'Christ, Petra, are you having some kind of midlife crisis?' said Marcus.

Pot, kettle, black, thought Petra. Who's having the midlife crisis, mister?

Her mother had prevented her going to meet David almost a quarter of a century ago. Now her husband despised her for it and her daughter said she was sad, which meant tragic, which meant pathetic or laughable, not sad, though sad was indeed what Petra was.

'So, you gotta go, right?' Carrie concluded briskly during one of their tea-breaks. Carrie hands her the last fig roll in the packet and points out that the Cassidy Vegas trip has all the ingredients of a very promising rebellion.

'Aren't they supposed to be for teenagers?' Petra asks dubiously.

Carrie shook her head. 'Listen, hon, rebellions are wasted on the young. What the hell have they got to rebel against? You and I, on the other hand, have a wide range of frustrations, disappointments and resentments, carefully accumulated over many decades. To my mind, the least we deserve is a little catharsis.'

Petra laughs loudly, though without conviction. Why hadn't she rebelled against her mother? Fear, obviously. Dread. But it was more than that; she had felt paralysed, unable to assert herself. Unable to locate a self to assert, that was it. Petra had experienced something like hatred for her mother's irrational outbursts of temper at her father, had sensed the awful unfairness of Dad being punished, not for who he was, but for who he wasn't. But there was nothing she could do to help him, or to help herself, that wouldn't make it ten times worse. So she withdrew into her music, which muffled the distant sounds of battle.

Now, in her own home, when Molly yells from the top of the stairs, demanding some missing item of

269

laundry or tells her mum she just doesn't get it, Petra tries to be glad.

You have a child who can call you an idiot and say that she hates you, secure in the knowledge she will still be loved, Petra tells herself.

It feels like progress, of a kind.

*   *   *

In her marriage, Petra played second fiddle to her husband, which was funny when you came to think about it. Second fiddle. Technically, as a cellist she was his equal. At college, they had vied for the same prizes, though Marcus always had the edge in drive and ambition. Anyway, it didn't really matter because she worshipped him and she was delighted and astonished to be loved in return by such a man, such a catch. A son-in-law who practically made her mother swoon with approval. At the wedding, it was Greta who mouthed 'I do' first.

She heard Marcus before she saw him. Exploring the college basement during her first term, looking for the coffee machine, she found herself in a long corridor lined with practice-rooms which had portholes set high in the dark wood doors. As she waited for the thin, tawny liquid to fill the plastic cup, the sound of a cello came from the room opposite. She stopped dead, seeking to place it. Yes. Chopin. Introduction and Polonaise, early Chopin. 'Drawing-room stuff,' one lofty fellow student had said to her once, tossing his hair, and she had thought: 'Not in my drawing room, mate.' Wished she had said it to his face. Not that he would have understood; he couldn't imagine a world where there were no drawing rooms. A world like hers.

270

And now, here it was again; shorn of the piano accompaniment, played naked on a damp Tuesday morning, with rain in the air outside. Just the kind of morning that was crying out for Chopin to come and rescue it. Who was playing? Her fingers tingled. Odd reaction, not so very far away from lust. A chord of different feelings: admiration, curiosity, the faintest touch of envy. The best musicians answer something in you when you don't even know the question. Petra couldn't resist. She walked up to the door and, on tiptoe, peered in through the porthole, like one passenger on a ship pursuing another. Marcus was sitting, half facing in her direction, head bowed, bow sweeping, eyes half lowered or closed, she couldn't tell. When he finished he opened them and looked straight at her, as if he knew she'd been watching. Probably had, the fiend. His lips were slightly parted, and he looked out of breath. It was to be another four years before she felt those lips on hers. Four years between the introduction and the polonaise. Dance with me.

Petra had other boyfriends in the meantime. All of them English, all of them out of reach. Top drawer. They were amused by her accent and, in the pub, they did impersonations of a cartoon way of speaking she had never heard.

'Well, look you, there's lovely, boyo.'

Boyo?

The proud daughter of a self-improver who swore by 'It Pays to Increase Your Word Power' Petra had never heard such a thing, let alone said it. To her ear, this sing-song mimic sounded not Welsh but Indian, though, like a good sport, she laughed anyway and accepted another shandy. Colluding with what other people thought about you felt easier than explaining

271

who you really were. The more English, the more cultured and the more alien the men, the more Petra wanted them. Getting the emotionally unavailable public schoolboy to become available to her, the girl from Gower, that was what gave her the special jazzed-up feeling, the feeling she craved. She hoarded their protestations of love like other girls hoarded jewels. Where was the thrill in conquering those who wanted you? She couldn't see the point. Pain and joy braided tightly together, that was what Petra craved. And no one played that tune as well as Marcus.

Oh yes, he had strummed her pain with his fingers, all right. Killed Petra with his song.

'Well, that's one of the most desirable properties off the market,' sighed Jessica, the viola player in her quartet, when Petra showed her the ring Marcus had given her in Florence. An emerald jealously guarded by two diamonds. The envy of other women sealed her happiness. She had never been the object of envy before and she noticed how it could fill you up, the same way thirsty flowers took in water. How had she, Petra, managed to win the unobtainable man? She felt blessed; better still she felt *chosen*. So the rest didn't matter. Second fiddle was the instrument she had always been destined to play, some small voice inside told her that. Besides, it was only practical; you couldn't really have two professional cellists in one house. So Marcus built his career on the public platform and, after a few well-received solo appearances, Petra began to scratch a living in the cracks—concerts with the quartet, session work, teaching. She did several lucrative stints as a backing instrumentalist on *Top of the Pops*, playing, as requested, in a short black skirt, which was meant to

272

look sexy, but ended up gynaecological when your instrument was gripped between splayed knees.

Marcus took out a bank loan to pay for a part-share in a very valuable cello to use in recitals, and they needed her money to meet the day-to-day bills. The magazines she rarely had time to read these days had some fancy new term for what she did—portfolio career—but Petra knew what she was. Second fiddle.

Everything changed when Molly Isolde was born at twenty-nine weeks. Her daughter was the size of a gym shoe. It was June, and Petra was due to play at the Wigmore Hall that lunchtime. Borodin, Second String Quartet. She was humming the Nocturne under her breath as she hurried to make up for time lost on a train delayed at London Bridge. The heat had taken the capital by surprise, just as London was always surprised, quite predictably, every summer by the sun and every winter by the cold.

It was so damned hot, and she was breathing for two. The air struggled to reach the farthest corners of her lungs. Alveoli. She hadn't thought of the word since she'd taken Biology. Lungs were structured like trees and alveoli were the little buds on the end of the branches. They played some key role in making the oxygen, she couldn't remember what, but they weren't making it now, or not fast enough anyway. Petra was always amazed how the present and the past could be going on in your head simultaneously, like hundreds of TV channels behind your eyes. Here she was in the thrumming centre of London, yet also back in the Biology lab in South Wales, which reeked of gerbil sawdust and jars of formaldehyde.

Oxford Street was packed, the shoppers moving

slowly, torpid as carp in an overstocked pond. Petra was in a hurry so she broke off the main road and took a short cut up the small L-shaped street by the Tube where she often stopped to buy a single mango from the fruit stall. She always took it to the square behind John Lewis. Mango-eating, she firmly believed, should be a solitary activity because of the dribbling problems. So Petra was inching her way up Regent Street, manoeuvring her bump and her cello like a plumber's toolbag, when she felt the water sluicing down her legs. It wasn't just a trickle of water, it was a comedy bucketful thrown by a clown.

Embarrassment came first—she was Welsh, after all. Then panic. Fear took a little longer to kick in. A security guard outside Broadcasting House took pity on the pregnant woman crouching in a puddle on his patch of pavement. An ambulance was called and within minutes Petra was in hospital. One of the best in the city, fortunately, with a specialist premature baby unit. When they were admitted—it was definitely *they*, she already thought of the baby as a separate person—they were surrounded by broken, bloody, tear-stained bodies.

The doctor stuck in a needle, a steroid injection to encourage the baby's lungs to grow faster. Undeveloped lungs could be a problem, he was saying. Alveoli again. But baby was already on her way; there was no stopping her.

'If You let her live, God, if You will please just keep her alive, I promise . . .'

Petra began that sentence many times during Molly's first few days, but she never completed it. It seemed beyond saying, beyond any words she knew at least, how much she was prepared to promise if her baby girl could pull off the miracle of survival.

Her own life Petra would have discarded in an instant for the sake of this tiny stranger.

She never knew a place called neonatal intensive care existed; most people are lucky because they don't ever have to know. When you first go in, the unit looks a lot like a museum, except the exhibits in the glass cases are alive, or at least being kept alive by the machines, and by the fervent prayers of their parents. When Petra was wheeled in for the first time, still woozy and wearing her green hospital gown, she saw transparent box after box containing these anguished sketches of humanity. One of them was her daughter.

Shrunken, with blue eyes the size of a five-pence piece, Molly barely looked like a baby at all. Her head was not much bigger than a light bulb, and to Petra the filaments of the brain inside seemed just as fragile. The bonnet that Greta had knitted as part of a beautiful layette swamped the baby, so, for the first month, Molly wore one of the matching woollen bootees as a hat. (Petra still keeps that lucky sock in her bedside drawer; a little yellow from the passing years and shockingly small.)

She lived in the unit day and night with background music provided by the beeping and sighing of the machines. Each time the machine breathed for her, Molly's throat gave a little froggy jump. As Petra found out, you learn a lot about yourself when you're so close to that much vulnerability. You learnt that if you're tired enough, you can sleep sitting up. That the unendurable is perfectly endurable, if you just take it a minute at a time, and when the alternative is no more minutes ever with your precious child.

Each of Molly's limbs was placed inside a tiny

275

doughnut of foam to stop them rubbing on the mattress. Any pressure on a premmy's skin could be painful, the nurse said. A boy called Andy, barely out of his teens, he had spiky, gelled hair and moved in his soft shoes like a dancer. At first, Petra hardly dared touch Molly. If she held her hand next to the baby's face, though, it did seem to calm her. Petra had this overwhelming impulse to fetch her cello and play; the baby had heard the cello every day for the seven months she'd been in the womb, so like her mother she must be missing it. Instead, Petra sang to her, humming the pieces they both knew by heart, her and the baby. The Bach suites, Elgar and the Borodin she'd been working on. Petra swore that Molly tried to turn her head.

In those first few weeks, Marcus came twice a day, bringing decent sandwiches and news and, best of all, simple animal comfort. Out in the corridor, Petra stretched her legs and recharged by burying herself in his arms, smelling the Marcus smell on his jacket. She saw that he was losing weight, his blue eyes stared out from damson sockets and he had stopped shaving so that he began to look like a holy man who has visions on top of a mountain.

James, who had been best man at their wedding, visited one Sunday and told Petra that Marcus had said the two girls in his life were suffering, and he could do absolutely nothing about it. The sense of impotence was terrible to a man who had always been able to fix everything with his hands.

One October afternoon, when Molly had just reached a normal birth weight, the consultant took Marcus and Petra into a side room. On the low pine table in front of them, there was an ominous box of Kleenex. The doctor offered water, which they declined. He was a big man, but sweet-looking; both burly and curly, with a snub nose. Petra thought instantly of one of those German teddy bears that fetch thousands at auction. If you pressed the doctor's middle he might have growled.

The consultant said that Molly was doing well. They were very pleased with her. The possible effects of oxygen deprivation, which had caused them concern, were no longer such a worry. Only time would tell for sure. Research suggested that babies as premature as Molly, even if they grew normally, could suffer some shortfall of confidence in adult life. It seemed the baby could carry a memory of its difficult start. Marcus and Petra should know, the doctor said, that Molly might experience some learning difficulties.

'We're not expecting her to be Prime Minister,' Marcus snapped.

Until that moment, she didn't know how angry he was.

Did Petra train as a music therapist because she had a premature baby who could have been brain-damaged? What Petra knew was that by singing to her daughter, a newborn who looked a thousand years old, she became convinced that everything we are starts with music, that maybe music has the power to mend things that can't be mended any other way. She sang to Molly and she believed the baby heard her song, that's all.

*   *   *

A few days after Petra and the baby got home, Marcus told her that he'd been to bed with someone else while she was in hospital. He'd been under terrific strain. Some girl in a northern orchestra, when he'd had to step in as soloist at short notice. The girl had become infatuated, clingy. It was nothing. He begged for forgiveness and Petra gave it gladly. Too quickly, she saw too late. Forgiveness needs to be earned, and thereafter, Marcus thought it was going cheap. Petra, for her part, could forgive but not forget.

The week after, her mother came up on the train to stay. She took charge of the bottles and the bedlinen and the shopping and the cooking. The house soon had the pleasant hum of a well-ordered hotel. Petra, still in her dressing-gown for long stretches of the day and leaking milk, was tearfully grateful. Greta was at the sink rinsing out the baby's bottles with a long narrow brush when Petra told her about Marcus and the affair. Maybe Molly's arrival was the opportunity to open a new chapter of intimacy and trust with her own mother.

Greta listened intently, and finally she said: 'You will have to make it up to him.'

'Make it up to him,' Petra repeated.

Her mother started fitting the teats back inside their white plastic surrounds with a rubbery snap. It was an unpleasant sound, oddly punitive.

'A man doesn't like feeling in the wrong, Petra. It makes him unhappy,' Greta said, working methodically. 'If you want to remain his wife really you will have to help him to forgive himself. Ach, it's the only way.'

The advice felt like it came from another age, one with gas lamps. Wasn't that the kind of thing women did in an era before choices? But what choice did Petra really have? She had a tiny baby and no income, she and Molly were wholly dependent on

278

Marcus's success.

This was not love as Petra had understood it, nor marriage either, but she saw that her mother's brisk advice was not simply hypocrisy, it was crude economics. She would have to make it up to Marcus for betraying her.

It would not be the last time. In an unwelcome moment of insight, Petra came to realise that, for Marcus, his affairs actually improved their marriage. He ran in late, his mistress's sweat barely dry on his body, and bent tenderly to kiss his daughter doing her homework at the kitchen table. He romanticised their vulnerability, Molly's and Petra's, their helplessness; it stopped him moving out, but neither did he stay, not really.

Many years after neonatal intensive care, Petra picked up a magazine in a dentist's waiting room and found a multiple choice quiz entitled: 'What Are Your Goals As A Mother?' It had honestly never occurred to Petra to have anything as ambitious as a goal for her child. Good health, holding close and staying alive, was what it had been about with Molly from the very start, and that never changed.

For the most part, Molly confounded the gloomy predictions about delayed development, although she never did learn to tidy her room. If I had goals for my daughter, Petra thinks, what would they be?

To feel pleasure and ease in her own body. Not to stand hot and ashamed on the beach in a prickly towel tent with sand chafing her legs. Good friends and rewarding work. A kind man to love and respect her, who will be a devoted father for her children. Not to walk around all her life with a weighted heart.

*   *   *

Love can take so long to die. You think it's dead, you think he's trashed all the feelings you ever had for him. One day, he hands over his dirty sheets to be washed, because his houseboat only has cold water, and you feel sorry for him so you're jamming them into the machine when you see that the sheets have these rusty islands on them, an archipelago of blood, her menstrual blood for Christ's sake, and you are so enraged, so humiliated that he didn't take care to spare you this fresh pain that you drop to your knees and you strike your head against the door of the washing machine. Better that you should hurt yourself than let him hurt you like this again.

This is what passes for logic when love has not died. You have sealed the chamber of the heart where the love for him used to live, sealed it in like nuclear waste, but there turns out to be another, smaller chamber where the love lives on. Stubborn, tenacious, enduring fucking love.

Why does Petra find it so hard to hate Marcus when hating him could set her free? It is the bittersweet knowledge that, if she accepts the man she has loved for so long is selfish and unkind, then the love itself may be rendered worthless. The love that brought Molly into the world, the love for which she has given up her life as a musician. A beloved child, a structure of shared friendships and obligations, birthdays, holidays spent on the Pembrokeshire coast and the Greek islands, everything that her marriage means made to look foolish and stupid and ugly.

So, stubbornly, Petra guards the love, refuses to give it up, even though the man who caused the love in the first place does everything in his power to erase it.

280

On the way to work, jostled in a crowded bus, its engine grinding and grizzling as it crests the hill, the soundtrack in her head is a wounded Joni Mitchell, singing a sad song about a love that's gone.

15

'Oh, Bill, this is Petra, today's makeover victim. Petra, this is William Finn, our editorial director.'

'Hello, Petra,' he says, holding out a hand and frowning. 'Petra as in the *Blue Peter* dog?'

'Petra as in the Baader–Meinhof terrorist,' she says.

'Ah. I stand corrected. Mind if I take a chair?'

'They're your chairs,' she says.

He perches awkwardly in the next make-up seat along from her, a padded black plastic recliner with a headrest. It reminds Bill of his dentist; after a recent episode of root-canal work, this is not a happy association. At the shattering memory of the drill, Bill begins to cross his legs, then changes his mind as he feels himself start to slide backwards. Before he knows it, they'll have one of those hideous lilac capes around his neck and twists of tinfoil in his hair.

He wonders vaguely what he can have done to offend this woman he has never met before. Even by his standards, it is quite something to cause a major chill after a single sentence. The *Blue Peter* dog line was obviously not as amusing as he'd hoped. Maybe she'd heard it before.

When readers come in for a makeover they tend to be embarrassingly grateful, gurgling with excitement at entering the HQ of a magazine that they treat themselves to in the supermarket, in order to lighten the burden of the weekly shop. Occasionally, coming down in the lift, Bill has bumped into a couple of the Before and After candidates: chirpy as canaries with their new blow-dries, they stagger out of reception with carrier bags full of freebies and a set of professional photographs, bathed in artful radiance, to astound the old man back home. Bill has always wondered exactly how well the old man will respond to the New You that women these days seem to be so keen on. As men grow older, they tend to see change as suspicious, that is if they notice it at all. Ruth used to tell him that she could switch all the furniture in their flat and he wouldn't notice, so little attention did he pay to his physical surroundings. That wasn't strictly true, although he did remember the day on which, dragging himself home after fourteen hours in the office, he poured, mixed, raised and drained an entire gin and tonic before realising that what he was drinking from was, in fact, a squat new flower vase in frosted glass from Heal's. In a panic, he threw the ice and lemon into the bin, dried the vase, and pretty much got away with his own folly, although Ruth, coming in ten minutes later with a fistful of carnations, had wondered out loud, in some puzzlement, why the glass was so cold to the touch. A narrow escape; the cretinism of the male was a subject on which women's research would never end.

Today's Before and After is a different sort of customer. Most of her predecessors have been happy to be treated as guinea pigs for a day, as long as they go home more glossy than when they arrived. This one is less of a guinea pig, more of a cat. Dark, composed and cautious. 'The Crazy Lady,' Marie had called her, but that isn't true, unless the madness is tucked away, buried very deep. Nothing ungracious in her movements, no shrieks of hilarity or whines of complaint in her voice. Hard to pin down. She seems almost to be observing the

283

makeover process at a distance, as though it were happening to someone else.

Bill wants to ask her about the quiz—*their* quiz, as he prefers to think of it. She had won it; he had compiled it, though she doesn't know that. Not yet. He is sure the news will come as a surprise, but he needs some time with Petra to work out whether that surprise would or would not be pleasant. He has a faint memory, a shadow of a memory, of Zelda telling him to put the quiz together, and to do it in haste to meet a deadline. The Ultimate David Cassidy Quiz.

'Make it hard, William dear,' Zelda had called across the office, or something like that, presumably to sniggers from the men around the room. Make it taxing enough, in other words, to sort out the hardcore fans from the mere dilettantes who were moonlighting from their dreams of Donny Osmond or David Essex. And now, here it was, unearthed, brought back into the light an epoch later, like a sword hilt from an Anglo-Saxon hoard, and no less easy to decipher. Marie couldn't find the quiz itself, but she had managed to dig up some old Cassidy material from the archive, bless her, and what struck Bill was how utterly impenetrable it was, even to someone who had once been steeped in Cassidy lore. Even to someone who, for eighteen months, had once been David himself.

Time had lent amusement, but no enchantment, to his time at Worldwind Publishing. Time in the slipstream of that squalid old shark Roy Palmer. Time with the redoubtable Zelda. Under her gentle prompting and, to be fair, her exacting standards, Bill had learned pretty much everything that had helped him to run magazines of his own. She would have been thrilled—genuinely moved, without the faintest shade of irony—to think of him reunited, now, with a devout reader of *The Essential David Cassidy Magazine*. It was Zelda who had warned him never to underestimate the primal power that the idol exerts over his fans, and here, in the chair next to him, her eyes firmly shut as her long dark hair is trimmed, sits the living proof that Zelda had been right.

How old is Petra? Bill is useless at ages. She had been a kid in 1974, that he knows for sure, so ... But it isn't about the maths. As he studies her in the mirror, Bill registers calmly and without any ignition of desire that she is beautiful. Great bones, great brown eyes, something drowsy in them even when they opened wide. A cellist, someone had said. A real musician, not like him.

Mind you, sitting and staring at her will not do. He is the host, his job is to offer welcome. Also, Bill has just decided, he is here to establish a connection, build some kind of rapport; has to, if he is serious about this Cassidy feature which is taking shape like an Airfix model in his head. Part memoir, part meditation on the phenomenon of the teenage pop idol. 'I Was the Real David Cassidy', that kind of thing. Might work well in Gavin's mag, you never know, for male readers who like to read. All three of them.

'I don't remember the Baader–Meinhof gang having a terrorist called Petra,' Bill begins, uselessly, five minutes after his false start. Christ, no wonder she was ignoring him. 'I know there was an Ulrika.'

'She was nineteen. Petra was. A hairdresser,' Petra says, with closed eyes. The lids are being painted a startling violet. 'Went out in a hail of bullets. Like

Bonnie and Clyde.'

'Ah, the hairstyles of the early seventies were certainly enough to drive a hairdresser to extreme lengths,' says Bill.

There is a laugh, but not from Petra. It rings out, strong and unabashed, from the blonde in the make-up chair on the other side of her.

'You're telling me,' the woman says. 'D'you remember that blimmin' feather-cut I had, Pet?'

'As if I could forget,' Petra smiles. 'You looked like a sheep sheared by a drunk.'

The cheery blonde, whoever she is, has a good effect on her slender, dark friend. Bill sees Petra relax as they chat.

'Don't think my hair's ever grown back right, to be honest with you. Did you have a feather-cut, then?' Sharon asks Bill.

'Oh, I'm sorry,' says Petra. 'This is my friend, Sharon Lewis. Sorry, Sharon *Morgan*. Sharon, this is Mr Finn who is the boss here and has come to have a laugh at the tragic women who are going to Las Vegas to meet their teen idol *just* in time for the perimenopause.'

'Not at all,' says Bill. His ear is still adjusting to her tone. She is too quick for him. 'I did have a Bowie cut, though. The plan was to look like Ziggy Stardust.'

'And how did it work out?'

'Not bad. I did actually end up looking quite like Ziggy. Just not the right Ziggy.'

'Which one did you look like, then?' Sharon asks.

'Next door's cat.'

*   *   *

When Petra first announced that they had won the competition, Sharon hadn't said, 'What competition?' or 'What are you on about?' or 'After all this time?' or, worst of all, 'So what? We've barely seen each other for the past ten years.' Although, God knows, any of those would have been a reasonable response. But Sharon, when the mood came upon her, or when happiness stole upon her, was ready to lose all reason. She had shouted, as if the years had fallen away, and it was still 1974, and Petra had just pushed open the bedroom door.

'You're joking me, mun. We won? We *won*!' Then she burst out laughing.

As Petra remembered instantly, you didn't really know how accurate the word *burst* was until you saw Sharon having a laugh. It sounded like a dozen paper bags being inflated and popped at the same time. Any louder and the neighbours would start banging on the walls. Lord knows what happened when she and Mal had sex; it would be like one of those major incidents where the police are forced to evacuate the area.

Armed with the phone number that Sharon had sent in a Christmas card, Petra had tracked her down to a modern cul-de-sac of detached homes. As Sharon had promised, it was a lovely spot. From the garden, you looked out across the beaten-silver sea to Pembrokeshire, where the mountains rose like smoke. The estate hadn't existed when they were girls; if it had, they would have said it was posh or way above their station. Petra had arrived there to bring the good news; a couple of decades overdue, of course, but better late than never. And Sharon, once she'd stopped laughing, promptly went into a

287

secondary burst, no less energetic than the first—into tears, this time, because it was impossible that Mal could be trusted to take care of their two boys while she was in Las Vegas.

'They'd get typhoid or something,' she said, kneading and tearing at a wad of paper tissues, which Petra had fetched from the bathroom as the burst began. 'Can't do it, sorry,' Sharon repeated, and went on saying so until Petra pointed out that missing out on the trip of a lifetime to meet David Cassidy was even *more* impossible than leaving Mal to deal with the kids.

They were surprisingly shy, the two friends. Each trying to measure what time had done to the other woman's face and body, without giving any outward sign that such an audit was taking place.

Sharon, who always had the plumper face, had no wrinkles at all. Definitely looks younger than me, thought Petra.

Petra looked tired, though otherwise had barely changed; still slender with that Snow White skin and dark hair, not yet flecked with grey. Definitely looks younger than me, thought Sharon.

In the big, ranch-style kitchen, with its breakfast bar and high stools, Petra admired the pictures on the walls while Sharon made tea for them. The prints appeared to be Japanese until Petra found her glasses and saw that they were watercolours on a kind of parchment, depicting views that she knew like the back of her own hand.

'These are incredible, Sha,' Petra said. 'That's Three Cliffs Bay. You could walk straight into those waves and swim.'

'Went up to London. Saw that big Hokusai show at the Royal Academy. *Beautiful.* Got me into calligraphy. Working with very fine brushes. Bloody mess at first, but I'm getting the hang of it now. Did my City and Guilds art foundation. Degree next. Bit more time now the boys are settled in school. Bachelor of Arts not housewife, I am. You'll be proud to know me one day, Petra.'

Petra felt a jolt of surprise that Sharon had done something like going to the Hokusai show without someone like her. Instantly, she rebuked herself. Christ, that was exactly the kind of patronising attitude Marcus had infected her with, describing Sharon as a 'colourful character' like she was something that came on in Shakespeare to keep the groundlings happy while the important tragic actors changed costume for their next big scene. Petra knew why she was there now. Not just because she needed company for her journey into the past to meet David. She was there to say sorry to Sha, to apologise for the missing years, for becoming the kind of woman who thought of Sharon Lewis as light relief.

'There's lovely you're looking,' said Sharon, placing her hand on top of Petra's and letting it rest there. 'From what you said, after Marcus finished with you, I thought you'd be a wreck, mun.'

All those years in London, Petra had thought of herself as the sweet Welsh girl, the innocent abroad. 'Little me from the Valleys in the big bad city—' that was her shtick among her new circle of friends, who had taught her words like shtick. But it wasn't her who was lovely. It was Sharon. That kind of sweetness was lost to her forever; Marcus had been her teacher in jaded worldliness and she had been a talented pupil.

'What d'you mean, emotionally he's still with you?' Sharon demanded. 'He's shacked up on a boat

289

with his fancy woman. Sometimes, for a clever woman you're bloody *twp*, you are, Petra. Honest to God. Bloody bastard,' she added, with as much malice as she would ever manage.

It was so hot they got in the car and drove to the beach. Sha put some sandwiches in a Tupperware and they bought a big bag of Quavers at the petrol station, and a bottle of dandelion and burdock.

'I didn't think they still made this,' Petra said.

'They don't. It's been out back since 1977. Land that time forgot, down 'ere. Hope you packed your own taramasalata.'

They were the only ones there, apart from a Jack Russell who barked at each incoming wave, greeting it with a darting fury, like a small and very indignant referee. After they had discussed how Quavers dissolved on your tongue, Sharon got down to the serious business of looking for pebbles.

'Apart from David and Steven Williams and Marcus, what men have you loved, Pet?'

Petra lay back and pressed herself into the stones, enjoying the way the warmth seeped into her bones through her clothes. 'Andrew Marvell. Romantic, witty, brilliant foreplay. Incredible insight into what makes women tick.'

'Sounds fabulous. What was wrong with him, then? Married, was he?'

'Died in 1678. Poet. Also Member of Parliament for Hull.'

'A *dead poet*?' Sharon gave a cackle of disbelief.

'The only kind you can trust,' said Petra firmly. 'You don't want to let a live poet near you. They're like locusts. Strip you of everything you ever felt, then use you for material in their sensitive first-person narratives.'

290

'Nice. And who else?'

Petra thought for a bit. 'The dark one in *Alias Smith and Jones*. Pete Duel. Always had a thing for him. Most gorgeous smile in history. Remember we used to watch it on your TV after you got colour for the Olympics?'

'Nineteen seventy-two,' Sharon confirmed. 'He topped himself, didn't he? Rest in peace, Pete Duel. Honest, Petra, I know you go for emotionally unavailable blokes, but alive would be a start.'

'I don't want to start,' Petra said. 'That's over for me.'

'What? Love, over?' Sharon pressed a pebble into her friend's palm. Petra opened her eyes. It was the palest greeny blue speckled with black dots.

'Perfect. You always found the best ones. Plenty more pebbles on the beach. I couldn't, you know. I just couldn't bear to tell my story to someone else ever again. The *effort* of telling my story to a stranger.' She sat up and shook her hair. 'Hey, we could advertise instead. "Damaged romantic Welshwoman, cellist, one careless owner seeks . . ."'

She was crying by then and her head was in Sharon's lap.

'It's all right, you know,' Sharon said. 'It's gonna be all right. We're gonna go to Vegas and meet David and he'll marry us both like one of those Morons—'

'Mormons, Sha,' said Petra, laughing tears and crying laughter. '*Mormons*.'

Back at the house, Sharon opened a bottle of wine, poured them a large glass each and got on with the boys' tea, quickly peeling the potatoes and cutting them into chips, while the two of them talked through travel arrangements and—far more important—what on earth each of them, come the great day, would wear.

'Retro, like,' said Sharon, firmly. 'Flares. Poncho. Just to freak David out. Like he just went through a time warp.'

'Well,' said Petra, it's a thought. But, look—' Here inspiration struck. 'No bra, mind. Nobody did in nineteen seventy—'

'Oh my *God*.' Sharon cupped her bosom in both hands. 'Are you joking? Two kids and twenty years later? Imagine this lot swinging around in front of the poor bloke. He'd be trying to shake hands with them.'

'Oh, I don't think you'd get them through customs,' Petra said. 'American security are very picky these days, anything that looks like it could be an offensive weapon.'

'All right for you, mun. Little Miss Pert. Look at them, all present and correct. Look at *you*. You're exactly the same shape as you were when that Steven Williams got it bad for you—'

'He did *not* . . .' Petra found herself blushing. For her, the unearthing of the past was part agony, part archaeology: so much effort, and unease, and so little pleasure for your pains. So much turning to dust Whereas for Sharon it was a trove, to be opened up and talked over, regrets all mingled with joyful recollections, everything up for grabs.

As if in answer to these buried thoughts, Sharon suddenly stopped in mid-conversation and put down her glass. 'My treasure box,' she said. 'I'm mad, me.' And with that she hurried up the stairs. She was gone quite a while. There were clatterings, a silence, two thumps and a string of Welsh oaths. Then she returned, arms laden with a cardboard box. The tape that held the lid down was wrinkled and dark brown, and had long since lost its power to stick. Sharon yanked it off and opened the box.

Inside was their archive, or its edited highlights: posters, postcards, flyers, newspaper cuttings, magazines. *The Essential David Cassidy Magazine*, stacks of it, held together with rubber bands that had hardened and cracked, or not held together at all. There were scrapbooks, the glue evaporated, the cuttings coming loose like snakeskin.

My God. That face. Petra was astonished. The eyes, with their heavy lashes. The parted lips. A face she had gazed at daily and longed to kiss. Even now, she knew that face better than she knew any of the world's great paintings.

'Hullo, lovely boy,' said Sharon, greeting a poster of David on a horse. 'Look at him, Pet. Gorgeous, wasn't he? How old must he be now then?'

'Twenty-four,' Petra said immediately.

'No, he was twenty-four *then*. Then's not the same as now, is it? So, how old are we? Ancient, we are. So he's eleven years older than us. When's his birthday, then?

'April 12th,' Petra replied without missing a beat.

She hadn't thought of David at all. Not once, not until that moment. It hadn't been about him. All of a sudden, the idea that they were about to journey back to meet him—travel through time, not just cross the Atlantic—seemed improbably strange. If the David she had loved was still twenty-four, but David Cassidy was now a middle-aged man, how old did that make the Petra who was heading for Las Vegas?

She thought of the thirteen-year-old girl—'Gillian's little friend,' that's what Gwennie the Grocer's had called her—who had filled in the

Ultimate David Cassidy Quiz, tracking down every answer as though in pursuit of the Holy Grail. And the prize didn't belong to Petra now, that was the thing. It belonged to the child she had been. And Petra had wanted her to have it. She wished she could give it to her: sneak past her mother keeping guard by the marble pastry slab in the kitchen, creep up the stairs and into that cold bedroom with the hard single bed and the brown counterpane and say, 'Here it is, darling. You won.'

How could Petra and Sharon, with their children, their adult bodies, their buried parents and their marriages, healthy and wrecked: how could they go and see David? It was impossible, she saw that now. The David Cassidy she had loved would not be there, and neither would the girl who had loved him.

'So, d'you think our hotel room will have a jacuzzi then, Pet? It's America so bound to, isn't it? *Petra?*'

'Sorry. Miles away.'

'You're telling me. I looked it up in Mal's atlas. It's in the middle of a bloody desert. You basically fly over sand for a while and then you look down, right, and there's David Cassidy, standing there waving up at you. Like an oasis.' Not a word they had much use for in Wales. The way Sharon said it, the vowels took about half a minute to come out.

'Typical,' said Petra.

'What's that, then?'

'Well, you just said I went after emotionally unavailable men.'

'No, I didn't mean that.'

'Well,' Petra sighed, 'I mean, you can't get more emotionally unavailable than a pop star who lives five thousand miles away. *And* you've got thirty million rivals for him.'

' 'S true,' said Sharon. 'But, you know, maybe it was better that way.' She paused, hearing an echo in her own words. Then she began to sing. Without any warning, Petra found herself sitting drinking wine with a George Michael impersonator. Sharon stopped and took another sip. 'Love a bit of George. No offence to David, mind.'

'None taken, I'm sure,' said Petra, wondering, for the thousandth time, at her friend's ability to go with the flow of her own thoughts and see where they led. Had that been the secret of happiness, all along? Sing when you feel like it?

'Tell you what, though,' said Sharon, skipping back to the past. 'If David had got off that horse and climbed down out of the poster into our bedrooms and made himself emotionally available, what would we have done, eh? We wouldn't have shagged him, would we? We'd never *kissed* anyone, mun.'

'Speak for yourself,' said Petra. 'I would have played him my cello. I had a bit I'd practised for him specially. He'd have been blown away, I'm sure.'

'From what I heard, he was keen on a bit of blowin' away,' said Sharon, with her witchiest cackle. 'Funny thing is,' she went on, 'I never did meet David, 'cept at White City, when he was half a mile away. But I still remember him a lot better than most of the boys I did, you know, know. I mean, just cos he wasn't available didn't mean he wasn't *there*. Right?'

'Right,' said Petra. She felt light in the head, with laughter bubbling up, as if the absurdity of the whole thing—this plight, this opportunity, this old joke—was only now starting to strike home. She knew that her obsession with David had been strange, unbalanced; a sign there was something missing in her childhood. Molly loved Leonardo DiCaprio, but

295

not in the desperate, all-consuming way that Petra at the same age had longed for David. Molly was happier, that was it. There was more in her life. Her need was not so great.

'Well, then,' Petra said, pretending to be decisive, 'since Mr Cassidy wouldn't come to us, we're going to go to him, aren't we now?'

'Bit late, d'you think?' asked Sharon, in a rare flicker of doubt. 'Look at me, Pet. I'm past it.'

'Come on, you're gorgeous,' Petra replied. 'Anyway, you know what they say. Forty's the new thirty.'

Sharon made a face. 'Try telling that to my backside.'

*   *   *

What do you wear for a makeover? Petra had decided to put on her patterned skirt and the black linen jacket she had bought for her mum's funeral, over a black camisole top. Black sandals. Around her neck was the fine, gold Wright & Teague pendant that Marcus had bought her for Christmas, with matching studs. Seeing it glint, she wondered how much guilt had contributed to the purchase. Assessing herself in the hall mirror before she left the house, Petra noticed that the shoes, fashionable two years before, looked a bit scuffed these days. Too late to do anything about it. She felt like one of those women who dashes around tidying the house before their cleaner arrives. You didn't want to arrive for a makeover looking like a wreck; on the other hand, you didn't want to primp and prettify yourself too much, in case the After photo looked worse than the Before.

296

Years of comparing herself with her mother had led Petra to nurture what the magazines identified as Poor Body Image. She probably didn't look too bad for her age, and divorce was turning out to be the best diet ever invented. Still, when it came to beauty, her mother had set the standard. All her life, Petra would identify with the plain daughters of beautiful women. What did it feel like to be one of those poor girls born to a supermodel mother and a beaky rock-star dad? The rock stars always left a trail of chinless, beaky daughters behind them. Girls doomed to live in the shadow of their refulgently lovely mothers. Petra sometimes wondered if those mothers found it hard, as her mother had clearly found it hard, not to have given birth to a girl in their own image.

On honeymoon in Egypt, Petra and Marcus had been browsing in a bazaar when they came across one of those revolving postcard stands outside a cafe. Instead of scenes of the Nile or the Pyramids, the postcards had featured row upon row of perfect, blond, blue-eyed babies; the exact physical opposite of the local children. If her mother had visited Cairo, they would have founded a religion in her name.

'You are not unattractive, Petra,' her mother had said, twisting her child's face towards the bathroom light. 'You know, you are really not szo bad.'

'It's *too* bad, Mum, not szo bad. I don't look *too* bad.'

'That's what I said, Petra. You don't look szo bad for a girl of this age.'

And so, when Petra, years later, found herself with her own girl of that age, she did her best to reverse the process. For every word of praise that had been withheld from her as a child, Petra found five to lavish on Molly. At first it came hard, mastering this new vocabulary of encouragement and admiration. She had to make her mouth do it, like forcing down a foreign food.

'You look lovely,' she said experimentally. 'Blue really suits you, love.'

'Stop it, Mum,' Molly would say, brushing off the compliment, but pleased nonetheless, perhaps.

Petra was so relieved that she could take uncomplicated pleasure in her daughter: the bloom of her skin, the surprising density of those slender limbs pierced her heart. She had worried that the mother–daughter struggle was doomed to re-enact itself down the generations, like the family curses in Greek tragedy, but it turned out that maybe, just maybe, the pattern could be broken. At least Molly would not be stuck, mute in the chrysalis of herself, as Petra had been at thirteen. She would not be szo bad.

*   *   *

'Could you leave the length, please?' Petra was at the mercy of Maxine, who did hair and make-up for the fashion shoots. Petra had been adamant that she didn't want her hair cut, but, once it was washed, she noticed that Maxine began snipping away. 'Just keep it as it is,' Petra added, to make quite sure. Maxine nodded intelligently and kept snipping. It was a clear case of selective hairdresser deafness.

When you got to Petra's age, people began to suggest an Annette Bening cut. A pixie crop was meant to be flattering. And, on Annette Bening, it *was* flattering. On anyone with less perfect features, however, which was every woman who had ever lived, apart from Audrey Hepburn, it lent a certain chipmunk bunchiness to the cheeks. Petra couldn't bear to watch as her hair fell to the floor. She closed her eyes. The whole place was like this, from the moment they walked through the door. She and Sharon had met at Paddington Station and taken a cab together; to arrive separately, they had agreed, would be far too intimidating. But the intimidation went ahead anyway, at full blast.

It didn't help having the magazine boss there, watching. William somebody, the editorial director, had come in and asked if she was named like the *Blue Peter* Petra. After all these years, there was still some twerp getting a laugh out of the TV dog. When she responded sharply, he went very quiet and sat there staring into space until Sharon made him laugh. William Finn, that was it. Bill.

'Great eyes,' Maxine said to Petra. 'We need to bring them out more.'

A memory twitched in Petra, like a nerve. 'It used to say in the magazines I read as a teenager that you had to use yellow eyeshadow on the lid if you had deep-set eyes,' she said.

'Oh, they said all kinds of shit back then. Still do.' Maxine dipped a small brush into her eyeshadow palette. It was as big as a bumper chocolate selection box. Her voice was flat, so that lines of admiration and sarcasm came out at the same pitch. 'Rinse your hair in rainwater as well, did you?' she said.

'We both washed ours outside in the rain,' said Sharon proudly, 'even though we lived in a steel town and the air was full of black specks.'

Bill, Petra saw, was paying close attention as Maxine applied mascara to Petra's lashes. With his fair, messy hair, and slightly shambling look he reminded Petra of some actor. Sharon would know. Petra noticed Bill smiling, too, whenever Sharon spoke. At first Petra felt a flare of anger, because she thought he was laughing at her friend as Marcus used to; then she calmed down and realised, to her greater surprise, that he simply liked Sharon, and had done on sight. They liked each other, after—what—three or four minutes? Sharon had always made friends easily, unlike her. Listening to her here in London, far from home, Petra could suddenly hear how strong Sha's Welsh accent was, and she felt the quick surge of homesickness, swaying within, like the swell of the sea. That's how Petra had talked for more than half her life, and she hadn't even been able to hear it. What are the other things about yourself that you don't know?

One thing she did know, for sure, was this: when you are offered the chance to meet a ghost, the man you were in love with a quarter of a century ago—half a life away—there is only one sensible thing to do. Just say no. Smile politely and say, thank you, but no thank you. I am a grown woman now, not a bit like the girl who loved that boy. I am a happily married woman . . . Correction: I am a soon to be unhappily unmarried woman, with a daughter of my own. Nothing could be more shameful than to seek the past; nothing could be more tragic, or more laughable.

And yet. First love is the deepest. You don't just fall in love, you *capsize*. It feels like drowning, but the thought of rescue is unwelcome. Other loves may come along, but the first breathes on inside you. And the things I still know about him; the date of his birth, his stepmother's name, his passion for horses,

300

his beach hideaway, the instrument he learned to play when he was lonely. Drums.

For two years I wore brown, because it was his favourite colour. Can you believe it? I was a sallow teenager. I looked terrible in brown. I looked *yellow* in brown. But it was a small sacrifice to make. For David, I knew, would be pleased. Thanks to me, he would never be lonely again.

'Julia Roberts.'

Petra woke from her reflections with a jump. 'What?' she said.

Sharon wasn't addressing Petra in particular, just anyone who would listen, which was everyone in the room. 'I was saying to Maxine, make me into Julia Roberts. You know, basically fantastic. Ringlets down to my waist. So if Richard Gere happens to be in Las Vegas, and he's driving down the Strip, like, he'll stop and go, "Hey, I know you!"'

'Sharon, my love,' said Petra, 'the character you are describing is a tall brunette from Los Angeles in thigh-high boots. She is also a prostitute. You are a blonde Welsh housewife, five foot three, and, as far as I know, nobody pays you for sex.'

'Depends.'

'Depends on what?' This was Bill, leaning forward, genuinely intrigued.

'Well, this one time, Mal bought me an ice-cream maker for Valentine's, a Friday it was, and I took one look and sent the kids away to their nan's until Sunday lunchtime.' She gave the dirtiest laugh that Nightingale Publishing had heard in twenty years. Then she said, by way of an airy afterthought, 'You should have seen my banana splits.'

Maxine dropped her scissors. Petra buried her head in her hands, feeling her new haircut, for the

301

first time, soft between her fingers, then looked up and met Bill's smile with her own. He said: 'Would you excuse me?'

'Oh God, I'm so sorry,' Petra said. 'We really didn't mean to be rude—'

'No, no, please, carry on. The ruder the better. I was just starting to learn something really interesting about dairy products. There's honestly nothing I would rather do than sit here pretending to be a hairbrush and listening to women's fantasies. Half the magazines we produce here consist of little else. I could literally take down everything Sharon says in shorthand and transcribe it directly into the next issue . . .'

'How A Knickerbocker Glory Saved My Sex Life, by Mum of Two,' said Sharon. 'With or Without Cherries? You Decide.'

'Exactly. You are clearly our perfect reader,' said Bill. 'Would you like a job?'

Sharon grinned at him in the mirror and wrinkled her nose. 'Gerraway with you, mun. Things to do back home. Thanks for the offer.'

'Any time,' said Bill, adding, 'No, it's just that I have a conference call in . . .' He looked at his watch. 'Ninety seconds.' He moved towards the door, then looked back at Petra. 'Um . . .'

'Petra, please.'

'Petra. When you're done, could you just nip down to my office? One floor down, turn left out of the lift. We just have boring paperwork to go through for the trip.'

'Sign my life away in blood.'

'That sort of thing. Shall we say half an hour?'

'More like five bloody hours with that lot in your hair,' said Sharon. The door closed. 'Ooh, Pet, how about that? Nip down and see me sometime.'

'Sha . . .' Petra looked in the mirror at her stylist, who shook her head in wonderment, as if to say: is she always like this, your friend?

'What's a conference call, anyway?' Sharon asked.

'Oh, you talk to a lot of people all at the same time, at once. Except you don't,' said Petra. 'You just talk across them and nothing gets sorted out.'

'Oh, I get it,' said Sharon. 'Well, he should come to Gower, shouldn't he? Get that for free round my way, no charge. Mal hasn't finished a sentence in twenty years. Poor bugger,' she added, with a voice full of love.

*   *   *

'How do you want it?'

'Oh, just milk, please.'

'Anything to eat? You must be exhausted after sitting in that chair all morning having your hair cut.'

'No, thanks. Sharon and I are going out for lunch in half an hour, and I think she may have some sort of medieval banquet in mind. We could well be rowing down to Hampton Court and having swan or something. I think her idea of London is quite . . .'

'Grounded in history?'

'I was going to say bonkers, but, yes, that sounds better. Just tea, please.'

They are sitting at a round table, in a booth at the back of the cafeteria. 'The throbbing heart of Nightingale Publishing,' Bill had said, as he led her downstairs from his office; they had gone through the details of the trip in less than ten minutes—so fast, indeed, that she wondered, for a moment, why he had bothered to summon her. His secretary could

303

have brought the papers up to the make-up room and done it there. Then he had invited Petra to have a cup of coffee. 'We like to think it's the strangest taste on the South Bank, and we want you to have something to remember this day by,' he said. So she had said yes, after a pause, hoping he wouldn't notice the fluster in her expression. Then she had chosen tea.

'So, what have you been doing all this time?' he asks.

'I'm sorry?'

'I mean, since entering the competition in—when was it?'

'Nineteen seventy-four.'

'BC or AD?'

'Now you're being the rude one.'

'I apologise. It's just that, you know, it was quite some time ago . . .'

Petra groans. 'Please don't remind me. Am I a mad old witch? Is that what you thought, when they told you I called up?'

'Honestly?'

'Honestly.'

'Well, I was hoping for witch, obviously. Samantha from *Bewitched*. With twitchy nose and spells and everything.'

'What about mad?'

'Oddly enough, I didn't think it was *that* mad. Remember, I'm old too. In fact I'm about twice your age.' Petra opened her mouth to protest, but he didn't stop. 'So I remember the whole Cassidy thing. I was right in the middle of it.'

'You can't have been. No boys allowed.'

'You'd be surprised.'

'What?'

'Doesn't matter. Anyway, I remember it well enough to know that it was mad then, and I would have been, you know, a little bit disappointed if the madness had completely gone away. Even now.'

'So you *do* think I'm mad.' For some reason, she finds she is enjoying this.

'No, I think the madness has . . . matured. Like wine. Deepened into something else, perhaps.' Bill studies her closely. Amazing hands. Long fingers. Cellist, he suddenly remembers. He tries to think of a piece he can talk intelligently to her about. Borodin, Second String Quartet. His mum's favourite. They had the slow movement played at her funeral. One of those bits of music so beautiful it soothes the cares of the world while telling you the world is too beautiful to last. Like Bill's mother. Petra is sure to know it.

'So I'm vintage mad.' Petra laughs.

'Perfect.'

'Like this tea.'

'Christ, I hope not. Is it really as bad as it looks?'

'Even worse. It looks like the Thames.'

She takes a spoon and stirs. Then she says, 'In answer to your question, I haven't spent the last quarter of a century thinking about David Cassidy, if that's what you mean.'

'I didn't think so.'

'Meaning?'

'Meaning you look . . .' Bill stops.

'Careful.'

'I am being extremely careful.' He sips his coffee. 'Meaning you are obviously someone who has widened her view of the world.'

'Is that so unusual?'

'Much more than you'd think, I'm afraid. I know

an awful lot of people who don't want to know any more than they did at fifteen. I mean really *know*. As if they'd taken one look at the world and thought: not me, mate. Mostly men.'

'Well, there are times you can't blame them,' Petra says. She is talking quietly now, almost too quietly, and Bill finds himself having to lean across the table.

'True,' he says. 'Never underestimate the wish not to know.' He looks at her, as she stares down into her tea.

'Or the wish that you hadn't had to find out,' she says, after a while.

'Ah yes, all the unsavoury truths. Mostly men again.'

'You mean men finding out about women?'

'Other way round,' he says. 'What do you see in your tea leaves, Gypsy fortune-teller?'

Petra dips her spoon and swills the tea around. 'Your future appears to be brown,' she says at last.

'My favourite colour,' he replies, and is taken aback when Petra looks up, sharply. But she says nothing, so Bill goes on.

'So what did you *want* to know? What have you learned all this while?'

'Well, I did music at the Royal Academy. Cello and a bit of piano. Then I played professionally, which earned me a fortune. Sometimes as much as twenty-three pounds a night. Now I do music therapy. That's my job.'

'Music therapy?'

'Yes, you know. Using music as an aid to mental and spiritual health.' She feels as if she is reading from a script.

'For troubled souls, you mean. Music hath charms

to soothe a savage breast,' Bill says.

'If you like. I see quite a few savage breasts. Damaged kids mostly.' Petra hates talking about her job. People always jump to the wrong conclusion. More cautiously, she tries again. 'When they hear about a job like mine people always call it "putting something back".'

'And it's not?'

'I feel I get more out of the kids, and the music, than they . . . It fills me up . . .' she trails off.

Bill smiles. 'So it's true then.'

'What is?'

'I knew it.'

'What did you know?'

'You *have* been thinking about David Cassidy all this time.'

Petra looks at him and narrows her eyes. 'Never stopped.'

Bill sits back.

'Tell me everything,' he says.

16

Getting To Know You: Music Therapy With Ashley

By Petra Williams, BMus, R.M.Th.

ABSTRACT
This case study describes weekly sessions over a two-year period with a 10-year-old girl with severe emotional problems. Ashley was referred to music therapy because of aggressive behaviour and learning difficulties at school. Her mother was taking part in a drug-rehabilitation programme at the time. Ashley had an excellent sense of rhythm and the weekly sessions became a place where we could improvise together and she could explore her feelings in a place she felt safe. The case study also illustrates how the child's defensive modes of expression were worked with musically, to help her communicate her needs without anger and to modify some of her destructive tendencies so that she could mix with her peers and start to enjoy a more fulfilling life. During the sessions, an unconscious accord between Ashley and the therapist was created to not speak directly of her personal story, which was too hard and too sad. Rather it was decided to let the music tell the story for her.

BACKGROUND INFORMATION

Ashley thinks of herself as The Girl That Nobody Loves. She was her mother's fourth child, but did not share the same father as her three older siblings. Ashley was conceived during one of her stepfather's periodic absences from the family home and it appears that he never accepted her, frequently telling the child she was a 'cuckoo in the nest'. Ashley's own father never lived with her mother and disappeared from his daughter's life altogether when she was four. He spent a period in prison, though she often said 'my dad's in heaven'. Social workers described the family as 'chaotic', and all four children had been taken into care for their own protection on two occasions.

Ashley is a graceful, pretty child who fought hard with her natural advantages to make herself as dislikeable as she feels she is. She shows moderate deficits in cognitive and language areas, generally functioning at between one year and 18 months behind the average for her age level. Her closest relationship was with her deceased grandmother—'Nana'—a pub landlady who played the piano and sang songs to Ashley throughout her infancy. Particular favourites were show tunes from musicals by Richard Rodgers and Oscar Hammerstein. Although her speech is often muddled, Ashley can incorporate song lyrics with great enjoyment and accuracy into conversation. Her teachers express surprise that such a 'challenging' child could show such glimpses of verbal precocity.

The death of her nana, six months before Ashley first came to me, seemed to be the

309

trigger for increasingly violent outbursts at school. Such background information as I had about her came from her head teacher, Rosemary, who felt the child showed signs of depression arising from erratic maternal care. Some mornings, she would turn up to school dressed for a party in brand-new trainers with ribbons in her hair, on others she wore grubby clothes and was teased by her peers about her personal hygiene. 'Smelly Ashley' is how she often describes herself in our role play. Rosemary felt that music therapy should be tried as a last resort after occupational therapy and swimming lessons had failed to make a difference.

Petra saves what she's done, closes her file and then the laptop. It is dark in the room except for the fuzzy orange glow cast by the lamp in the road outside. Through the bay window, freckled with late-summer dust, she can look into the house opposite, an exact copy of her own solid Victorian semi, and watch the shadow play of another family. Observing how other people's families work has always fascinated her. She reaches for the switch on the desk lamp, but changes her mind. Hello darkness, my old friend.

When she was making music with Ashley she felt she knew exactly what she was doing, which made a change from the rest of her life, but now she finds she can't write it up. A case history requires her to impose the technical language of her profession— cognitive deficits, transference reactions—onto the living child who came into her room one freezing February afternoon. Ashley refused to speak, yet was simultaneously shouting her distress. Undersize for her age, the girl wore a crop top with a Playboy bunny motif and dirty white towelling shorts; the puppy fat wobbling between the two garments was mottled blue with cold. It was towards the middle of their fourth session together, with Petra guiding the child's hands over the piano keys, that Ashley took out her chewing gum and sang 'Getting to Know You'.

The crystal-clear diction of Deborah Kerr's governess in *The King and I* had travelled down forty years or more, via Ashley's nana on a pub piano, to a child-woman who probably had a vocabulary of no more than two thousand words. Petra made a point of not breaking down during sessions. The child's emotions were always more important than any she might have, but that day with Ashley it was a struggle to compose herself sufficiently to be able to echo and answer the child's song with the bit about getting to like her, getting to hope that Ashley liked her back.

And then the final verse together, the girl's and the woman's voice twined together in a silvery helix of sound.

Music can reach the parts that language can't, it can perforate the armour that a wounded self builds very early to protect itself; that is why the therapy works, if it does work, and maybe the fact that the process is mysterious and beyond language is what makes it so hard to write down.

Bill Finn could write it down, Petra is suddenly sure of it. At the makeover, Bill asked about her job, questions that suggested he might even be interested in the answers, which he couldn't possibly be. Petra knows that metropolitan type. Actually, she doesn't know them, not personally. But she's read about

311

them. Always flitting between the latest book launch and opening night, everything is marvellous or incredible or terribly interesting, if only as a ploy to make yourself interesting to the other person. Maybe that was unfair. Maybe Bill was more than the sum of his glossy magazines. They were sitting in the canteen at Nightingale Publishing when Petra found herself telling him about Ashley's laugh, the most joyful she had ever heard, and thus the most crushing because it came from a place with no previous record of joy. Bill wanted to know exactly how the music therapy got through to a kid like Ashley.

'It's not an exact science,' she said. 'There are a lot of theories about how it works.'

'And what's yours?'

'They think that Early Man may have communicated by song, don't they? Sort of grunts with tunes. So maybe we were like birds and we lost it. Except we didn't really lose it.'

'Birdsong is pretty strange stuff,' Bill said. 'You think it's all territory and sex. But it turns out they're doing it because they love it.'

'You mean the birds.'

'This one guy, biologist or something, takes his clarinet to play in a forest. Flocks of thrushes around. At the end of it all, his only conclusion is they're making thousands more sounds than they actually need to. Just for the joy of it, improvising as they go along. Like Charlie Parker.'

'You mean Bird.'

'Yeah,' Bill said. He paused. 'I thought you were a classical girl, not a jazz fiend.'

'Just a general fiend,' she said. 'If you get brain damage in your right temporal lobe, which controls higher auditory processing of sound—speech on the

312

left, music on the right—'

'You're losing me,' he said.

'No, you're OK. Right temporal lobe, just behind your ear, *here*. I'm guessing yours is pretty well developed. If it's injured, patients exhibit a complete failure to recognise recently heard songs, although they can still respond emotionally to them. It's called amusia.'

'Amusia. Great title for a book. I love it.' When Bill smiled he looked like a different person.

'So what if humans sang before they spoke?' she said. 'I mean, music may be profoundly instinctive to us, maybe it's our truest form of communication.'

'You haven't heard me in the shower at six in the morning.'

'Like I said, Early Man.'

'Ouch,' Bill said. 'Where did you come from?'

As Petra thinks this over, she is returned to her living room by a loud rhythmic pounding coming through the ceiling above. Molly. Still awake and on her keyboard. At 10.25. On a school night, for God's sake. She pinches the bridge of her nose, the part that's supposed to take away headaches, or so the magazines say. All their worst fights these days are about bed. Not going to bed early enough, not being able to go to sleep, then not being able to get up the next day. Bedtime, her daughter announced loftily, is babyish. Petra thinks back to the baby Molly in her cot, curled tight as a cashew nut, her tiny fists clenching and unclenching. That had felt like the hard bit; the night feeds, the bedside clock's beady green digits telling you it was 3.15; back then, it always seemed to be 3.15. Sleep deprivation made you light-headed at the same time as your feet felt like they were shod in lead. During a concert at the

Albert Hall, Petra had nodded off for a few seconds, which would have been just about OK, except she was one of the performers. Petra always reckoned she could play the cello in her sleep, though only motherhood had given her the opportunity to test that hypothesis.

Then, the baby years passed, like an April shower, and the hard bit turned out to be the easy part, only you didn't find out until it was over. Motherhood was like being in a play and only ever having the lines for the scene you were in at any given moment. By the time you figured out how to play the part, the curtain dropped and it was onto the next act. Some days, she felt so nostalgic for that little baby.

'Being a parent doesn't get any easier,' Carrie said. 'It just gets hard in a different way.'

Petra was the family disciplinarian, a role that Marcus had been quite happy to delegate. No, happy to abandon, she thinks, and then checks herself. She can't stand being bitter, the taste of it like cheap mouthwash. Walking away from the solicitor's office after discussing an amicable settlement—Mr Amos used to be *their* solicitor, but suddenly he was Marcus's—she retched up the bile that had been accumulating in the back of her throat into a green wheelie bin.

I have become the kind of woman who spits in the street and doesn't carry a handkerchief, she thinks. If her mother were alive, it would have killed her.

Now Marcus is gone, Petra must somehow be good cop and bad cop for Molly. Cagney *and* Lacey.

Which was which? She never did get that straight, though the blonde was definitely harder, the brunette rounder and more maternal. You didn't see enough portraits of women who loved and depended

314

on each other like those two; in real life, it was female friendship which kept most women going, in her experience, especially once the rivalry over men had fallen away.

Every weekday at ten to seven, Petra goes into Molly's room and stumbles across the carpet. With its scattered heaps of debris, the room is like a beach after the tide has gone out. She switches on the radio—some jackass DJ irritating enough to raise the dead; then, fifteen minutes later, she yells up the stairs, by which time her daughter is usually in the shower. This morning, though, she had literally had to shake her awake. Molly, her features snared in a mess of golden hair, surfaced like a marsupial from some deep burrow. This was not sleep, it was hibernation. Petra had got angry. 'Lost it', in Molly's tearful accusation.

'And if you're going to wear your hair long, young lady, you're going to have to learn to brush it every night or we're cutting it off.'

Young lady? Where did that come from? How prim and predictable are the words that travel down the maternal line on the reproachful gene. Did Darwin guess that survival of the fittest involves a hairbrush? No, but mothers do. Greta used to grab Petra by the hair and say: 'Ach, it's szo greasy.' So many of her mother's sentences began with that guttural *ach* of disgust. She thought it was because Greta was disappointed in her daughter's looks. Now she has a girl of her own, Petra sees with frightening clarity how the world will judge Molly, and it won't be for her dry humour or her wonderfully mobile hands which straddle complex chords like bridges made of flesh and bone.

She loves her daughter passionately, but she is

highly critical of her. With a son it might have been different; she always wonders about that. Instead she has a teenage girl, a creature with a whim of iron. Will of iron. No, whim of iron is better. The way Molly juts that heart-shaped chin of hers, determined to have the last word in any argument, most confident when she is most ignorant. And it stings when she accuses Petra of not understanding her. Compared to her own mother, Petra feels like a limbo dancer of flexible compassion and comprehension. Greta could have taught those ayatollahs a thing or two about rigid intolerance. At least Molly has not inherited the relish for gloom and disaster. Petra was brought up to believe that anything invented after 1959 would give you cancer. Still does.

'Not the old days again,' Molly sighs if Petra dares to suggest that, once upon a time, there were mothers even stricter and more annoying than she is.

'That was like twenty-five years ago,' says Molly.

Not for Petra. 'I am approaching the middle of my life,' she thinks. 'I am a grown woman. A mother. I have a home in a pleasant suburb of London with a south-facing suntrap patio where I grow surprisingly good tomatoes and basil, which I tear with my hands to release the fragrance and then strew over the chopped tomatoes with a little balsamic vinegar. I have come to like the word strew. Strewth. I have a job which I love and which may even do some small good in the world, I am supposed to be a mature person anchored by all the trappings of a decent, slightly dull life, yet increasingly I feel like a child who suspects that the past is sweeping round in a big circle to ambush her.'

316

She has only the faintest grasp of Einstein's theory of relativity, but she knows that something strange has happened to time since she found the letter from the David Cassidy magazine in her mother's wardrobe. Her brain, which generally spins through a Rolodex of worries, has started making dramatic leaps between the years and decades, as if some invisible director were putting together a package of Petra highlights for an awards ceremony. While she was reading in the bath the other night, it was Steven Williams's penis that surfaced. She saw it for the first time when she was babysitting, for her geography teacher and his wife, and Steven dropped round unannounced. (Petra and he had just started seeing each other after Gillian grew tired of Steven. She had never wanted him; she had wanted others not to have him.) Petra remembers, for example, how, when she opened the door, he was standing there in the pebble-dashed porch with a bottle of Woodpecker cider and a hopeful grin. How he took off his leather jacket and threw it over the banister as if it were a saddle and the buckles jangled like stirrups. The way they both padded upstairs to check that the two little girls were asleep, and how it felt as though they were trying on adulthood for the first time. How she found herself scrutinising Steven's face in the glow of the toadstool night light and realised, to her mild astonishment, that she was looking to see what kind of dad he might be. She can only have been fifteen.

She startles herself by recalling things she didn't know she'd noticed. How, when they'd been kissing on the settee, he lifted himself onto one elbow to keep his weight from crushing her. The way she liked being crushed by his weight. Her heart pounding like she'd run a hundred miles. When his mouth found

317

her breast it sent an electrical signal Down There, a spasm of longing that created a new pathway as it convulsed. He undid the button on his jeans, adjusted himself with a single movement, and there it was. Huge and unmanageably alive. No Chinese whisper in the needlework room, no biology lesson, not even Carol's mime with a *saucisson* on the fifth-form trip to Paris could have prepared her for the thing itself.

She didn't know whether to laugh or faint, though neither would have been right because it was unmistakably a solemn moment. Knowing that something had to be done about the erection, done with it to be exact, and finding out what that was just at the moment the geography teacher put his key in the front door. Steven leapt to his feet, tucked himself back in and scooped her bra up and into her bag with a single movement, years of training on the rugby field paying off.

Petra said the girls had been no bother. No bother at all. The teacher knew, and they both knew that he knew, but they were saved by mutual embarrassment.

Steven gave her a lift home on the back of the bike, along the seafront. Petra felt happy simply to be alive. The salty wind on her raw, kissed lips, her hands laced round his middle, her body and his leaning together to take each corner. Her first brush with sex left her feeling drugged, hugging the secrets of womanhood to herself.

*   *   *

One whole wall of Molly's room is wallpapered in boy. The same boy, in picture after picture. A boy on

318

the prow of a ship, a boy on a beach. A boy with cool, blue eyes and a prominent, dimpled chin. A boy whose floppy, too-long fringe is parted to the side and threaded with blond streaks. Petra doesn't think much of him, this boy. With his button nose and round eyes, he looks like a child's drawing, not entirely real. She dislikes the fact her daughter's bedroom looks like some kind of Renaissance chapel dedicated to the cult of this youth, but she doesn't say so. Instead, in a pleading voice she dislikes, she says: 'Mol, I've told you before, if you use Sellotape to stick posters up it'll bring the paint off when you take them down.'

Molly doesn't respond. She is in bed, listening to her Discman and writhing with the duvet as if it were a sea monster.

'You know we can't afford to redecorate.'

As so often with her daughter, Petra finds her tongue keeps talking when silence would be the wiser course. That's not what I meant to say, she thinks. This is not who I am.

'But I'm not going to take the posters down, am I? Duh,' says the shape under the duvet.

'Don't say duh.'

'What's wrong with duh? Honest, Mum, I don't get you sometimes.'

'There's no need to get me. I'm your mother.'

Petra bends to scoop up an armful of tights and pants.

'Is that the boy from *Titanic*?'

Molly sits up, incredulous with disdain. 'Leonardo DiCaprio, Mum. He's world-fay-mous.'

'How did he end up with a name like that?'

'His mum was pregnant with him and she was in Italy and she was looking at a painting by Leonardo

319

da Vinci.'

'How on earth do you know that?'

'Because I read it in a magazine.'

Petra sighs, exasperated. 'You can't believe everything you read in magazines, darling.'

'It happens to be a true fact. Ac-tchew-ull-ee.'

Petra bends forward slightly to allow this falsehood to go over her head. 'You know, when I was your age I wasn't allowed posters on—'

Molly doesn't wait for her to finish. 'And your point is?'

The awful, hand-on-the-hip sarcasm she has learned from those American TV shows she watches.

'Molly, please don't talk to me like that.'

'Like what?'

Along with the rest of her generation, Molly is bored by foreign languages, but somehow manages to speak fluent Beverly Hills brat. 'It's sooo gross,' she will say, wrinkling her nose. Petra, who still thinks of gross as a pay packet before deductions, feels old and weary.

'Always try to remember you're the adult.' That's what a neighbour with older children told her when Molly started nursery. It seemed such a strange thing to say—who was the adult, if not the mother? Now her baby girl is a teenager, Petra knows exactly how hard it is not to be provoked into childish retaliation. *'Well, how do you think I feel?'* is what she finds herself wondering.

Molly doesn't care how Petra feels. Petra's job is to absorb whatever Molly feels.

'Mol?'

'OK, I'll use Blu-tack.'

'Good.'

320

'Fine.'

'It's so late. I hoped you'd be asleep by now, my love.'

Petra perches on the edge of the bed and strokes her daughter's forehead with her index finger. Over the past few months, the child's features have been going about their urgent task of morphing into a woman's; right now, they are slightly too big for her face—eyes, nose and pillowy lips, all slightly out of scale. Molly complains that she is not even pretty, but one day she will be beautiful, her mother thinks. The prettiest girl in class seldom grows up to be the beauty. A sudden image of Gillian at their school reunion, four years ago. A Home Counties wife and mother now, living in one of the shires—Berks or Bucks—pleasant features under a neat bob with expensive caramel highlights, just a millimetre too wide. Gillian Edwards as a grown woman, talking about their place in the Algarve, the palms of her hands stained a telltale Darjeeling by self-tan. Gillian. All her fearful magic gone.

'Can't sleep. I keep telling you,' Molly says. The bags under her eyes are a livid damson. Her lids, fluttering as if a moth were trapped beneath.

Petra bends to kiss them. 'Is everything OK at school?'

'Fine.'

'Hannah OK?'

Said casually. Tricky Hannah, the volatile one in Molly's group. Hannah, whom Petra long ago spied as a threat to her daughter's happiness, though she keeps that thought to herself lest she make Hannah more attractive to her daughter. Tricky Hannah, the queen who moves the other girls around the board. Every group has one. Hannah who regularly

321

demands to be Molly's bestest friend, hers alone and no other. More demanding than any lover.

It's just teenage girls, Petra tells herself, but she knows the other things that teenage girls can do, so she stays alert. Petra counsels Molly to maintain a wide circle of friends. She doesn't say that the more friends you have in different groups the less chance there is of being abandoned. Adolescence is a worrying time for mothers, but Petra knows she worries more than is strictly reasonable. Her antennae for rejection are overdeveloped; even though she seems to have produced a popular, well-adjusted kid, she can't switch them off.

'Mu-um, it's no big deal, OK?'

That's what Molly says whenever Petra enquires why she isn't part of a shopping trip the other girls are going on or has, inexplicably, been left off the guest list for some disco. Petra experiences every snub to her child, both real and imagined, with a lurch in her belly. She can't help it. Even Molly hates it if they're running late for a sleepover, yells at Petra when they're stuck in traffic; hates the other girls to get started without her. Fear of missing out is married to the twin dread of not being missed at all. Some things never change.

Petra adjusts her position on the bed so she is lying alongside Molly, their two heads next to each other on the pillow. The cushion between them is Molly's breasts, a recent addition and swelling fast. She is glad about her daughter's breasts, proud even. Is that normal? Recently, Molly has become very private, banning Petra from the bathroom when she is in the bath. Not long ago, they used to chat about their day, with Petra perched on the loo and Molly lying back in the water like the girl in that Millais painting, hair a skein of seaweed floating behind her head.

She wonders now if she will ever see her daughter's naked body again, the body she grew inside her own; probably not. The next person to see it will be a boy, a real one, not the Leonardo kid in the posters on the wall.

As she puts her arm around her, she feels all the fight leave Molly. When she was a toddler, Molly would go quite rigid during a tantrum, until the demon departed and she allowed herself to be cuddled and soothed by a warm drink from her bottle. She liked to have the bottle held for her so she could twirl her hair with one hand and clutch her blanket with the other. How easy it was back then, Petra thinks. You could comfort her, smooth it all away, tell her everything was going to be all right. And it was. Because you could control the world. You *were* the world, pretty much.

Drifting now, Molly burrows closer. If she's honest with herself, this is what Petra misses most about Marcus. It's not the sex. It's another body which can, as if by osmosis, drain all the tension out of your cells. She has to hand it to him, Marcus was good at massage; his cellist's fingers powerful and nimble, finding the knots.

'I *knead* you,' he said, turning her over and pressing his way down the rungs of her spine, springing each vertebra like a catch. He always was terrific at vibrato.

By the end, she couldn't bear him to touch her. Tried to get the sex over with as quickly as possible; hating herself for even letting him near, still thinking maybe he'd stay, and hating herself for that also. She'd read somewhere that the higher the pitch of

323

the woman's cries the faster the man climaxes. Well, well, well, it turns out that, sometimes, you *can* trust what you read in magazines. It was that easy, and that hard.

'When you and Sharon are in America you can go and see Leo,' Molly murmurs.

'Who's Leo?'

'Leo DiCaprio.'

'Oh. The most famous boy in the world.'

'Such a cool name. I love him so much, Mum.'

'Yes, my darling, I know.'

*   *   *

Downstairs once more, she needs to get back to the computer, but the air in the living room is hot and sullen, so she lets herself out through the patio doors. The dark garden twitches with scents. Earlier, eager for distractions from writing up Ashley's case history, she'd wasted at least an hour out here watering her plants, picking her favourite sweet peas and some tomatoes which she put on the kitchen windowsill to ripen. She likes the dusty green smell they leave on her palms. Absent-mindedly, she starts to deadhead the nicotiana in the terracotta urn by the back door. The withered blooms feel like parachute silk to the touch. Fingers poised to pinch, Petra suddenly feels the terrible power of life and death. She hesitates over one collapsed flower. No, let's give the poor thing one more day.

The cream trumpets only open in the late afternoon and release their musky, throat-constricting fragrance throughout the evening. How strange to think that nicotiana, pretty and blameless as a Victorian nightdress, is a little sister of the tobacco plant that kills millions. Helped to kill her father, took what was left of his lungs after pneumoconiosis, and his glorious voice. If Petra kneels down next to the container she thinks she can smell Dad's pipe and hear him tapping it on the top step in the garden at home to loosen the thick tarry molasses that gathered at the bottom of the bowl.

Several times, Petra has tried to tell Molly about her grandfather. *Ei tad-cu hi.* By the time Molly was old enough to be aware of him, Dad was half the size of the man who worked in the steelworks, a whiskery husk under a trembling sheet, scarcely able to shave and struggling for breath, though still holding out his arms to his granddaughter.

'Come by y'ere, lovely, and have a *cwtch* with your grandad.'

She desperately wants Molly to carry that template of a good man in her heart, but when Petra tries to describe Dad to her daughter it just comes out as words. He was so lovely. Gentle. Kind. Wonderful baritone. Dancer. Dean Martin. That's Amore.

How was she meant to sum up the human being who sheltered her as best he could from her mother, as the blows rained down on him? Occupational hazard.

At least, Petra thinks, her own daughter doesn't feel she has to hide—not her Leonardo DiCaprio posters, not her feelings. Molly may not like her mum to come into the bathroom any more, but she knows she has a vagina, not some indeterminate, shameful place called Down There which it's not nice to touch. *Achafi!*

Petra is glad about that. She rarely allowed Greta

to see her feelings, knowing they would only afford an opportunity for disapproval or even gloating. One day, she was walking along the breeze-block wall in front of the bungalow they were building opposite and she fell, cutting open her knee and grazing her new shoes. The toecaps, glossy as a conker, were scarred with angry pink streaks. She came in crying, because she knew she'd be for it, but crying also for her poor new shoes, as the blood trickled down one leg onto her white sock.

'There you are, *see*,' her mother said.

Pain was there to teach you a lesson, although what that lesson was she never learned. Greta's self-appointed role in life was to toughen up her daughter.

'Taking control of your emotions, please, Petra.'

When Petra thinks of herself as a child she sees a mute who dare not speak. Music was her way of speaking, her therapy, too; William Finn, Bill, had said as much to her at the makeover. She'd never thought of it quite like that before.

'I must move house,' Petra thinks suddenly, closing the patio doors behind her and sliding the bolts across. It was in this room that she had her last outbreak of grief for her marriage, the only one the world knew anything about. But it was terrible, flinging herself at Marcus's legs and giving herself up to her misery. Promising him things, begging. He had shaken her off, wanting to get away from her, eager to get back to what had taken him away. He told her that he had tried to let her down gently. You have to be cruel to be kind. Why? Why not just be kind?

After he'd gone, she sat in the dark sobbing and talking to herself. 'There, there, you'll be all right.' As if she were her own mother. Even then, she had listened for his steps on the path, thinking that perhaps he might come back, as he always had before.

Now, for the first time since Marcus left, she feels a faint stirring inside, the sense that she might have a future. The day after tomorrow, Molly will go to stay with Carrie round the corner, and she, Petra, will go to Vegas to meet David. Petra and Sharon and David. Sharon and Petra. And Bill. It no longer seems like quite such a mad plan. She finds herself singing. 'Breaking Up Is Hard To Do'. The lyrics as fresh as paint in her memory. Still humming, she consults her notebook and begins to type, the words coming easier now.

Every week for the first few months we worked together, Ashley said, 'I donwunna tell you my story, Miss. I don't have to if I donwunna.'

As the work with Ashley evolved, using a combination of the showtunes she knew so well and free improvisation on cello, keyboard and percussion, she began to speak differently, to show a sense of self-worth and to be able to admit her desire to be safe. The familiar song structures offered her a certain predictability in which she began to trust our relationship. Ashley started to find another way to communicate and began to realise that her behaviour could be a conscious choice, not just an angry reflexive response.

By mimicking clear phrase structures in songs that matched her moods I could 'hold' her feelings, musically transforming them into normal excitement and pleasure.

327

CONCLUSION

Music therapy is a very important activity in Ashley's life: the one time when she can safely release all of the feelings, including the rage and the distress, which she has been locking down. Most of the grown-ups she has met have dealt with her unsympathetically, often aggressively, and I have been in the privileged position of being able to offer something better. The one advantage she brought with her was a rich trove of musical memories; the show tunes learned from her beloved grandmother equip Ashley with one of the few constant and reliable structures in her experience. Among all the children I have taught, I can think of nobody for whom music has been a more vital outlet.

Ashley has had to say many goodbyes in her short life. By singing 'So Long, Farewell' from *The Sound of Music*, I took on the role of the many adults who have left her. When she started to sing the words back to me at the end of each session, her confidence growing every time, tears came to my eyes. She had obviously taught herself how not to be hurt by the act of saying farewell.

17

I was the real David Cassidy. Oh, sure, there
was this other guy: the one who sang the songs,
who got the girls, who wore the shirts, who
broke the hearts. But the story of David Cassidy
really had very little to do with pop music, or
pop culture, or even the culture of fame; it was
something much simpler than that. It was a love
story. And I wrote it.

I left university in 1973 with a degree, a
girlfriend, and a half-share in a Mini Clubman.
It turned out that I only had a half-share in the
girlfriend, too, and that she preferred the other
half, but it took a shouting match in a mews off
Bayswater, at three o'clock in the morning, to
learn the truth. My degree was in English, with
particular emphasis on the Romantic poets.
Proof that I had gained it came with a diploma,
in a roll of fake vellum, and a blank space where
my future was meant to be. Not only did Keats
fail to get me a job: he practically guaranteed
that no one would employ me. Employers would
sit there with my one-page, double-spaced CV
on the desk between us, curl their lips, and
pronounce the words 'English Literature' as if
they were saying 'criminal convictions' or
'known perversions'. Clearly, they thought that I
would arrive on the first day with a cape and a
quill pen. Whereas what I wanted, more than
anything, was to put Keats behind me: to escape
from the cage of his life and loves into the
freedom of my own. And, if that meant making

329

the coffee, that was fine by me. Girls drank coffee. That much I knew.

Bill closed his file, and then his laptop. This simple action, as always, triggered a twofold reaction within him: the need for a cigarette, and the deeper need for a drink. The fact that he hadn't smoked in twenty years, and hadn't been drunk in ten, was of no consequence at all. What mattered was that smoking and drinking were the kinds of things that writers were meant to do—reflex behaviours that were supposed to kick in at the foot of every page, or even the completion of a paragraph. They were badges of bad conduct, pinned to the writing to give it some extra shine. When you saw a photograph of a novelist, and he was seated at a typewriter, breathing though a Marlboro, with a tumbler of Scotch at his elbow, and the light of early morning at his back— well, it was sixty per cent proof, was it not? The guy had *earned* his style; his books must be hard won, ground out on a battlefield of booze and badly injured hearts. How could you take seriously the thoughts of a writer who survived on tea and biscuits?

Bill was ashamed of himself, automatically thinking *he*, but there was nothing he could do about it; when he thought of writing, it was the image of his fellow man that fell into his head. Part of him, he guessed, was stuck in 1973, when an author was still a guy in jeans, or, if dead, in a frock coat with a well of black ink to match the Scotch. Imagine George Eliot, growling over her uneaten breakfast, fumbling to slit open the day's first pack of Lucky Strikes, one hand rubbing her stubble, trying not to sniff the reek of last night's breath, her own bad atmosphere . . .

All the smartest people Bill knew were women. He thought of Marie in the office. Women alone seemed to keep the traffic flowing smoothly between their brains and mouths, whereas men were all gridlock and diversions and dead ends. When it came to communication, men were manholes. And, it went without saying, they didn't read; they didn't read men, and they sure as hell didn't read women. A few men, like monks, still read, but they didn't talk to other men about the books they'd read, and, if they read *good* books, they stashed them away like pornography. Just think if they read *poems*: under the bedclothes, with a torch, while their wives slept uneasily beside them.

When had men stopped reading? When had men become anti-reading, or reading become anti-men? Maybe the rumour had gone round, Bill thought, that books were good for you, like fruit or yoga or going to church. They nourished and sustained you. In other words, they were a bad idea. Maybe the only way that men would ever read, now, was government action. The government could start banning books, beginning with the good ones. Ban them and burn them, deny them and shred them to bits. Then men would want them again. A book would be like crack, or adultery, or treason; a book would be bad for you. And that would be a good thing.

And through it all, licking a forefinger and turning a page, the women would go on reading. Of all the smart women Bill knew, most were readers. And what they read, for the most part, was other women. When they weren't too busy with their own lives, which was most of the time, they read about the lives of other women, most of whom, as far as Bill could work out, were even busier than they were, though

331

whether that was meant to rebuke them, or console them, he had no idea.

His flat was in a converted warehouse near Tower Bridge, a seven-minute walk from the office and with a partial view of the river. It had been a convenient stopgap; eleven years later it sometimes felt like home. Bill looked around his living room. It was tidy, he guessed, and welcoming; there were no carpet stains or unidentified burns or food remains; it was, recognisably, the place where a professional adult would seek to unwind, at the close of the day. But it was also, in some unmistakable way, a place where women did not come—or had not come of late, or come enough. There were books, but none left lying face down, their spines cracked, the wings of their pages crinkled and spread. That was another thing he would never understand about women: how they could bear to read in the bath, a novel propped in the soap tray, with steam rising and turning the fiction to pulp.

Here, though, in this room, the books were sentry-neat, like an army of knowledge. Only one was missing; you could see its place on the shelf, a dark gap. Now it was laid flat on the coffee table with a marker in it, beside the stack of magazines, and Bill couldn't read its title from where he was sitting, at his desk, though he knew it as well as his own name, and he knew where the author had taken it from, under cover of darkness. Other people's thoughts and feelings, long before, grew into poems, and bits of those poems drifted into the minds of novelists, and the novels sat on the coffee tables of men too tired and preoccupied with other things, like bringing out magazines, to think about the feelings that they themselves might once have had, long before. 'When

332

youth grows pale, and spectre-thin, and dies . . .'

Bill went to the kitchen. Last year, he had had a new one put in. German. It cost only slightly less than his father earned over ten years when he was trying to keep a family of five. He ran his hand over the granite worktop and smiled weakly at the folly of the industrial mixer tap, like a python made of steel. Who was he kidding? A tap that had enough pressure to douse the Great Fire of London would only ever be called upon to sluice Bill's morning toast plate. He looked at the shelf of bottles, some never opened; who, in the course of human history, had asked for apricot brandy? All those drinks for guests, lovers, partygoers: people who liked to reminisce at length, others keen to forget. There were no cigarettes in the house. He made himself a cup of tea, took two biscuits, sat down at the table and began to dunk. Nothing was in his head. When he had finished, he tipped the dregs of grainy swill down the sink, and paused. Then he left the kitchen, trailed past the living room like a sleepwalker, pushed open a door and flicked a switch.

Music ran round the room; along and up and down, as though on a stave. LPs at the far end, huddled together in stacks, their spines rubbed and unreadable even if you went up close. Elsewhere, CDs by the hundred, the thousand. And out of sight, in sliding drawers, at ground level, cassettes, in heaps of six, some of them ringed with elastic bands. Cassettes, what a joke: plastic shells with broken corners that rattled like dried peas. Designed to be dropped and lost down the sides of car seats; but designed, too, to contain everything that you loved about a band, or, better still, everything that you could cook up by mixing one band that you loved

333

with a dozen others, to make a compilation that you would pass on to friends. In mid-1972, Bill had felt the same way about compilation tapes that others felt about the National Gallery; in some ways, he still did. He opened a drawer and took out a batch of tapes. There was an index card, visible through the clear casing, with a song on each line. The first words he read were 'Floyd, Pink'. Bill snorted, and then looked round quickly, as if an intruder had broken in with the specific purpose of watching a middle-aged man laughing at his pompous younger self.

Christ, had he really been that bad? It didn't say much for the frenzy of Mr Finn. How could music send you, spirit you out of yourself and into the stratosphere, if you filed it away afterwards under 'Floyd, Pink'? Bill wondered what on earth he must have done with Crosby, Stills, Nash *and* Young: four separate catalogues, presumably, or maybe four cubed. Sixty-four. What had happened to his record collection when one of them peeled away and became Young, Neil? A surprise, really, that the whole system hadn't melted down.

Once, some years ago, he had brought a woman home. They had met at a party just before Christmas, and talked, not about music but about plenty of other, less contentious things. He remembered, for some reason, that she had worn a black velvet jacket, cut like a man's tuxedo, with a white shirt and a double string of pearls; someone in passing, carrying drinks, had told her she looked lovely, and she had said, 'I feel like a male impersonator,' and seen Bill's smile. She offered to give him a lift home, and had said, as her car dawdled at his kerb, 'Well, aren't you going to ask me to come in? It is Christmas, you know.' Flustered, and not quite seeing the connection, he had done as she said. In her breezy, confident manner, she had walked around his flat, inspecting it, before committing herself, while he wrestled with the coffee machine in the kitchen: the standard rigmarole, more sad than funny, of consenting adults who have already decided to go to bed, and know it, but must nonetheless go through the motions of a cursory, well-mannered courtship, even though the coffee will, in all probability, remain undrunk.

She had called out comments on her brief tour, pausing to laugh, as was required, at the spartan fixtures of his bathroom. Then there was complete silence. He had said her name. (What *was* her name? Bill was dismayed at his memory these days, with its rough patches and holes. Helen? Harriet? He could see the pearls, still, but the name had lost its lustre and disappeared.) Then he had turned off the coffee machine and gone in search of her. She was standing in the doorway of the music room, gazing at the massed ranks, and at the hi-fi that squatted, like a black stove, where a fireplace had once been. 'Your music,' she had said, 'is all in *order*.' 'Yes,' Bill had replied. That was when he'd made his mistake. He had thought order was something to be proud of.

'Chronological within thematic within alphabetical. So, taking Bob Dylan, say, first we go to D . . .' He had stopped. She'd looked at him oddly, and tilted her head, like a mother considering someone else's strange child, and said: 'I think I better go.' And she had gone. He had listened to her car drive away, then made the coffee, and listened to Dylan till dawn. On Desolation Row . . .

Bill hadn't thought of the Pearl Woman for a long while. He was sure she hadn't thought of him once,

335

after that evening, other than to raise him as a comical species, a full-grown punchline, among other women, for a week's worth of lunches and drinks. ' "First we go to D" . . . No we don't, matey. You're not even getting to A tonight, believe me . . .'

No chance of finding her now, ever, to say sorry, and to confess that now he, too, had got the joke. Better late than never. How could you retrace your steps like that, back into the past? Not hook up briefly, or rekindle, but truly find the old path, into the woods? He replaced the tapes, turned off the light and closed the door, then ambled back to his laptop. Its screen glowed at him, in the dim-lit room, like a window in a city by night.

I replied to an ad in the *Evening Standard*. I didn't expect to get the job; I'm not sure I even wanted it. I remember leaving the interview, where the exact nature of the work—and the name of the pretty boy at the heart of it—had, for the first time, become clear. I could have stood up and declared to the interviewer, 'Madam, I spit on your offer of toil, be it ne'er so well remunerated. I bid you good-day.' Instead of which, I said yeah, OK. The music meant nothing, I reasoned, but the money sounded good.

That evening, I went to see my girlfriend. I shall call her Rachel. Knowing that I had been for an interview, she asked how it had gone. Well, I said. Offered the job on the spot. From now on, she could introduce me as a music journalist. Result: the very words made her melt. Her own job was steadier, and better paid, but this—and remember, we are talking 1974—had the edge in glamour.

'Who will you get to write about?' 'Oh, you know: Plant, Page, Clapton. Maybe Hendrix, if he's over.'

Consider the scene: not only was I lying about the strength of my wish to meet proper, hairy rock stars; I was lying in the full knowledge that I never would meet them, because I would be too busy writing about a smooth-chinned pop goblin whom I fervently hoped I wouldn't have to meet at all. My secret boy, of whom she must never know.

A couple of weeks later, I was sitting at my desk, staring at a heap of correspondence. 'Zoe,' I said to my boss, 'these are from girls to David.'

'What do they want?' she asked.

'Oh, nothing much. Promises of undying love for them and them alone. Offers of marriage. His hanky. His horses in Hawaii. His favourite colour. Things like that.'

'Yes,' said Zoe, 'the usual.'

I asked her what to do with them.

'Do?' she replied. 'Answer them, of course. Not personally. Just draft some general replies and give them to me. I'm having the page made up in a mo. We just call it "A Letter from David"'.

I looked at her, like a child being prodded onto the stage in a nativity play for the first time. Then I said, in a small voice: 'But I'm not him.'

And Zoe smiled back. 'You are now, darling,' she said.

And so I was.

And you know what? It was easy. I took the first letter. It was the one about David's

337

favourite colour. Obviously, I would have to dig around to find the answer; there had to be one, after all. Everybody had a favourite colour. I went and asked a colleague. 'What's Cassidy's favourite colour? Where can I look it up?' He sneered at me and said something like: 'Don't look it up, wanker. MAKE it up.'

Still, I was uneasy. This was journalism, after all, not fiction. Wasn't it? As a compromise, I gave David my own favourite colour, forgetting that it might not be the most convincing choice, because I was colour-blind. I turned back to my typewriter and wrote: 'Hi there, girls! People often ask me for my favourite colour. So I have to tell you my favourite colour is brown.'

Bill sat back and thought about Ruth. What would happen if she picked up a copy of the magazine, in three months' time, and saw his article, and recognised herself? Bill didn't know whether he was revolving this idea in his head because he feared the consequences, or because he wished for them—wanted her to think of him in return, search for him, find a number, call him up . . . 'Bill, hi. It's, um, Ruth. Ruth from before. You know, David Cassidy days. I read your piece, and I couldn't help . . .'

There was more. I didn't just deliver the holy writ of David Cassidy. I put together the Bible. I learned to design a page and lay out text. I learned how to cut and paste, though not with a scroll and the click of a mouse; in those days, cutting meant scissors and paste meant a pot of something so white, rank and gloopy that we

338

convinced ourselves it must have come from a sperm whale. To me it stank of boiled bones, but that was not disgusting enough for my fellow pasters. 'Probably the sperm,' one of them put it; 'sperm whale sperm.' And from that moment on our pot of adhesive was labelled Moby Dick. 'Pass the Moby,' we would say to one another, breathing through our mouths. When millions of human beings remember David Cassidy, they think of a voice, and then of—I don't know, the burning smell of their old hairdryers, perhaps, from the time when they got themselves dolled up for this unavailable pop star while reading our magazine. And me? Well, I must be the only person who, whenever the word 'Cassidy' crops up in conversation, thinks 'Moby Dick'. And vice versa.

Bill felt a key turn inside his head. Something like that; something released. He hadn't found that glue smell at the back of his senses, under all the other rubbish, for twenty-five years, yet here it was, set free by a few idle words. Bill didn't write these days, not unless you counted Post-it notes, stuck on the side of the computer or the front of a fridge. And emails, of course: the rosaries of the twentieth century—an endless clicking of fingers, unique to each soul, sending off complaints, regrets and pleas into the unknown, hoping they find their mark. But that wasn't writing. He hadn't written anything longer in years, not even a letter of condolence; a letter of any kind, in ink, would be as unthinkable, as physically unmanageable, as writing the kind of poems he tried to write at college, to girls whose names never seemed to rhyme with anything. What word chimes with Bethany or Jenny? Or Pippa, except a stripper? Or Amanda, outside a limerick? Or Ruth, forsooth?

Ruth. Bill had no idea where she was living these days. He tried not to put an even more fearful suggestion to himself, the kind that came at night: what if she was not living at all? Contact had been lost soon after they split, and, without many mutual friends, it would have been hard to restore.

One true love. Is that the ration, allotted to everybody? There was that old myth, wasn't there, some creaky Greek legend about each person being a half, like half of a broken pot, and life being a question of watching and waiting, wandering the earth, hoping for your other half to show up and slip into place. A perfect fit, to make a whole. If that was so, Bill was still waiting; whether he was still watching was another matter. He had ceased to look. Ruth had come as close to anyone, but they both knew that the edges had not really locked together; there were shards missing, it was not quite right.

Bill had read enough of his own women's magazines to know that it's *never* quite right, there *is* no perfect fit, and your best bet is to spend a lifetime with someone, smoothing the edges, making repairs, getting used to the cracks. Then, with luck, as the end nears, you might suddenly realise that the pot has been finished, and that two have become one.

And what about those girls, the ones who read his David Cassidy thoughts each week? They had been sure of their one true love; the fact that millions of them had the *same* true love didn't seem to bother them. Clearly, David was the perfect fit for all sizes. That woman who had come into the office the other

340

day: the batty old Welsh girl, one of the receptionists had called her; except that, when she arrived, she didn't seem batty at all. Or old. One of the least mad people that Bill had ever met, though the Welsh part was true. Petra. And the way she talked about her past, her Cassidy days, as if she *knew* how mad she must have seemed at the time, and yet was not prepared to disown it now—refusing to take the easy adult option, and dismiss her yesteryears. Better to cling to one's youthful foolishness, surely, and argue for its importance, for its lasting place in the heart, rather than pretend it had never happened ... Love had been true, for Petra, utterly true, even if the truth was made up. Bill wondered what would happen when and if she found out that he, a lout of a literature student, had done most of the inventing. He hoped she wouldn't scratch his eyes out. She didn't look the type. She didn't look any type at all. She seemed like herself.

So, where did it all go wrong? David and me? Did he go cool on me, or find someone else; or did I force the issue, saying I needed the space?

I really did need the space; when I found myself crammed into White City, in May 1974, at David's final London concert, with teenage girls all around me, fainting not with excitement but because the crush was breaking their bones and, in one case, squeezing the life from their bodies, I wanted out. I remember walking away that night, away from the stadium, gulping down lungfuls of air.

Not long after that, David Cassidy quit. Not long after that, *The Essential David Cassidy Magazine* also called it a day; the right choice, I guess, on the grounds that it's hard to maintain a church when the god has announced his retirement.

Where, I wondered, did the congregation go? Into their grown-up lives: taking exams and jobs and husbands; first filing away their David posters and clippings, with their copies of my magazine, and then, somewhere along the way, just losing them, in attics and house-moves. How appalled they would have been, as thirteen-year-olds, to think that there could ever, ever come a day when they wouldn't know, or even mind, where their most treasured possessions were—that three-speed record player, that unscratched copy of *Cherish* . . .

I never did have that album. I never bought a David Cassidy record; to be brutal, I can't swear that I ever sat down and listened to a David Cassidy song—not all the way through, from intro to fade-out. Oh, I knew the songs all right, but that's because I had photocopies of the inner sleeves Sellotaped to the wall above my desk. Whenever inspiration flagged, I would raise my eyes to the lyrics in front of me, steal a phrase, and hammer it into my latest piece of Davidry. 'Cherish is the word I use to describe all the feeling that I have hiding here for you inside.'

How hard is it to work that into a letter? Christ, it sounds like a letter to begin with. The guy was doing my work for me.

Bill stopped, and went to a cupboard next to the bathroom, pulling it open to reveal a heap of suitcases. He yanked them out, one by one, taken aback by his own haste. At the back, under a rolled sleeping bag, there was a cardboard box. He lugged it back to the living room, and delved. It was full of clippings, as yellow as old skin. He flicked through them fast, dropping some onto the carpet. At last he paused, a small magazine in his hand. He took it back to the desk, smoothed it out, and began to type again.

It's so fantastic to feel the cool water closing over my hot, citified body! And then I just lie there on the side of the pool, drying off and looking down across the valley. It sure is a magnificent sight . . .
Not me drying off! The valley, I mean!

Only now, at this distance, could Bill grasp the full strangeness of his first job. Petra had got him thinking about it. Who would he rather have been, himself or David? By the age of twenty-four, Bill's career was taking off. Cassidy's, having flown a thousand times higher, was over, or in free fall. Not for him the normal arc of a life: a stumbling start, moving towards some distant peak that you finally reached in your middle years, even though the goal, once attained, might not seem worth the climb.

What must it be like to enjoy your finest hour before you turn thirty? Keats. All those books of poetry, scrawled upon by night, and shelved in shame when Bill put away childish things to enter the world of work, turn out to have been right all along. They held the clue, to love and fame alike. And the pop star, burning bright and fading fast, turns out to be little more than a rewrite of the Romantic poet. If Cassidy had died at White City—if he, not his fan, had been smothered in the crush—might it have been for the best? Wouldn't he have been made immortal, trapped at his moment of perfection?

The fate of the teen idol is the fate of beautiful girls down the ages. The idol has to be seen as virginal but highly desirable. Desirable, yet untouched.

Mind you, Cassidy was still alive, older and wiser with some sharp things to say about his condition, and good luck to him. He had got married, Bill knew that much. Two times, maybe three. The first must have been when he was still in his decompression chamber, recovering from global celebrity. Kay someone. A small blonde with cheeks like a peach. 'Peachy-creamy,' as Bill's Aunt Rita used to say, when asked how she was. Rita, in summer frocks for two-thirds of the year, married to Uncle Douglas, who used to stoop down, as if his waist were hinged, and gravely present Bill with a birthday fiver. One year, the banknote rustled a little as he placed it in the boy's grateful hand. A year later, the rustle was a shake, the paper trembling and rattling against Bill's palm, and then Douglas was not there any more; his tall frame confined to a chair, and finally a bed, the spasms— so Bill heard from a whispering cousin—grown uncontrolled. Rita, by then, was a ghost of a woman, soot dark around the eyes, exhausted by the love she had given to her man, once lofty, now quaking and unhinged. Yet still, at Christmas, unaccompanied, she wore butter yellow or Mediterranean blue, and smiled as she handed round the plates. 'Peachy-creamy, thank you, Bill,' she would say.

Who had Bill loved? Who did he want to take care of, once Ruth had disappeared? He had *made* love, God knows, sometimes not for weeks, or even months, and then in a fever of entanglements and five-timings; dressing quietly at dawn, in an Edinburgh hotel, while one woman slept, in order to catch a train to London and a lunchtime tryst with another, who stood in her hallway as he came in, wearing court shoes and nothing more, and received him there, pulling him into her, against the rain-damp coats. Then dinner with an old friend, unhappy now, requiring consolation. Bill had gone to bed that night, alone, feeling like an exhausted oil well, and slept for thirteen hours.

Or that Italian beauty, too beautiful for him, no name; maybe she hadn't seen him well, maybe that distracted mist in her violet eyes had been a myopic blur; finding themselves in front of the same painting, in, where was it? Milan, perhaps, when he had ninety minutes of museum-graze between meetings? Talking *sotto voce* about the picture, as you do, as if in church, she in her halting English, Bill in his backward Italian; then a pause, a look passed back and forth, then downstairs, don't rush, quiet marble corridors, heels clacking, finally an unlocked room, found and opened and locked from inside, Bill knocking over a mop or a broom, the beauty trying not to laugh out loud, then turning her face to the wall and raising, almost primly, the hem of her dress. What was it, seven, eight years ago? Didn't feel real, now, from this distance.

That was the thing with making love; over time, it took on the finished feeling of a story, or the gleam of a film, like something that had happened to someone else. (With love itself, the true love of legend, the opposite was true; as it grew, you could no longer imagine yourself without it. The love made you.) Sex opened up a rift from the world, rendered it redundant for a minute, or a month. Three days on the trot, once, in London, 1981, missing the royal wedding completely; getting out of bed to pee in the basin, hungry as lions, with no time to eat; who had been that devourer? Mary, that was it, saintly Mary, with the haircut of a principal boy, like Peter Pan, who had been with him for six weeks in all, and had never met any of his friends.

Then there was Melody. Lord help us, Melody. Bill still smiled, when he thought of his mate Pete the Pimple, informed over a pint that Bill had met a girl named Melody.

'You have *got* to be kidding,' Pete said. 'Bill, that's not a girl. That's a record label. That's a shampoo. That's half a fucking *magazine*.'

In those days, everyone, but everyone, read *Melody Maker* and *New Musical Express*, and so, of course, from that day in the pub to the end of the relationship, Pete and all his mates had called Melody 'NME'. To her *face*.

'How's it going, NME?' they would chorus as she drifted in, long skirt frilling the floor, and drank her barley wine. One time she came to a football match carrying a flute. Melody believed that in a previous life she had been an Egyptian cat, and her lovemaking was certainly feline, all sensual, selfish ease mixed with mad voracity. 'Sleeping with the NME,' as Pete observed. Bill, despairing of her finding a job, had forced her to fill in a careers questionnaire, only to come back three hours later and discover that, under the heading, 'Where do you see yourself in ten years' time?', she had written the single word 'Waterfall'.

Melody had wafted off, like a cirrus cloud, one afternoon, and such had been the relief that it wasn't until two weeks later that Bill, checking his bank balance, realised she had taken the lot.

By then, Bill was busy working for *Puzzle Time*, which sold more solidly, and made more money, for Nightingale Publishing than all but three of its other titles. He managed six months before moving sideways to another journal, and then, a year later, to another, but always within the same parent company. He was becoming a corporate child. And still, on dank Friday evenings, without even time for a bath, he would lug his guitar case from behind the sofa, or from under the vacuum cleaner, and hurry to Kentish Town or unfindable church halls off Tooting Broadway, to play in bands that seemed to change name, identity and purpose even more frequently than his jobs.

The most enduring, from 1975 to 1978, and still the most inexcusable, had been Green's Leaf, Bill's one and only foray into prog rock. He had been bandless and uneasy for a year, with Ruth gone and his other love, Spirit Level, cast to the winds. Spirit Level had lasted so long, and weathered so much, and put such heroic effort into never improving, despite an unceasing change of cast, that Bill presumed it could never die; for him, it was like playing in goal for a hopeless but venerable football club that would never rise beyond the Fourth Division. Then came the news: not one but two of its members, secretly and independently, had decided to sit accountancy exams, and had in fact met, face to face, at the door of the municipal sports hall where

347

the exams were being taken. Both wore suits. The horror of this coincidence had, not unnaturally, finished the band.

And so Bill had drifted, and played Hendrix records, until introduced one day to a trio of public schoolboys. Of *course* they were public schoolboys: that was the deal, with prog rock. It was easier to fantasise about mystical England if you could look out of your dormitory window and see Glastonbury. Or Wenlock Edge. Bill's secondary school had been directly opposite a pet-food store called Rruff Trade.

The public schoolboys were the same age as him, but still boys; still looking, behind their sheepish manes, as if waiting to be told to get their hair cut. When only fifteen, with voices barely broken, two of them, Roger and Miles, had formed a folk duo by the name of Pendragon. Then a third, Piers, had come in the sixth form, with his own drum kit, and they had grown—or 'matured', as Miles liked to say—into Stone Circle. Now, with Bill, their pet proletarian, on bass, they were Green's Leaf, and none of their songs lasted less than nine minutes. Sometimes Miles would go away in the middle of one of Roger's yowling, interminable guitar solos and change costume, re-emerging for the finale dressed as an ash tree. For 'Golden Bole' he hummed the middle eight with a light bulb inside his mouth, switched on. Bill would be at the side of the stage, defiantly clad in T-shirt and jeans, twanging along, his mind continents away. 'David Cassidy was better than this,' he said to himself, out loud, to the mirror in the backstage toilet, and then bowed his head in shame. Because it was true.

For one thing, Cassidy kept it short. Maybe not always sweet, but short. Say what you liked about

'Cherish', it was all over inside two and a half minutes. No wonder a pop song was called a number. Green's Leaf didn't have numbers, they had equations; and the sum of those equations was, as Pete the Pimple pointed out, 'zero shagging'.

By now, the room was nothing but shadow. Bill groped back to his computer.

Life can be brutal for the teen idol who tries to grow up. His job is to remind his fans of lost innocence, not their advancing years.

Donny Osmond recalled that, once the posters were torn down and 'Puppy Love' had faded, he was ridiculed for his lack of cool. Desperate to shed a goody-goody image, Donny engaged a publicist who suggested faking a drugs bust to establish some street credibility. The problem was, Donny didn't do drugs or caffeine or even premarital sex.

'Do I need to make mistakes to be thought of as interesting?' he asked. 'In my mind, I've been to the darkest places you can possibly imagine, but physically I don't want to go there.'

Teen idols can still go on touring into their thirties, forties and even fifties, but, as the hairline recedes and the waist thickens, the venues diminish in grandeur from stadium to concert hall to school gym to pub.

It would be a mistake to think that David Cassidy was something new. He was, for a heartbeat, the biggest thing in the world, but, when he stopped beating, others replaced him, just as he himself had followed earlier beats. When millions of girls screamed for Cassidy— and, trust me, this was real screaming, cavegirl-crazy—they thought that there had never been or ever would be anyone like him, just as their desire for him was unique and unrepeatable, every girl's howl and sob as particular to her as her own sneeze or—still to come—her orgasmic cry.

Whereas, of course, the poor bloke was perched uncertainly, in his spangly catsuit, on the shoulders of giants. Before him there had been—to take only the unembarrassing examples, and leaving aside the Monkees and Johnnie Ray—the Beatles, and then Elvis, and then Sinatra.

The bobby-soxers who waited in line for the young Sinatra felt the planet tipped in their favour by his presence. There was a day in wartime, October in New York, when they were allowed to keep their seats, for an all-day session of Frank on-screen and Frank in person, as long as they continued to occupy them. This was not a wise ruling; most of those girls would happily have stayed in those seats, leaned back, given birth, raised mini-Franks, and died there. And so, of the thirty-six hundred who began the day, only two hundred and fifty departed. You don't walk out on Frank. To their eyes, and on the evidence of their ears, he had been put on earth to pitch his woo at them, and they were born with a view to catching it, and hugging it close, and yelling back that, yes, they were all his.

And David Cassidy? Same deal—with a fraction of the Sinatra voice, but with the same Bambi appeal. The screams remained the same. And what if David had stopped and turned round, mid-chorus, and pointed a finger at some likely lass and said, 'All right, then. If you're mine, can I have you?' What would she have done, apart from swooned? Well, as a matter of fact, we know the answer to that.

I was one of the few male buyers, I suspect, of Cassidy's autobiography, *C'mon, Get Happy*, when it came out in 1994. That makes me, I would also guess, one of the few readers who were undismayed. It seems safe to presume that most of the people who rushed to get the book were fans of the artist formerly known as David; they didn't particularly want to know about his marriage, or his comebacks (which they would avidly attend, nevertheless, in any city, any time); they weren't interested in now. They wanted then. They wanted reports from the front line of 1973, when the battle for David was in full spate. They wanted reassurance that their love had been, though unrequited, worth every tear, every sleepless night beneath the giant poster, and every scream.

And what did they read? Stuff about how David was fascinated with women who really enjoyed the art of oral sex. That he rarely had any emotional connection with the girls he slept with, even comparing it to masturbation.

Forget unrequited love. The guy was requiting all over the shop. He was requiting backstage, in his hotel suite, on the hoof. And what I longed to know was this: what was it like for the women who crossed the threshold? Were they disillusioned to the core, devastated by the brief reality, or did they realise that this was, logically, where all the illusions he sang about were bound to conclude?

351

It's important, at this point, to get our demographics right. Cassidy confesses to a great deal of action, most, if not all, of it from people down on their knees, like worshippers; but he also, by his own admission, went for older fans—women of the world, not young girls new to it. He recalls turning down a beautiful fourteen-year-old who wanted her first time to be with David Cassidy. For a deity, he was remarkably kind and considerate. So maybe the mystery is doomed to be unsolved; we never can know what the teenaged fans, the readers of my magazine, would have done, if presented with the flesh of true romance, because they never had access. They were free, in other words, to shout out their desire, because it would never be satisfied. Their screams were dreams.

Beyond this point, I find myself in the dark. No man has ever known a woman's thoughts . . .

Bill stopped. Once you find yourself admitting defeat in a piece, it is always time to stop. And if you don't, he thought, his tired mind twisting back on itself, you get Clare. Clare, light of my life, fire of my loins; 'waste of your time, more like', as Pete preferred to call it, once the whole thing was over.

Brisk and bracing as a walk on a frosty day; Clare with her portfolio of international clients and her regulation three orgasms, one before, thank you, one during, one to finish, together if possible please. Hair pinned up with no need of a mirror as she spruced herself in the morning, catching the Tube to Bank before Bill was even awake. An affair, yes; a stretch of efficient pleasure, in the capable hands of Clare; but *married*, for *ten years* . . . How had that happened? How had Bill allowed it to happen? Even now, he could barely summon the era, recreate its contours in his head; it was less of an event, more of an absence, a desert where two people, compatible enough, were said to have been together, by no means unhappily, but where they seem to have left no trace.

What was that Fitzgerald story? Last one in the book, where one guy meets another, a former acquaintance, and tries to work out where he's been for so long, out of the fray. Abroad, or sick, or just away? Turns out he'd been drunk. How did the line go? 'Jesus. Drunk for ten years.' Well, that was how Bill felt, sometimes; not resentful, quite mild in his way, but sad and quizzical nonetheless. *Jesus. Married for ten years*. 'The Lost Decade', that's what the story was called.

Clare had been quite firm about not wanting kids. And he had gone along with it, not wishing to force the issue, as it were, while noticing, as if out of the corner of his eye, how much he enjoyed being Uncle Bill to his six nieces. From the outside, Clare and Bill had the gleam of success. They had risen through their ranks; she, to high office in the temple of investment, a priestess whose rites he never claimed to understand; he, 'Magazine Man', as Clare would say with a third of a smile, leafing his way through the ever shinier pages of one title after the next, until he was senior enough—'sufficiently wanky', in the words of Pete, when they met up near work—to take off his shirt and tie and wear a top of black knitted silk instead, buttoned to the neck, beneath his suit.

He had seen the Welshwoman, Petra, looking at him the other day, and sizing him up; taking in the clothes, the loafers (soundless, on the office carpet),

353

even the lacquer of his fountain pen, and—he had never felt the force of the phrase before now—getting the measure of him. Like an entomologist with a beetle, still alive. She would have tapped his shell if she could, to find out if there was anything inside. There was a look in her eyes he couldn't place. She was the polar opposite of a groupie, that was for sure. Whatever those older women had done to David Cassidy, wanting him without knowing him, without knowing *why*, it was the opposite of what Petra was after, with her visitor's pass and her twenty-five-year-old letter.

She was not on her knees; Welshwoman stood straight and looked at Magazine Man. She did not altogether like what she saw, he was sure of that. But then Bill did not always like what he saw, whenever he caught sight of himself. In a glass, darkly. He had put away childish things, and he kept fearing—half-hoping—that they would start to reappear. Flashes and eruptions of young William, in the sagging face of Mr Finn. Did Petra think such thoughts? Can two people think the same thing without knowing it?

Strange that he should wonder about her. Met her for—what?—an hour or two at the most. Yet she had struck him—really struck, in the way that you do a gong, or a chord—and the sound would not die away. He could see her now, in detail; conjure her more exactly from those few minutes than he could Clare, his other half, with whom he had spent a decade. Clare was misting over, and this stranger—this *other* other—was growing clearer by the hour. Petra. Lost and found. Tender is the Night. Ruth and Melody and Clare. The Pearl Woman. Spirit Level and Green's Leaf. David Cassidy and Puzzle Time. Petra. I claim my prize.

354

18

'Are you alone?' asked Petra. 'Is there just one of you? I thought there were going to be more.'

'Me too,' said Bill.

They were standing at the coffee machine in the British Airways lounge. It was a while since Petra had flown, and she had half forgotten the crush of travellers at the check-in desks, the long lines of thrumming anxiety, everyone on the hard verge of complaint; having forged a way through, she found her need for coffee, here on the other side, almost overwhelming. Coffee and somewhere to sit down. Sharon, on the other hand, who had flown only twice before, and had never been in an airline lounge, was in heaven. She was eating a slab of soft cheese on a Ritz cracker, and devotedly studying the labels of the three available brandies, like an art historian at a show of lithographs. It was nine o'clock in the morning.

Bill waited until they were seated. He stirred his tea, sipped, and said to Petra, as she raised her cup to her lips: 'Yes, I was going to send one of our writers to cover you.'

Petra snorted into her coffee. Some of it slopped into the saucer.

'I'm sorry,' said Bill. 'I'll start again. What I was trying to say was, I asked one of our lot, very smart lad called Jake, to fly out with you and write up the story. Ideal chap; did a really nice cover story for us last month on Emmylou Harris.'

'The most beautiful woman in the world,' said Petra.

'God, yes. Most of the survivors from that era, they look a bit, you know, lived-in. And she just seems to have sailed through without a scratch. And the voice with it. Amazing. Anyway, when I said about you, and, and . . . the David Cassidy thing, Jake jumped at it. Said it was a brilliant idea.'

'So where is he?'

'Well, it was him who pulled out. I mentioned that I was thinking of doing, you know, the deep background piece. An oldie speaks. And he says, go on then, Boss, you do it. Do the whole thing.'

'Do they really call you Boss?'

Bill made a face. He broke a biscuit in two and dunked one half in his tea. Petra was glad her mother wasn't there to see it.

' 'Fraid they do, and it always makes me feel like I'm going to be rumbled at any minute. Because I am really the least . . . bossy boss you can get. I mean, I'm sure I'm a nightmare to work for. But I don't do shouting or throwing things or threats. I just doodle a lot and change my mind. Although I did staple my thumb to an A4 pad last week.'

'Ouch.'

'Very ouch. And how about you?'

'What about me?'

'Are you the bossy type? You don't look it, but then . . .'

'Well, I'm organised.'

'Not the same thing. Who do you organise?'

'My daughter,' said Petra. 'And me. I mean my days. I used to organise my husband, but then he organised himself into being with someone else.'

'Idiot,' Bill said.

'Who, me?'

'No, him.'

356

'Not all men are idiots, you know, just because they leave women.' Petra poured herself more coffee.

'Well, I left,' said Bill. 'Because I didn't know what to stay for. Or who, actually.'

'At least you didn't leave to go and live on a houseboat with someone half your age.'

'God, is that what he did? He really is an idiot.'

'So there was no houseboat with you.'

'No, and no someone else either. I just went. My dishwasher-stacking skills were becoming the most interesting thing about me. I thought of turning pro.'

'Me too.'

'Dishwasher?'

'No, cello.'

'Oh, cello's much easier. You don't need rinse aid.'

Petra smiled. 'No, we use rosin instead.' She looked across at Sharon, who was busy slipping a complimentary KitKat into her hand luggage.

'Why did you give up?'

'Oh, because of my husband, I suppose.'

'Come on, he didn't make you? Nobody does that nowadays. It's not 1913.'

'No, but he's one too. A cellist. And he's better than me.'

Bill sighed. 'Modesty gets you nowhere.'

'But it's true. He's a star, and I . . . I mean, he's like a planet and I'm just a moon, circling round. So I gave it up and went into music therapy, where I still use my, you know, my—'

'Gifts.'

'I was going to say skills. He has a gift, I have skills. Anyway, you can't have two soloists in one house. People think we played duets all the time, making beautiful music and so on, but it's not like that at all.

357

I mean it wasn't. It was more like a . . . like . . .' Petra, not wanting to go on, was relieved to find Sharon coming near, hauling her hand luggage. She was waving a leaflet.

'Pet, we can get a massage on the flight. For free.' She sank down into one of the chairs and puffed her cheeks, as if at the end of a long day, not the start. 'Can't decide whether to have the neck rub or the herby facial. Look, says here, "cleanses and refreshes with subtle oils of lavender and sage to rejunev, renuj . . ."'

'Rejuvenate?'

'Yeah, brilliant, "rejuvenate *and* brighten your looks, enabling you to step off at your destination ready to go and enjoy". Well, that's us, isn't it? Don't know about you, but I haven't had my looks brightened since 1981. Royal wedding. Only I would put a bloody face-pack on just to watch TV.' She looked at Petra, then at Bill. 'What you two nattering about, then?'

'Music,' said Bill.

'What, David's music?'

'No, Petra's. She was saying she doesn't have a gift.'

'I—' Petra began.

'Oh, you don't want to listen to her. I mean, you do want to listen, when she's playing, like, but once she starts going on about how rubbish she is . . . Haven't changed, have you, Pet? Never one for blowing her own trumpet. Cello.'

'She's as good as I think she is, then?'

'Bloody brilliant, Pet is. Better than her bloody husband, I tell you.'

Petra sat through this with the flush gathering on her face. She hated to be talked about, even in

358

praise, and especially when she was sitting right there. Who would like it? Pop stars, maybe, but nobody normal.

Their flight number was announced. Sharon and Petra stood up at once and started to gather their belongings. Bill stayed where he was.

'Give it a few minutes if I were you,' he said. 'They're trying to herd us. Won't even open the doors for another twenty-five minutes.'

'Don't want to miss it,' said Sharon, seriously concerned.

'We won't, I promise. We're near the front, anyway.'

'There's posh,' said Sharon, sitting down again.

'All part of the service, ma'am,' said Bill, in a bad American accent. Petra sat down, too, though still uncertain.

'Do this a lot, do you?' said Sharon. If anyone else had asked, Petra thought, there would have been resentment at the edge of the question, like a stain; but Sha had no resentment in her soul. Not now, not twenty-five years ago. She took the world on its own terms, laughed out loud at its stupidities, and waited patiently for any joys that might come along. Whenever, at any stage in life, Petra heard the phrase 'counting your blessings', she always thought of Sharon, aged thirteen, kneeling on the carpet in the Lewises' lounge, emptying a pack of Spangles onto a copy of *TV Times* and sharing them out: one for you, one for me . . .

'I do quite a lot of flying, yes, for the job.'

' 'Spect you get bored, don't you?'

Petra watched Bill. He smiled at Sharon and said, 'You know what? I don't. Some blokes do, and it's not that good for you, being cooped up in a tin can,

359

but I'm still enough of a little boy to think that getting into the can at one end and coming out the other end in New York, eight hours later, is a kind of magic trick. And it's . . . When you take off, it's still quite, I don't know, liberating, leaving all the usual stuff behind. You just know that for the next few hours nobody's going to knock on your door or ask you about cover design or bollock you for not making a phone call. The only boring thing, I guess, is not getting to share the liberation. Normally it's just me. One time I had to go to Hong Kong, and I left my book on the Gatwick Express, and ended up running for the plane, and spent fifteen hours reading the in-flight shopping mag. So now I know nothing about Raymond Carver but I know all there is to know about furry padded 747s and what the difference is between Diorissimo and Miss Dior.'

'Go on, what's the difference, then?'

'Um, one comes in this handy atomiser, for all your fragrance needs on the go . . .'

Sharon actually barked with laughter. She reached out and took the undunked half of Bill's biscuit.

'Well, now you've got us, haven't you? So you won't be bored.'

'Exactly.'

'Bang goes your liberation.'

'Exactly. Thanks a bunch.'

Petra watched the two of them, enjoying themselves. It looked as easy as a game of ping-pong: to and fro, nothing to it, no hard feelings, almost no feelings at all . . . Why was it always harder for her—cautious, loaded, heavy with spin? Why could she just never play the game? And she had noticed how deftly Bill had ducked the danger. If he had admitted that yes, he was bored by the travelling (and he had to be, like all businessmen were), it would have undermined the pleasure that Sharon was taking in this day. Not that Sha would have minded, or even noticed much; but to her the trip was something special, a big hilarious one-off. The right thing to do, the good thing, was to respect her feelings and play along. That's what Bill had done, and, for the second time in as many weeks, Petra found herself thinking: I like him.

'What was the book you left on the train? Carver something,' she said.

'Raymond Carver. Short stories. Just the best. Perfect for leaving on trains.'

'I think I read some, in a collection. I'm so useless, if I really like something I remember the plot and the characters and these silly details, like the colour of someone's lipstick, but I forget who wrote it.'

'The least important thing. Lipstick matters much more.'

'What was the title? Of your lost book.'

'*What We Talk About When We Talk About Love.*'

'Oh, I can tell you that,' said Sharon, taking an apple from a bowl on the table and rubbing it on her sleeve. 'People in love don't sit around chatting about it, like "ooh we're so in love", do they? Waste of time. I knew this boy once, and all we ever talked about was who we'd really hated in school and what the best kind of ice cream was to go with what meal, like if you have roast chicken you have to have rum and raisin, right?'

Bill liked listening to the way her voice swooped up at the end of a sentence: rai-sin.

'And once, we spent a whole afternoon talking about how we'd live in space. And I was asking how you get the needle to stay on the record when there's no gravity, if you want to have a listen to a song, and he was worried about flushing the toilet, and you know what he means, don't you? All that wee floating round.' Bill and Petra looked at each other, trying not to laugh. 'And so we split up, right, and it wasn't until after that I was in the post office, and I thought, ooh he was lovely, that Gareth. I think I loved him, and I never said. Never knew. Nor did he, poor bloke. All we did was talk, like. Don't know what happened to him, mind. Probably weeing in space. Might see him this morning if we look out the window, eh, Pet? Give him a wave.'

Petra shook her head in wonderment. 'Your brain, Sharon *fach* . . .'

'This is a last and final call for passengers on BA174 . . .'

'There we are.' Sharon jumped to her feet.

'Don't worry,' said Bill, getting to his feet. 'You don't start running till they ask for you by name.' He picked up Sharon's hand luggage.

'Bloody hell. What have you got in here? *Who* have you got in here?'

'Gareth,' said Petra. 'All tied up.'

'Get you,' said Sharon. 'Anyway, I thought we had another boy coming? Didn't you say there was a writer?' They left the lounge and started walking, three abreast, towards the gate.

'That's what I thought,' said Petra. 'But the other one dropped out. Just the three of us. Bill's the writer now.'

'How's that, then?' Sharon was asking Bill, but Petra answered first.

'It's his field. You know, Professor of Cassidy Studies. World expert on batty old ladies who want to be fourteen again.'

362

'That's not quite fair,' said Bill.

'On who?'

'Ermmm . . . hang on, left here. Gate 26. Down there.' He had quickened his pace again, Petra almost sprinting in his wake, but now he slowed. 'Told you. Ages to go.' There was a small crowd around the gate, gradually filtering through in single file. 'Wait till this lot clears.'

They stood there, while Sharon frisked herself for her boarding pass. 'Had it somewhere.' She found it, at last, stuck against the KitKat. 'There we go. So,' she went on, addressing Bill, 'what makes you the expert anyway?'

'What, on batty old ladies?'

'No, on David.'

'Oh, you mean batty young ladies. Oh, well, believe it or not, I used to write, a hundred years or so ago, for something called *The Essential David Cassidy Magazine*. And my—'

'Oh my Gaaawwwd,' Sharon and Petra cried out together. Bill looked startled.

'That was our Bible, that was.' Petra gazed at him with an earnestness he hadn't seen before, though it didn't seem unexpected, or even out of place. As for Sharon, her mouth was still ajar.

'Meaning?'

'Well, we believed it.'

'Not all of it.'

'Every word.'

'Still do,' said Sharon, regaining the power of speech.

'But,' said Bill, who was struggling with these latest revelations, 'but, if it's like the Bible, don't you? . . . I mean, not everything in the Bible is true. Not literally.'

'It is to a believer,' said Petra.

'Yeah, but—'

'To one of them,' said Sharon, 'them fundy, what are they? Fundymentals.'

'Fundamentalists.'

'Yeah, that's the boys. That's us.'

'You mean it *was* you back when you were kids,' said Bill. 'You can't still believe it. Not now. If you read that stuff now, you'd see in an instant that it was all cobbled together.'

'Gerraway with you, mun,' said Sharon. The crowd was thinning now, and they were beckoned towards the gate. 'If you believe something, you have to go on believing, don't you?'

'Like what?'

'I dunno.' Sharon handed in her boarding card, then presented her passport. 'Look at me,' she said, showing Bill the photograph. 'What a mugshot. Like I'm wanted by the cops or something.' Petra came next. She was quiet.

'Well,' Sharon continued, as they filed down the tunnel towards the plane, 'like the letters he wrote. David. You know, the every month ones, signed by him. You're not going to say those were made up, are you? I mean, we knew those were actually him writing. Sounded just like David. We could feel it.'

Bill stopped. 'But that was me.'

'What?' The two women stopped as well. Latecomers bustled past them. Up ahead, cabin crew held open the airplane door and smiled.

'That was my job. I wrote those letters. I was David Cassidy.'

Without hesitation, Petra swivelled round and started walking straight back the way they had come.

'Pet?' said Sharon.

'Petra, come back,' said Bill.

'I'm not coming,' called Petra over her shoulder. She went on walking.

Sharon nudged Bill with her elbow. 'I think she likes you.'

*   *   *

Outside, the blue was so pure it felt like a special effect. A fake backdrop, surely, thought Bill; not real sky. Petra, sitting beside him, hadn't given it so much as a glance. She didn't want to be here. The cabin crew had taken her aside and explained why she had to get on, talking calmly to her about luggage and security and departure slots. But still, she could have gone, just walked on out of the airport and back home. Wanted to in a way. The absurdity of what she was doing suddenly overwhelmed her. It wasn't that she, Petra, the woman of thirty-eight, had been upset by Bill's bombshell, but the girl inside her, the one who still wanted to meet David, was shocked. All her life she had been lied to about love and the man sitting next to her, tapping on his laptop, he had started it.

'Why did you do it?' she asked, looking down.

'Somebody had to.'

'But why?'

'Because . . . because there were thousands of people like you, I mean not just like you, but thousands with the same kind of—I don't know, the same sort of love. The same craze. And we didn't know what to do with you.'

'What d'you mean, do with us?'

'Well . . . we called it feeding the lionesses. Your appetite was, I mean, there was no end of it. You

365

wanted more of him, every week, on every conceivable subject, than we could possibly supply. It was hard enough for us to churn it out, so the idea that he could have done it himself . . . It just wasn't possible.'

'What about, what's it called, syndication? He writes one letter, back in California or wherever, and it gets printed in all the different magazines all over the world. It wouldn't have been ours alone, but at least it would have been true.'

'Not a bad idea. You should mention it to him when you see him on Wednesday.'

Petra said nothing. She knew she was being ridiculous, like a child; but then that, after all, was what was at stake here—the right to defend the child you used to be. The child who was trying out love, real love, for the first time. To be cheated in love later on, well, it happened, happened to the best of people; it had happened to her, with a vengeance, just this past year and her heart was ripped apart. But to be cheated at your first attempt, by someone trying on the disguise of the person you loved: what kind of betrayal was that?

The flight attendant went past with the drinks trolley, on her second run. Petra had shaken her head when she came round before. Now she ordered a vodka and tonic; not a drink she had ever ordered before in her life. Why now, then? It seemed as good an occasion as any. The attendant gave her two small bottles of vodka and two cans of tonic. Petra opened them and mixed them, half and half. Bill was drinking tomato juice. She wondered how it would look all over his white linen shirt.

He was staring into his plastic cup, saying nothing. Then he said, 'Sorry.' He looked at Petra properly

366

and steadily, admitting his guilt, hoping to see a flicker of merciful humour in those eyes of hers. Deep brown, her eyes. He took a breath and continued.

'But which would you have preferred, honestly? To read David's letters, every month, and believe in them, and, I don't know, draw strength from them in some way; or never to hear from him? To sit in your bedrooms and giggle and swoon over the nonsense I wrote on his behalf, and it was nonsense, believe me, or to sit there and look at a blank space in the fan mag, maybe with a few words from Zelda, saying, "We're terribly sorry, but Mr Cassidy doesn't have the time, the inclination or the punctuation to write you the message you want to hear right now. Nor will he have the time in the immediate future; not until you've stopped loving him, at which point he will suddenly have all the time in the world." Think about it, Petra. You're a brilliant woman, so you tell me. Which would it be? The happy fib, or the sorry truth?'

Petra swallowed half her drink in one long draught. She could feel it going straight to her head, siphoning directly from her stomach. She was blinking oddly, too; fizzy eyes, one of her friends used to say when they first had a girls' night out.

'Who's Zelda?' she asked eventually. The consonants were fizzy now as well.

'Oh God, she was my boss. Extraordinary woman, in a way. A sort of human galleon. Everybody took the piss, but I liked her a lot. She taught me how to be picky, for one thing.'

'Picky?'

'You know, check your spelling, lineation, pagination, dropped caps, contents page matching

367

actual contents, picture credits. All the gubbins. Get your quotes right.'

'Unless you've made them all up,' she said.

'Yes, and even then they need to make sense, and sort of gel together. Believe it or not.'

'So picky was good.'

'Picky is always good. All the maddest poets were complete pedants, the madder the better. Byron, Baudelaire, all the Bs, all the wild boys; whoring and drinking, then back to the proofs and the semicolons. Come on, you're the cellist. Without picky you haven't got a hope, you know that.'

'Yes,' said Petra sadly, 'I know that.' She thought of her mother, the Kaiser of Picky, and of Miss Fairfax, her own personal galleon. The world felt a lot less safe and rigorous without Jane Fairfax in it. The only consolation was that you could hand on the pickiness, pass it on to those who would live after you, so they, in their turn, would pass it on. 'Bach never wastes a single note, Petra. You *must* play every note consciously.'

They said nothing for a while. 'What became of her?'

'Who?'

'Zelda. Did you keep in touch?'

'Oh God. It was awful.'

'What was?'

'Well, we lost touch after I left the job. You know how it goes. The more you promise to stay in touch, the more guaranteed it is that you'll never hear from each other again. I was waiting for her to make the call, and she was probably doing the same with me. And then a couple of years ago, by sheer chance, I was in Stratford. Not Shakespeare, the other Stratford, Stratford East. And this tiny little bloke

368

comes up to me in the street, taps me on the arm, and I sort of veer away. Cos he looks a bit of a mess, bit smelly. And he says, "'Allo, Bill." And I look at him, and I swear I genuinely don't know who it is. And it turns out to be this chap called Chas, who was our office boy, back in the, you know, the Cassidy days. I was always a bit mean about Chas, and I'm pretty sure he hated me, thought I was a snob and a college git.'

'And were you?'

'Totally. And it turns out, of course, that Chas was the one who kept in touch with Zelda. Not me, the nice boy with all the promises and the big career coming. Fat lot of good I was. But the dogsbody with no career at all, you know, a lifetime of doing other people's dreary stuff for them, he was the good Christian soul. Met up with Zelda three, four times a year; lunch, pub, talk about old times. Which of course were her best times, as far as she was concerned. And she got ill, and refused to leave her flat, and Chas would take round the groceries, you know, heat up the soup.

'And I said to him, "how's she doing now? Is she still alive?" And he looks at me and says, "Oh no, died ten years ago." He went on hols, first trip ever, been saving up for it, and while he's away she took some sleeping tablets. He comes back from Spain and finds her in bed. Been like that for two weeks. Just the most dreadful thing. Imagine how I felt.'

'Imagine how *he* felt,' corrected Petra. 'Imagine how *she* must have felt.'

'Yes.' Bill looked down at his drink. This woman seemed to be peeling him apart. It was like going to confession.

'What would Zelda say,' asked Petra, a few
369

minutes later, 'if she knew you were going to meet David Cassidy? And that you were bringing two of your readers along?'

'Oh, no question. She would be completely thrilled. That would be her idea of heaven. To have arranged it so that other people could be happy.'

'Even though she wasn't.'

'Well, she was on her own ground. It's just that elsewhere she seemed, I don't know, marooned.'

'Not like our girl there,' said Petra, nudging him and glancing over at Sharon. The flight attendant had come to ask what they would like for their lunch, and Sharon was deep in conversation. The attendant was forced to kneel down beside her and go through every detail, so that Sharon, who had been reading the in-flight menu ever since they took off, could savour all the possibilities before landing on the right one. 'Is that real cream with the pineapple cake?' she was saying.

'I have to tell you, Petra,' said Bill, in great solemnity. 'I'm in love.'

'Oh, please, Mr Finn. And we've only just met. This is so sudden.'

'With your friend. I honestly think Sharon is the most lovable person I have ever met, I mean properly able to be loved. Like it's her vocation or something. Of course most of the people I work with are total shits, so she does have a head start, but still.'

'Well, I loved her first, so hands off,' said Petra. 'You're right, though.'

'Has she always been like that?'

'Always. From when she was—well, she was never a slip of a thing, but from when I first knew her. I was always glad she put up with me, she's just a much better person than me.'

'Rubbish. How can you say that?'

'It's true. She's better and she's happier.' Petra sipped her vodka. 'Better because she's happier.'

'Is that how it works?'

'Oh yes. People always say, oh, do good and it'll make you happy, but that's the wrong way round, isn't it? Contented people are just more likely to do good, they're more . . . equipped for it. They don't have to work themselves up to it, it just comes naturally. I mean, look at her. Look at them.'

The attendant had departed, deeply bewildered by the in-depth discussion of salmon roulade, and Sharon was talking, with great animation, to the couple across the aisle. They were matching human beings: outsized but cheery, the bulk of them overflowing the seats, even these larger ones in business class. Both wore shirts of a deafening loudness, as if they were already in Las Vegas, not nine hours away. Both were drinking small bottles of champagne, their second bottle each. Their free hands, the ones not holding their drinks, were clasped together on the armrest.

'I think they might be married,' Bill said.

'Noooo!' said the woman to Sharon. She turned to her husband. 'Hear that, Mr J?'

'There you go,' said Bill quietly. 'She's Mrs J.' Petra stifled a laugh.

'Guess what this lady's doing in Vegas. You'll never guess.'

'Gamblin'', said Mr J, and shook merrily at his own wit.

'No, silly, much better than that. Guess who she's going to meet, her and her friends here.'

'Give up,' said the husband, instantly.

'Only David Cassidy, in't it? David bloody

371

Cassidy. I love that little fella.'

'Number fifty-three,' said Mr J.

'Is it really? Fifty-three? Well, there you go, then. He's coming back up. Well I never.'

It was Petra's turn to lean across. 'Excuse me, but I couldn't help overhearing. Who's number fifty-three?'

'David is. Sorry, love, sounds a bit mysteeerious, don't it?' The woman had an audience now. Half the cabin was listening intently, and the other half had no choice. 'My husband here, he's, well, he's in the ringtone sector. You know, like on mobiles. "King of the Ringtones", that's what the local paper said. And we have a chart, like, which songs are people choosing this week to put on their phones. And Mr J was just saying that your David Cassidy, he's up to fifty-three this week. Not bad, eh? I mean, especially seeing how old he must be. Wearing well, is he?'

'Bloody well hope so,' said Sharon, opening a packet of pretzels. 'Not going all that way to see someone who looks like my grandad, are we?'

'Which song is it?' Petra asked. 'In your chart.'

' "I Think I Love You". Obvious, really,' said Mr J.

'Completely,' said Petra. 'Great song. Never dates.'

'Mind you,' he went on, 'someone told me this funny thing at the office last week. Happened to a friend of his, his wife, right? Big Cassidy fan, all the way back. Anyway, she's at the doctor's, OK? Not just any old doctor's, either. Gyny whatnot.

'Mr J!'

'So, she takes off her togs, puts her handbag down, with the phone in it, not switched off, and the gyny fella's got his little, what do they call it?

372

Speculation?'

'Speculum,' said Petra, who knew it well.

'That's the job. Anyway, he's got his speculum, right, and he's having a proper feel, like you do—no, Marjorie, they got to hear this, let me finish—and he's just saying, "Does it hurt", you know, "I do hope you're not feeling any pain," all polite, and at that moment . . .' Mr J paused to wipe his eyes, already overcome. 'At that exact moment her phone, the one in her bag, starts going, "I think I love you" . . .' Mr J sang it to them, in a strong bass. 'And this bird, she hears this ringtone, right, number fifty-three, and it's just so wrong, for where she is, that she laughs, like really, really loud. And the poor doc, he gets shot out of her backwards, like a cork out of a bottle, she says, and his speculator comes flying out too, and he bangs his head on the door. And she says, quick as a flash, "I do . . ."' Mr J was uncontrolled by now, quivering in every corner of his frame, his wife beside him doing the same. 'She says, all polite like, "I do hope you're not feeling any pain." I mean, you've got to laugh, an't you?'

Sharon was spraying pretzels over the aisle. Petra sat back.

'I'm not sure I'll ever be able to hear that song in quite the same way again.'

Bill looked at her and said: 'All things considered, I don't think we should tell David Cassidy what happened to his song.'

'Oh, I don't know. He might be thrilled. He always wanted to reach out to his fans. Just not into them.' Petra had finished her drink, both bottles. Her tongue felt loose. She rattled the ice. 'Anyway, what's the plan when we get there?'

'Well, tonight, just as your body wants to go to

373

sleep, your spirit has to get up and go and see David sing.'

'Oh, I think I can manage that.'

'And then tomorrow morning, at eleven thirty, depending on whether or not we can drag Sharon away from her all-night blackjack session, we go and meet David. Meet and greet, take a few snaps, sign autographs, that kind of thing. We won't have that long with him, I suspect, but still. The good news is he's staying at the same hotel as us.'

Petra closes her eyes. A quarter of a century ago, the news that she would be spending the night in the same hotel as David Cassidy would have made her faint clean away.

'Tonight is a special,' Bill was saying. 'One-man show, I guess; he stands there and belts out all the golden oldies.'

'You mean to all the golden oldies.'

'That's us. Most nights he's in some stage show called, wait for it, *EFX*.'

'*Effects*?'

'No, spelt out, like E-F-X. Lots of dry ice and lasers and new songs. That's why we timed the trip to coincide with the show he's doing tonight. More your thing.'

'Very good of you.'

'Oh no, purely selfish. Gives me more to write about.'

The meals had arrived. Sharon had already dropped half a roll and was trying to open a sachet of salad dressing.

'Take cover,' said Petra to Bill.

Across the aisle, Mr and Mrs J were clinking glasses and proposing a toast to the assembled company.

374

'To David Cassidy.'

'To David Cassidy,' said Petra, raising her empty glass. 'Bill?'

Bill gave a long sigh, as if suffering from an old wound, and lifted his tomato juice.

'To David Cassidy,' he said. 'And Zelda, who art in heaven.'

Petra smiled, and touched her glass to his. 'To Zelda.'

19

He is five minutes late. Five minutes and twenty-four years. The Welshwomen, for the second time in their lives, are surrounded by their love rivals. It's not as big a crowd as turned out for David at White City, maybe only a few hundred, and there are no screams tonight, just the occasional shriek, as if someone had seen a mouse, followed by gales of embarrassed womanly laughter. Looking round the audience, Petra is surprised at how emotional she feels. Jet lag may be making her feel a bit weepy, but it's more than that. Many of the women here look like survivors. She can see at least two whose tufted baldness shows they have had cancer, and may still have it. All of the Cassidy girls have entered the age of grief, that time when life's losses start to stack up. Few will have been spared. Count yourself lucky if you get to your mid-thirties without knowing death, divorce or other species of grief.

Some of the fans have brought their daughters along and Petra suddenly wishes Molly were by her side. When they spoke on the phone earlier, Mol reported happily that Carrie had made her waffles and maple syrup for breakfast. She loves anything American because it brings her closer to Leo diCaprio.

'Love you, Mum,' Molly said. It was worth flying thousands of miles just to hear that. Petra thinks of emotion recollected in tranquillity, of all the women like her in this auditorium who are looking back on their thirteen-year-old selves, on the pressure of all that yearning. Wanting to be loved so badly. That was the great engine of life, revving up back then, if only they'd known it. And how many are thinking of what happened, and what didn't happen, in the years between then and now? David's album, as it happens. Good title. *Then and Now*.

'Where is he?' she asks. 'Why isn't he here yet?'

'Oh, he'll be here,' said Sharon. 'Don't you worry.'

'Oh, I'm not worried. He's a grown-up, he can take care of himself. D'you think *any* men are really grown up?'

Sharon thinks about it. 'Well, I thought my dad was, but then I caught him on the PlayStation with David—'

'*Your* David. Not this one.'

'My David, yeah. We don't really get David Cassidy coming round too often to play Donkey Kong. Funny, that.'

'Marcus never came to any of my recitals. I mean, what else is he doing with his life? What's so important that he couldn't come and listen to a thirty-year-old Welshwoman playing Debussy on a Tuesday lunchtime? In a crypt?'

'Too busy with his Donkey Kong, that's what I heard.' One of the best things about Sharon, Petra had long thought, was that she genuinely found her own jokes more appealing than anyone else's. There was no ill will towards other people, not a trace of selfishness; in her eyes, she was just funnier. She laughed now, and the sound of it—clear as a bell, dirty as a rugby match—turned heads all along their row.

'Shh now, everyone's looking at us,' said Petra.

'Pet, this is Las Vegas. There are lions in the lobby. Real live ones. No one's gonna look at us, are they?'

377

'They're not *in* the lobby. Not like chatting to the concierge.'

'No, but did you see them in that bit with the glass ceiling? Got the shock of my life, I did, when I looked up. Like bloody *Daktari* in here it is.'

'It's because it's MGM.'

'What?'

'You know, like the lion that roars at the start of the films? That's why they have them here.'

'Oh, right you are,' said Sharon. 'Tell you what—lucky it isn't J. Arthur Rank, eh? Look up and see some nudie bloke in a nappy banging his gong.'

'I'm sure it can be arranged, ma'am.'

'Ladies and gentlemen, the MGM Grand Las Vegas is proud to present . . .' As the voice boomed, the lights died down.

'Where *is* he?' Petra said again.

'Just coming, isn't he? Just getting into his catsuit. Probably a bit tight these days. Needs a shoehorn.'

'Not him. Bill.'

Sharon considered her friend through the gloom. 'Get you.'

*　　　*　　　*

Bill was lost. That put him one step further down the line than most of the people around him, who were merely losing. Some were losing their savings, their mortgages, their plans for the future; other were losing twenty dollars and calling it a night, although night and day had no purchase in this place, no meaning at all. Some were just losing their shirt, and, it had to be said, most of the shirts were worth losing. 'The size of four football pitches,' the brochure had said, and, indeed, the greensward of baize, table after

378

table, stretched out to a horizon that you would never reach; was there one lonely guy, somewhere over there, peacefully playing craps against a wall? At least in football there were time restrictions, but here there was no end of play; no midfield, no defence, no more than the illusion of a win, just one damn loss after another. Everyone was having a fine time.

Just to add to the confusion, Bill had left his watch in the room. He was due to meet Petra and Sharon at seven thirty, for the start of the concert. They had checked in, left their bags in the room and headed straight out, Sharon having announced that she would be dining out on the next two days for the rest of her life and that, not unreasonably, she would not be wasting a second of them, certainly not on anything as dull and wasteful as sleep. Bill, meanwhile, had collapsed on his bed and lain there, hands by his sides, eyes closed, as if in a well-appointed morgue.

Flying drained him, but it was more than that. He hadn't quite understood his own reasons for coming on this trip; there was no need for him here, he didn't *have* to write a piece, there was a decent writer already lined up. Now he knew the reasons. You drift along, he told himself, into the doldrums of your mid-forties, with a job you like but could never love; with a loud, distracting marriage behind you, a marriage that ran down like a radio; with an address book of old girlfriends whom you think about and very occasionally call, but who, you can be fairly sure, hardly ever think of you at all (listen to their voices when they hear yours, surprised without joy); with everything to live on and precious little to live for; with more of a life, in short, than millions have, and

379

to claim otherwise would be ungrateful, and yet . . . It wasn't the life, was it, for which you had hoped, and of which the old songs sang? And then, out of nowhere—

'I beg your pardon, sir. Coming by!' A waitress sailed past with a tray of drinks. Bill stopped her.

'I'm so sorry, do you by any chance have the time?'

'Are you British? You are *so British*.' She said this with good humour, no scorn in her tone at all, despite having identified him as a joke. And England *was* a joke, wasn't it? Sport that went on for five days without a result, non-mixer taps, hotels without lions . . .

'It's a quarter of eight,' she said, pointing out the large clock ten yards away, above a dealer's head. She didn't get why Bill hadn't noticed it; was this British guy trying to pick her up? He looked kinda nice. Jeff Bridges before Jeff took to hiding that gorgeous face of his behind weirdo beards. Another time. He thanked her, she thanked him back, and sailed on.

Christ, he was late. Where did the time go? You could buy most things in this town; maybe you could buy back time here, too, stake everything you had on retrieving that all-important twenty minutes . . . You could get married in twenty minutes here and regret it for twenty years. Or never regret it. He turned and ran, not too fast, he didn't want to be collared and stopped for stealing chips. A security guard blocked his path.

'Sir? May I help you.'

'Yes, I'm sorry. The Cassidy concert, I'm late. I'm meeting my, my friends there. Is it far?'

'OK, you want to go past *Kà*.'

'Past a car?'

380

'*Kà*, sir. Our world-famous effects extravaganza by Cirque du Soleil, exclusive to MGM Grand.'

'Fine, where is . . . car?' Bill found it hard to speak at moments like this.

'You want to make a left past those doors, then a hundred yards down, past *Kà*, like I say, then follow the signs. Our automated walkway will assist you—'

'Thanksbye,' said Bill, in one breath, and took off. He found the entrance to the concert, and was told to wait at the back until the next break in the songs. After the dazzle of the gaming floor, and the permanent noon of the hotel corridors, it felt like midnight in here, and Bill was glad for the rest, not wanting to grope his way through the dark as if newly blind. David was onstage, under a couple of spotlights, with a band half hidden behind him. He was singing something that Bill hadn't listened to, intentionally, for twenty-four years.

'You don't know how many times I wished that
    I could hold you.
You don't know how many times I wished that
    I could mould you . . .'

Not bad. The voice was in good shape. Taken the melody down a tone or two, perhaps, so as not to risk a strain or a crack on the peak of 'hold you, mould you'. Never the best rhyme in the world, that one: made girls sound like pots. Bill looked at David's audience. How many men out there? A couple of dozen, among the hundreds of women? Who was it, which bunch of guys had landed on an island populated by women only? Something in the furthest nook of Bill's memory turned up the word 'Argonauts'. That was it: Jason and the boys, landing

381

on Lemnos, outnumbered by the other sex but unable to hang around, having to move on. There was a golden fleece to find . . . How many guys had accompanied women to see David Cassidy down the years in the faint hope that some of that cherishing might come their way? Crumbs off the love god's table. Crumbs would be OK, no shame in crumbs if you were famished.

Where was she? He couldn't find Petra. Petra and Sharon, that is. Must be there somewhere. They wouldn't have been late like him, not after waiting this long. At last he picked them out, half visible beside a row of five large ladies in matching green T-shirts. He sidled a yard down the aisle for a better angle, so that he could see Petra from the side. She was gazing at the stage with gleaming eyes, hands in her lap, swaying gently. He couldn't see her feet, but he guessed they were tapping up and down. Sharon's too, most likely, but she was leaning further forward, half out of her seat, hands clasped tight together at her breast, like a young girl at her First Communion. She wore a smile of unmistakable rapture. As the song closed, the two of them, together with the rest of the crowd, took to their feet as if springs had gone off underneath them—hands over their heads, a blur of clapping right across the room. The singer took it well, his gratitude uncomplicated, nothing wistful about it; what did David's expression look like, right now? It looked like Sharon's.

With a glance at the usher, who nodded, Bill set off. He passed through the cheers, ploughing a path down the aisle between waves of adoring women; none were looking at him, or were even aware of his passing, but yet, for a fraction of a second, he had a fraction of a sense of what it must be like—how it was, to be among the wants of the world. The only people who sneered at acclaim, he thought, were those who had had it and lost it, or grown too old and weary to enjoy it; or shy souls who shrank from the very thought of being known by more people than they knew. The ones you never heard from were the figures at the heart of the applause, the ones who could have told you, not in retrospect or hope, but face to face, with the fans going nuts: look at me being loved. Be honest now; tell me you do not want this madness for yourself.

He found the row and inched along, past the large ladies, ranged there like five green bottles. 'OFFICIAL DAVID CASSIDY FAN CLUB OF IRELAND', their T-shirts said. 'Scuse me, scuse me.' Petra hadn't seen him yet, even though he was feet away; her gaze was still fixed on the stage. The lights had risen for the applause, but now they dimmed once more, as the audience resumed their seats, and Bill was bewildered for an instant by the dark. He tripped over someone's legs, and began to stumble, reaching out to stop and steady himself, heading for a fall. A hand took his, fitted into his, and drew him up, as dancers draw each other to their feet. He didn't fall, just slid neatly into his seat, with far more grace than he'd ever mustered in his life before. Petra smiled at him and didn't let go, even when he was safely in his place. 'Thanks,' he mouthed. Sharon leaned forward, from Petra's other side, and greeted him with a busy wave, as if she were fifty yards away.

Up onstage, David was apologising. He knew they wanted the songs from before, but, just once, he wanted to try something newer, you know, a little more up to date; a little number that explained how he was feeling *now*, at this wonderful juncture in his

383

life, with all these great folks around him. The great folks shifted a little; you could feel them, brimming with goodwill (couldn't blame the guy, could you, for wanting to break free of the past; give him a chance, right?), but also aware that any eagerness they could work up for this unknown song would be contrived—marks for effort, not freely given from the heart. And the man onstage took a breath, and sang softly into the mike:

'*How can I be sure . . .*'

And of course the place erupted. The old ones *were* the best, that was the point! The past is *never* dead! Not so long as they were alive. David, *their* David, was saying so, to them! Sharon was shaking, laughing, although if you had taken a photograph of her at that moment, and looked at it later, the next morning, you would have sworn that it showed a woman crying. She turned to Petra and Bill and shouted, 'Oh, he's a blimmin' *teeease,* he is!'

Petra laughed back and shouted something to Sharon that Bill couldn't hear. At last, the riot subsided, and the song was under way. Petra looked at Bill and began to sing. No act of memory was needed to summon the words; they poured out of her from the place she had kept them for a quarter of a century.

'Together we'll see it much better.
I love you I love you forev-vah . . .'

Bill gestured towards the stage. 'He doesn't know the words.'

'I know the words,' she said. Her hand was still in his.

They sat on a bench, all three of them, eating ice creams, in the heat of the night. Bill had chocolate and vanilla twist. Petra had strawberry, topped with something orange-brown that she hadn't ordered and couldn't identify, even after she'd licked it. Sharon had an Atomic Test Site, a speciality of the Nevada Ice Shack, which she *had* ordered; you needed two hands to eat it, since it came in twin cones, the mounds of unnatural flavour sprinkled with tiny silver balls. It was served with a lit sparkler, but that was long gone. Now she sat there, gripping it tightly, making an odd crackling sound. 'Popping candy,' she explained to Bill. 'And when you're nearly done, you pull the cones apart. Something to do with fishing, the man said.'

'Fission, I think. Like the bomb. They tested them round here.'

'What, ice creams?'

'Atomic bombs.'

'Same thing, Bill *bach*, from where I'm sitting.'

For a minute, they said nothing, happy just to lick and crackle. The streets were crammed. Some people had children with them, even though it was ten to eleven at night, and none of them could go near a casino.

'It's like Oxford Street,' said Petra. 'During the sales.'

'Yes, except that when I last looked,' said Bill, 'Oxford Street didn't have a live volcano. I always thought it lacked something.'

'Where's that, then?' said Sharon, talking through a mouthful.

'Well, this is Caesar's Palace we're outside now, as you can tell from the large garden sprinklers in the front. And the volcano is at the Mirage, I think, so I think it must be somewhere . . . *there*.' Bill pointed. 'Hang around and wait for the wisps of steam, apparently. They tell you she's about to blow.'

'Don't talk about my friend like that,' Sharon said.

'And don't mind *my* friend,' Petra said. 'She can't help it, poor love. Cooped up for decades in a small Welsh town. They go bananas when you let them out.' She licked her pink fingers. 'Just asking for trouble, bringing her to a place like this.'

'Gerraway with you, I'm thinking about staying,' said Sharon. 'Saw this ad in the programme for David—it said you can train as a dealer, do it in a month, and then you start. Raking it in, you are. Or you can serve cocktails, at the Palace. And I get to wear this Roman goddess outfit, mind, with my boobs in a breastplate.'

'D'you think they're, you know, actively looking for short Welsh blondes of thirty-eight?' asked Petra.

'Thirty-seven, if you don't mind,' said Sharon. 'Until next Friday.'

'What have you got planned?'

'Rissole and chips and I get to choose at Blockbuster.'

'Mal will take you out somewhere nice, won't he?'

'Nah, save the pennies,' said Sharon. 'David needs a new bike.'

She seemed to be able to traffic back and forth, Bill thought, between her life and her fantasies without changing gear—without *minding* too much. If more people in the world were like Sharon . . .

'So, when you become a roller-skating Roman gladiator-cum-cocktail waitress,' he said, 'what will

386

your husband do? Mal, isn't it? And your little boys?'

'Oh, they'll be fine. Boys, you know. As long as they wash their socks and comb their hair.' That seemed to settle the matter. Bill guessed that Sharon would die a hundred deaths rather than leave her family, but she didn't need to say so.

'So, Boss,' she said to him, 'what d'you think of it, then?'

'Which bit?'

'The concert.'

'Oh, I quite liked it, actually. Very professional. Good crowd. There was just this one thing that, you know, really got to me.'

'What?' Petra asked.

Bill went quiet. 'I don't know how to say this, quite, and at the risk of being serious . . .' He looked up at them and frowned. 'Which one was David Cassidy?'

'Oh, *stop* it,' said Sharon, and pushed him off the bench.

*   *   *

'How's the jet lag?' Petra said to Bill.

'Well, I can't feel anything below my knees, and I think my head may be facing the wrong way, but, apart from that, OK. You?'

'I don't know, it's odd. I don't know whether to go to bed or have breakfast.'

'Don't be daft,' said Sharon. 'Gotta keep on going, girl. City that never sleeps and all that.'

'That's New York,' said Bill.

'Well, it's all America, isn't it?'

It *was* all America. They had, at Sharon's insistence, wandered over the road to Harrah's, and watched the bartenders. 'More like jugglers, mind,' Sharon said, by way of encouragement. She had read Petra's guidebook, and tried to summarise her findings in advance. 'Shake the cocktails, right, but with these things on fire on their heads.'

In the end, it wasn't a bad description. Bill stood and watched the juggling, and found himself thinking of the Dog & Cart, in Turnham Green. There, years before, after Spirit Level hadn't played too badly, he had tried ordering a Martini for a girl called Serena Tombs, the most sophisticated girl he knew, and the angry old barman had looked at Bill for a long time, and then *spat* at him. Now, here he was, in a desert, and the barmen were in flames.

'Another world,' he said.

'Sorry?' Petra stood at his side.

'Just thinking. Sorry.'

'Can't hear you.'

Music and shouting walled them in. A right old racket, Bill's parents would have called it. Can't hear yourself think. That's how *he* thought of it, too, nowadays, much to his shame; was that all middle age boiled down to—an irritable quest for peace? In front of him and Petra, Americans half their age danced in a superheated squirm like bacteria under a microscope.

'Shall we get out of here?' he said to Petra. He had to bend down to make himself heard, and his mouth all but brushed her ear. He felt her hair against his face. She smelt of oranges.

Petra nodded. 'Just let me tell Sha.' She leaned in close and spoke to Sharon, pointing outside, and Sharon nodded back. At least she *seemed* to be nodding, though it was hard to tell, since she was also jumping up and down, as if on an invisible

388

trampoline.

They stood on the sidewalk, outside Harrah's. The air was thick and warm, as if they were standing in a laundry, but it still felt refreshing after the fiery bar. That was like standing over a barbecue.

'Mustn't move from here. She'll panic if we do.'

'Absolutely. God knows where she'd end up if we weren't here.'

'Oh, she'd be fine. Probably have more of a laugh, without us oldies.'

'Speak for yourself,' said Petra.

'So long as she doesn't find that waterslide that goes *through* a pool of sharks.'

'Jesus Christ.'

'She doesn't have a swimming costume with her,' said Petra.

'And if she decides she doesn't *mind* not having a costume, then our problems will *really* start.'

'Americans are a most polite people who are not standing for vulgarity,' said Petra. She never guessed she'd end up quoting her mother, let alone agreeing with her.

They sat opposite the Mirage. The city seemed to tilt in Petra's head. Damn this lag.

'Anything you want to do?' she said at last.

'Lots,' he replied.

'I meant here.'

'So did I.'

Petra took a bottle of water out of her handbag, drank some, wiped it on her shirt and offered it to Bill. He took it and drank.

'Rather tragically, I do actually want to go to this place called Auto Collections.'

'To hire a car? In the middle of the night?'

'No, to look at cars. Very old ones. Best collection

389

in the States, someone said. A weakness of mine, although, as weaknesses go, it's not too bad, since I could never afford one.'

'But you're a big cheese.'

'No, just sort of medium Cheddar. I don't own the company, I just run it. And I don't want to *drive* a Lamborghini Espada or anything, actually, I just want to look at it. When I was little, I wanted to drive one more than anything else in the world. Took me a long time to realise that what mattered wasn't the driving—not with all the idiots on the roads—it was the wanting.'

'Like me and David.'

'Oh, come now, gentle reader, that's not fair. You really *believed* he was yours. I mean, he was your *destiny*. That's why you got so pissed off with me at Heathrow yesterday. Because part of him had turned out not to be him.'

'I'm sorry about that. I was such an idiot.'

Bill smiled and looked down at her. Something inside him tilted. He decided not to observe the feeling, for once, but to let himself go with it.

'What did you think of him tonight, honestly?' she asked, after a while.

'Honestly?'

'Mm.'

'Honestly, I spent the time . . .' He paused. 'I spent the time asking myself what *you* were thinking. Of him.'

Now it was Petra's turn to smile. 'Well, of course I was dreading it. I couldn't bear to feel sorry for him. I didn't want all those women to look at him and feel disappointed. I was sort of cringing for him, you know. And then he came on and started singing, before you turned up, and everything just sort of fell into place. How can I—'

'Be sure?'

'Watch it. No, it's just that he . . . he both was and wasn't him. The voice is there, even if he does look older, still pretty fantastic, though. That beautiful smile. But the aura or whatever you call it, that's gone.'

'But *you* made the aura, not him,' said Bill. 'That was *your* job, back in 1974. I did the fake version on the magazine, but you did the real thing. You told a story to yourself, about a boy you all loved, and you did it so brilliantly, with all your heart, that it didn't matter whether it came true. It just *felt* true.' Bill drank from the water bottle, and passed it back to her. She took a swig. 'Sorry, I'm putting it badly,' Bill went on.

'No, that's better than I could ever do,' said Petra. 'That's why, when I saw him tonight, I didn't feel like crumpling, I didn't feel stupid or disappointed. I really loved hearing the songs again, and David seemed pretty, you know, balanced, considering—'

'That's what I thought.'

'—but I just said to myself, well, young Petra, the story's over, girl. And the funny thing was, I didn't *mind.*'

'What a swell story it is.'

'Yes.' Petra repeated the line, hearing the faint echo of a tune her dad had sung all those years ago. 'Sinatra.'

'Ah. Now *there*, excuse me, is a *real* star. That is who I came to Las Vegas to see.'

'He's not here?'

'God, no. Alive, more or less, but not here. But just imagine, to have been here when he *was*. You could have come dressed like Ava Gardner.'

391

'The bargain-basement Welsh version.'

'Not at all. The spitting image.'

'And what would you have come as?'

'Oh, a very unsuccessful mobster. Machine gun jammed. Losing all my money in minutes.'

'Not the Boss?'

'Not the Boss.'

Petra looked round, at the door of Harrah's.

'Talking of losing money, where's Sha?'

'Shall I go and see?' Bill asked.

'No, because then we'll be split up, and it'll be a disaster. Give her three more minutes, and then we'll go back in together.'

'They do have a separate karaoke bar in there, you know.'

'Oh God.'

'She's probably doing "I Am A Clown" right now.'

'In clown make-up. If there's any of my friends who can get hold of a red nose at midnight in a foreign country, it's her.'

'Is it midnight? Jesus. What's the time in England right now?'

Petra looked at her watch. 'Seven in the morning.'

'That means I have been up for exactly twenty-four hours. Bed, I think.'

'I think so.'

There was a pause. Bill, as he often did when confounded, took refuge in mock formality.

'Anyway, my dear, thank you for a most enjoyable evening.' He gave her a gentlemanly nod.

'And you, sir. It was most pleasant.'

Bill looked at her, and said: 'Back at the Grand, when you were watching him. David. When you said that thing about it being both him and not him . . .'

'Sorry, it sounds rubbish.'

'No, it makes perfect sense. In its rubbish way.' She laughed. 'And what I want to know *is*,' he went on, 'was it the same for you? Did you feel like Petra One and Petra Two, you know, before and after? What did the screaming teenager have to say to this lovely, perfect, grown-up cello therapist with a tiny bit of strawberry ice-cream on her cheek?'

Petra put a hand to her face.

Bill said: 'Come on, who is this I'm looking at right now: you or not you?'

Petra, for once in her life, had no doubt.

'Oh, it's me all right,' she replied. 'Just the one of me.'

Bill leaned towards her. She breathed in and closed her eyes.

There was an almighty sound. A roar went down the Strip.

'Oh *please,*' said Bill, and put his head on her shoulder. Opposite, the volcano had exploded outside the Mirage. Smoke and fire burst from the crater. False lava flowed down the flanks.

Bill and Petra leaned together and laughed, and hoped they would never stop.

'Bloody *hell*!' It was Sharon, who had herself erupted from the doors of Harrah's. She was carrying a bunch of flowers in one hand and a poker chip in the other. '*Fireworks.*'

20

When Petra and Sharon were thirteen, they made a promise. If they were still unmarried when they were old and on the shelf—twenty-nine or thirty, say—they would move in together. So that they would never be alone.

'Like those two ladies of Llangollen,' Sharon said. She was standing in front of the bathroom mirror, doing her eyes. After all these years, she still had a soft spot for blue mascara.

'I used to think it was common until I saw Lady Diana wearing it. D'you think Diana read *Jackie* on how to open out your eyes with blue mascara?'

'Course she did,' said Petra.

'Even posh girls?'

'All girls.' Petra tucked her shirt back into her skirt, having experimented with wearing it hanging loose. In twenty minutes they would meet David, and the girls—the women—were keen to make the right impression.

'Gorgeous blouse,' Sharon said.

'My mother's. Must be twenty years old. Hasn't dated, has it?' She had decided to wear Greta's white silk blouse and her pearls. It felt right. In the weeks since she found the letter from *The Essential David Cassidy Magazine* in the wardrobe, her attitude to her mother had altered. She was no longer angry with her. Like many mothers of her generation, Greta had a harshness which already felt as though it belonged to a lost, more brutal age. It was as if particles of steel, floating in the air of their Welsh town, had entered her bloodstream. Greta had been trying to prepare her daughter for a better life, a life that offered more than the narrow, ugly existence she hated. Petra saw that now. Wanting to stop your child making the mistakes you had made. Just as she was doing with Molly.

'Christ, Pet, don't look in this mirror.'

'What?'

'Magnifying *and* illuminated.' Sharon leaned foward. 'I've got more open pores than Mars, mun. If I end up in a coma, will you come by with tweezers and take my chin hairs out?'

'Only if you do mine.'

'Course I will,' said Sharon happily. 'Don't want Mal seeing my beard. Got to keep *some* mystery in a relationship, that's what they say.'

'Come on,' said Petra, 'time to go.'

'I'll be down in a minute. Necd a wee now, or you don't know what might happen when you see David, do you?'

'I'll go and find Bill and we'll see you downstairs,' said Petra.

*   *   *

In the lift on the way down to the lobby, she counted ten Petras in the mirrored walls. 'Really not szo bad for a woman at your age,' she told her reflections. Past and present were so close now they were practically breathing the same air. What would the other girls in Gillian's group think if they knew that Petra and Sharon were about to meet David Cassidy?

Last night, after the ice-cream and the volcano and Bill, a sleepy Sharon had mentioned that Carol was a grandmother. Ryan. Gorgeous little boy. Bit of a handful, mind, like his mamgu. Carol brought him along whenever she and Sharon met for coffee. In the new place where the Kardomah used to be. They had herb teas there now. Carol fell pregnant at sixteen and ended up behind the till at the Co-op. 'She's so proud of you, Pet. Well, we all are. You're our star, aren't you?'

Angela had gone back to England, no one was sure where. Olga did brilliantly in computer sciences and was working in America, Silicon Valley. Married a software engineer called Todd and they had two boys. Autistic, both of them. Tragedy, really, though Olga loved them to bits. Now she was pregnant again and they were praying the third baby would be a girl, you know.

And Gillian? Last thing Sharon and Carol heard, she had parted from her husband and set up some kind of dating agency in Maidenhead. Not just for any old lonely hearts. You had to be good looking, with a high net worth. Gillian would see to that.

Just because she could.

* * *

'His favourite colour was brown.'

'Sorry?' Bill looked up from the display cases in the hotel lobby. He was inspecting the jewellery, and doing the sums. You could fly here, get lucky, win a hundred and fifty thousand dollars at the roulette tables, nip out to the lobby, purchase a platinum and white-gold watch of blinding monstrosity, its face inlaid with so many diamonds that the hands were barely discernible—you couldn't, in fact, tell the time, which more or less took away the point of the watch—and still get two dollars and fifty cents change, just enough for a twin-pack of Juicy Fruit for the flight home. Neither richer, nor poorer. A nice, well-rounded weekend that would be.

'I said his favourite colour was brown. David's.' Petra looked at him, as he straightened up. Then she saw the expression on his face. 'Oh dear God,' she said, 'don't tell me you made *that* up as well.'

' 'Fraid so. At least, I *think* so.' To his intense relief, Petra shook her head and laughed. This time yesterday, he thought, she would have kicked me. Or should have.

'Is there anything about him that is *actually* true? Anything not made up by you? I'm starting to believe he doesn't exist. That he never did. You made up the boy I loved. He's all yours.'

'No, no.' Now Bill was shaking *his* head. 'No, that's going too far. For one thing, you saw him yourself last night.'

'Hologram.'

'And you heard him.'

'CD player.'

'And you cried. Or Sharon did.'

'Weakness. Welshness.'

Bill took a moment to think.

'OK, what about the bloke I saw at that press conference in 1974? The one who—'

'You *saw* him?' Petra was thirteen, again, in an instant; the years peeled back, and there she was.

'I met him. I went up to his hotel room, too, and we sat and—'

'You went to his *room*?' She actually had her mouth open, like a goldfish. 'You mean, only one of us got to go to his room, and it was *you*? Why not me? I knew him better than you.' Petra had to check herself; she was losing her sense of play. Bill felt as much, and gently rescued her.

'Well, *that's* true,' he conceded. 'My David poster collection was pitiful. Did you kiss yours, on the wall?'

'Well, we did at Sharon's. My mother, hardcore Wagner woman, she didn't really do pop stars, so no posters in our house. But Sharon had this David shrine and we, you know, genuflected, and the odd snog.'

'Mm-hm. You see, as a general rule, boys don't kiss walls. We knock them down, with a tank if we have one, but we don't kiss them. It's like the songs. I only played the records when I wanted to nick a line for the mag.' He paused. 'And who knows? Maybe his favourite colour *was* brown.' He shrugged, and added: 'Not that I could tell.'

'What d'you mean?' Petra said.

'Well . . .' Bill realised that he had opened up a trap for himself, and was now stepping into it, up to his knees. 'I'm colour-blind.'

'No.'

'Yes.'

'So you didn't even know what brown was anyway.'

'Well, that would be green to me.'

'You mean the world is full of cows eating brown grass.'

'The brown, brown grass of home,' Bill said. 'I suppose so.'

'That is the saddest thing I ever heard.' Petra seemed upset on his behalf, more than he would have bargained for. She said, 'What colour are my eyes?'

Bill came close and looked into them. She didn't blink.

'They're just right,' he said.

'You sound like Goldilocks.'

'And there's two of them. And they match.'

'Thank you.' She held her gaze, under his. Only with an effort, it seemed, did she raise it, and glance over his shoulder, and say, 'Here comes trouble.'

Sharon was coming towards them on tiptoe, as if the lobby were full of sleepers whom she was trying not to wake. 'My heels're giving me a headache,' she said, without preamble. 'They've got this really loud clack, like.' She was wearing the largest pair of sunglasses Petra had ever seen. Jackie Onassis could have lived behind them, incognito, for months.

'Sha, what are they like? You look like you've got two tellies strapped to your face. And the label's still hanging down the side.'

'Great, aren't they?' Sharon said, drinking in the praise. 'Georgie Versace.' She turned to Bill. 'Morning, David.'

'I—'

'Oh come off it, we know you're him really.'

Petra chimed in. 'That's what I was just saying. And he can't prove any different. We're going to go up to David's suite in a minute, when his PA or agent or whatever comes down to fetch us, and it won't be David Cassidy at all. It'll be him.' She looked at Bill. 'Better be off. Why not take the service lift and get a head start? Got to get into your white catsuit and everything by the time we arrive.' She frowned at him. 'We won't accept anything less, you know.'

' 'Sright,' said Sharon. 'Or maybe the red tails, like he wore at White City. That'd suit you.'

'Possibly,' said Bill. 'I mean I *packed* them, of course, but I thought, in the end, no, they're a bit quiet for the occasion. Just not enough rhinestone

399

for the kind of impact I was hoping to make. Also,' he said ruefully, 'I forgot the bow tie.'

'Well, of course it's useless without the sparkly tie,' said Petra. Sharon nodded eagerly at her side, like someone convinced that this was genuinely going to happen. 'Nice research, though.'

'What?'

'Remembering the bow tie. We've got the photos to prove it. You had to cut out the pictures and stick them in your magazine, did you?'

'Oh, no,' said Bill. 'I was there.'

'What?' This was both of them: Petra and Sharon, in chorus.

'I was at White City. You know, the awful night when that girl got crushed. I was right there. I saw the sparkly tie and everything. It was madness. Like a war.'

'But we were there,' Petra said. 'We both were. We went with Gillian and Carol. And Olga and Angela.'

'Were they OK?'

'Well, Carol was love-ly'—this was Sharon now, her accent strengthening and rising as the memory swept back—'but Gillian, she was a right bloody cow, wasn't she, Pet?'

'Pretty girl, though,' said Petra, distantly. She looked at Bill again. 'Were you really there? Did you stay for the, you know, the bit when it all collapsed?'

'God, yes, I was right there in the press enclosure beside the barrier. Had to help some girls over. Some of them looked pretty beaten up, I remember that. Funny, most of it's a blur now. Must be my great age.'

'Of course.'

'The one thing I do remember is this shoe. Don't know why. Just this clunky shoe, sort of reddy-brown. Wandering round with it in my hand, trying to find who'd lost it. Like that really mattered, when there were girls being squashed. Spot the idiot, trying to find a foot to fit a shoe.'

'Cinderella man,' said Sharon. Her shades were slipping down.

Petra was very still, staring hard into the past. Playing it frame by frame, then freezing it and trying to zoom in. The sensation of Sharon's hand slipping from hers. The crowd's monstrous thrashing, going down among the thousands of legs and spotting her. A bracelet of bright hair about the bone. Grabbing the hair, pulling with all her might. And Carol pushing the crowd back like the champion prop forward she was. Then she said, 'I lost a shoe.'

She and Bill were like divers now, groping through the deep; each waving a hand in the dark, hoping to brush against the other. One boy with a shoe, and one girl without: it could be a scene from a fairy tale. They had been so close, once upon a time, and now they were so close again. Reason told them it was pure coincidence; not *that* amazing, anyway, if it were true—a pop star had put them in the same stadium, so why shouldn't he wait twenty years or so and place them in the same hotel? But reason cowered before romance. According to romance, there was no coincidence. That was the word that non-lovers used, sad souls in the everyday world, to account for the workings of destiny.

We were meant to be here, thought Petra and Bill, both of us, right now. There are two of us. And we match.

'Told you,' said Sharon, who had left reason behind in Gower, with her husband and children, and was in no hurry to return. 'Prince Bill.' She pushed the enormous sunglasses up her nose.

'Magic, mun.'

'Mr Finn?'

A Tiggerish young guy was bouncing towards them, hand outstretched. His smile was so bright it belonged in the jewellery case.

'Hi, I'm Edouard.' He pronounced it the French way, *Ed-warrh*, though neither Petra nor Bill had ever seen a more complete American.

'And you must be Petra,' he said to Sharon, who rocked him back with a guffaw straight from the Valleys.

'Fat bloody chance,' she replied graciously, and for half a second, Bill thought that Edouard's smile might start to crack. Two of her first three words had set off alarms inside the boy's head. Nothing bloody, and certainly nothing fat, had crossed his path in many, many years. But, like a pro, he came back strong.

'So you must be Sha-*ron*!' he exclaimed, pressing down hard on the second syllable, as if she were a part of the Holy Land, or an Israeli general. Sharon screamed. Her joy was unconfined.

'Sha-*ron*-ron-ron-ron,' she sang back.

The greeter, defeated by he knew not what, turned to Petra. 'We are so honoured to have you here,' he said, not risking her name, and holding on extremely tight to her hand, as if seeking protection from the madwoman at their side. 'David could not be more excited. He is upstairs now, and, if you are ready, we'll go right up!'

They moved, as a little group, towards the bank of elevators. Petra asked politely, 'Does, um, Mr Cassidy know why we . . . ?'

'Oh, totally,' said Edouard, who was always happiest when asked to confirm something that he

402

knew, or believed, to be true. 'He just loves your backstory. *Great* backstory. Both of you,' he went on, with a nervous grin at Sharon. 'He loves you.'

Sharon started singing again. Bill and Petra stood next to each other, waiting, and stared silently down at their shoes.

* * *

Sharon was kneeling on the floor of the bedroom. David was smiling up at her.

'No, it's better like that,' she said. 'Fits better. What d'you reckon, Pet?'

Petra considered. 'No, that one goes better in the middle. Then he's with both of us, together.'

They had a sheaf of pictures, and Sharon wanted to make an album right now, before they even got on the plane. There had been a proper photographer when they went with Bill to meet David. A burly, beaming man from a local company called Cyclone Images, with a picture of a tornado on the back of his shirt.

'How d'you do?' said Sharon, shaking his hand.

'Hi, I'm Cy,' he said.

'Oh my God, like the clone!' she shrieked. Cy looked confused. He set to work, arranging the tripod and lights, so that when David came in they would be, as he put it, ready to roll.

And when they were done, and the roll was over, and David was chatting with Petra and Bill in the corner, Sharon asked Cy—cheeky, mind, him being a pro and everything—if he would take some extra ones with her new camera. For her collection. And, for once, it went according to plan: Cy did as he was asked, and David posed a few times more, with each of them in turn. Sharon kissed the photographer as he left, saying, 'Thank you, Cy,' as loudly as possible, to see if she could make Petra giggle. And when they had said goodbye to David, who was due at a soundcheck for the evening show, Sharon had gone—no, she had run—out of the hotel to the camera shop across the street. They could do them in an hour, but you had to pay more. She paid more, refusing Petra's offer to chip in. It was as though, if Sharon didn't get the photos printed now, the memory of the morning would fade in her head, and with it the proof that it had actually happened; she would have nothing to show that she had ever been here, with him, hand in hand. He had given her a hug. Three decades, waiting for a hug.

'God, he's lovely, isn't he? Brilliant. The whole thing.' Sharon sat back and admired her handiwork.

'Yes,' said Petra. She had been thrown, for a second, by vertigo. Not space vertigo, although their hotel room was number 2147, twenty storeys up, with a view down over the Strip; more like time vertigo. A sudden plunge, which she wasn't expecting, and could hardly cope with—back through the years, almost violently, to something . . . that matched where they were now. Where had that been, and when? Something about the carpet under her fingers, now, rich and scratchy, as she knelt beside Sharon; and, in the air—not this air, Vegas parched, air-conditioned air, but wafted in, on the air of the past—the weirdest smell. Like you get from burnt hair, with a cheap hairdryer; a smell so sharp that it hit you between the eyes, and behind the nose, and stayed for a while, and everything in you reeled. And then it was gone.

'Sorry?' she said to Sharon, who had spoken while

404

Petra was in a dream.

'Hello, *twp* face, I said I could die happy.'

Petra smiled. 'Live happy. Better for you, *bach*.'

'Yeah, you're right. And cheaper. Better chips. You don't get decent chips when you're dead. What they call them here? Fries.'

They bent over the photos again.

'I like this one of you and me,' said Sharon. 'See how young we look.'

'Camera never lies.'

'And I like this one of me and David and Bill, although Bill's got this kind of goofy look. This is better of him, just with David. Oh, and this one's even better. You and Bill. This is the best.'

Petra was silent.

'D'you know what David said to me, when you and Bill were posing for Mr Clone?'

'Don't tell me.'

'He said—looking at you two, right?—he says to me . . .'

'What?'

'He says: "I think she loves him."'

Petra laughed. 'David Cassidy did not say that.'

Sharon hesitated, then wrinkled her nose and laughed back.

'No, but he could have done, couldn't he? Just because I made it up doesn't mean it's not true, does it?'

'Well . . .'

'And it *is* true, so there. You do love him.'

'Who? Who do I love?'

'And David Cassidy brought you two together. That's his, what you call it. His destiny.'

'Whose? Now I'm really confused. Sorry, there's too much loving going on round here.'

At once, Sharon started to sing. 'There's a whole lotta lovin' goin' on, in my heart . . .' She reached out and gave Petra a hug. 'More for me,' she said.

Petra pulled back. 'What d'you mean?'

'Well, now you've got Bill—'

'Excuse me, I have not got anyone—'

'Now that you have, Pet, well then. David's mine now, isn't he? Fair play. He's all mine.'

Petra moved to embrace her friend, and as the smaller woman's fine blonde hair floated sideways onto her blouse it delivered a familiar shock.

'All yours.'

21

Petra sat at her kitchen table, quite still, holding a mug of coffee in both hands. She watched the steam rise from it, in the morning light. The day was still young; their flight had landed not long after dawn.

She took a sip, then frowned at something. Her suitcase, in the doorway, airline tags attached. Just waiting for Molly to go tripping over it when she came in.

Petra rose and carried the case upstairs, bumping its bulk on every step, then swung and heaved it onto the bed. She breathed out, and was about to leave the room, to go downstairs and finish her coffee. She paused. Better hang her new linen jacket up before it got too creased. She went back to the bed, and clicked the two clasps on the case.

It opened, she swung back the top, and stopped. Her first thought was that she had taken the wrong suitcase at the airport. But no, there was the jacket, neatly folded, and the edge of her mother's blouse underneath. But on top was something that was not hers. Yet it was meant for her, because her name was on the front.

Petra took the envelope and looked at it. The flap was not stuck down, just tucked in. She opened it, and slid the letter out. She read it for the first time in her life. Then she read it again to make sure.

Dear Petra,

How can I be sure, in a world that's constantly changing, where I stand with you?

I'm beginning to think that man has never found the words that could make you want me.

Nevertheless, cherish is the word I use to describe all the feeling that I have hiding here for you inside.

As somebody once sang, I forget his name: life is much too beautiful to live it all alone.

Believe me, you really don't have to worry. I only want to make you happy and if you say, hey, go away, I will. But I think, better still, I'd better stay around and love you. Do you think I have a case? Let me ask you to your face: do you think you . . . etcetera.

I believe you know the rest.

Yours,
sincerely,
Bill x

Petra put the letter in her pocket and went downstairs. Passing the hall table, she noticed a jug of sweet peas. The scent was so strong, intoxicating. On a Post-it note stuck to the wall, she spied Molly's girly, looped handwriting: 'I picked them. Told you!!!'

Petra smiled. The daughter, unlike her mother, was going to lead a three-exclamation-marks kind of life. She thought of Molly, obeying the request to pick the sweet peas while Petra was in Vegas, to keep the flowers coming, an instruction Molly's mamgu had issued more than thirty years ago to Petra herself, and, who knows, maybe Greta heard it from her own mother in Germany. Things being passed on; habits, scents, beloved melodies, a heart-shaped chin: motherhood and memory forging a slender

408

handrail to cling onto down the generations.

She wondered what Greta and Molly would think of Bill. It took a second to remember that one of those meetings would never take place now. Too soon, she thought. It's *too soon*. And yet, we cannot choose those moments when two people are suddenly wide open and the merest glance has the power to console or heal.

In the years to come, the only thing they would find it hard to agree on was whether they had actually met at White City. Petra always said they must have because she loved the perfect symmetry of it. Bill was the first man to take her in his arms and, if life was kind to them, then he would also be the last.

Bill, who had made up the story that brought Petra to him, was perfectly happy for his darling wife to write whatever ending she liked best. *Cariad* was the Welsh word for darling. This Petra taught him, along with so much he had never known before.

She was so tired that morning she got back from the Cassidy trip, but old habit and new desire sent her into the living room. She bent down and flipped the catches on the case. Bill's letter was in her pocket. Pulling the cello to her, she answered it. Urging the music on. Each note like a pearl. Each phrase like a string of pearls. One little phrase, and so many ways to say it.

AFTERWORD

In 2004, I was asked by the *Daily Telegraph* Saturday magazine to interview David Cassidy. As I prepared to travel to Florida to meet my teen idol, several unexpected emotions crowded in. Panic about what to wear was high on the list. Should I go dressed as the fan who had worshipped him so ardently from afar or as the wife and mother of two I now was? I felt like a time traveller. If David was still twenty-four in my heart, how old did that make me?

While I was packing and unpacking the suitcase, my husband sat on the bed and sang an aggressively tuneless version of 'Could It Be Forever'.

'Why on earth would you want to *meet* him?' he asked. 'David Cassidy sang flat and, let's face it, he was basically a girl.'

I defended David, exactly as I had defended him thirty years earlier from the taunts of the boys at school. Just as I would always defend him.

David lived in Fort Lauderdale with his wife, Sue, and his son, Beau. In the cab on the way to his house, everything I had been feeling coalesced into a single thought. 'Please don't let me pity him.'

I realised I could bear just about any kind of awkwardness, embarrassment or disappointment, but I never, ever wanted to feel sorry for the man who once bestrode my world like a colossus in a white catsuit trimmed with silver studs.

David Cassidy was about to turn fifty-four. He looked at least ten years younger, but that still made him twenty years older than the beautiful boy millions of girls like me believed we were in love with. That comparison was clearly a source of pain to him. He who had once turned on half the world was

413

now doomed to disappoint. He was not Peter Pan, nor was he meant to be. David was about to embark on another farewell tour of the UK. The fans, now women in their forties and fifties with young girls of their own, would still turn out for him in enthusiastic numbers, but I sensed in him a great weariness that he needed to exploit for money a period of his life which in different ways had cost him so dear. His bitterness at the record companies and merchandising people who had managed to spirit away the hundreds of millions of dollars that his records and his image generated was clear and well justified.

As David posed for the photographer, I said he should be careful the camera didn't take his soul.

'I had my soul stolen a long time ago,' he replied. As an actor, and the son of two actors, he can be prone to self-dramatising statements; still, if anyone on the planet can claim to have had his soul stolen, it is David Bruce Cassidy.

The interview turned out to be more fascinating and moving than I could have hoped. David was thoughtful, intelligent and extremely honest in his responses. At times he became angry, at others he was close to tears. We laughed a good deal as we recalled the strange, compelling experience we had shared, though separated by age, gender and thousands of miles. He was generous enough to scream at me, as I had screamed at him all those years ago, which proved he was a true gentleman. Being able to prompt David on the lyrics of one of his own songs, which I knew better than him (naturally), was a moment from fan heaven.

The David Cassidy that millions of us loved did not exist, not really; he was a brilliant marketing invention, though the man who has both the pleasure and the burden of bearing his name was not a disappointment. On the contrary.

I want to thank David for giving me such a fantastic interview, and for helping me to recapture the way we were. No girl could ask for a finer teen idol. This is the transcript.

AP: David, your agent told me that some of the more aggressive fans still move towards you like you're a meal. How do you feel about the fans now?

DC: It's a great compliment that they still care. I've never once thought otherwise.

AP: Really, so it's not been a burden to you?

DC: Oh yes, it's been a burden, but I've never thought it wasn't a blessing, flattering. Yes, lots of aspects have been terribly difficult to cope with. Has it altered my life? Dramatically. Has it changed me? Yes, dramatically. But, it is pretty extraordinary if you can view it somewhat objectively.

AP: Your last farewell tour was in 1974.

DC: Yeah, and I said, that's it. They went, 'Oh right, he'll be back next year.' Before I started it I announced it to the world, this is IT. My final tour. Stadiums all over the world. Started in New Zealand, Australia, Japan, Europe, UK [he snores in mock boredom]—nine months in all.

AP: Someone got killed at that last concert in London, didn't they?

DC: Next to last concert. A girl died, wasn't killed. She *died*. Clarify it. There was no violence going on, there was incredible pushing and crushing. She was

415

way up in the back. She had a heart condition. She died. It was very sad, but of course, the press made it out to be like, you know—it sells newspapers, right? I called the parents and spoke with them and said, because of the media circus that I attracted wherever I went, out of respect for their daughter I will not come to the funeral. I sent flowers. You know I had no responsibility. There were 45,000 people there, I didn't know where she was. She was half a mile away. I had no idea that she had died.

AP: It must have been shocking?

DC: It was really sad for me because it was a celebration for me and it was the next to last day, which was up in Manchester City Main Road, I remember.

AP: Were you ever frightened?

DC: For them?

AP: For you.

DC: I can't say I wasn't ever frightened. It happened so many times in five years. In the car, girls crawling all over it. Black. Darkness, pfffwwwrr, smothered. You just had to make sure you had a really smart driver because it's a mob. It's a mob. It has its own consciousness, its own mind. Instead of one or two or three, it's fifty, a hundred, then they start piling on top of each other, then it becomes crazy.

AP: Do you remember the first time it happened?

DC: It was 1970, shortly after *The Partridge Family* had aired in America. I went to Cleveland—the show has been on the air ten times. I was Grand Marshall of Cleveland Parade. I'm on like a 1950s fire engine.

416

Reporters said they'd never seen anything like it before or since. There were 40,000 kids following me down the streets of Cleveland and it was cold. It's like Glasgow. To get off it and get into a safe place I had a minder with me. I'd never had a minder before. It was just starting. I went from the top of the fire engine and into this car. The police were not on top of the situation. The car was instantly smothered. It was chaotic. They were grabbing at my hair and my clothes. It was not comfortable.

AP: If they got hold of you, what did you think they would do?

DC: Well, I think they wanted to take a piece of me home so they could have it next to their bed or something. Like a scalp for their wall.

AP: Did it feel primitive?

DC: It *is* very primitive. I've had a lot of time to think about it. I've observed young girls at events since then, like cheerleading events, and when they get excited, the pitches in their voices go way up and their emotions. It becomes like, well, imagine the level of intensity standing at the focal point of the most emotional thing for them, the most exciting thing for them, and being at the focal point of 40 or 50,000 people. What that feels like vocally to have that come at you—it's a *powerful* weapon, it's a *powerful, powerful* experience. I remember saying I wish everyone could stand in my shoes for just five seconds and feel what that feels like because it's the ultimate expression of love. But it's spoken in a way—it's *screamed* at you. I LOVE YOU! Intensify that ten thousand times and imagine how that feels. It's overwhelming.

417

AP: But it was something the fans were projecting onto this figure called David Cassidy because they didn't know you. I was one of the ones screaming at you, by the way.

DC [smiles]: If you were screaming, Allison, you know what that emotional pitch was like for you. For me it was like, wow, it was so fantastic to feel people letting go, letting you know that you touched their lives, that you meant something to them. It's the greatest compliment that someone who does what I do can get.

AP: OK, as I once screamed at you, David Cassidy, it's only fair that you should scream at me.

DC [laughs and screams]: I LOVE you—sorry, can't quite get that pitch.

AP: No, that's very good, thank you. I can see how you could get used to that. It's as though the fans were on the cusp of a pre-sexual feeling. Sex is implicit in it, but maybe it's not yet sexual?

DC: It's *all* sexual, but because it's very naive, extraordinarily romantic and it deals with fantasy, it's sex before it becomes overtly sexual. You can define it better than I can because I haven't ever been in a female body. Intellectually now I see it, but I couldn't see it then.

AP: What did you think then?

DC: I thought it was just hysteria. Like they were seeing me as this demigod. I was just a guy who played the guitar.

AP: Did you feel like a demigod?

DC: No, never.

AP: Come on, when you had all those young girls screaming at you?

DC: Do you want to believe me or do you think I'm making this up?

AP: I just think you wouldn't be human unless you felt pretty pleased with yourself with that many girls throwing themselves at you.

DC: I can't tell you I wasn't happy with myself. I can't tell you I wasn't aware that people found me attractive. But I never felt like a sexual person. I mean, I was a sexual guy, but I never thought of myself as being sexy, you know what I mean?

AP: Yeah, but I think that was partly because you were lovely, but you weren't . . .

DC: Threatening?

AP: There was nothing threatening or aggressively masculine about you.

DC: See, but I don't think you knew that at that age. I didn't know that then either.

AP: I certainly didn't think, Hey, here is David Cassidy, my Transitional Love Object.

DC: Correct, it's a phenomenon. I was very male, but there was an androgynous part. When I see pictures of myself, I was skinny, my hair was long, I looked kind of feminine. I wasn't a big bully kind of guy. Girls between the ages of seven and seventeen would show up at my concerts. In America, the audience was 80:20 girls to boys. I guess in Britain it was not cool for boys to admit to liking me.

AP: No, you were a fairy, I'm afraid.

419

DC: A fairy? [He laughs a little uncertainly.] I knew there was jealousy. I knew what the guys were saying, I knew they were, like, drawing moustaches on my picture and blacking out my teeth. I understood it. I would have felt the same way.

AP: If I had met you thirty years ago . . .

DC: You would not have been able to speak. I had that happen many times. It was very sweet. These girls, they'd just stand there, they'd start crying, it was overwhelming. I have to tell you I was doing a benefit in a TV studio two weeks ago. Backstage, one of the heads of department, she was about thirty-seven years old, walked into the dressing room, held my hand and began to weep. She said: 'You don't understand this,' and I said, 'Of course I do. Believe me, I get it and I thank you, I'm glad it still means something to you.'

AP: But there was this gap, wasn't there? The David Cassidy I was in love with wasn't you, was he?

DC: If you read the magazines, bought the merchandise, of course that wasn't me. That was a scripted character. On *The Partridge Family*, they didn't let me play [Jimi Hendrix's] 'Voodoo Chile'. Trust me, that's what I was playing at home. I was playing B.B. King.

AP: Did you ever feel uncomfortable with that velvet suit you had to put on?

DC: Terrible discomfort. Terrible. I was much older, hipper than Keith Partridge. I was going with women who were in their late twenties.

AP [laughing]: Oh, *really old*!

DC [laughing also]: Yeah, *realllllyyy* old . . .

AP: I remember when I knew you were in your early twenties—to me that seemed impossibly grown up.

DC: When I toured in '74, I was twenty-four years old. Imagine someone who has lived three lifetimes by the time they're twenty-four. What kind of a guy was I compared to whatever your preconception was? The line is very smeared. For me, I didn't go out and act onstage. I performed as a musician. I really cared about that even if nobody listened. That was me. It was the only part of the day I enjoyed.

AP: I think for the fan there was this aspect of knowing some of your background; there was a sense of you being wounded by your childhood that distinguished you from the other teen stars.

DC: Well, I was wounded. I hadn't thought about that. That's a new one. You are dissecting why I exist, Allison. I think you're right. I think I need to get seriously wounded again. If you want the girls to like you, go out and hurt, motherfucker!

AP: Isn't that the Michael Jackson story?

DC: You could only imagine what a talent has been destroyed and wasted there. I'm thinking about *Off the Wall*, the best album ever made. I've met Michael a few times. It's all gone so terribly wrong.

AP: Does it make you shiver slightly?

DC: Yes it does, but it doesn't and I'll tell you why. He didn't have a perspective internally to make the choice to go, 'So long, kerpow!' I pressed the ejector button. He bought the Elvis dream with the belt over the bed. I said ten years ago about Michael Jackson,

421

you have no idea how tragic this is going to get. I had a choice of saying no more and I don't want to buy this dream because it's a miserable dream. It's a sad, empty, lonely, shallow, self-absorbed, narcissistic existence. If Michael Jackson isn't the height of narcissism—look at that face. It's like anorexics—they want to stay a child. Doing your face like Diana Ross? It's so terribly tragic and it's a difficult choice to make. Let's see: fame, money, adulation, being God or being happy. Hmmm. That other thing, being God, is so alluring. I thought: I've got to try and take this road for happiness.

AP: But you didn't know it would make you happy.

DC: Oh, I did. I knew the only way for me to survive and be a human being again was not to live like that. I lived in a vacuum like Elvis, like John, Paul, George and Ringo did, for five years.

AP: I love the story of you meeting John Lennon and singing his songs to him because he was drunk and he couldn't remember them.

DC: I was reteaching John the Beatles lyrics. It would be like you playing my songs to me.

AP: I probably know your lyrics better than you do.

DC: You probably do because I forget them all the time. Actually, there are a few I get confused.

AP: Could you please sing 'I Am A Clown' as a special favour to me?

DC [puzzled frown]: 'I Am a Clown? I can never remember . . . they're so similar.

AP: You say that you bailed out, but isn't the lifespan

of the teen idol over in a blink?

DC: Well, mine lasted much longer than most and it could have gone on for an indefinite period of time. Not forever. I saw I could leave this at the top. There was nothing more to experience. I had the biggest fan club in history. What else can I do with this? I'm not happy. I'm alone and—

AP: In interviews at the time you said—

DC [getting angry now]: They weren't accurate. I read things I never said.

AP: So, lots of that stuff that I thought I knew about you was made up by other people?

DC: All of it. Pretty much all of it. They're going to write 10,000 stories in a hundred magazines that are all contrived for their audience of young teenagers so, at the beginning of the year, they'd come in and I'd give them all like an hour. They'd ask me a bunch of questions that were so silly—What's your favourite colour? What's your favourite drink? After a few times, you start making stuff up. What do you eat for breakfast? 'Oh, ketchup and ice cream.' You think, I can't do this shit any more.

AP: Is it a hard thing to recover from?

DC: You don't ever recover. It's how you understand it, address it and move on from it. There's always the scar, it's just that when I push on it now it doesn't hurt me so bad. If you're in a corporation you climb up and you become head of department. They don't give you a gold watch in my profession. You're a god who no one wants to employ any more, because you're too old. That's the saddest thing for me

423

watching the Oscars and seeing people you idolised so much getting treated like that because they're old.

AP: What was it like after you quit?

DC: I said, no more recording sessions, no more TV. It's very dark. It's like you've fallen down the abyss and it's very strange. I stayed a lot indoors in my little compound. I wasn't a very happy camper at the time and was kind of lost.

AP: When I come here and meet you after all this time . . .

DC: I'm just some fifty-year-old guy. You don't give a shit, right?

AP: On the contrary. We're all getting older. One day, years from now, I'm going to be in my kitchen at home and I'm going to turn on the radio and they'll say that David Cassidy, the seventies teen idol, has died. It will be an incrediby poignant and resonant moment for me and for millions of other women around the world. You are one of the ways we measure out our lives.

DC: A small part of you dies with me?

AP: I believe that.

DC: That's why I've never taken it lightly. I think it is meaningful.

AP: Do you feel stuck in time? There must be moments when people are pestering you to do the old songs. You wouldn't be human if you didn't want to move on?

DC: I spent ten years going, No, no, I won't do that cos I don't want you to think that I'm still back there.

I'm not there. I don't want to stay there just to make *you* feel good. I have to have a present, otherwise I'm just a relic. And I'll never be a relic. That's why I won't be in an oldies show, I'll never do that.

Will I do my hits? I'd love to sing them, they're great songs, but I couldn't do them till I had a present, understand? For me, saying this is what I do now, this something that may not have the impact the other stuff had, but it'll never have that impact because you'll never be thirteen again, I'll never be twenty again.

AP: If you sing 'Could It Be Forever' now, are you reconnecting with the young David Cassidy or are you singing it with an adult sensibility?

DC: I didn't do my hits from '74 to '85. Never. I had to relearn them. Seriously. Two years ago, I went back and re-recorded all my hits on the *Then and Now* album—going in the studio and singing songs you haven't sung for twenty-five years. Same studio, same microphone, same players—it was emotional. I'm singing these songs as a different guy, I can't possibly sound like I sounded when I was twenty-three, twenty-four. I have to sound like I'm fifty, fifty-two.

AP: Actually, your voice hasn't changed that much.

DC: No, but it's impossible for me to be nineteen again, to be that innocent in life, [so open] to hurt and pain and relationships. I have so much more voice now, to be able to find that purity, like your skin is at nineteen, you'll never get that back. I tried to be true to the material, I tried to be gentler.

AP: Which songs from that period do you really like?

425

DC: 'How Can I be Sure', 'Cherish', 'I Think I Love You'.

AP: How come from all the record sales and merchandise your face sold you didn't make gazillions of dollars?

DC: Record companies are set up to steal. They do it at every point, from packaging to promotion. It's a corrupt business and it always has been. They've never, in the history of the recording business, made a mistake in the artist's favour.

They say to you, OK, you can audit us. It's going to cost 150,000 to 250,000 dollars of your own money to audit us. If you're lucky. So we'll settle for X amount instead of going through that nightmare. In the end, they have ways of stealing you don't really know. They're making money on everything and you never know what the real sales were . . .

AP: They owned your likeness.

DC: I should have made a hundred million dollars based on the merchandising. If the corporations had a conscience they'd write me a cheque today, but not a dime. I said, I have eleven compilation albums here and you were allowed only *four* in my original contract.

AP: You can sue them?

DC [plaintive and sad]: Well, how do you prove it? This record company was bought by that record company . . . I was in three lawsuits at one time. I just want what it says on the paper. Don't do this to me . . .

AP: Do you think getting older is harder for you

because people have this perfect memory of you?

DC: Yup, I think it is harder. It's not like, poor me because what I have and what I get to do . . . [He starts twiddling unhappily on a guitar.] Yeah, it is hard.

AP: People judge you?

DC: 'Hey, how come you don't grow your hair back? Have you ever thought of getting your hair back?' [He winces.] I get it all the time. Same with Farrah Fawcett, icon of a generation. That's the problem. They say, 'Oh, I saw a picture of her recently, it's sooo sad.' I can't stand the idea of that being said about me. Hey, people get older. People relate to Robert Redford because of the way he looked at a certain age when he was a young man. That's the thing he has to constantly be measured against. Sixty happens. They do it maliciously and it's cruel, it's mean-spirited. People love to be shocked and they love to see other people come down. 'See, he's not that handsome [any more]!'

AP: Do you ever meet people and think they're disappointed in you?

DC: Yup. 'Why don't you look like I remember you at nineteen?' Well, I *tryyyy*. Dare I say it, how old are you? I've got fans with pics of me meeting them back in the seventies—these sweet little innocent girls, twenty-five years have gone by and they don't look anything like that. NOTHING like that. I was already a full-grown person. Can we ever look like we did when we were twenty when we're fifty?

AP: All right, there's something I need to check with you before I go. It's really important. David Cassidy,

427

was your favourite colour ever brown?

DC: Brown? Never. No.

AP: For eighteen months I wore nothing but brown because I read in a magazine it was your favourite colour.

DC [explodes with laughter]: Allison, it was all made up!

AP [laughing also]: That poor trusting girl living in South Wales . . . I looked terrible in brown. So help me God, I looked *yellow* in brown.

DC: It was never a great colour on me either. Do you see brown on me? Do I look like someone whose favourite colour is *brown*?

ACKNOWLEDGEMENTS

Writing a novel is a long and lonely business. Certain people make it less lonely. Joanna Lewis was a constant comic inspiration and a reminder of the country we were both so lucky to be born in. While I was in South Wales worshipping David Cassidy, Sharon Dizenhuz was kissing his picture in Cincinnati, Ohio. Sharon's American perspective, along with her glorious wit and wisdom, were invaluable in helping me get started. When it looked like I might never finish, Louise Swarbrick propelled me across the finishing line by sheer strength of character.

Caroline Michel at PFD has shown incredible patience and never stopped believing. I don't know *how* she does it. Jordan Pavlin, at Knopf, worked her editorial magic and made this book the best it could be. As did Clara Farmer at Chatto & Windus, who held her nerve—and mine.

I want to thank David Cassidy himself for his kind encouragement. David's autobiography, *C'mon Get Happy* (Time Warner), was an invaluable source of information. Thanks must also go to all the Cassidy fans who shared their memories, particularly Judith Frame. I would love to hear from any more fans out there. You can reach me via the Allison Pearson page on Facebook, follow me on Twitter @allisonpearson or email me at allison.pearson@virgin.net

Special gratitude is due to Barry McCann, a walking encyclopedia of popular culture. Barry's email on 'Swearing in the Seventies' deserves a book to itself. Tim de Lisle, another expert in the field, led me to Bill. Many others offered support and valuable suggestions: my American agent, Joy Harris, Cara Stein, Alison Samuel, Miranda Richards, Emma Robarts, Catherine Humphries, Jane Bird, Christobel Kent, Naomi Benson, Belinda Bamber, David Bamber, Julia Bamber, Lisa Collins, Caroline Dunn, Mary Hitch, Carolina Gonzalez-Carvajal, Philippa Lowthorpe, Laura Morris, Daniel Newell, Ysenda Maxtone Graham, Jane McCann, Anne McElvoy, Isolde Ivens, Professor Jon Parry, Anne Polhill Walton, Hilary Rosen, Christine Ford, Jeffrey Carton and Natasha Walter. In Wales, I need to thank my mother, who made this book possible, and to salute the memory of her friend Jean Thomas, a fine artist and a lovely woman. I am also grateful to Eiry Evans and Edna and Dafydd Jenkins. *Cymru am byth*!

Nicola Jeal provided a fascinating insight into the world of magazines. At the *Daily Mail*, Tobyn Andreae and Maureen O'Donnell gave a five-star service to the struggling author.

The case history of Ashley, which Petra writes, is purely fictional, though I drew on the remarkable *Case Studies in Music Therapy*, edited by Kenneth E. Bruscia (Barcelona) and, from the same publisher, *Psychodynamic Music Therapy*, edited by Susan Hadley.

For thoughts on teaching and playing the cello, I am indebted to the great cellist Natalie Clein. Trevor Robbins, Professor of Cognitive Neuroscience at Cambridge, shared stimulating ideas on music and the brain. The wonderful Nordoff Robbins centre in north London helped me to understand the transformative power of music therapy.

430

At home, my own personal music therapy was provided by the songbirds, Evie and Thomas Lane. 'Have you finished your book yet, mum?' I have now, and I'm all yours.

While I was failing to write this novel, my agent, Pat Kavanagh, died unexpectedly. Pat would have been a remarkable woman in any century. Not just because she was beautiful, although she was certainly beautiful, but because she didn't fear the truth and spoke it on a regular basis. I have missed Pat's cool judgement, her praise, all the more precious for being hard-won, and the ripple of amusement in that lovely low voice.

Finally, I am lucky to have personal access to one of the world's great critics. Lucky and unlucky. Anthony Lane sets the bar very high. I can never repay his love, encouragement and furious margin notes.

Picky is always good.

Allison Pearson,
Cambridge, Easter 2010

PERMISSIONS

Every effort has been made to trace or contact all copyright holders, and the publishers will be pleased to correct any omissions brought to their notice at the earliest convenience.